REFLECTION
of the
MOON

Elyn Eden

National Library of Australia Cataloguing-in-Publication Data available.

ISBN 978 0 9953938 0 6 (Paperback)

ISBN 978 0 9953938 1 3 (eBook)

Cover: Blue Wren Books

Image: Keremgo, Dreamstime.com

Formatting: Integrity Formatting

elyn.eden@gmail.com

This book is dedicated
to Love

*Grateful thanks to my wonderful family and friends
who have supported and encouraged me.*

Chapter 1

THE MOMENT ELLIE SAW THE ancient site she felt it: a sense of power and significance. She stopped and stood transfixed, overwhelmed by the enormity of all that had happened to bring her here. Excitement but also trepidation spiralled through her body. This place had called to her across time. What it meant she did not know.

Marked out in white lines in the grass, the outline of the giant man stretched almost the entire length of the steep hillside in front of her. He stood with his arms open wide, each hand holding a long stave. Created by an unknown people for an unknown purpose, his origin lay far back in the distant past. Countless generations had lived and died in the village beneath his steadfast gaze.

Suddenly the heavy clouds that billowed across the sky drew back and the sun bathed the figure with gold. Intense light spread out over the fields, caressing Ellie with its warmth. A great wave of love arose in her chest and flowed outwards to embrace the beautiful landscape of hills and wooded valleys surrounding her.

After a few moments, the clouds drew together once again and the scene darkened. As it did so, Ellie became aware of tall trees behind her, their leaves whispering in a timeless conversation with the wind. The sound intensified as a strong gust swept over the countryside, bringing with it a sense of foreboding.

Shivering, Ellie turned and walked towards an old wooden gate a short distance away into a graveyard where an ancient yew, its weary limbs supported by heavy beams of wood, stretched its gnarled roots among the tombstones. She stopped at a grave by the sprawling tree and stared at a headstone worn by weather and time. The inscription read: Thomas Marshall 1868—1892.

She laid her hand upon the stone and her heart ached. She had loved this man, loved him with a passion born of walking together in the wilderness, of laughing and talking and feeling his naked body moving with hers as they made love, hidden by the trees, in the old oak wood.

Ellie loved this land, the vibrant living land of England, always green, and she loved him because he had shared it with her. An indescribable sorrow welled up as she stared at the ground that had drawn him into its cold embrace. A dry oak leaf blew across the grave. She picked it up but it broke into fragments. The wind caught the pieces and scattered them over the graveyard.

The call of a crow echoed on the wind. She turned to look at the stone church behind her. The door stood open. Leaving the grave, she walked through the entrance into silence and shadow.

Moving down the centre of the church, she took in the wooden pews on either side, the altar draped with white linen, the simple cross. As she walked past a small side chapel, a flash of colour drew her attention. Going in, she saw a vibrant stained glass window showing the standing figure of a man in red robes holding a key in his hand. Several circles surrounded him, each containing a different butterfly, except for the one beneath his feet. In this, the artist had painted a bee. In the lower section of the window, a bright red phoenix spread its wings. But this disturbed her. The bird should not be there. She didn't understand.

As she gazed at the window, the image intensified.

The brilliant colour of the phoenix expanded to fill Ellie's vision but then she realised it was the sun burning red through her closed eyelids. Cold despite the heat on her skin, she shivered and sand shifted beneath her body. She opened her eyes and saw a vast expanse of blue sky. The sound of laughing and the crashing of breaking waves came from nearby. Pushing herself up into a sitting position, she stared out at the glistening sea. A few people swam.

Ellie stared around, disorientated. The dream remained vivid in her consciousness. It seemed more real than the beach on which she sat. The giant outlined on the hillside still glowed with sunlight in her mind as did the beautiful window in the dark church. After a few moments, the scenes faded to be replaced by the image of the grave beneath the tree and a profound sorrow welled up. Someone she loved had died and her body cried out for his touch. There had been a name on the headstone but Ellie couldn't recall it. She only knew she longed for the man buried there with an intensity she still felt. Touching her cheek, she found it wet with tears.

Slowly the hot Australian sun warmed her but it did not ease her strange grief. She'd been fine before falling asleep. Why had this dream affected her so much? It wasn't real, just images created by her brain as she slept. It made no sense. Why was she mourning a man who did not exist?

Without warning, a football slammed down nearby and sand sprayed everywhere. "Damn!" she exclaimed.

A young boy dashed up. "Sorry," he muttered, grabbing the ball and leaving Ellie to stand and shake off the sand. It was time to go. She felt alienated from the people on the beach. They made her feel all the more alone. The sight of a young couple, their arms clasped around each other as they kissed, didn't help. Ellie stuffed her towel into an old, frayed basket and walked up the beach.

Tall and thin with wavy, shoulder length, light brown hair and dressed in a long blue dress that flowed softly around her legs, Ellie attracted attention as she passed. She looked younger than her twenty-six years, despite the strained expression on her face. She made her way up the concrete steps to the road and found her car. The feelings of loss and loneliness from the dream intensified and her brown eyes filled with more tears. She didn't understand why she felt so bad but perhaps it had something to do with the vague sense of unease that had been bothering her the last few weeks. It was ridiculous, though, life was good. She'd been living with James for three years now. They were having a house built and getting married in a few months. That very evening they planned to go to a party at a house in the Adelaide Hills owned by one of James's clients. She *had* been looking forward to it, but now wasn't so sure. For some reason, the thought of the evening filled her with apprehension.

"What the bloody hell's happening to me?" Ellie said aloud as she turned the ignition on. The car sputtered and fell silent, which did nothing to alleviate a growing feeling of depression. This is ridiculous, she thought.

The engine flared into life on the second try and Ellie drove the short distance to her flat. She shrugged off her clothes and took a hot shower. She hoped the water would wash away the sadness brought back from the beach but it didn't.

Ellie wove her way through the crowd of milling people. The party was in full swing, the large house bright and noisy. Set in the middle of a large area of natural bush, no neighbours would complain. Her eyes scanned the room and she wondered where James had gone. She poured herself a glass of wine and found a place to sit on a sofa. Her thoughts drifted back to her earlier dream. The profound sense of loss still lingered but she also remembered the love she had felt in the presence of the strange figure on the hillside. It left her with a sense of wistful longing for something she couldn't define. At that moment, a man dressed in a dark suit sat down. He leaned towards her, his breath reeking of beer and stale cigarettes. As his attention fixed on the curve of her breasts, she stood and walked away.

A trickle of sweat ran between her shoulder blades in the hot, humid atmosphere. Ellie scanned the room one more time but James had vanished. She moved through an open door to the outside and felt the blessed relief of a cool breeze waft over her body.

Thinking James might also have felt the need for fresh air, Ellie searched through the garden but soon slowed, entranced by its loveliness. A full moon dusted the leaves and flowers with silver. The further she went, the quieter it became.

Ellie heard trickling water and followed the sound down a narrow cement path surrounded by shrubs. Coming around a turn, she discovered a stone fountain. Water poured out of an urn held by a naked woman standing in the centre of a round pond. Lights beneath the figure lent her an ethereal quality and Ellie felt she had come across a magical scene from some other world.

She continued on but soon came to a halt. A couple kissed in the bushes off to one side, oblivious to everything but each other. She half turned, intending to retrace her footsteps, but, at that moment, the man drew back and Ellie saw his face. She wanted to run away but her body lost its ability to move. No one seemed capable of reacting so they all stood frozen in a kind of bizarre tableaux. The woman with James came out of it first. She touched his arm, whispered something then hurried away. Ellie only had time to notice her short blonde hair and long red dress.

James looked uncomfortable. "I'm sorry," he said, after a moment. "I *was* going to tell you."

"Tell me what?" Ellie said, her voice icy cold.

"I'm sorry but it's over between us. Catherine and I, well . . ."

Ellie stared at him. "How long has it been going on?"

"Not long," he said, "*really*. Look, it just happened. I didn't mean it to but . . ."

"So that's it, then," Ellie said, her body tense, her hands clenched. "What about everything we planned?"

James looked as if he might be sick. "You can keep the ring."

Suddenly, Ellie could take no more. She turned and fled through the garden, angry tears streaming down her face. Oblivious of anything except the huge pain of betrayal, Ellie ran for a long time, heedless of her direction and that she had entered an area of dense woodland. Branches raked across her body and she stopped, aware now of the distance she had come.

As she stared around her, thick clouds drew over the moon and plunged Ellie into complete darkness. To make matters worse, rain drops spattered on her face. Soon a heavy shower thundered down. Frightened, Ellie turned back. She walked for a while then stopped again. The trees seemed as thick as ever. She should be out of the wood by now, she thought. She had gone the wrong way!

Panic surging inside her, Ellie started in a new direction, pushing though wet branches. She stumbled on a stone and pain sliced through her ankle. Tears streamed down her face but she paid them no heed and kept going.

After some time, Ellie came out of the undergrowth and sensed space around her. The rough earth gave way to small stones that shifted beneath her feet. Exhausted, she sank down onto the ground, grateful it had at least stopped raining.

Ellie's breathing slowed and her heart stopped pounding. Enfolded by complete darkness, she could not see. Where was she? Ellie listened but heard only the sound of raindrops dripping from the bushes. Her flight had taken her a long way from the house. She heard a distant splash and realised she must be near water. Then she saw a flickering white shape.

A frisson of fear ran down Ellie's spine. She felt vulnerable, aware of being out alone in the middle of nowhere but then realised she could now make out the landscape around her. She looked up and saw the clouds parting in the sky. Lowering her gaze, Ellie sighed in relief. The mysterious light was the reflection of the moon on the shifting surface of a lake. Something had disturbed the water.

She relaxed a little and stared out at the shimmering pattern of light. Above, the full moon gazed down upon the earth. Ellie wished she too could float above it all, look down on her life and perhaps understand it. Nothing made sense anymore. Something she'd thought so special had turned out to be an illusion. Anger and pain were her new reality.

Ellie stared at the lake as the flickering shapes slowly stopped shifting and merged into a perfect circle of reflected light, capturing her attention. It called out to her and she had the sudden impulse to wade into the lake. It would be so easy. Let the water and light ease her pain. They had the power. She didn't want to live without the man she loved. Her whole body ached for him. She wanted to follow him into death.

She struggled to her feet and stepped into the water going some distance before her mind kicked in. What was she thinking? James hadn't died and, anyway, at that moment she hated him.

He was a bastard; she wasn't going to kill herself because of him. Then the realisation hit her.

It wasn't James she mourned!

Her whole body ached for someone else. The dream she'd had earlier surged forward in her mind and she stood again by the grave. This time she saw the headstone clearly and the name carved into the stone: Thomas Marshall.

"Thomas," Ellie whispered. She shivered and realised she stood thigh deep in water. She splashed back to shore then turned and looked back. A breeze ruffled the lake, once again breaking the image of the moon into scintillating shapes. Thomas. Somehow she knew he had died in water. A wave of sadness washed through her again. Why did she feel this way about someone from a dream? Why did she walk into the lake? Had she gone mad?

Ellie stood for a while, staring at the reflection of the moon, but then the present predicament penetrated her consciousness. Wet through, she couldn't stay where she was. She looked around and in the moonlight made out the shapes of trees surrounding the small lake. Behind her, the wood looked dense. She did not know in which direction the house lay. She fumbled in her bag for her mobile, scared it might not be there, but her fingers found the phone. Its glow eased her fear as she keyed in James's number. She didn't want to see him but needed help.

Nothing happened. Ellie stared in disbelief at the display. No signal. She carried on pushing buttons in the futile hope of a miracle but it soon became obvious God wasn't watching.

She didn't know what to do. Which direction should she go? Ellie wished she had paid more attention when they drove to the house. She stared at the moon hanging motionless and serene, inviolate and remote, far above the world. Well out of it all, she thought with bitterness. Reasoning that the house must be through the woods behind her, she started walking but hadn't gone far before the scene dimmed as clouds devoured the pristine shape of the moon. Soon she'd be unable to see her way.

Ellie stumbled on as fast as she could through the trees. Her skin crawled with fear as the clouds closed in, engulfing her in darkness. Desperate, she continued on. After about twenty minutes, she found herself again walking on stones that shifted under her feet. A splash in the distance told her what she didn't want to know, she had come full circle.

She collapsed onto the ground and gave herself over to the fear and grief battling within her. Alone in the darkness, her life in ruins, Ellie lay down and allowed her feelings full expression. They washed through her body and out to touch the landscape. The world was pain; everything was pain. An endless stream of tears poured from her. She cried for the loss of her illusions, her hopes and dreams.

Her neatly mapped out future dissolved before her. The shining image she had cherished for so long of standing with James at the altar in a beautiful old stone church with stained glass windows faded into darkness. She saw the house they were buying disintegrate and merge into nothingness, the children they planned to have turning and walking away. But, muddled in with it all, she also mourned someone she did not know, a man whose grave she had only visited in a dream yet who held a strange power over her heart.

Chapter 2

A BITTER COLD PENETRATED EVERY part of Ellie's body. She lay in a foetal position. Although unable to move, she still lived. When she lay on the ground last night in the darkness she hadn't expected to wake, hadn't cared whether she would or not.

Ellie opened her eyes to the grey light of dawn. Brown mud and small stones filled her vision. She watched an ant walk past until it wandered out of sight, a comfort of a sort, something living.

She flexed her hand then shifted her arm a little. Her body had seized up, as if she *had* died and rigor mortis had set in. Bit by bit, however, she straightened her legs and eased herself up. She looked around and gasped with unexpected joy. A burst of brilliant gold hovered above the trees surrounding the lake. A sudden cry echoed across the water and a bird swooped down. It skimmed the surface and sent ripples expanding out over the pristine surface of the water. The intense emotion of the night before had scoured her out but now the world rushed in to fill the void. For a moment, she sat transfixed by wonder until she remembered James. Pain and humiliation flooded back.

The image of James kissing the woman had burnt into Ellie's brain. When they'd arrived at the lovely old country house for the party there had been no indication that things would soon crumble around her. She'd had so much to live for but now her life was over. Ellie wished it *had* ended in this beautiful spot. The idea appealed to her sense of the dramatic—spurned fiancée dies of broken heart in the bush.

A parrot screeched and Ellie's attention came back to the present. She watched the sun rise higher. It permeated the scene in front of her with golden light. The sound of the bird died away and everything stilled as if waiting. To her surprise, her pain faded as she sat absorbing the experience of the landscape. Maybe it wasn't really the end of the world. Life went on. Surely she didn't need a man to validate her existence? She certainly didn't need one who messed around.

Ellie's eyes felt gritty and sore. Mud and leaves matted her hair and her damp clothes clung to her body. She struggled to her feet and brushed herself down as best she could.

She looked around. At least she still had her bag. She noticed an opening through the trees on the other side of the lake and walked in its direction along the shore. It could be a track away from the area. Perhaps it would lead to a road where she might be able to get a lift back to civilisation. Ellie knew she looked dreadful but didn't care. She just wanted to get home, have a hot shower and a cup of tea then climb into a soft bed. This thought gave her the energy to keep moving.

After an hour and a half, Ellie lost it. Tears coursed down her cheeks but she struggled on and eventually saw a road up ahead. Her mobile phone still had no signal so she had no choice but to keep walking. After twenty minutes, she heard the drone of an engine. No longer caring for her safety, she ran out in front of the approaching truck and flagged it down.

It screeched to a halt. "For God's sake, love, what happened to you?"

Ellie peered into the truck. She hadn't expected a woman in the beaten up looking vehicle. She stared into concerned brown eyes in a weatherworn face. "I got lost. You haven't by any chance got a mobile that works so I can call a taxi?"

"No, don't like them fiddly little phones. Hop in. I'll give you a lift. Where d'you live?"

"Adelaide. Somerton Park, actually. It's by the sea near

Glenelg."

"I know Glenelg."

Ellie clambered into the cab and took a better look at her rescuer, an enormously fat woman dressed in an ill-fitting floral print dress.

"No problem. Drop ya back there in no time."

"No, really, you don't need to. It's too far." It had taken at least an hour to drive to the party yesterday.

"You look like you need a break. What happened, if you don't mind me asking?"

Ellie explained about the party, how she'd gone for a walk and lost her way in the dark. She didn't want to talk about James. The woman gave Ellie a long look but said nothing, guessing there had to be more to the story. She revved the engine and the truck surged forward. Ellie gripped the worn leather seat as they hurtled around the curves at breakneck speed. She couldn't locate anything that resembled a seatbelt.

Christ, Ellie thought. Maybe it hadn't been such a good idea to get a lift. Walking might be slow but at least she stood some chance of survival! Her stomach churned. Fortunately, they soon reached some buildings and the woman slammed on the brakes in front of a garage.

Ellie's heart stopped pounding and she looked around. They had stopped in a small village. Perhaps she could get a taxi here. In the garage forecourt an old man tinkered with the engine of a truck even more dilapidated than the one they were in. The woman rolled down the window and entered into a short discussion with him. Before Ellie had time to get out and do something about finding a taxi, the woman said, "See ya, Jack," and put her foot down. They raced off, raising a cloud of dust with their hasty exit.

"Just told me husband where I'm going. I'm Sue, by the way"

"My name's Ellie."

"You feeling all right?"

"Just a little stiff."

"Sorry, I'll try and take it easy." To Ellie's great relief, the truck slowed down enabling her to relax to some extent.

She noticed junk piled everywhere in the truck: old newspapers, books, beer cans, rags, ropes, tools, wrappers, even bits of dried up sandwich. Ellie felt like rubbish herself—cast off and tarnished, something to be replaced with a newer, better model.

Why? She and James had been happy, or so she'd thought. What did she do wrong? It was so unfair. Tears welled up in Ellie's eyes. One trickled down her cheek.

"He isn't worth it, love."

Ellie turned to look at Sue who grinned, her face creasing into wrinkles of brown skin."

"How can you tell?" Ellie asked.

"Been there, done that," Sue laughed. "There'll be another along soon and you'll wonder what you ever saw in this one. You don't need 'em anyhow. Sex is overrated if you ask me."

Ellie found herself smiling.

"Give me chocolate any day." The old woman cackled with laughter. "Speaking of which," she thrust her hand into a bag on the seat beside her and held out a small chocolate bar. "Have one."

Ellie's stomach churned from lack of food. Grateful, she accepted the offering. Her mouth filled with saliva as she chewed. God, this is good, she thought, swallowing the last bite. Sue definitely had a point.

She relaxed and glanced at her companion again. Sue hummed to herself. The hands that gripped the wheel were fat and brown and covered with age spots. Sweat glistened on the coarse skin of a face dominated by a large nose. Certainly not an attractive woman, Ellie thought, but then Sue turned and smiled and Ellie revised that decision. Sue emanated an animation, a joyous energy that lit up her features. Ellie could not help but respond and her mood lightened.

What was it about this woman that lifted her spirits and made Ellie want to smile despite all that had happened? She suspected nothing ever bothered Sue very much; she probably let the storms of life rage on around her as she barged through.

"Have some more, you must be hungry." Sue felt for the bag and held it out. Ellie gratefully took it and helped herself.

"Mmm," she said, "I think you're right."

"What, love?"

"About chocolate."

The woman laughed and accelerated. The old truck swerved at breakneck speed around the curving roads of the Adelaide Hills but it no longer bothered Ellie. She felt a lot better. She trusted this old woman who was kind enough to take her home. With gratitude, Ellie thought of a hot shower and the warm softness of her bed coming ever closer.

The truck lurched. Ellie had chocolate in her hand. It slipped from her fingers and lost itself in the debris covering the floor. She leaned down and sifted through the stuff. Something caught her eye. The chocolate forgotten, she stared at a postcard showing a painted phoenix. The brilliant red and orange feathers resembled flames. As she picked it up, heat passed into her fingers. The sensation flowed up her arm to her face. The feeling intensified and Ellie felt faint.

The picture reminded her of the phoenix window she dreamt about on the beach. The image swelled into her consciousness again, the feathers becoming moving flames that took on a life of their own. Jesus, Ellie thought, why couldn't she get that bloody dream out of her mind?

"You OK?" Ellie felt a cool hand on her arm and raised herself up, still with the postcard in her hand. The image in her mind faded and reality took its place. "Yes, yes, I'm sorry, I was looking at this."

"What's that? Oh yeah, got it from my daughter. She's travelling around Europe. She's an artist. I suppose that came from some gallery somewhere. Angie's always sending me postcards of paintings she's seen, bless her. Be glad to have her back. Twenty-nine she is, been away two years. She's in England at the moment."

England. The word resonated in Ellie's mind, evoking green hills and dark trees and a cold wind that whipped around her body. The heat dissipated and she felt cold, like death. She shuddered, that bloody dream again!

"You don't look so good." Sue said.

"I'm feeling very tired."

"Don't worry, we'll have you back home in no time."

Ellie nodded off. She remembered nothing more until Sue shook her arm. "Sorry to wake you, love, but what street do you live in?"

Opening her eyes, Ellie saw they had arrived at Somerton Park. She gave Sue directions to her apartment.

They continued on a bit further then Sue braked so fast they both almost went through the windscreen. "Sorry," the old woman said with a sheepish grin.

"That's OK." Ellie felt relieved to be home. "Look, thanks so much for doing this. Would you like to come in for a tea or coffee perhaps?"

"No, thanks, sweets, you need your rest. I'll just be getting back."

Ellie climbed out and stood on the pavement.

"Take care, love," Sue said and waved, revved the engine and drove off in a cloud of fumes. Ellie watched her disappear.

Now alone, she became aware of a clamp of pain encircling her head and a flush of heat pulsing through her body, signs that, perhaps, she had caught a chill from sleeping out in the rain. Anxious to rest, she let herself into the apartment, unsure of what she would find.

The place was empty. Ellie felt relieved but then realised James would be with *her*. What on earth would she say to him when next they met? At the moment she felt numb and exhausted. All she wanted to do was to have a hot shower, climb into a warm bed and forget the whole mess. The light blinked on her answering machine. Someone had left a message. She wondered if it had been James. Ignoring it, she went into the bathroom, slamming the door behind her. Let him worry.

Ellie turned on the hot water and washed away the debris from her night in the open. Appalled, she watched a large mangled spider whirl down the plughole. Thank God she hadn't known she had *that* on her. Spiders made her flesh crawl. A sick feeling ran through her body. She could have so easily stepped on some poisonous snake in the dark.

As she came out of the bathroom, the phone rang. She hesitated for a moment then picked up the receiver. "Ellie, thank

God. What happened to you last night? I was so worried."

"Not that worried, I'm sure." Ellie gripped the phone tight.

James answered her with silence.

So tired she couldn't think straight, Ellie said, "I don't want to talk to you right now. I'm exhausted."

"Are you all right?"

"What do you care?"

"Of course, I care. Where *were* you? Why didn't you answer your phone?"

"I was lost in the bloody woods, if you must know. I spent the night on the ground. I tried ringing you but there wasn't any signal."

"Oh Jesus, I'm sorry, Ellie. I just thought you'd called a taxi and gone off to a friend's. How did you get home?"

"I got a lift from someone on the road." Anger surged up. "Where are *you*? With Catherine, I suppose. Christ, James, it's been three years. We had everything. Just tell me why? What did I do?"

"You didn't do anything. It's not your fault. Oh, I don't know. Catherine and I just have more in common."

Ellie thought back to the scene in the garden. She remembered how elegant Catherine looked in her red evening dress and long sparkling earrings, how much in contrast to Ellie in her charity shop treasures: a purple tie dye skirt and soft, blue blouse. She knew James sometimes didn't like the way she dressed but hadn't worried about it. Obviously she should have. Ellie swayed, tiredness threatening to overwhelm her. "Look, James, I just want to go to bed. We'll talk later." She paused. "Are you coming back here?"

The silence at the other end of the phone told her what she already guessed. "So, you *are* at Catherine's."

"I'm so sorry. I'll come and get my stuff tomorrow. We'll talk then. There are things we'll need to sort out. The house. . . . ." His voice trailed away.

"Fine." Ellie couldn't keep back the tears as the finality of his words pierced her heart. He wasn't coming back. It was all over.

"Well, I'll let you get some sleep. I'll ring you tomorrow

morning. Bye."

"Goodbye." Ellie put down the phone. She felt dizzy. Her stomach rumbled and she realised how hungry she was. She went into the kitchen to make some tea and toast. It tasted wonderful. She remembered Sue's comments about chocolate. She'd have to make do with food for the time being. Ellie ate several more slices, stuffing her body in the hope they would fill the emptiness inside her.

Ellie stood and walked into the bedroom. She swept James's things off the dressing table to the floor and collapsed onto the bed. She fell asleep before she had time to cover herself.

A cold wind swept over the grass pushing her skirt against her legs and throwing her long, dark brown hair into abandon as she climbed the hill. Grey clouds billowed overhead. A few drops of rain fell. Sheep grazed all around but they scattered as she passed. Reaching the hilltop, she turned and looked out over the countryside that lay spread out below, a patchwork of green fields separated by hedges and trees. She loved this view.

She shivered in the wind but stayed still, waiting, waiting for Thomas. She sensed him come up behind her long before she felt his warm arms encircle her waist. He turned her around and his lips came down on hers. Their kiss stirred a passion that urged their bodies closer. She put her arms around his neck and ran her fingers through his curly, black hair. How was it possible to yearn for someone this much?

Asleep in the apartment, Ellie stirred. She flung her arm over to one side and knocked a small wooden box off the bedside table onto the floor. Its contents spilled out but she did not wake.

Chapter 3

ELLIE SLEPT UNTIL LATE IN the afternoon. With the memory of the hard stones of the previous night still vivid in her mind, she appreciated the soft warmth of her bed. She couldn't bring herself to get up for a long while. Vague impressions of a green hillside and a man who came to her there still lingered from her dream but she couldn't remember any details.

Eventually hunger motivated her to struggle out of bed. As she stood, she felt something cold under one foot. She lifted it and saw a small silver key. Ellie picked it up and stared at it in her fingers. She had loved this key as a child. It was rather lovely with an intricate design of interwoven leaves at its end. She had found it many years ago whilst sorting through her mother's jewellery box.

The box contained cheap plastic necklaces and brooches with sparkling coloured glass stones but to Ellie it was "treasure." The key had been mixed in with it all. Something about it had appealed to her. It had looked important as if it should open something special. She had asked her mother what it opened. "I'm afraid I don't know, sweetheart. I found that key in your grandmother's things when she died but I never did find anything it fitted into."

"Can I have it, then?" Ellie asked.

"Yes, of course."

Eight-year-old Ellie treasured the silver key. To her it was magical. Just to hold it filled her with a special feeling. She felt light and wanted to dance. Sometimes she did, twirling around and around until overwhelmed by dizziness.

It featured in a number of games, opening many a secret door or box of hidden treasure. Ellie's favourite book then was *The Lion, the Witch and the Wardrobe* by C.S. Lewis in which a number of children found their way into another world through a magic wardrobe. Ellie climbed into several wardrobes but found no magical world, only smelly old clothes and shoes. Disappointed, she sought solace in worlds of her own imagination.

Dressed in her mother's old dresses and scarves, she wafted around the backyard as a fairy princess and used her magic key to open doors into places where she had the most amazing, imaginary adventures. She lived in a timeless world of infinite possibility. Ellie wasn't comfortable in the real world. Ever since she could remember, she had struggled with deep depression. It lifted at times but not for long.

She found solace in food but this only exacerbated her problems. She became fat and no one allowed her to forget it. The other girls at school taunted her every day but, in order to escape the pain of not belonging, Ellie resorted to more chocolate and cake. Later, Ellie became anorexic. It took her several years to overcome this and even now couldn't tolerate being overweight. Depression still clouded her life but she had learnt to live with it.

To Ellie the key symbolised all of this: alienation and rejection but also the liberation found in her imagination. How bizarre life was, she reflected. One moment the world seemed bright and wonderful, the next nothing but shit. She clutched the key, wishing she could gain entrance to another world now, one where Prince Charming hadn't run off with another woman.

A ringing distracted Ellie's attention. "What did I do with the bloody mobile?" she muttered. Her handbag lay on the lounge floor where she flung it earlier. "Oh yes." She scrabbled inside. As she did so, the key fell out of her hand into the bottom of the bag. Ellie found the mobile but, typically, it stopped ringing the moment she pulled it out. The key forgotten, she read the display. Oh God, Ellie thought, how am I going to tell Mum? She'd been so thrilled when her daughter became engaged to James, an up and coming lawyer, an ideal "catch." Ellie replaced the phone in the bag. She didn't have to tell her yet.

Ellie felt awkward and conspicuous in the bright lights of the bar and the loud music drummed through her skull. She would have turned around and left but couldn't face the emptiness of the flat. Up until now she and James had spent their evenings together watching TV or going out. Ellie didn't like being alone. It made her feel empty inside so she'd rung a friend and arranged to meet up. Ellie saw Claire on the other side of the room and attempted to squeeze through the mass of bodies in the way.

"Excuse me." Two men, fat stomachs thrust out in front of them, were her last obstacle. They laughed and leered at Ellie as she pushed between them. Relieved, she reached Claire.

"God, it's busy in here tonight," Ellie said.

"I know. Here, I saved you a seat."

"If you don't mind, I'd prefer to sit outside. It's so noisy in here."

"Sure."

They bought some wine and pushed their way through the crush to a table outside with a great view of the sea. Ellie sighed as she lowered herself into a chair. "That's better."

Claire sat down opposite. "Well, how're things. You look dreadful, Ellie."

"Thanks."

"What's up?" Claire knew something had happened.

Ellie turned away and stared out over the ocean. The moon floated high in the clear sky; it reminded her of the previous night. She had been unable to stop herself walking into the water of the lake to reach the reflection of the moon. Crazy! She shivered but continued to stare up with a strange feeling the bright circle had something to tell her, that, if she waited long enough, its secret would be revealed.

"Ellie?"

She tore her gaze away and focussed on Claire. "Sorry, I was miles away."

"Yes, you were and it's not like you. What's the matter? You sounded upset on the phone."

Ellie briefly outlined the events of the previous day.

"The absolute bastard! Oh, Ellie, I'm *so* sorry." Claire's eyes filled with compassion.

That made it worse. Ellie hated people feeling sorry for her. "Don't worry. I'll get over it. Why, it's been a lucky escape. He could've done this when we were married with two kids and then where would I have been?" Ellie took a sip of her drink then replaced it on the table. Her hand shook.

"You're right," Claire agreed, "but knowing that doesn't help much, does it?"

"No." Ellie agreed.

"What are you going to do?" Claire asked.

"I don't know," Ellie answered, staring down at several circular stains and a blob of red sauce on the table. She felt depressed. Things were just so horrible. The table represented her life—all messed up.

"I've already ordered the wedding dress. And the invitations have been sent out. Everyone will have to be told."

"Don't worry, I can do that for you."

"And the house, my God, the house, what of that?" Now she would never get the chance to live in the house she and James had designed together. The builders had rung last week to say they could move in soon.

Ellie pulled her attention back to Claire. "I'm sorry. I'm not good company tonight. What about you, how are *you* going?"

"I'm fine. It's taken a while but I'm a lot happier now." Left alone with a young daughter after a bitter divorce, Claire knew how devastating the break-up of a long-term relationship could be. She longed to ease the pain in her friend's eyes. "You'll get over this, you'll see."

The two of them stayed chatting for a long time. Claire tried her best to cheer Ellie up but failed to free her from the storm of sadness and anger assailing her friend. After two hours she stood to leave. "I'd better get going. I don't want to leave Chloe with her grandmother for too long."

"Are you sure you can't stay for another drink?" Ellie asked, reluctant to return to the empty flat.

"No thanks. I've had too much already."

They walked through the now almost deserted bar to reach the car park on the other side of the building. Ellie noticed a man leaving at the same time. He came over as they stood by her car in the carpark. He staggered and nearly fell but righted himself and stared directly into her face. "I know you," he said.

"Er, I don't think so," she replied, taken aback. The man smelled of beer and stale cigarettes. Ellie shrunk away but he moved closer.

"Yes," he repeated. "I do. You killed him. It was *your* fault."

Ellie gasped in shock. "Killed who?" she stammered. "I don't know what you mean."

"My son." The man swayed and almost fell again but leaned on the car just in time. "He loved you. You were his world. If he hadn't been with you he wouldn't have died."

Ellie felt sick. "I'm sorry but I don't know what you're talking about." She looked closely at the man. He couldn't be more than twenty five or so. A light wispy beard dusted his chin. She had never seen him before. He stared at her with hate in his eyes. She felt Claire tug on her arm. "Come on, let's go back to the bar for a while. *Now!*" They hurried back into the building.

"Hey," shouted the man. "You can't walk away from me. You killed Thomas."

Ellie stopped and looked back. Thomas? The strange dream that, even now, still haunted her mind had involved the death of a man named Thomas. And now this man accused her of killing someone with that same name. His son. It was an obvious case of mistaken identity but odd all the same. She felt sorry for him. Losing a child must be awful. She understood why he'd be upset.

The man started to cry. As she stood there looking at him, the colours of the surrounding hotel blurred and spun as if the two of them stood in the centre of some strange vortex. As quickly as this feeling came, it evaporated when another man appeared. "Come on, mate, let's get you home. Sorry, love," he said to Ellie. The friend supported the drunk under his arms and led him off up the street.

"Thank God," Claire said. "I was a bit worried there. Poor bloke, completely off his head."

"Yes," said Ellie but the incident left her with a feeling of unease. Why should a man she didn't know accuse her of killing his son, Thomas, the same name as the man she had dreamed about? It had to be just a bizarre coincidence but still. Ellie's head spun and started to ache as a wave of exhaustion hit her. "Oh well, I'd better get home."

Claire gave Ellie a brief hug. "I'll ring you tomorrow. You take care. Let me know if I can do anything." She walked off to her car parked a short distance away.

Ellie drove back to her apartment. Unable to keep her eyes open any longer, she climbed the stairs and let herself in. She needed to get to bed. She had to get up early for work tomorrow.

Ellie felt terrible in the morning, having cried herself to sleep the night before. In misery, she stared at her swollen eyes and the red blotches on her skin in the mirror. She couldn't face them all at work. She rang and told them she felt unwell but then sank down on her bed wondering what to do. The flat felt so empty. Noticing the sun shining through a nearby window, Ellie decided to go for a swim. She changed into a bathing suit, grabbed a towel and drove the short distance to the seafront.

She stepped onto the sand and stared out over the ocean. Tiny wavelets rippled the calm surface, flattening out on the sand as they reached the beach. Ellie laid down her towel and took off her shoes. Without hesitation, she waded out into the crystal clear sea and started swimming. The shock of the cold water soon passed with the exhilaration of slicing through the water.

A good swimmer, Ellie scythed through the ocean for some distance. Always mindful of sharks, she swerved around and returned to the shallows where she turned over and floated on her back. A perfect blue sky spread above her. With the sound of lapping water inside her ears, Ellie shut her eyes and relaxed, allowing the sea to support her body, which rocked in tune with the gentle motion of the tide.

For a few minutes Ellie felt at peace, needing nothing more than to float, but then her mind cranked in and she remembered—he had gone. An intense grief welled up inside and tears filled her eyes. "Thomas," she whispered, "no, *James*." Oh Jesus, this is insane, she thought, her body tensing. Ellie sank, her communion with the sea destroyed. She flailed around for a while until she found a firm footing on the seabed. It was *James* she'd lost, *James* who had run off with someone else. It was *James* she missed. Not bloody Thomas.

The perfection of the moment was broken. Angry at herself, at James, at the stupid illusory Thomas and the rest of the whole stinking world, Ellie swam back out to sea. She carried on for a long time before shark anxiety prompted her to slow. Turning, she realised how far she had come. Fear flooded her body, her imagination filling the ocean around her with lurking predators waiting to bite her dangling legs.

She panicked and swam back to the shore as fast as possible. Why had she come so far out? She didn't want to die. Ellie tired but dare not stop. The beach and safety looked so distant, out of reach. What if she couldn't get back? She swam slower and slower, her arms aching so much they became impossible to move. Oh God, I can't take much more of this, she thought. Got to keep moving, keep moving, keep moving. The words echoed in Ellie's brain. The whole thing took a few minutes but it seemed like hours before she lowered her feet onto the sea bed. She waded in and collapsed into the shallows, taking long, heaving breaths. With relief flooding her body, life had never seemed more precious.

Soothed by the warm water and gentle motion of the waves, Ellie calmed down and relaxed. Her energy slowly returned. After a while she rose and walked up the sand to her towel. She sat on the beach and stared out at the far horizon, reflecting on the fact that a short time ago she had been out there, at risk, afraid. Now, back in normality, embraced by safety, everything felt precious and beautiful: the softness of the sand, the blue sky, the warmth of the sun on her body and other people, laughing and talking.

Ellie noticed a small child. He sat watching grains of sand run through his fingers. She marvelled at his intense concentration. A grin of pure joy lit up the little boy's face. Ellie smiled too. How bizarre, she thought, she had passed from absolute fear to joy in the space of a few minutes. What *was* life? One minute it held disaster and darkness, the next, warmth and safety. Was it hell or heaven? Or both?

At this moment she felt happy to be alive and yet still miserable over Thomas, no, *James,* she corrected herself. Christ, she'd done it again. Could she be losing her mind?

She remembered the previous night. Why had that young bloke accused her of killing his son, Thomas? It still felt weird. Ellie remembered the agony on the man's face and her mood saddened.

Ellie decided to return home but a feeling of disquiet followed her. After a shower, she sat down in front of the television wanting only oblivion. She watched the morning chat show and even sat through an American soap opera.

At lunchtime, James rang. "I'm coming at six to collect my stuff. Is that OK?"

"Fine," Ellie answered and put the phone down. She resumed her position on the sofa. She dozed off then watched children's cartoons until the doorbell rang.

Ellie opened the door. As soon as she saw James, pain gripped her chest. He looked just the same, expensively dressed, not a hair out of place. He avoided looking into her eyes and she felt physically sick. How could he do this to her? It made her feel so worthless. She hadn't been good enough for him. She also missed the bastard. The thought of being alone, lying in an empty bed, listening to silence with no one to talk to, hold her, laugh with from now on filled her with a sense of hopelessness.

James walked in; his face tight and closed. "You're leaving, then," Ellie managed to say.

"I'm sorry," James replied. "It wasn't working between us. I think you know that, really. Think about it. It hasn't all been a bed of roses. You were depressed quite often. It got me down, too, you know."

Ellie held her feelings inside, maintaining a cold, controlled exterior as James walked into the bedroom and took out his things. He had several large plastic garbage bags with him. She watched in misery while he went through the whole place, removing himself and his possessions from the flat and her life. She realised that somewhere, deep down, she had hoped he'd change his mind, realise Catherine wouldn't make him happy, but obviously it wasn't going to happen.

Soon four sacks waited by the door. How appropriate, Ellie thought, James and his things had become the refuse of her life, stuff to let go of. In no time at all, the number of bags increased to six and a coffee table he'd always liked. She let him take it although it made the living room look bare. But then James opened the front door and heaved everything down the stairs to his car. When only one sack remained, James paused. "Well," he said, "that's almost it. I was wondering . . ." James looked at Ellie nervously. "I was just wondering, would you mind, well, if I bought your half of the house? I'd like to keep it if I could."

Ellie couldn't stand any more.

"Get out," she said, her voice full of bitterness.

"Ellie . . ."

"Just GO." James looked at her face then hefted up the last bag and hurried down the stairs. How *dare* he? Ellie fumed. That house had been her dream. They had intended to raise their children there. She had put a lot of time into picking out the things she wanted for it. How dare he? She couldn't bear the thought of him moving in with Catherine.

Ellie slammed the door and stood with her back to it until she heard James's car driving off down the road. A deep silence filled the flat. She moved like a zombie into the kitchen, made a coffee then went into the lounge. She slumped onto the sofa and stared at the television. Nothing moved across the screen. Although turned off, Ellie still watched it. She sat there immobile, consumed by hatred, the feeling so huge she didn't know what to do with it. All she could do was sit and scream in silence. She couldn't cry, couldn't do anything. Ellie sat there for a long time but in the end fell asleep and slipped into a vivid dream.

She walked over the hill. A freezing wind clutched at her clothes and stung her face. Snow lay on the ground. Her feet left a trail of footprints as she made her way down to a small village of stone cottages. Smoke billowed from the chimneys and she thought with longing of the warm fires within. She looked behind her. The giant on the hillside lay hidden beneath a carpet of snow.

She reached one of the cottages and opened the door, slipping in away from the reach of the wind. She stared in surprise. Thomas! He sat in the old armchair by the fire. He turned his head and looked at her. His black hair curled down almost to his shoulders and his deep brown eyes bored into hers with an intensity that sent a shiver down her spine. He wore brown trousers and a white linen shirt. His feet were bare.

"Anne," he said, and smiled. He stared at her, his gaze travelling over her body and heat rose to her face.

"You shouldn't be here. Someone might have seen you."

"I was careful." Seeing the anxiety did not abate on Anne's features," he continued, "I promise. Come here."

Anne stared at him and all restraint evaporated. Even though the whole village would condemn her if they knew, what she and Thomas felt for each other did not feel wrong in this moment. It felt right in every part of her." She laughed and threw her shawl onto a chair. "I have food to prepare."

"It can wait."

"Well, there are clothes to be put away, wood to get in for the fire."

He rose in an instant and grabbed her by the wrist, pulling her down onto his lap. He put his hand behind her head, brought her face to his and kissed her with a strength that wrecked her composure and she returned his kiss with a sudden urgency of her own. It was always like this with them. Right from the start, they had been hungry for each other, the physical attraction between them a powerful force neither could resist. He started undoing the buttons of her blouse but she stayed his hand.

"Let's go to bed." She stood and stepped up the narrow stairs in the corner of the room. He followed. They did not eat that evening.

Ellie's eyes flew open in the darkness. Night had fallen. She still lay on the sofa. This time she had a face in her mind. She saw him so clearly. She also remembered what happened next. Every detail of the night of passion she had shared with Thomas! Her face flushed. Where had all that come from? She'd never had such a powerful sexual dream before. Ellie replayed it all and felt her body respond. Christ, she thought, it had never been like that with James.

Thinking of James brought *his* image to mind. Irritated, Ellie returned her focus to the dream. She wanted to think of Thomas, not James. The pain of the desertion fell away; it no longer mattered. She hadn't lost anything important at all. James had been right; they'd had their problems. Ellie wasn't sure if she'd ever really loved him; she felt more for the man in her dream. But that was insane. *He* wasn't real.

Chapter 4

Ellie dragged herself into work the next day despite exhaustion. After the dream she spent most of the night tossing and turning, the feel of Thomas's body, warm and strong, naked against hers, intense in her mind. No, it felt more real than that, her body itself remembered the experience. She drowned in the feeling of his mouth on hers, the scent of his skin, the gentleness in his voice as he murmured how much he loved her. The look of his face in the candlelight, the desire in his eyes as he gazed at her, stirred her in a way she had never known before.

How could her imagination have created something with so much power to affect her? It must be the grief over James but she didn't believe it, not deep down. The night had been long and silent. The dream intensified the loneliness she felt. She had no one *real* to be with, to hold her close, to love her. Ellie longed to talk to someone. Walking through the warehouse to the office where she worked, the realisation came she needed to step back into life. Perhaps then she could forget about Thomas.

She arrived ten minutes late but no one noticed. The other office workers had all gathered around a colleague, Maggie, to hear about her new granddaughter and look at photos. Ellie listened without interest, her head full of cotton wool.

The office manager walked in and Maggie put the photos away. Ellie sat down at her desk to start work but could only stare at the empty document on the computer screen, captivated by the flashing curser but unable to remember what needed to come next. She had to write a report about . . . something. What was it?

Her gaze fell onto a red file. Of course, she had to write up the latest catalogue of the company's products: office supplies. All the prices needed to be updated and new items added. Ellie forced herself to focus. She found the information required and started typing.

Constantly distracted by images of her night of passion with Thomas, the catalogue took most of the day. Ellie spoke to no one until lunch-time. In the staff room she told one of her colleagues about James. Later, her co-workers' expressions told her the news had done the rounds. By the time five o'clock came, Ellie felt drained. She shut down the computer, desperate to go home and sleep. Several people expressed their sympathy and invited her out for a drink. Ellie felt warmed by their concern but, dizzy with tiredness, declined their offers.

On the way home, Ellie remembered she needed to buy food so stopped at a shopping mall. She picked up a few items then joined a queue at the supermarket checkout. Someone came up behind her. She turned and looked right into the eyes of the man who had accused her of killing his son! Rigid with shock, she stared at him.

The man recognised her right away. He returned her gaze with an anguished expression but said and did nothing, fighting to bring himself under control. Ellie watched as anger, followed by fear and uncertainty, wove across his face. They passed and he relaxed. She had no idea what was going on. They carried on staring at each other, neither able to turn away.

"I'm sorry," the man said, after a while.

"What?"

"About the other night." A look of desolation flooded over his features. "I'm sorry," he said again, "but you reminded me of someone."

Ellie stared at him, taking in his straw coloured, straggly hair and the sweat glistening on his blotchy face. He didn't look well.

"Who?" Ellie asked.

The man looked uncomfortable. He stared at his feet then put down his shopping basket. He looked round at the shop entrance as if looking for a way to escape. "A friend," he said.

Ellie knew he was lying.

The checkout became free and Ellie loaded her few pieces of shopping onto the conveyer. She paid and moved aside. She waited until the man had put his purchases through but he ignored her and walked away. Ellie, however, knew she couldn't leave it like that and ran after him.

"Tell me about Thomas?" she asked.

The man looked at Ellie intently for a moment. "You don't want to know," he said and continued on.

"Wait. Please. I realise it's crazy but I want to know about Thomas."

He stopped and the two of them stood together in the glare of the shopping mall. The sound of people talking, the rattling of shopping trolleys and the background music faded into silence. A bubble of stillness settled around them and, in that moment, Ellie knew the two of them were linked in some strange way far beyond her understanding.

She broke the spell. Although nervous and unsure, she asked, "Look, would you like a coffee or something?" She expected him to refuse but he sighed and nodded.

They moved to a nearby cafe. Her companion looked dazed so Ellie ordered two coffees while he sat down in a corner. She looked at him as she waited for the drinks. He slumped in the chair and fiddled with his sleeve. He had an air of hopelessness about him. All of a sudden, Ellie felt a profound sorrow and guilt, almost as if she *had* done something to hurt this man. But that made no sense. She had never met him before the other night.

The coffees ready, she sat down opposite the man. "My name's Ellie," she told him.

"I'm Adam," he replied, reaching for his drink. Ellie watched as he tore open a packet of sugar and poured it into the mug.

"Why did you accuse me of killing your son Thomas the other night?" she asked.

Adam touched the creamy foam on the surface of his coffee and stared at the white bubbles captured on the tip of his finger. "Why are you so interested?" he said without looking up.

Ellie sipped her coffee. The hot liquid scalded her tongue so she replaced the mug on the table. She took a deep breath. "To be honest, I'm not sure. This is going to sound stupid but I have this strong feeling I should talk to you. I've had some odd dreams these last few days." She paused, uncertain how to continue. "Dreams about someone called Thomas." Ellie watched Adam, trying to gauge his reaction, but his face remained impassive as he focussed on his drink. She carried on. "It seems weird that you should accuse me of . . ." she hesitated, "well, of killing your son, Thomas, right now."

"What dreams?" Adam asked.

"In the first one I stood in a churchyard looking down at a grave. The headstone had a name on it: Thomas."

Adam said nothing.

"Ever since then, I've felt this inexplicable sense of loss for Thomas as if he is real. And now I seem to be dreaming of being with him alive. I know this will sound insane, it *is* insane, but I can't get him out of my mind. I'm sure it's all coincidence but when you came up to me outside the bar accusing me of killing someone called Thomas, I got the strangest feeling. I'm sorry, this doesn't make much sense."

"*Nothing* makes sense, I think you'll find," Adam said.

Ellie took a sip of her coffee, burning her mouth again. "Tell me about *your* Thomas. You said he was your son."

"You'll think *I'm* crazy," Adam replied. "Well, to be honest, I have had some problems."

"Problems?"

Adam shifted in his seat. He picked up his spoon and stirred his coffee, staring at the spinning foam. Ellie watched it too as she waited for him to speak. When he did, his voice cracked but he cleared his throat and continued. "I thought I was someone else for a while. I had to be. . . . counselled."

Ellie felt a wave of compassion for Adam. Whatever happened to him hadn't been easy to cope with.

"It started about two years ago. I was at university but it all got too much. I couldn't handle the work and started drinking and doing drugs. My life fell apart. You know how it is." He looked at

Ellie, at her clear complexion and bright grey eyes staring into his. "Well, maybe you don't. Anyway, one day I took some stuff. I don't even know what now but it had something wrong with it. Damn near killed me. I was out of it for days.

"When I came to, I thought I was someone else, an older man. I didn't feel my body fitted me anymore, it felt *wrong*. I checked in the mirror and I still looked the same but when I shut my eyes I felt the weight of fat on my stomach although I've always been thin. And I felt a pain in my back. I was *old*, man, *old*. My hands shook and my chest hurt. I could, kind of, still see where I was and move around but it felt alien. I remembered what I did in this other life and it had nothing to do with being a university student. I even knew my name: Mathew.

"Well, I just couldn't cope. The feeling didn't go away. It lasted the whole of the day. I fell asleep off and on but each time I woke up it was the same. I couldn't function. I tried drinking and more drugs but they made it worse. I couldn't eat or sleep, did nothing but stare into space, so my mates got worried. I couldn't relate to the real world around me anymore. They got a doctor in, and he admitted me to hospital."

Adam stared at Ellie, his eyes full of anguish. "People thought I was crazy. Well, I was in a way. I couldn't handle the truth."

"And what was that?"

"That it wasn't just some mental illness." Adam paused. "Tell me, do you believe in reincarnation, that we've actually lived before?"

"Well, I know there've been some quite well documented cases of it." Ellie had watched a TV program once about a young Indian girl who had vivid memories of being an old woman who used to live in a village the girl had never visited. When taken there, relatives of the dead woman verified everything the girl recalled. The story had been quite convincing. "You're saying you were remembering a past life?" Ellie asked.

Adam's eyes took on a distant look as if he saw a different landscape. "Yes. I know it sounds incredible but I knew I was experiencing memories of being someone else. Perhaps the drug stimulated a part of my memory inaccessible under normal circumstances, I don't know. The memories were so real, more real than what I saw around me in the present. The problem was,

I couldn't control them. All this stuff kept intruding. It was bloody awful.

"Nothing made sense. I just felt in the wrong place, that I should be back on the hills with my sheep. I knew I had been a farmer, you see, who lived in England over a hundred years ago. I had more sheep than any others in the neighbourhood." Adam's manner changed. His body straightened and Ellie sensed the pride in his voice. "I owned more land, too." Adam slumped again. "I had a wife," he paused, "poor Mary. She died but I had my son to help. Thomas."

Ellie struggled to come to terms with the implications of what she was hearing. She gripped her coffee mug, something real to cling to in a shifting universe.

Adam looked through her, his attention back in the past. "I had another son but he died as a baby so Tom was special. We were close. He took over the farm when I fell and hurt my back. He was a good lad, meant everything to me. He was all I had. We tended the sheep together. Often they'd escape and run all over the Man. We would have to chase them back."

"What do you mean, 'all over the man'?"

"Man? Oh, yes, the Long Man. That was the name of the giant drawn on the hillside above my farm. You could see it for miles."

The image of a huge pale figure on a green hillside filled Ellie's mind and shock ran the length of her body. Surely it couldn't be? "The figure, did it have two large poles either side?"

Adam looked at her curiously, "Yes, why?"

"Because I remember it, too." They stared at each other. Adam looked uncomfortable. Ellie's mind reeled. Had she looked into this man's eyes before?

In another life?

Ellie picked up her coffee and took several sips, struggling to come to terms with what had just happened.

"Tell me what you remember," Adam asked.

"I told you I've been having dreams, well, I saw the figure on the hill in my first dream. It was so vivid. I remember staring at the giant then I walked away into this churchyard and found the grave of Thomas. I knew I'd loved him and felt the most profound grief and yearning for him. I haven't been able to get this sorrow out of my mind. It's followed me out of the dream and into my life."

Ellie described all that had occurred at the party, how she'd got lost in the woods. "I found myself by a lake and all this grief for Thomas welled up. Something about the reflection of the moon on the lake started it, I think. All I knew was that I wanted to follow Thomas into death. I actually walked into the water. It was insane."

"Thomas drowned."

"What?"

"My son, he drowned."

"Oh my God," Ellie whispered. She looked at Adam. His eyes had glazed over and Ellie knew his attention had returned to that other time. His face took on a look of extreme pain and she became afraid. What if he reacted badly again? Adam reached for his coffee. His hands shook as he raised it to his mouth and drank but he stayed calm.

Ellie struggled to comprehend what had happened. The man in front of her had experienced what he believed were memories of an actual past life, memories that seemed to link to experiences she herself had been having. If it were true, it meant she was remembering a real life lived before she had even been born. The image of Thomas came into Ellie's mind and she felt again that now familiar longing and sorrow. Could it be true? Was the man she saw in her mind real? It would explain why her dreams had affected her so much. Why couldn't she remember more? All she had were a few glimpses and emotional reactions. Ellie looked at Adam, at the tension on his face. Maybe it was just as well, she thought.

"Adam," Ellie said. "Tell me about Thomas."

Ellie knew it might upset Adam to talk about his past life but she *had* to know more about Thomas.

Adam shifted uncomfortably in his seat and sucked on his bottom lip. "He was such a lad, always up to mischief as a child. I never knew where he was most of the time. He loved to be out on the hills, climbing trees or playing in streams. He'd come back covered in mud or with some animal. He found a badger once, mauled by a fox it was. Tom had blood all over him. I had my

Mary then and she made such a fuss about it. Anyway, it died. The boy was upset for days.

"Mary was a good woman. When Tom was eighteen she took sick and died. She got a fever." Adam fell silent, a mixture of emotions playing over his face. "We buried her and carried on. That's what you had to do. We had sheep to care for. Thomas took it bad but he kept going. If it hadn't been for him I'd have let it all go, drowned myself in ale. No, he took over a lot of the work for a time and eventually the pain passed. Thomas grew into a man that year. We worked the farm together until I fell from an oak tree in the autumn. I had to rest in bed for months. I never walked properly again. Thomas took on the whole farm after that.

"We got on really well together." Adam's voice grew gruff and he cleared his throat. "Then he met a girl."

Ellie couldn't breathe. Could Adam be talking about her? Ellie tried to sense something but felt nothing. It seemed her mind only leaked memories under certain conditions, unlike Adam's whose memory had been torn completely open by his drug use.

"What was she like?" Ellie felt nervous. What would happen when Adam remembered the part where Thomas died? Adam believed Ellie, or the woman she had been, at least, had been responsible.

"He started going away. Oh, not for long, just for the day. At first he wouldn't say where but then he told me. He'd met someone he liked. She lived in a nearby village. He'd seen her at a fair one day and they'd got talking. It grew from there. He began to visit her more and more. He didn't neglect his work but he didn't have time to spend with me. I missed him but I didn't mind. I wanted him to marry. He needed a wife.

"One day he brought her to meet me. I liked her, a pretty little thing with light coloured hair and a pale complexion. Her name was Helen."

"What did she look like?"

Adam picked up a paper napkin off the table. He folded it into a concertina shape as he talked. "She was short and quite thin with straight light coloured hair," Adam smiled, "and so nervous she hardly said a word to me at first but in time we got on well. She laughed a lot. They looked good together; everyone said they made a perfect couple.

"They courted for about six months and had a spring wedding in the village church."

The church, Ellie remembered it from her first dream on the beach. Thomas lay in the graveyard. The image of the grey, stone building returned with its beautiful phoenix window. So they had been married there. Ellie wished she could remember their wedding. She tried to imagine how it might have been but could not.

Ellie turned her attention back to Adam.

"She became a good wife to Tom. Right from the start she made the old farmhouse into a home again. Tom and I hadn't bothered with it much after Mary died, only doing what had to be done. A house needs a woman. She cleaned and scrubbed and brought laughter back. And she helped take care of me. She was an angel, so kind and gentle, never making me feel a burden although I knew I was."

How bizarre, Ellie thought, he was talking about *her*. It sounded as if she had been a nice person in this other life. She ached to know more.

"Yes, she was an angel," Adam repeated. "They were so happy. I loved them both a great deal, they were my life." Suddenly he screwed the napkin into a ball. He gripped it so tight his skin turned white at the knuckles. He raised his head and glared at Ellie. She gasped at the look of hatred in his eyes. "That is, until *you* came back." He spat out the words.

Ellie gaped at Adam as the implication of his words sunk in. She hadn't been Thomas's wife. All further thought dropped from her mind as Ellie noticed Adam's hands now shook and his face looked distorted. Some kind of internal struggle raged inside. Ellie became afraid. The persona of the old farmer now had control and meant her harm. Adam stood and his hands lifted as if he might reach for her throat. Ellie pushed her chair away from the table ready to make a run for it.

"You stole him away from Helen and then you killed him," Adam snarled. A trickle of spit flowed from his mouth. Ellie watched in fascinated horror as it ran down his chin.

"No, I didn't," she found herself saying. "I loved him. I never would have harmed him. I never meant for any of it to happen. Believe me." Adam stared at her and must have seen the truth in her face because the vehemence left his expression and his body slumped.

Ellie relaxed, sensing the crisis had passed but saw Adam's eyes now stared vacantly and she became afraid for another reason. Maybe it had all been too much and her questions had pushed him over the edge into insanity. He obviously found his past life memories hard to bear and she'd brought them all into his mind. Ellie desperately wanted to know more about her and Thomas but knew she couldn't ask Adam to go through it all again.

A deep sadness welled up. She'd been responsible for destroying a marriage and somehow killing a man. How ironic, Ellie thought, that now in her present life the tables had turned and *her* relationship had been destroyed by another. Was it some sort of poetic justice? There was a special word for it, yes, karma. Ellie couldn't think any more about it, though, for Adam worried her. He looked dazed.

Adam?" she said, "Are you OK?" Instinctively, she reached out and gently touched his hand. The physical contact brought him back into the present and he looked at Ellie, staring into her eyes for a long time. She held his gaze, wanting him to see her remorse even though she herself had no recollection of the actual events.

"I'm sorry," she said. "I'm *truly* sorry." Ellie spoke from somewhere deep inside. She felt she had to say this. In a past she could not remember she had been directly involved in events that caused Adam to lose his son.

They sat for a while, her hand on his, held in a moment that spanned time. Adam continued staring into her eyes, searching for the truth. The compassion Ellie already felt for this man grew stronger. He had carried his suffering for so long. She wished she could help him.

"You have to let the pain go," she said. "It's over. Thomas isn't dead anyway. How can he be? You and I are here. *We* have come into new lives; surely he must have as well." Ellie squeezed Adam's hand. He relaxed and some of the anguish left his eyes.

"You're right," he said. "Of course, you're right. I don't know why I've never seen it that way before. I guess, I tried to block out the whole experience and the drugs and alcohol screwed up my mind."

Ellie smiled. "You have a new life now, so do Thomas and Helen. Life doesn't stand still. You've been so busy trying to fight your past life you've forgotten about the present. You need to focus on what's happening now. Do you have a wife, girlfriend?"

"Yes, no," Adam said. "Well, I had a girlfriend, Mia, but she got fed up with me, couldn't handle the way I was. I don't blame her."

"Did she care for you?"

"For a while."

"Could you give her a call? Perhaps the old memories will fade if you make new ones."

"Maybe."

"Do you still take drugs?"

Adam nodded. "Not as much since being in hospital but yes."

"Get help to give them up."

Adam stared at Ellie. "Maybe you're right." He carried on staring at her. "You don't remember, do you?" he said.

"What?"

"How he died?"

Ellie looked at Adam, afraid the conversation would bring back his hostility. She scanned his face but he looked calm and relaxed. "I only remember snatches of stuff: just being with him on the hills, that we were . . ." she paused a moment, "close and that he died somehow. I know I loved him, still love him now. I can see his face, feel his touch and I miss it as if it was yesterday but everything else about that life, his life, his. . . . death, no, I know nothing."

"I'm sorry for. . . . just now, I scared you, didn't I?"

"Just a bit," Ellie said with a rueful smile, "but don't worry about it."

"It wasn't fair."

"It's OK."

"Your name was Anne."

Ellie stared at Adam. "Anne?" He nodded.

"Anne," she repeated. Yes, it fitted somehow. The name sank

into her mind and permeated throughout her body. Anne, Ellie, Anne.

"Thomas was obsessed with you."

Ellie looked at Adam, gauging his mood. "Can you tell me about it?" she asked.

"Helen and Thomas had been married for two years before you came. They were happy but one day he changed. He became distracted, tense. He denied anything was wrong but started being out a lot, working, he said, but sometimes Helen went looking and couldn't find him. Then one day she did; he was with you. It broke her heart."

Ellie felt sick. She had obviously ruined Helen's life. Ellie wasn't sure she wanted to listen to any more of this story.

"She begged him to stop seeing you. He agreed and we all tried to go on as before. I think he did try to keep away but, as I said, he was obsessed with you. You were so alike; you both loved the countryside. Anyway, Helen changed, became bitter and angry and Thomas became sad and quiet. The happiness went from our lives."

"I'm sorry," Ellie said. "I don't know what to say. This is just so strange. I don't remember any of this. I wish I could. Tell me, what was I like?"

"You weren't like other people. You lived in the village but were always out on the hills. You had been like that even as a young child.

"You were about seven when you first came into our lives. I remember how tiny you were, so delicate, with very long dark hair and fine features. You were a fey little thing, wild, always out in the woods, like a nymph, playing in the streams and the rivers, dancing over the hills. That's how you got to know Thomas. He was the same, always wandering around. You and he got on well as children, always out in the country together, climbing trees, running and playing around the farm and the woods."

"We knew each other from that young?"

"Yes. Those were good days. I had my Mary and the farm was doing well. Thomas was happy. Mary didn't like you two spending so much time together. She said you were too wild and would get Thomas into trouble. Some in the village said you weren't quite normal, maybe even touched."

"Touched?"

"Odd, you know, mentally. I don't think you really were," he added hurriedly, when he saw Ellie's dismayed expression, "but you were just a bit too strange for them."

"What do you mean?"

"Well, you used to play in the church but you wouldn't go to the Sunday service. People didn't like that. You also wandered around the countryside at night quite often."

Ellie felt more and more intrigued as Adam spoke. Then, all of a sudden, the brown décor of the café faded and her mind filled with a bright image.

Anne ran up the green hillside past the outline of the Long Man laid out in the grass. She laughed out loud with the joy of the wind in her hair and the strength in her body as she climbed. When she reached the top she lay breathless on the ground for a moment then allowed her body to roll down the hillside, over and over, scattering sheep in all directions. Elated, she came to a standstill and lay face down in the grass. It tickled her skin and the odour of damp earth and green, growing things made her feel light headed. When she raised her head, she noticed a yellow flower and softly touched its stem, moved by its fragile beauty: a cowslip.

She flung herself over and stared up into an infinite blue sky. It was summer and the day would last forever. Anne knew she should go home but the woods and fields were more her home than anywhere else. She adored their living beauty.

Anne scrambled up and ran across the meadow until she reached the village. She continued running through the graveyard and into the church. In the building she savoured the cool darkness. The stained glass windows shone in the dimness. She loved their vivid colours. She walked into a side chapel and sat down in front of a small window. It was her favourite. In the centre stood the figure of a man, St Peter, holding a key. All around him were circles, each one with either a flower or a butterfly inside it. Beneath his feet a square shaped section held a bee.

That's odd, Ellie thought. She had seen this church before, in her dream on the beach, but the window had been different. A phoenix had been beneath the man and the butterflies. Why weren't the windows the same? The question faded away, however, as the memory of sitting in the church intensified.

She felt a deep feeling of peace and something else: an indefinable sense of subtle vibrating energy. The whole church felt alive and filled with a love that gently drew her into itself until she could perceive no distinction between her and it. Tears came into Ellie's eyes at the holiness of the feeling. She had never felt anything like it before, at least, not in her present life.

"Ellie?"

"What?" Ellie became aware again of sitting in the café.

"You seemed miles away, were you remembering something?" Adam asked.

"Yes. I was just imagining what it must have been like for Anne as a child." But it had been more than just fantasy, Ellie thought to herself. The whole experience felt real, especially what she experienced in the church. She longed to reconnect with that time but the memory slipped away from her. She turned her attention back to Adam. He could tell her more about her life as Anne. "You said Thomas and Anne grew up together, what happened? How come he married Helen?"

Adam screwed up his eyes in an effort to remember. "You got sent away when you were about thirteen. I don't know why. All I know was that one day you stopped coming to play with Thomas. He missed you badly, took a long time to get over it. You two had gone everywhere together for years.

"I don't know where you went but we didn't see you for a long time. Thomas met Helen and, as I said, they were happy."

Adam stared into the distance. "I was in the garden the day you came back. I watched you walking over the fields, all grown up, your long dark hair blowing in the wind. I can see you now, tall and thin like a reed but graceful. You had something about you that drew the eye. You came to the garden wall and asked if Thomas was in. I told you he had gone to Eastbourne with his wife, Helen. You looked shocked then smiled a wistful smile and turned away." Adam's face took on a hard look. "Some time after that Thomas started being away lot and then Helen saw you two together. After that our lives were never the same. Thomas and Helen started arguing."

"Tell me how Thomas died. I have to know," Ellie whispered.

"I told you, he drowned."

"But how?"

"It happened when Helen tried to kill you."

"What?" Ellie gasped.

"Bitterly jealous, it all turned her head." Adam's pain showed in his expression but he continued. "One night Thomas said he had to go out. Helen suspected him of going to meet you. Something snapped inside. She took a kitchen knife and followed. When she found you with Thomas down by the lake she tried to stab you but Thomas got in the way. He took the blow and fell into the water. He drowned."

Ellie couldn't speak. The room went dark and she felt faint.

An ink black lake stretched before her. The perfect reflection of a full moon floated on its surface. She stood with Thomas looking at it but then a woman with long fair hair and a twisted expression of anger and hate on her face came out of the darkness. She lunged at them. Thomas fell into the water and the moon's reflection broke into a thousand flickering lights.

Anne plunged in to help him but he sank. Desperately, she pulled him back up but he did not breathe. She shook him, trying to will the life back into his limp body but to no avail. In despair, she held him in silence and stillness. In time, the water stopped churning and the fractured reflections on the water merged back into the shape of the moon. Anne stared at it as she held Thomas to her. It became so cold she lost consciousness and darkness filled her mind.

Adam's voice brought Ellie back to the present.

"Helen ran crying and screaming into the village. It took a while to get out of her what had happened. Some of the villagers went to the lake. They found you both in the water.

"You were nearly dead, too, but you recovered. They brought Thomas back to the farm. I will never forget that day. He was my only son. I didn't want to live after that.

"If it hadn't been for you, Thomas and Helen would have had

a life together, the farm would have prospered. Because of you, Thomas died. Because of you, I was left alone."

Tears fell down Ellie's cheeks and her hands shook as she remembered holding Thomas in the cold, dark water.

"I saw it," she said, her voice trembling. "As you described it, I saw myself there. Oh God, it was so real."

Ellie couldn't stop crying. She felt raw. Her grief had become fresh and new. She had just relived Thomas's death.

"I'm really sorry. I. . . . I really loved him. I never meant for anything bad to happen. I know I should have stopped seeing him but I couldn't." Ellie scrabbled in her bag for a tissue and blew her nose. "Christ, I can't believe I'm talking like this but it's true. I know it's true."

"It's a bit hard to take, isn't it?" Adam said.

"Yes. You know, if it's any comfort to you, my fiancé just left me for another woman. It's probably some sort of karmic justice."

"You know, it's odd seeing you so upset," Adam mused. "I feel sorry for you now. I'm actually glad we've met like this. I feel a weight's been lifted from me. You're right, Thomas hasn't gone. He's probably out there somewhere living a new life, and my Mary, too. I hadn't looked at it that way before. Maybe now I can finally move on. I'll try to ditch the drugs, perhaps give Mia a ring."

"That's a good idea." Ellie smiled. But what was *she* going to do now? With everything she had relived still vivid in her mind, both beautiful and terrible, Ellie knew she would never be the same again. Somehow a doorway from the past had opened and memories of her life as a woman named Anne were seeping through. She wondered why.

As she did so, the image of a figure looking out over the countryside holding two staves drifted to the forefront of her mind and Ellie had the strongest feeling that in her life as Anne there existed something she needed to understand, to experience again, something linked to the place where it had all happened, the place she, as Anne, had obviously loved, the hill of the Long Man. But that wasn't all: her grief and yearning for Thomas had intensified. *Was* Thomas out there somewhere? Ellie wondered, and what were the chances they would ever meet again? She had met Adam. Had she already unknowingly met Thomas? Could he be James? She quickly dismissed the idea; it didn't feel right.

"Adam, the other day, outside the bar, how were you so sure I was Anne? You didn't know about my dreams or anything about me then. Do I look like her?"

"No, you don't, although there is something about the expression in your eyes but I didn't see that then. No, I sensed it. I instinctively knew you were Anne."

"I didn't recognise you at all but then my memories have been buried deeper," Ellie said. "It's only now that they seem to be surfacing."

They both stared at each other for a few moments then Adam said, "I had better get moving." He stood and reached down under the table for his shopping.

"Just one thing before you go," Ellie said. "Do you know where it all happened, where you lived on the farm?"

"England somewhere."

"Can you remember the name of the village?"

"Unfortunately not, I only know for sure that the figure on the hill was called the Long Man, that's clear in my mind."

"I wonder if it's still there."

"I would expect so."

"Then I should be able to find it. There can't be many figures like that in England."

"No." Adam looked at Ellie. "You're not thinking of . . ."

"Yes," Ellie said. "I'm going to go there."

Chapter 5

AFTER EXCHANGING PHONE NUMBERS AND saying good-bye to Adam, Ellie went straight home, turned on her computer and got the Internet up. Once born, the idea of visiting the actual area where her past life had occurred had grown. It was the right thing to do. She *knew* it. She needed to know more and felt the answers would come if she were back where it all happened. All she really had to search for were "Long Man," and "England." Ellie typed them into the search engine on her computer and waited to see what the Internet would throw up. The screen filled with sites after only a few seconds.

It was just so easy, as if destined. Ellie brought up the site at the top of the screen: *Hill Walking in South East England* and up came a list of hills to climb in the Sussex area. She clicked on the first one, Windover Hill, and a photo filled the screen. There was no mistaking it. The scene was just as she had "seen" it in her dream—the huge white outline of a man holding two poles on a green hillside.

Ellie stared at the image on the screen, the back of her neck tingling. It looked so familiar. She had walked up that hillside. She and Thomas had spent time together there. In that moment, she became aware of the past in her mind as a jumble of feelings and impressions she had been unconscious of before. A wave of excitement ran through her body. If simply looking at this photo had this effect what would happen when she actually walked over the Long Man?

She read the caption underneath the photo: The Long Man of Wilmington, Windover Hill, East Sussex. The only information about it was a brief description of how to get there so Ellie went back to the site list. She knew the name of the place now, Wilmington, so clicked on a site that said Long Man of Wilmington and the now very familiar figure again filled the screen. This site had a lot more information.

Ellie scanned through the text, intrigued by what she read. The Long Man of Wilmington, also sometimes known as the Wilmington Giant, was the huge figure of a man holding two staves cut into the turf on the slope of Windover Hill above the village of Wilmington, six miles north-west of Eastbourne in East Sussex, England. Measuring 226 feet high, it was apparently one of the largest representations of a man in the world. It was first documented in 1710 but thought to date much earlier.

It had originally been picked out in chalk. Grass growing over it made the figure only visible in certain conditions and gave rise to one of the Long Man's other names: the Green Man. In 1874 a Rev W. de St Croix of the Sussex Archaeological Society made it more visible using yellow bricks. These were replaced with white bricks in 1891. During the Second World War they were painted green to prevent enemy planes using the Long Man for navigation. It was now picked out with concrete bricks and regularly repainted white.

Fascinated, Ellie continued to read. The Long Man had been constructed so as to appear in proper proportion on the ground. Some people believed it had been altered over time, possibly once having facial features.

The origin and purpose of the giant was unknown. Various theories dated it anywhere from the Neolithic period to the late medieval. Some believed it to be a fertility symbol or a representation of some god or hero. Roman remains found on the site led some to think he was a Roman standard bearer. Other people thought the figure resembled figures on old Templar carvings or that it had been created by the monks in the Priory at

Wilmington, either as some sort of religious symbol such as a pilgrim or even simply for amusement. Some believed the Long Man was the guardian of a gateway and linked this to the church in the village, which was dedicated to St Mary and St Peter, guardian of the gates of Heaven.

As she read these words, Ellie had a sudden sense of something impossible to define yet which made her feel strangely uplifted, lighter somehow and more alive. She scrolled back up to the photo of the Long Man at the start of the site and stared at the man drawn on the hillside. "Guardian of the gates of heaven," Ellie repeated aloud. She liked the sound of that. The words had a ring to them that evoked a feeling of magic and mystery and made her long to travel to Wilmington more than ever.

Ellie returned to the text and read that many ancient religious sites had been Christianised by relating them to saints with similar attributes.

Another local legend had it that the Long Man was the outline of a giant who had died in the area. An actual burial site known as Giant's Grave existed on the hill. Several other prehistoric burial places were to be found in the area.

Ellie discovered that many ancient sites were in alignment with one another, the lines connecting them known as ley lines. The Long Man was apparently positioned on one of these lines connecting two ancient burial sites with the priory and the church in the village. A theory held that the Long Man could be a representation of the legendary being, the Dodman, who had laid out these lines.

The more Ellie read, the more interested she became. Going back to the site list, she clicked on one that featured Wilmington church and caught her breath as she stared at a photo of the Church of St Mary and St Peter in Wilmington. It was as familiar to her as her own apartment building. There were the dark stone walls, the porch, the small steeple and the spreading shape of the old yew in the churchyard just as she had "seen" them. Scrolling down, Ellie's mouth fell open as she saw a photo of a stained glass window identical to the one she had visualised whilst with Adam earlier. The caption told her it was called "The Bee and Butterfly Window" and depicted St Peter holding the key to heaven surrounded by images of local butterflies. She soon discovered the reason for the window in her dream on the beach being different as a photo of it came up next complete with the vivid phoenix. The text beneath explained that in July 2002 a fire had significantly damaged the church, including the Bee and Butterfly Window and described how fragments of the earlier window had been used to create a new one.

How could she have dreamed of the more recent window? Ellie wondered. She saw the old window in her life as Anne and so it had featured in her flashback but she had never seen the new version before. It made no sense.

Ellie went on to read about the ancient yew tree in the churchyard, so old it had to be supported by props and chains. Some believed it had existed for two thousand years. Near the church stood a priory built by Norman Benedictine monks. Both buildings had been constructed around the 12th century and were reputedly linked by an underground passage.

On this site Ellie found photographs of the surrounding area. It all looked so familiar it brought tears to her eyes: the soft green downs, the woods, the hedgerows, the wooden fences and sheep dotted on the hillsides. The images intensified her longing to go there even more.

Suddenly Ellie's mind filled with light and in her inner vision she saw a golden field.

Tall ears of corn scratched her legs as Anne walked. A hot but gentle breeze softly played across her skin. Twelve years old, she loved the feel of the earth beneath her feet, the power and strength in her physical body. Intense happiness flooded through her as she moved, one with a world filled with vibrant colour: blue sky above, yellow corn splashed with the fragile red petals of poppies below. In the distance, a skylark sang.

Anne reached a gate and entered the church-yard. Stepping over the gravestones, she laughed. Too afraid, the other children did not like this place. They whispered that the dead walked here in the middle of the night but she knew they did not. There was nothing to fear. One night she'd sat on a tomb waiting to see if anything would happen but the darkness remained peaceful with only the rustling of the old yew tree to disturb the silence. For her that night, the churchyard had been filled, not with dread, but magic—the beauty of a full moon floating serene amid a sprinkling of stars in the clear sky and the deep peace and joy she felt as she sat on the cold stone.

But now sunlight filled the graveyard and she could only see it as a place of life not of death. The hand of nature had clothed it so beautifully with trees and grass and flowers.

Ellie stared into space, no longer seeing the images on the computer screen but the ones that lived in her memory.

Anne walked over to the church and pushed through the heavy wooden door into the building. She loved it here and moved over to the altar, her gaze on the religious figures glowing with sunlight in the stained glass windows. The smell of polish permeated the air and dust glittered in a sunbeam falling upon the stone floor. She sat on a pew and relaxed into the tranquillity she always felt in the church. But then she heard a grating sound and a rush of air moved over her skin. It disturbed the flowers on the altar and a single red petal fell, looking like a drop of blood on the stone floor. Anne turned and smiled. They were there again.

The scene in the church faded and Ellie came back to the present sitting at the computer. She couldn't move, her mind reeling with the power of the images she had just experienced. Who were *they?* Ellie sought to recapture the scene but her inner vision remained dark. The peace and joy of the past evaporated, leaving Ellie with a wistful longing to experience that quality of happiness again. The vividness of the world in that former time shook her. The present seemed faded in comparison. The past had more reality, a brightness that did not exist now and she knew that in Wilmington she had lived a very special life, one in which she had known things she had now forgotten and yearned to understand again.

And in that place she had known and loved Thomas. He had shared the magic with her until tragedy overtook them, replacing her joy with a deep sadness and a sense of loss that had persisted into the present. There in the churchyard was his grave. Perhaps her body lay there, too. How would it feel to stand upon her own grave? How would it feel to actually enter the church and walk upon the hillsides around the village in reality? No doubts remained in Ellie's mind. She had to go to Wilmington and soon. She would not know peace until she had.

England. It seemed so far away. It *was* the other side of the earth. Just how, Ellie wondered, could she do it? She had no money but, as she had this thought, the answer came. James wanted to take over the house they had been building together. He would have to pay back her share. It would be more than enough for the trip and she could take long service leave from her job for a few months. So that was it. She could go to Wilmington. Her heart lifted. It was the right thing to do. She had never been more certain of anything.

Ellie went to the phone and rang James. He didn't answer his mobile at first. When he did, he was laughing and Ellie heard a woman's voice in the background. Catherine? Probably. A few days ago this would have filled Ellie with intense pain but now she accepted it. She and James hadn't been right for each other, not at a deep level, she knew that now.

"You can have the house," she said.

"You mean it? Oh, Ellie, I don't know what to say. You know, I'm really sorry. I . . ."

Ellie cut him off. "I want the money. How quick can you arrange it?"

"I'm sure I can do something within a week or two."

"I reckon you owe me at least forty thousand." It was quite a bit over half of what they had already paid for the house. She was surprised when James agreed. Guilt, she thought.

"I hope you'll be very happy in it," she said sarcastically but then felt sorry. Life wasn't that simple, she knew that now. Ellie remembered Thomas. How could she judge Catherine and James when she herself had stolen another woman's husband? She knew now how hard it was. She hated the idea that, as Anne, she had caused so much pain for Thomas's wife, Helen.

"Look," she said more sincerely, "I hope things work out. If you could get things moving as soon as possible I'd be really grateful."

"I'll do my best," James replied.

Ellie put down the phone.

No, Ellie thought, Catherine and James probably hadn't meant to hurt her, just as she had never meant to hurt Helen. With this realisation, a tendril of memory curled out from the darkness that shadowed her past life. As she shut her eyes, it unfolded into a full vision.

She stood on the hillside above the farm where Thomas lived watching him and Helen down below. Guilt cut through her body. She had to leave. How could she have happiness at another's expense? Tears trickled down her cheeks. But she loved him so. Her body ached for him that very moment. In his arms she knew a happiness that could not be measured. Somehow with him no barriers existed; she could be herself completely. He did not think her odd. He understood.

Ellie came back to the present with the windswept hillside still in her consciousness. Obviously she hadn't left for eventually Helen had discovered their affair and Thomas had been killed. But how had she and Thomas become lovers in the first place? Ellie longed to know.

There was so much she didn't understand. Ellie wasn't even sure when her life with Thomas had taken place. Her memories were so fragmented. She ran through what she could remember from her past life searching for more information in the kind of clothing she and Thomas wore and what had been around them. She remembered wearing a long skirt of rough material and had a brief impression of the interior of the house where she and Thomas had made love. There had been an old iron range that made it likely she had lived well over a hundred years ago at least. Adam had said that, too, Ellie suddenly remembered. She thought back to her first dream. Thomas's headstone had been inscribed with dates but she couldn't remember them. She would have to wait until she got to Wilmington.

And that would take a lot of organising, Ellie thought. First, she had to ask for leave from work then, never having been abroad before, she needed a passport. She would have to find a hotel near the Long Man and then book a plane ticket. A sick feeling bubbled up inside her at the thought of flying. The flight would be long to England. My God, Ellie thought, how can I do it? She hadn't flown before. Images of disaster whirled into her brain and she saw herself lost in a foreign airport, losing her luggage or, worse, the plane plummeting from the sky. A band of fear tightened around her chest but, as it did so, she became aware of something else, the gentle sound of rustling leaves. The room around her faded to black and once again a memory of the life she had lived before birth rose up out of the past to take over her mind.

She stood in the centre of a circle of trees on a hilltop at night. In the daytime, the whole countryside could be seen stretched out all around. It was one of her special places. Anne had come in the afternoon and kept company with a group of sheep, loving the soft breeze caressing her skin and the sound of the birds singing in the sky above. In time, made drowsy by the hot summer sun, she lay down and drifted off to sleep, not waking until night fell.

Even though unable to see in the dark, she could find her way home. Her feet knew the trails through the fields. The earth was her friend; it loved her as she loved it. Anne started walking but noticed lights coming up the hill. She watched them bobbing up and down and, as they came closer, saw they were lanterns carried by four men in long robes. Afraid, she hid behind a tree and waited.

When they reached the hilltop, she risked a look. She had seen three of them before. They came to the church. The other she did not know, an old man dressed in white. What were they doing here? Anne stayed hidden, uncertain what to do, but then the man in white turned and looked in her direction. She froze as he walked towards her. Eyes wide with terror, she stared up at the ancient face revealed in the lantern light.

But then he smiled and all fear fell away.

As Ellie sat at her computer in the present and looked into the eyes of the mysterious figure in white, she felt the presence of an indescribable power, and had the strangest feeling he could see *her*, Ellie, now, and not just the young child she had been, standing on the hill all those years ago! She continued to stare at him, held in thrall by his hypnotic gaze, and felt a profound love emanating from the old man. It reached out through time, drawing her into its welcoming embrace, and all her anxiety about travelling to England evaporated as if it had never been.

All too soon, the memory faded and a veil once again descended over the past, leaving Ellie shaken and wondering at the mystery of it. Through her memory, she had connected to someone who had the ability to move her, to reach into her deepest nature and ease her fear. Who *was* that man? Ellie ached to remember more. These tantalising glimpses into her previous life only created more questions but she had the distinct feeling that, hidden in the gaps in her memory, lay something important for her to know. What could it be?

Ellie hoped the answers she sought would be found in England but, for now, what she needed most was sleep. It had been a long day and so much had happened. She'd had enough. After eating a light meal, she went to bed.

Chapter 6

*A*NNE WALKED ON THE DOWNS *just above the Long Man, the soft grass yielding under her feet. She stopped and stared out at the huge expanse of countryside laid out before her. The morning had started out damp and gloomy but a strong wind had blown away the mist hanging in the valley. Now the sun shone warm on her child's clear, smooth skin. She wished Thomas would come so they could roll down the side of the hill. It was one of their favourite games. She watched him in the distance helping his father. She ran down the hill alone and walked on to another of her special places—the old oak wood.*

Running in and out of the trees, she whirled around and around until overwhelmed by dizziness. She stopped and stood still, laughing as the world spun around her. Holding onto a nearby tree for support, she sensed the life flowing in its trunk. She felt the energy of the earth beneath her feet and imagined being a tree herself with roots thrust down into the soil. They held her firm until the spinning stopped and her senses steadied. She felt she could reach out her branches and touch the sky.

A deep happiness welled up. She loved this wood so. The feeling flowed through her body and expanded to embrace the whole countryside beyond. Her body tingled and she felt grateful to be alive, to be able to run and dance and feel the wind in her hair. She started moving again, weaving in and out of the trees, swaying in time to the melody she felt in her body.

After a while Anne stopped and stared up at the leaves, a shifting mass of exquisite shades of green flickering in the sunlight. Their rustling merged with the sound of distant birdsong to create the music of the wood. The air smelled of damp earth and fresh grass.

Ellie woke in the morning with the memory still vivid in her mind and feeling incredibly alive, just as she had running through the oak wood in a distant time. The room glowed with a subtle light she had never noticed before and she became intensely aware of everything around her: the soft texture of her bedding, the feel of her own body, the beauty of the shells displayed on a nearby shelf.

The gentle light of dawn filtered through the curtains. Ellie dressed and went out, savouring the freshness of the air, untainted as yet by the usual car fumes of the city. Ignoring her car, she walked in the direction of the beach. Twenty minutes later, she stepped onto the sand, uplifted by the magnificent pink and blue sky. A gentle chill caressed her body and, as it did so, Ellie felt a peace that echoed the calmness of the ocean which stretched before her, a vast expanse tinged with the glow of the rising sun. Only tiny wavelets gently flattened out over the smooth sand. She removed her sandals and stepped into the icy water. Looking down, Ellie saw a white shell. She picked it up, captivated by its exquisite beauty. Wet, it sparkled with captured sunlight.

She loved the feel of the sand shifting beneath her bare feet and, just as she had in her dream earlier, felt an intimate connection to everything around her. Ellie realised she was looking at the world as if she were still Anne. No trace remained of the depression that had haunted Ellie even as a child. In that moment she felt light and clear. A seagull screeched above. Ellie looked up and followed its swooping flight then became aware of a gentle rumbling sound. She turned her gaze in its direction. The first of the morning flights had lifted off from the airport. The plane angled out away from the land and over the sea disappearing into the sky on its journey beyond. Soon she too would be on a plane like that. A thrill of excitement ran up her spine.

Ellie heard a car drive along the seafront and realised she had to get to work. As she walked back to her apartment, the enhanced perception brought back from her dream faded and the world returned to normal. Sadness reasserted itself and Ellie felt a sense of disappointment. She longed to recapture the joyfulness she had just experienced.

Late for work, Ellie found it hard to concentrate, her mind still caught up in a different place and time. She took an early lunch hour and went to a nearby travel agent. "Can I help you?" a smiling sales assistant asked.

"Yes," Ellie said. "I want to find out about going to England." She sat down in front of the young woman who handed her a glossy brochure. Ellie flicked through it, staring at photos of green hills and old buildings similar to those she had seen in her visions. She felt a strong inner pull towards what she saw.

"Whereabouts do you want to go, do you know?" the assistant asked.

"Oh, yes, East Sussex. I'd like to stay at a place called Wilmington, if that's possible."

"Let me see." The assistant's fingers flew on her computer keyboard. "Ah yes, there is a place in Wilmington, The Green Man Hotel. It's only small, does that matter?"

"No, no, that's fine."

"And when would you like to go?"

Ellie had talked to her office manager that morning who had agreed to let Ellie take some time off in a couple of months. "End of May."

"Yes, it'll be nice in England then." The assistant asked a few more questions about the flight and soon had a provisional itinerary worked out. "All you have to do is pay us a deposit and the balance closer to your departure. Do you want to go ahead with this now?"

Did she? Ellie wondered. Was she *really* serious about going half way around the world? The image of Thomas came into her mind and a powerful love for him and the countryside of Wilmington where they had lived swelled in her chest. She longed to walk there again. Hopefully by doing so, she'd be able to access more of her life as Anne. It had such a special quality about it, almost a touch of magic; she *had* to know more. "Yes. Yes, I do."

That night Ellie dreamt of being Anne as a young girl again.

She sat quietly in the church watching dust motes drifting down in a shaft of sunlight. The familiar smell of polish and old wood hung in the air. Anne felt happy. The old man she had seen on the hill with the ring of trees sat beside her. She looked at him. His face was deeply lined and his long beard almost white but he did not seem old. He looked at her with his smiling eyes and warmth spread throughout her body.

Anne looked behind her. Five monks of varying ages sat in the church with them. They wore long brown robes and remained motionless, their eyes shut. She stared at them for a few seconds, wondering why they did not move.

"Let us sit in stillness," the old man said. Anne turned back to him. He closed his eyes and an expression of peace spread over his face. She felt confused and uncertain. What should she do? She sat there for a while staring at the old man. As she did so, she became aware of the deep peace emanating from him. The sense of it grew and filled the church. Anne wondered what was happening but then the peace crept into her very body and she became quiet inside. Suddenly the old man spoke, "Open to the light within you."

Anne did not know what he meant so just continued to sit quietly, listening to the birds singing outside the church. After a while she shut her eyes and then it happened. She felt the aliveness of her body but also something else, a sense of space inside her, not empty but filled with life and light. It felt vast, as if it reached out forever. She somehow knew this was her essence existing within, but also somehow beyond the limits of her body.

Her relaxation deepened and she felt incredibly light and free, as if she could fly but without moving from the church.

Anne sensed the presence of the old man at her side and instinctively knew he was experiencing the same thing, that it was because of him she felt it.

She had no idea how long she sat in that state but Anne finally felt her arm being shaken. Opening her eyes, Anne found herself looking into the angry face of Edie, the woman who cleaned the church. The monks had gone

"What you doing here young Anne? Your mother will be after you."

Anne was afraid of this woman. Edie often gave her the harsh sting of her tongue when she found her in the church and had once even chased her outside with a broom. But, as Anne stared at Edie now, she suddenly knew that underneath the unpleasant scowl Edie felt alone and afraid and that the lines on her face were the scars of tragedy and sadness. Anne felt Edie's pain as if it were her own. She realised the poor woman couldn't feel the presence of spirit, her inner essence. Anne didn't know how she knew this, just that it was so.

"What's the matter with you?" Edie said. "Why're you looking at me like that?" Her expression turned from anger to fear.

Anne laid her hand on Edie's arm. "Don't be afraid." Anne's fingers tingled and a vibrant, loving energy flowed from her to Edie. The old woman's face softened and she looked as if she might cry. The sensation continued for a few seconds then Anne withdrew her hand. She slid off the pew and walked away. At the door she turned. The old woman stood motionless, staring after her.

Edie never chased Anne out of the church again. She would gaze at her thoughtfully but leave her alone.

When Ellie came back to waking consciousness, she still felt a sense of the incredible spaciousness she experienced in the dream and lay for a while, a loving energy surging through her body. She hadn't known it was possible to feel like this. It brought tears to her eyes. She felt intimately connected to everything, not just an isolated fragment in an alien world. Ellie thought about the old man in the church, wondering again who he was and how he'd been able to open her up in this way.

The alarm rang. As Ellie got ready for work, the feeling faded, leaving only a subtle trace. She longed to experience it again and couldn't forget the dream. The memory pervaded her day and fuelled her conviction that going to Wilmington was the right thing. Maybe there she'd be able to reconnect with the way she felt in the dream.

That night Ellie fell into bed, exhausted after a long day. She slept deeply but just before dawn images of Wilmington once again swirled into her brain.

She sat by a lake watching tiny insects walking on the surface. Her knees were green and scraped for she had fallen on the stony path whilst running away from a group of other children from the village. Why did they call her names? She had never done anything to them. Anne looked down through the water and watched the lazy passage of an old grey fish. Her sadness soon faded for, as she looked around, she felt the energy of spring in the air. Yellow primroses opened their petals to the sun everywhere and she sensed the vigour of the trees in the wood as they brought forth their new leaves after winter.

Anne heard the sound of footsteps and saw the old monk in white walking towards her. He stopped and smiled. She liked the old monk. She had sat with him several times now whilst he prayed in the church and knew they were friends. She called him Old Father. She felt happy in his presence although they rarely talked. He had told her she was spirit, not only flesh, and as spirit she was free and could know love and communion with the world. Anne felt it when she sat beside him but more and more she experienced it when she was out alone in the countryside and it had brought great joy into her life.

"Let us walk together," Old Father said. Anne scrambled to her feet and they ambled companionably over the fields and up past the Long Man where they stood looking out over the landscape.

Anne decided to voice something she had been wondering about, "Old Father, where do you live?"

"Ask the man on the hill," Old Father replied.

Anne stared at him in confusion, "Who?"

Old Father pointed down the hillside.

"Do you mean the Long Man?" Anne asked but the old monk merely looked at her with an enigmatic smile playing on his lips.

"There's your young friend," he observed.

Anne noticed Thomas at the bottom of the hill. He waved.

"Go," Old Father said, "he waits for you." The old man laughed. "There are trees to be climbed."

Anne ran down the hillside to Thomas. Two years older than her, he was tall and gangly with long, curly, black hair and brown eyes. He often laughed at her but not in ridicule like the other village children. He loved nature, too. The marks of a life spent out in the open were evident upon him now for mud and grass stained his trousers and a leaf clung to his hair.

He grinned as Anne came up to him. "Look, my aunt gave me some cake." Thomas held it out but as she reached for it, he pulled his arm back and ran off. "You'll have to catch me first," he shouted.

They ran over the green fields. Thomas moved fast. Anne didn't catch up until they reached the oak wood where she reached out and grabbed his shirt. He stumbled and she knocked into him causing them both to fall. They lay on the ground laughing. Anne took the cake from Thomas and ate it, savouring the sweetness of it in her mouth.

"Anne, look," Thomas whispered and pointed. Anne gazed entranced at the small grey squirrel that sat upright under a nearby tree. It grasped a nut in its paws. The small animal nibbled at it for a while until startled by a sudden noise. It froze then bounded away through the wood. Anne and Thomas smiled at each other. They both loved the birds and animals that shared the countryside with them.

Ellie woke with a feeling of joy. She smiled as she remembered the dream. She and Thomas had obviously been very happy as children. A sense of that bright spring day in the distant past stayed with her as she showered and dressed. At work every so often another impression from it filtered into her mind as she tried to concentrate: the feel of the gentle breeze blowing through her hair, the sound of sheep, Thomas laughing. At lunch time she lay back in an armchair in the staffroom and nodded off.

And this is how it went on for the next few weeks. She continued to have dreams about her previous existence at night but impressions also intruded into Ellie's waking life. Sometimes they came as images but at other times subtle sensations or feelings. It was as if a door had opened in her mind allowing the past to seep through and colour her experience. Ellie lived in two worlds, Australia in the present but also England in the past.

These flashbacks centred around her childhood from age ten

to about thirteen. She and Thomas could always be found together in the daytime, except for when he had to help his father on the farm. At those times Anne wandered around the countryside alone or spent time with Old Father and the other monks. She never saw them in the village, only around the hills and in the church. She welcomed their presence with her there and joined in their prayers, easily sinking into silence beside them. She would sit in stillness, open and intensely aware, feeling a powerful connection with everything around her.

Ellie experienced this heightened awareness and feeling of communion more and more. It characterised her experience as the child Anne, often remaining for a while when the flashbacks ended. It always faded but she found herself becoming increasingly sensitive and aware. She found it harder to watch TV with all its violence and took to walking on the beach and just sitting quietly. She stopped going out with Claire to noisy nightclubs and bars and longed for the nights when she trod softly on the cool, green hills of Wilmington.

She wore dirty, ragged clothes made of a coarse material in her dreams and visions and remembered often being cold and hungry so Ellie knew money had been scarce. She had a vague impression of a grey haired woman with a face heavily lined with care, perhaps her mother, but most of the memories centred on Thomas or the monks. She only saw very vague impressions of the village of Wilmington. The women there wore full length skirts or dresses and horses and carts seemed to be the only transport so Ellie guessed her life as Anne had taken place sometime in the eighteen hundreds.

It felt as if she were being pulled further and further back into the past away from present reality. She had a strong feeling she needed to remember something about her life as Anne, something important and yet it remained elusive. What could it be and why did she need to remember it? Although she now knew quite a lot about her past life as Anne, much of it remained fragmented or shadowed as if the past was reluctant to surrender some of its secrets. The image of the Long Man, the strange figure carved on the hillside, featured strongly in her flashbacks. She knew it held great significance but could not fathom why. She longed to get back there.

Arrangements for the journey to Wilmington fell into place. James paid Ellie for her part in their shared house. This enabled her to pay for the trip. She obtained a passport and told her parents she was going on holiday to England. They voiced concerns about her going so far away alone but she assured them she would be fine. She told no one the real reason for her journey, not even her closest friend, Claire. Ellie simply said she needed to get away for a while to recover from her break up with James. She wanted to keep her past life secret. It felt too sacred to expose to the inevitable disbelief of others. They would only think her insane.

The sunlit memories of her childhood as Anne eased the grief Ellie still felt over Thomas's death. One in particular stood out.

Near the end of a hot summer day she and Thomas lay next to each other staring up at the blue sky watching small white clouds drift by. They had been out most of the day and now lay resting in the sun on the summit of the hill with the ring of trees. Skylarks sang in the atmosphere above. The warmth, the peace and the music of nature lulled Anne's mind and her eyes closed. When she awoke sometime later, she saw Thomas sat staring at her with a strange expression on his face.

"What is it? Why are you looking at me?" she asked.

"I was just thinking how pretty you are." he said. She felt like laughing, but the look in his eyes stilled her voice and she blushed, unsure of what to say or do. His gaze flicked briefly to her chest. At thirteen, she felt self-conscious about her blossoming womanhood so sat up and pulled a handful of grass as a distraction, letting it fall through her fingers.

Looking back at him and seeing he still stared, she punched him gently, "Hey, stop it." Thomas laughed then and the moment passed but the way he looked at her stayed with her for a while. She felt unsettled, as if something she didn't understand had changed and yet it felt good, somehow exciting, but what it meant she did not know.

After this the dreams and impressions stopped. For more than a week Ellie felt a profound sense of disappointment and loss. The memories had become part of her life.

Then, one night, the memories of being in Wilmington started again.

Chapter 7

*A*NNE'S BACK ACHED WITH THE *weight of her heavy bag but she did not care. She was home. She walked through the main street of Wilmington and stared around her. It had been so long. Nine years. A few wisps of dark hair had escaped from the bun on the back of her head and she pushed them away from her eyes. A gentle rain speckled her face. She felt hot and restricted by her tight clothes and the smart brown leather shoes she wore pinched her feet. She longed for the loose blouse and skirt she wore as a child running barefoot and free here on the hills but she was a woman now.*

The scene changed and she found herself walking up over the Long Man. A day had passed. She felt sad for a reason which remained out of focus but Anne, nevertheless, delighted in the sight of the fertile, green landscape and it soothed her distress. She had missed it so. Pulling the pins from her long hair, she allowed it to fall down her back. The wind blew strands over her face but she did not care. She felt relaxed and free as her awareness expanded to embrace it all. She pulled off her shoes and walked barefoot through the lush grass. Thomas's home lay in the valley below. She longed to see him. What would he look like now? Would he be pleased to see her?

As Anne approached the farm, she saw Thomas's father in the garden. He stood leaning on a walking stick by a low flint wall and watched her approach.

"Mr Marshall," Anne said. "How are you?"

He stared at her in confusion for a few moments but then recognition dawned and his eyes widened.

"Why it's Anne. I didn't know you had returned."

"Just yesterday."

"My, how you've grown. You're so different." His gaze flicked over her narrow waist, taking in the smartness of her dark blue dress and the close fitting jacket, fine clothes, not often seen in the village. His gaze rested for a moment on her full breasts before returning to her face.

"Is Thomas here?" Anne asked.

"No. I'm sorry. He's in Eastbourne today with Helen."

"Helen?"

"His wife."

Anne didn't falter. She simply said, "Oh, I see. Well, I'll be going, then. Thank you," But as she walked away from the farm, the words "his wife" echoed in her brain. Thomas had married, how could that be? She hadn't expected it but why not? Most people married.

Ellie's eyes flew open in the darkness. A week ago she had been dreaming about being thirteen and living in Wilmington. Now she was remembering returning as a woman. Where had she been for all that time? Nine years. The dream had given her another glimpse into her past but also raised more questions.

The next came two nights later. Ellie lay down on the settee after a particularly busy day at work. Her eyes closed and the sound of the TV news faded from her consciousness.

She walked into the churchyard at Wilmington. A man stood outside the entrance of the church. Anne recognised him instantly although he'd been a youth the last time she saw him. Thomas. He stared out over the fields and did not notice her. Anne stopped and looked at him, shy and uncertain. What would she say to him after all this time? He was taller and gone was the gangly thinness she had known and gently teased him about.

He had filled out and exuded a strength born from hard years working on his father's farm. His dark hair still looked the same, curling down to his collar but his face, shadowed with stubble, seemed different, displaying a seriousness of expression she had not seen before.

Anne moved towards him but then a slender young woman with light coloured hair tied back in a blue ribbon came out of the church. She slipped her arm in his and looked up at him. He said something and she laughed. Although she longed to see Thomas again, Anne felt too awkward in that moment so slipped behind a tree and waited until they passed.

Helen was pretty, Anne thought, as she watched them walk away together into Wilmington. They made a good couple. She felt sad, even though the affection between her and Thomas when she last knew him had never developed into anything more than a childish friendship, she had always thought she and Thomas would be close for ever. The idea of him marrying someone would have been unthinkable to her then but what else could she expect, she had been gone a long time. Feeling sad, Anne walked into the church. It lay empty. She sat awhile there, hoping that perhaps her friends the monks might come but they did not. Where were they? She hadn't seen them anywhere since coming back. Anne waited until the light began to fade then hurried outside. She needed to get home. She had been away too long.

Ellie woke feeling anxious, remembering vaguely there had been some problem at home that day in the past but couldn't bring it to mind. Her thoughts turned to Thomas and Helen. They had seemed so happy. Ellie wondered how her affair with Thomas had started. She soon found out.

The next night Ellie had one of the most vivid dreams she had so far experienced.

She walked back home from a trip to a nearby village along a narrow winding road. Suddenly the sunlit day darkened. A few minutes later, dark clouds piled up in the sky and heavy drops of rain fell. An angry rumble echoed over the hills. The rain increased and a fork of lightening arced down across the downs followed by a loud crash of thunder. A gust of wind travelled up the valley and whipped Anne's long skirt tight around her legs. She ran towards a wooden barn. As she reached it, the rain poured down.

Inside it smelt of hay and animals. Grateful for the shelter, Anne stood by the door and watched the storm. A strange muted glow lay over the countryside. A violent wind swept across the open fields pushing down the corn and surging through the trees. They thrashed wildly as if alive with some demonic force. Anne smiled. She loved days like this, when nature played rough and wild. A rustle came from behind her and, startled, she turned. Someone stood in the shadows at the back of the barn. Anne held her breath as the person walked forward.

Thomas stopped and stood staring at her. "You're back," he said after a moment.

"Yes. I came to the farm one day but you weren't there." She paused. "Your father told me you're married."

Thomas said nothing but carried on looking at her, his gaze travelling over her body.

Anne flushed.

"You are so different and yet," Thomas smiled, "just the same." A look of pain passed over his face. "I missed you."

"I'm sorry. I didn't want to go."

"I heard you'd been sent to London."

"Yes." A loud crash of thunder sounded outside and she fell silent as heavy rain poured down. Neither could think of anything else to say. They both felt awkward and unsure. So they just looked at each other. But as they did so, memories came swirling out of the past, encircling them and linking them back to when they had last been together. They both remembered how it had been between them as they ran wild in the countryside, their hearts full of joy. The time apart disappeared as they recognised and reconnected with each other. They smiled.

"It's good to see you, Anne," Thomas said.

"And you."

A flash of lightening lit up the barn. Anne and Thomas stared outside. The fields were flooding. The strong wind blew the rain in, wetting their clothes, so they moved further inside. Another gust swirled into the barn, tossing loose straw over them. They *laughed, an easy laugh of simple happiness as they used to do. But then they looked into each other's eyes and the awkwardness returned. For some time neither could look away. They were no longer children but man and woman, and, in that moment, the bond that linked them before transformed into something else. As it did so, Anne turned away and walked back to the entrance. She could no longer meet his eyes as a great sorrow filled her. Thomas was married. He loved another. There could never be anything between them.*

As suddenly as it started, the rain stopped and the clouds rolled away from the sun. Brilliant light broke through, illuminating the countryside. Up over Windover Hill and the Man a rainbow shimmered into existence. Anne felt Thomas come up behind her but couldn't look at him, for in her there had awakened something she dare not let him see.

"The rain's stopped," she said, simply. "I must go." With these words, she ran off through the meadow and down the road, heedless of the floodwater and mud. She felt Thomas watching her but did not look back. As she hurried home, all Anne could think about was Thomas. She longed to go back to the barn and ask him to walk with her to their favourite places. But she knew it wouldn't be right, her feelings would betray her. What happened in the barn had burned itself into her mind. When she looked at Thomas, saw the boy she knew now turned into a man, she longed to reach out and touch him in ways that had never occurred to her as a child all those years ago.

Ellie found it difficult to concentrate on her work the next morning. The scene in the barn and the moment her passion for Thomas ignited kept replaying. She couldn't stop feeling again and again the sadness and frustration that this man she felt so drawn to should be denied her.

As Ellie sat in the staffroom at lunchtime, she closed her eyes and found herself walking through Wilmington.

She saw Thomas standing by the village shop. He turned and looked at her. She nodded at him and went past but he remained in her thoughts as she made her purchases and the brightness of her day diminished when she came out of the shop and found he was no longer there.

A little later, as Ellie sat at her computer struggling to maintain interest in a financial report, a wave of tiredness overcame her. She shut her eyes and once again a memory rose up to dominate her consciousness. The past, it seemed, would not be denied.

Anne walked over the Man. She saw Thomas coming up the hill. When he reached her, he stopped. "How are you?"

"I am well," she answered. They stood there for a moment, looking at each other, but then they both walked on. They who had been so close for so many years were acting like strangers. It tore at her but it had to be. At the bottom of the hill she looked back. Thomas had stopped. He stood motionless, staring down at her.

Ellie spent that evening alone trying to watch TV but could not concentrate. Thomas lived constantly in her thoughts. She went to bed early in the hope she might see him again. The life of her dreams had come to mean more than her present reality. She was not disappointed.

Anne walked into the old oak wood. She often came, finding it a place of sanctuary and peace. As she passed between the great oaks, she stopped in surprise. Thomas sat against a tree. He looked to be asleep. What was he doing here? It was her special place. But then she remembered. It had been his special place, too. As children they had gone there together, spending hours watching the squirrels.

Going as close as she dared, Anne hid behind a tree and looked at him. Relaxed in sleep he looked more like the youthful Thomas she knew before although, as she gazed at him, she became more aware of how his slight frame had strengthened into that of a full grown man. How beautiful he was, she thought. She found herself wondering what it would be like to run her fingers through his hair and explore his body with her hands. She, who had never known the kiss of a man, suddenly felt the desire to place her lips on his. What would it feel like?

Heat flushed her face. What was she thinking? This man belonged to another. And yet he was so dear to her how could she stem the flow of these feelings?

As if sensing her presence, Thomas stirred. Anne turned and ran off through the trees, praying he wouldn't see her.

Ellie had a headache when she woke. She looked at the bedside clock. It was only four am so she relaxed back against the sheets and allowed her mind to drift back over the images she had experienced. She soon fell back asleep.

Anne came out of her house. As she walked along the lane, she saw Thomas coming towards her. She quickly changed direction down a small alley. Why did she keep seeing him all the time? It made it so hard. She looked back. He hadn't followed. Anne continued upon her errand, wracked with disappointment.

In the morning Ellie couldn't get Thomas out of her mind. She tried to focus on household chores but they seemed so meaningless. She no longer cared about her present life. Only the past had relevance now. It was starting to drive her mad. Why? Ellie asked herself. Why was all this happening to her?

She went for a walk on the beach but found herself wondering how she and Thomas had started their affair. Ellie knew she'd tried her best to keep her distance from Thomas but somehow he'd always been around. At some point, though, she had stopped trying to avoid him and they'd become lovers. How had that happened? She hated that so much of her life as Anne remained hidden.

Ellie couldn't wait until bedtime when she might find out. However, to her intense disappointment, she had no dreams that night, nor the next. When two more nights passed without any flashbacks, she tried meditating in an attempt to find out more about her affair with Thomas but the doors to the past remained firmly closed. It became apparent the memories had a timing all of their own. She had to wait five days before she finally found out how she and Thomas came together.

She stood next to a grave in the far corner of the churchyard. She gently laid a bunch of wild flowers on the freshly turned earth. It had been just a week since the funeral. Anne felt sad but also thankful her mother was now at peace. Her last days had not been easy.

As Anne walked from the graveyard, she ached to walk in the wilderness. She didn't want to return to the empty cottage just yet. Her footsteps led her to the oak wood. Relieved to find it deserted, she walked among the trees, sensing the aliveness around her and listening to the sound of the birds. Her sadness fell away in the peace she always felt in the presence of nature.

She stood underneath an oak tree and shut her eyes, listening to the leaves rustling. A soft breeze wafted across her skin and she relaxed against the rough trunk and drew strength from the tree's solidity. It roots went deep into the ground and held firm despite all the storms that came and went.

The living peace and stillness of the wood settled around her like an embrace, holding her within it. Anne smiled. The years fell away and she remembered how she had felt here as a child, full of love for nature and powerfully connected to the earth beneath her feet. When she opened her eyes a few minutes later, Anne still had a smile on her face but it fell from her lips as she saw Thomas standing close by. Their eyes met and, in that moment, she knew that he too shared the feelings that flooded through her body at the sight of him. They stared at each other and the truth was revealed. They could no longer deny the strength of their love for each other, birthed from their shared past. Thomas walked towards her.

"No," Anne said, "no," but her face betrayed the lie in her words and she did nothing as he came closer. He did not hesitate, nor did she stop him, as he laid his mouth on hers.

And so it began, a kind of divine madness that consumed her and drove all thought of the morality of it into oblivion. They both became helpless under its spell. Their passion arose, swept them up and carried them away.

All thought passed from their minds as they kissed beneath the oak tree. Anne slid her arms around Thomas's neck and he pulled her to him. They kissed for a long time, stopping briefly to look into each other's eyes. It had been so long and they who had grown up together now found their way back. They were oblivious to everything except each other.

They sank down onto the grass but then Anne pulled back as a thread of remorse ran through her body. "We cannot do this. You are . . ." But Thomas's mouth came down on hers and she never finished. She could not pull away again. And so they surrendered to the strength of their feelings, there on the ground, the trees and creatures of the wood bearing witness.

Ellie awoke in the morning with the powerful love she felt for Thomas burning in her chest. She couldn't believe how happy and alive she felt. She held the memory of her night of passion with a man long dead close to her all day, reliving it over and over. Everyone at work wondered what had happened to cause the soft smile that hovered on her lips.

Another dream came that night.

She and Thomas walked along a small track along the edge of a meadow. They spent time together whenever Thomas could get away from home without arousing suspicion. They met well away from the village, often in the oak wood. They took care not to be seen. Anne lived alone but in a cottage right in the village where everyone would see.

Suddenly Anne ran on and into the wood ahead of them, twirling around and around laughing. Thomas ran after her. He grabbed the edge of her cloak and she fell, pulling him down with her. They tumbled over, landing in a pile of brown autumn leaves. They laughed but then stilled as they stared into each other's eyes. Anne reached up and touched Thomas's cheek. His skin felt rough to the touch. He hadn't shaved that day. He turned his head and touched his lips in the palm of her hand then leant forward and, with great tenderness, kissed all over her face until he reached her lips.

His mouth moved on hers with exquisite gentleness, teasing her, lingering then drawing back before allowing a deeper kiss. She moaned as desire surged through her body. She moved closer and wrapped her arms around him; her whole being yearned for this man. How was it possible to love him so much, she wondered, before all thought left her mind. Heedless of the chill in the air, they pulled away each other's clothing until they became naked.

The reality of their situation fell away as the intensity of their passion increased and their bodies came together. No barriers existed between them. They opened to each other fully and completely, losing all sense of their separate selves yet gaining a connection to something greater and infinitely more powerful.

Oblivious to anything else, the sky darkened into twilight before they drew apart, their passion spent. Thomas pulled Anne's cloak over their bodies and held her gently. They lay like that until the darkness deepened and stars pierced the blackness.

They stared up and listened to the sounds of the night. They could only be together in secret places like this out in the wilds but they both loved the land and so it became part of it all. When they met together their love reached out to embrace not only the other but the earth beneath and the trees, plants and animals that surrounded them.

It grew cold and so they stood and dressed. Thomas held her to him one last time. She didn't want to let him go but knew she must. They parted at the edge of the wood.

When she woke, Ellie knew why she mourned for Thomas with such intensity and longed for him even after death, for theirs had been no ordinary relationship. She and Thomas had shared an intense physical passion but it was more than that. In each other's arms they found a profound transcendence, letting go so much they touched the heart of life itself.

After this, Ellie had several other dreams of being with Thomas. They knew great joy when they were together but she soon discovered she paid a heavy price for their happiness.

She walked with Thomas from the oak wood, her wet clothes clinging to her body after a recent rain shower. Anne shivered and thought back to when Thomas recklessly climbed in through a back window of her cottage and she found him waiting there. That time they lay together in a bed. It felt strange but so wonderful to be warm with the soft sheets enfolding them. She longed for a real life with Thomas as man and wife but they did not want to hurt Helen.

The thought saddened her but she reached for Thomas's hand and drew strength from his warm grip. She felt so alive and energised with him. He set fire to her senses with even the merest touch. She had no choice but to cherish the brief time they had.

At the edge of the wood, they stopped and held each other but then Thomas moved away. "I have to go."

"Not yet," Anne said, still holding onto his hand.

"I must. I'm sorry." Thomas pulled away and Anne's hand fell to her side. She watched him as he walked away, back to his life, back to Helen.

Anne returned to her empty cottage.

The price for Anne's love for Thomas had not only been loneliness but guilt. Betraying Helen weighed heavy on Anne's mind and during one dream Ellie discovered she had tried to end her affair with Thomas.

Coming out of a shop one day in the village, Anne came face to face with Thomas and Helen talking to the vicar.

"Good morning, Anne," the vicar said.

"Good morning," she replied. Keeping her gaze averted from Thomas, she continued walking but the vicar stopped her.

"Oh, Anne, "the vicar said. "I couldn't prevail upon you to help on the cake stall at the fair tomorrow, could I?"

"Oh, I. . . . ." Intensely aware of Thomas and Helen standing there, Anne found it hard to speak. "I . . . er . . . I'm not sure about working on the stall but I could bake a cake perhaps."

"That would be splendid. Splendid."

Anne turned to leave but Helen said, "We haven't met. I'm Helen. "

"Pleased to meet you,' Anne replied, forcing herself to look into Helen's eyes. They were clear and smiling. Helen didn't know Anne lay naked with her husband. Anne's guilt stabbed deeper, right through her heart. She stood there, desperate to get away, but the vicar was talking to her again. None of his words made any sense. All she knew was that Helen stood close to Thomas, her arm linked with his. Thomas stared at the ground.

Helen obviously loved him a great deal, Anne thought. She saw it in the way Helen looked at him. She herself looked at him that way.

After what seemed an eternity, the vicar left. Anne said goodbye and walked off as fast as she could, her mind in turmoil. Helen seemed like a nice woman. She didn't deserve to be hurt.

That night in the wood Anne told Thomas they had to end their affair.

"But I cannot stay away from you. You are my life, my joy, everything." Thomas put his arms around her but Anne pulled away.

"Please don't. How can we have happiness when we hurt another? How? It goes against all that is right. You know it's true."

Thomas ran his hand through his hair and a look of intense anguish passed across his face.

"She loves you." Anne said in a quiet voice.

"Do you think I don't know that?" Thomas retorted. He slammed his fist against an oak tree. "But I cannot be without you. I cannot!"

"You must. Can't you see it will destroy us in the end? I'm sorry." Anne turned and ran away out of the wood. Afraid Thomas might follow her, she didn't go home but to the hill with the ring of tree, hoping Old Father might come there although she hadn't seen him or the other monks since her return to the village. She missed him and wondered where he had gone.

She waited a long while with only the sound of the trees blowing in the wind to comfort her. Strangely it did. As Anne sat on the grass, she calmed and sensed the open space around her even though she couldn't see it in the dark. She became aware of the light that shone inside her. It helped her bear the pain she felt. She relaxed and lay back on the ground, poised between heaven and earth, staring up at the sky. The clouds drew back and she glimpsed the moon and a sprinkling of stars shining in the darkness.

The next morning Anne baked the cake she promised the vicar. As she approached the village green, she heard the sound of music and people laughing and talking. She saw Thomas with Helen. She clung to his arm as if afraid of losing him. Did she perhaps sense something? Anne wondered.

Anne couldn't stay there. She left her cake at the stall and hurried away over the fields and up over the Long Man. At the top of the hill she sat looking out over the valley below. The view soothed her mind but the hot sun made her long for the shade of the old oaks and so she ran down the hillside, the wind flying through her hair, arriving breathless at the edge of the wood.

She sat underneath one of the huge trees and shut her eyes. Her path became clear. She had to leave Wilmington. She couldn't go on living so close and unable to be with Thomas.

But then she opened her eyes and saw him standing looking down at her. Anne scrambled to her feet. "Go back to your wife," she shouted. She tried to walk away but he grasped her arm and pulled her close. As she looked up into his eyes, her resolution fell into dust and she realised she could go nowhere. Thomas touched her cheek with his fingers and kissed her then nothing else mattered in that moment except being together.

During the time Ellie dreamed of her life with Thomas she never thought about her former relationship with James. It was as if *that* had been a dream. Only Thomas had reality for her.

Then one night came a dream in which another element entered the story, one that had been inevitable right from the start but it still shocked Ellie when it revealed itself.

She sat on the hill with the ring of trees and looked out at the landscape she loved. A deep sorrow flooded through her veins. Anne laid a hand on her abdomen. Soon everyone would know—when the child grew larger and could no longer be hidden. The thought of parting from Thomas tore her heart in two but she knew she had to leave the village.

Ellie's eyes flew open in shock. There had been a child! She became pregnant with Thomas's child. Unable to sleep after that, she made herself a cup of tea, her mind full of questions. Did she have the baby? Could there be descendants of her and Thomas still alive today? Would she perhaps be able to trace them? She glanced over at the newly purchased blue suitcase sitting in the corner of the room. Soon she'd be flying to England. Hopefully she'd find the answers there.

When Ellie went back to bed and fell asleep she returned again to the past.

She waited for Thomas at the oak wood. She intended to tell him about the child but he did not come and Anne waited for a long time, her cloak pulled tight around her against the cold night air. She almost gave up but then heard him walking through the wood. He came to her and held her close. They kissed. She didn't know how to tell him about the child, that their time together must end for she had to go away, so she said nothing, just returned his kiss. She just wanted a few more minutes to be with him.

When they broke apart, Thomas stared over her shoulder. "Look, what's that?"

Anne turned and saw a light flickering through the trees.

"Let's go and see," he said and started walking towards it.

They found themselves at the lake and saw the light was the reflection of the full moon shining in the water. They walked out onto a small wooden jetty and stood staring at it, transfixed by its beauty but then Helen came crashing through the undergrowth and brought out a knife. Their expressions turned to horror.

It all happened so fast. Helen lunged at Anne and Thomas moved across and took the blow. He fell into the water and sank. Anne plunged in and managed somehow to lift his head up above the surface, praying he would take a breath but he did not. She willed life back into his limp body but he remained inert. In despair, she continued to hold him as the fragments of the shattered reflection of the moon glittered chaotically in the water around them. Even when the lake became still and the moving lights merged once more into one, she remained with him, her tears falling onto his beloved face as he grew cold.

Ellie woke in the morning with her own tears on her face and the image of the moon in the water etched into her mind. Having spent so many nights in a bright world with her memories of the living Thomas, remembering his death intensified the grief and longing she felt for him, the fact that the dreams suddenly stopped after this made it worse.

As the days passed and she had no more dreams, Ellie's sense of loss and disappointment grew. She desperately wanted to know what happened after Thomas died but the memories remained locked away out of reach so she worried the answers would never come. Fortunately she had a lot to occupy her. In just a few more days she was flying to England.

Chapter 8

E LLIE STARED OUT OF A window at the airport terminal. Several planes gathered on the tarmac. She glanced up at the clock, only a few more minutes to go. Her stomach churned with fear but also a deep feeling of excitement. She was going to Wilmington.

Neil, her father, and brother Luke, stood off to one side chatting about planes. Her mother, Liz, who questioned the wisdom of her daughter travelling alone to England, hovered at Ellie's side looking tense. "Are you sure you've got a safe place for your money and passport?" she said.

"Yes, Mum."

Neil looked over at Ellie and smiled, "You have a good time, love. You'll be fine."

"Don't forget to ring," Liz said. "It'll be hard for us here not knowing if you're all right."

Ellie sighed inwardly. She refused to feel guilty. This trip was very important to her. Fortunately at that moment the sound of the airport announcer echoed around the terminal calling for passengers on Ellie's flight to board. She took a deep breath. "OK. This is it."

"Bye, Ellie," Luke said. "Good luck." Ellie hugged him, then her mother.

"Oh, love," tears filled Liz's eyes.

"I'll be fine, Mum."

"Yes, yes, OK."

Ellie hugged her dad. "Take care," he said gruffly.

"I will." Ellie lifted her cabin bag up from the floor then walked over and through the gate. She turned and waved at her family standing watching. As she passed down the link-way from the terminal building, Ellie looked out at the sleek shape of the white plane then around at the surrounding airport. How would she feel when she saw Adelaide again?

Ellie passed through the door and down the aisle to her designated seat, which was by a window. She stowed her bag in a locker above and sat down. Her hands felt clammy and her mouth dry. Relaxing music came from the speakers, merging with the sound of people laughing and talking. A man in a dark suit came and sat next to her but did not acknowledge her smile so Ellie looked out of the window at the runway and suburbs beyond. She felt separated from them already, as if she no longer belonged, cast adrift from all she knew. She put on her seatbelt and pulled it tight, telling herself very few flights crashed, but her stomach wasn't convinced.

Finally everyone boarded and the doors shut. A few gentle bumps vibrated the plane as it moved slowly away from the airport terminal. God, she was actually going!" Ellie looked around. Everyone else looked as if they did this every day. They sat chatting, reading or dozing. But *she* didn't. This was her first time ever.

Cabin staff demonstrated the safety equipment, describing how to get out of the plane, where the oxygen was if needed. But they *wouldn't* need it, Ellie told herself. A voice came on the loudspeaker telling the staff to prepare for take-off. But the plane had stopped. Was something wrong? Ellie gripped the armrests. She saw another plane take off beside them. They started moving again and turned onto a different runway. The plane slowed then started accelerating. The sound of the engines increased. They went faster and faster and then it came: the subtle shift in her stomach, a weird pulling sensation. They had left the ground.

The plane tilted upwards and climbed. Ellie saw the earth fall away and then she was staring at blue sky. Higher and higher they went. She looked down below and saw familiar streets then the sea with several tiny boats. The water glistened with light.

Soon they turned and headed back over land bound for Sydney, where she would join an international flight to England. It was simply amazing. Her fear completely forgotten, Ellie stared out of the window, overwhelmed with wonder at seeing the world spread out beneath her. She couldn't believe how small everything looked. They gained greater height and moved away from the densely populated areas. Tiny cars sped along the roads. Captivated, Ellie continued to watch. Sunlight flickered in a lake surrounded by soft, folding hills covered with miniature trees then the ground flattened into a brown expanse only broken by occasional fences or roads.

As the plane sped on, the view from the window darkened. By the time they arrived at Sydney, night had fallen and the city had become a vast expanse of twinkling lights. Ellie felt as if she were looking down on a fairy kingdom. To complete her excitement, she saw the famous opera house and bridge lit up in the distance as the plane came in to land.

A few moments later, Ellie entered Sydney Airport and followed signs for the international terminal. She felt good, buoyed up by a sense of aliveness and peace. She didn't need to worry, everything had been organised. She only had to follow the path where it led.

Ellie knew she had to catch a bus to the international terminal. One came fairly soon and she found herself staring out at a surreal world as they travelled through the airport area. Empty planes stood waiting for their turn to take to the skies. Tiny figures worked on others inside huge brightly lit hangars. Vehicles sped here and there, some loaded with luggage, perhaps hers. It was like a scene from a science fiction film and Ellie marvelled at the ingenuity of human beings to create such things.

At the terminal, Ellie passed through customs. From there she came out into the departure area. Despite the lateness, several cafes and shops remained open. She wandered through them, staring at all the things for sale: gifts and souvenirs, electronic equipment, books, cosmetics. Past the shops, she saw the gates where people sat waiting for their flights to all manner of different destinations.

Ellie found the gate for her own flight. Through the large windows, she watched the plane being prepared, in awe at the size of it. Except for a short stopover at Singapore, this plane would take her all the way to London, a trip of at least twenty hours. How was it possible the huge machine could lift off from the ground and carry her and all the other passengers up into the atmosphere half way across the world? Ellie walked around the complex until the staff called her flight then joined the queue waiting to board. All these people would be her companions for the next few hours. Ellie felt a kinship with them even though they were strangers drawn together only for the journey and would probably never meet again.

After a long tiring wait, the queue moved forward and Ellie boarded the plane. It was packed. She squeezed past all the people loading their belongings in the storage containers, stowed her own bags and settled down in her seat.

Ellie no longer felt afraid of flying, it excited her. She looked forward to the take-off, that moment when the plane accelerated and broke through the bondage of gravity. It took some while before the doors shut and everyone settled down but then Ellie felt the plane bumping as it moved away from the terminal. A few minutes later they lifted off and the long flight began.

They were given a meal shortly after take-off. Ellie had a window seat again but this time saw only darkness outside. The lights in the cabin dimmed. She pushed back her seat and tried to rest but felt too excited to sleep. Her whole life had changed and now she had embarked on the biggest adventure of her life: leaving Australia and all she had known behind.

Images from the dreams replayed through her mind: running down hillsides, climbing trees, wading in the stream then being with Thomas later as an adult. And the Long Man carved on the hill watched over it all. She wondered what Wilmington would be like and whether it would provide the answers she sought. Her logic told her not to expect too much but this was a journey of the heart, not the mind, and deep within her Ellie knew it was the right thing to do.

She wondered where Thomas was. Had he too been reborn?

Would she know him if they met or would they pass by oblivious to each other as two strangers? Perhaps they already had. Ellie knew meeting Thomas again was unlikely but the fact she had met Adam, Thomas's father, tantalised her. Why had *they* been drawn together? Surely it was more than chance. There had to be forces at work behind the scenes and, if that was so, who knew what might happen. The thought that perhaps she and Thomas could possibly meet again sent a shudder down her spine. But what if he were a woman in this life? She chuckled. The whole thing was absurd. Perhaps she *was* crazy after all.

Ellie sneezed. She bent down and pulled her handbag out from under the seat in front where she had placed it. Putting on the small overhead light, she scrabbled in the bag for a tissue. Something glinted at the bottom. Curious, she pulled it out. It was her special key, the one she played with so often as a child. How on earth had it got into her bag? As Ellie stared at it in her hand, a memory surged up from the past.

She stood as a young girl in Wilmington looking up at the bee and butterfly window. Tears streamed down her face. She did not want to go. How could she leave Thomas and her home? She could not bear it. But then Anne felt a hand on her shoulder and warmth flooded through her body. She turned and saw Old Father standing there. He looked at her with great love and compassion.

"My mother wants me to go away, leave Wilmington." Anne said, her voice breaking. "What shall I do? Can you help me?"

"Alas, no, my child, your life is your own. I cannot interfere."

"But . . ."

The old man pointed at St Peter in the centre of the stained glass window. "Look, he holds the key to heaven. You too have the key. Remember it always."

The scene faded out and Ellie became aware again of being in the plane, the drone of the engines loud in her ears and the much loved silver key in her hand. In her childhood games it had been the imaginary means to access a world beyond reality. It was ironic, Ellie thought, because now, in a way, it had done the same thing. It had opened another door into her past life.

Ellie wondered about Old Father. What had he meant when he

said: "Look, he holds the key to heaven. You too have the key. Remember it always." Did the words imply that Anne did not need to suffer, could access heaven herself or, at least, happiness, despite being forced to leave her home? Ellie didn't know what it meant but was happy her memory had opened up again. Quite a while had passed since the last flashback or dream and she had feared no more would come. The key had been a trigger. Hopefully, Wilmington would be, too.

She looked down at the key and wondered, as she had done countless times before, what it had opened. It was so odd she'd accidentally brought it. Ellie's grandmother, Nancy, the original owner of the key, had emigrated from England to Australia with her husband. She left behind a sister, Laura. Ellie's mother, Liz, spoke to Laura regularly on the phone and had arranged for Ellie to visit her. The key was so old and unusual, there was just a chance the key dated from Nancy's childhood and Laura might remember it.

Ellie replaced the key in her bag and turned her attention to the small TV screen on the back of the seat in front of her. Using the remote, she searched for a film to watch. She needed something to distract her from the long, tedious plane journey that lay ahead.

Ellie came awake. Shortly after the refuelling stop at Singapore, exhaustion had taken over and she fell asleep. Her right leg had gone numb but she felt somewhat refreshed. She shifted as best she could without disturbing the woman sleeping in the next seat. Ellie checked the route map on the TV screen front of her. They were only four hours away from England! Instantly alert, she sat up and raised the window shutter gasping at the breathtaking scene that met her eyes.

White and blue extended in all directions. High above the plane, the pale sky darkened into eternity; below her, stretched a vast expanse of fluffy looking clouds frozen in countless strange formations. They caught the sunlight, creating the impression of a majestic celestial city tinged with gold.

Ellie had never experienced anything so beautiful or exciting as this. To fly was simply amazing. People couldn't survive this high in the atmosphere and yet here they were, supported by technology. In that moment, she felt proud to be a member of the human race that had created such a miracle.

She felt a profound joy and a wonderful sense of freedom as she stared out at the vast panorama. She had been lifted above mundane existence. All the fetters which had previously bound her fell away. Nothing else mattered except being here, now, looking at it all.

Cabin staff brought round a meal. She didn't enjoy the first course but then noticed the dessert. Ellie smiled. Her bliss became complete as she enjoyed tea and chocolate cake while flying over the roof of the world.

After a while, the clouds broke up and Ellie caught glimpses of land. She saw towns and roads and thought of all the countless human dramas being enacted down below. How strange it was to be so high looking down like a god at the people on the surface. Ellie felt a sense of dislocation. She couldn't really know or touch their world. She no longer felt a part of Australia but hadn't yet connected to any other place.

Ellie found it hard to imagine how far they had travelled but with every minute they drew closer to her goal. The atmosphere in the cabin lifted as people realised the end of the journey approached. They started talking, organising their luggage or walking about. Ellie felt incredibly excited. She was so close; how unbelievable. She continued staring out of the window and watched as they passed over an ocean again but soon a green edge of land came into view. Ellie looked at the route map; it was England.

It gave Ellie a strange feeling to look down on the country she had dreamed about. It had the appearance of a patchwork quilt of fields separated by hedgerows or roads. Soon she would be a part of this world but not quite yet. They flew over London and Ellie saw some of the famous landmarks as the plane circled, waiting for permission to descend. After a while a voice on the loudspeaker told them to prepare for landing and to set their watches to London time: 6.10 AM.

Ellie felt the now familiar sinking sensation and soon the plane made contact with the runway. They had arrived! Rain spattered against the window. The world looked dull and grey below cloud level. "Typical English weather," she heard someone remark and laugh. Ellie didn't care what the weather was doing; she was in England.

She couldn't wait to leave the plane but it took a while as everyone gathered their belongings and filed off. Ellie's first experiences of England were long corridors leading to the customs area, queuing at passport control then waiting at a luggage carousel. After what seemed like ages, she saw her blue suitcase moving towards her. She hauled it off and made for the exit.

Rounding a corner, she came face to face with a whole crowd of people, friends and relatives of her companions on the flight. Knowing no one waited for her, Ellie became overwhelmed by a feeling of intense loneliness. Her family, with the exception of the elderly aunt, were many thousands of miles away. All Ellie's exhilaration drained away. Here she was in England, walking on its very soil, but she just felt tired and empty. What had she expected, to feel at home? Well, she didn't. It was just another airport and she was exhausted. She still had to make the journey to her hotel in Wilmington so couldn't relax for a while yet.

Ellie looked around, searching for directions to the trains. The travel agent had explained what to do: catch an underground train to Victoria Station and then another train to Eastbourne where she would be able to take a taxi to the Green Man Hotel on the outskirts of Wilmington. Ellie found a lift that took her to the underground station and managed to purchase a ticket to Eastbourne. A map on the wall told her how to get to Victoria. Her confidence grew and her spirits lifted. She would be OK.

Rumbling echoed down the tunnel and a train eased into the station. Ellie lifted her luggage on and sat down. Only two other passengers kept her company. After half an hour or so and a change of trains, Ellie walked through a tunnel and up some stairs into the mainline station of Victoria. She felt excited again. This was London.

As Ellie came out onto the surface, she walked outside the station. Hundreds of people milled about in the forecourt and distinctive red double-decker buses moved along the street. A queue of black taxis waited to pick up passengers. It looked just like her tourist brochure. Ellie looked forward to exploring the many famous landmarks here. She definitely intended to make the most of her time in England but first she had to get to Wilmington, the main object of her journey.

Ellie headed back inside, in awe at the enormous size of the station. It even had an upper level shopping area. She would have liked to look but couldn't face it with all her luggage. She checked a large noticeboard detailing departures and discovered an Eastbourne train due to leave in a few minutes. She located it and found a seat in a rather shabby carriage just before the train pulled out.

Heedless of the dirt on the window, Ellie stared out in fascination at London, interested to see how tall and close together all the buildings were. They passed over the Thames and out of central London. Her first impression was of drabness. The grey sky did nothing to dispel this reaction. The graffiti decorated walls, large blocks of flats and billboards advertising mobile phones beside the railway line depressed her and she felt a pall of gloom descend again.

What had she done? For the first time Ellie questioned the wisdom of her decision to come. She had been carried along by her inner conviction she would find something important in the beautiful green countryside of Wilmington. But the scene in front of her now couldn't be further removed from it. Rain pattered on the glass and Ellie noticed rubbish on the floor of the train. She felt a great weariness. Her eyes ached to shut but she dare not sleep in case she missed her stop.

Ellie stretched out her legs, grateful to have the carriage to herself after the packed plane. Outside the window the scenery improved, the train now passing through the outer suburbs of London. She found the rows and rows of small terraced houses, many quite old, fascinating. The large number of chimney pots amused her. It all looked very different to Adelaide where she lived, everything smaller and more condensed.

The train passed by playing fields and parks and trees. Ellie continued to look out as green hedgerows and fields replaced the houses. The trees with their denser, greener foliage looked quite different to those in Australia. It seemed like a gentle landscape, soft and undulating. This was more like the England she remembered. Her tiredness evaporated as she drank in the view but all too soon another town engulfed the countryside and this characterised the trip: stretches of fields and woodlands interspersed with built up areas.

They passed through several tunnels and over a viaduct from where Ellie saw a wonderful expanse of beautiful open land. As the train progressed, more people got on and the carriage filled. Ellie continued focussing on the scenery, fascinated by it all, until the train pulled into Eastbourne station. Ellie gathered up her belongings and climbed out. A chill wind blew against her body. She shivered and regretted not unpacking a coat at the airport. Hopefully, the weather would improve. She scanned the grey sky and thought that maybe she was being too optimistic about that but at least the rain had stopped.

Ellie came out of the station building and looked around. She stood in the centre of a busy town full of shops and offices. She located a taxi waiting by the side of the road and attracted the attention of the driver. He loaded her stuff and she climbed in.

As she settled in her seat, Ellie realised that soon she would be in Wilmington, the object of her journey. She felt ridiculous all of a sudden. The cab driver would think her mad if he knew why she had come. Most people would. Was she? Ellie stared at the busy modern street. This wasn't part of her vision of the world she experienced in the past. It seemed alien. Did she ever come here as Anne? Ellie wondered. It wouldn't have looked as it did today.

"Where to, Miss?" the driver asked, breaking Ellie's reverie.

"Oh, yes, sorry, the Green Man Hotel at Wilmington."

The driver, a thick set man with a very English accent, put the car into gear and drove away from the station.

Ellie felt sick. What if Wilmington had been modernised, perhaps become part of Eastbourne? Towns spread out and engulfed smaller villages. What would she do if her instincts had been wrong and she felt nothing when she got there? She tried to convince herself it didn't matter, that she could still enjoy sightseeing in other places, but knew that it did. The closer they got to Wilmington, the more nervous Ellie felt. To her relief, they came out of the suburban sprawl of Eastbourne and into open countryside. They drove fast along a main road and she saw soft rounded hills in the distance. Suddenly the driver turned down a narrow road and pulled into the forecourt of an old building, the hotel. They had arrived in Wilmington.

Ellie saw a lot of trees, several attractive old buildings and a lane leading off up a hill. This was it. She couldn't see the Long Man or anything she recognised like the church but knew they were at the other end of the village. It was lovely but did not look familiar. A wave of disappointment flooded through her. Ellie climbed out of the car and took a deep breath of cool, fresh air. The Green Man Hotel, an old brick building with a red tiled roof, looked pleasant. Away from the main road, it was quiet and peaceful. The driver unloaded her luggage. She paid him and he drove off. She watched him disappear down the road before turning and pulling her luggage in through the front door of the hotel.

Chapter 9

Ellie sank into an armchair in her room, grateful to relax fully for the first time in nearly two days. It had been such a long way. The room was lovely, not large, but fine for her. Pale pink and green floral patterned wallpaper covered the walls. The hotel itself must be many hundreds of years old, Ellie thought. It thrilled her to be in such a place. She peered out of the small window. The room overlooked a stretch of lawn surrounded by trees. Ellie glimpsed a curve of green hillside. The sky looked a lot lighter now with even a small patch of blue sky.

A knock sounded on the door and Ellie let room service in. At check in the staff had offered to send up some sandwiches.

Ellie saw a kettle, some tea bags and small containers of milk on a chest of drawers so made herself a cup of tea. She stared out of the window while she ate her lunch. As she looked at the trees and small stretch of hillside, her exhaustion faded and a new vigour entered her body. She couldn't possibly rest until she had seen what she came here to see. The time was now. Leaving her tea half drunk, Ellie put on a coat taken from her suitcase and slipped out of the door.

She smiled at the woman behind the reception desk and walked out through the hotel entrance. Ellie stared up at the sky.

More blue had replaced the grey. It seemed like a good omen and she turned right and walked along the narrow road that led up the hill, fascinated by the lovely old houses she passed. She drank in her surroundings, thirsty for it all.

However, as she progressed along the road, Ellie felt a growing sense of disappointment. Nothing looked familiar. She had feared this might happen. Most of the buildings looked as if they had been there for several hundred years so why didn't she remember them? But then she reached an area where the road cut through the hill and a footpath carried on up along a bank beside it. She knew it here.

The street was deserted. Ellie suddenly felt conspicuous, as if acting a part in a film with everyone else off set watching her play out the drama. As she thought this, she saw the steeple of the church behind some trees. She stopped walking, feeling disorientated and dizzy, unable go on. What would happen when she walked into the graveyard and actually saw the grave of Thomas?

Standing motionless, Ellie's heart beat faster and she found it hard to breathe. She had waited a long, long time for this moment but now it had come felt afraid. She suddenly had an insane urge to walk back down the village street, take her bags and return to Australia where everything would be normal and predictable. She had the strong feeling that if she walked forward her life would never be the same. She stood on the edge of something she didn't understand. If she turned away she could go back home, pretend none of it had ever happened and stay safe and secure. She could have a good life, meet someone new, have a family. Perhaps she *should* go back.

She hesitated, caught between two opposing destinies. But then the face of Thomas came into her mind and she knew the missing parts of her memory held something important. If she turned back she would never find out what it was. She *had* to know. She *couldn't* go back. Her decision made, Ellie walked on. The safe life in Australia fell into dust and blew away on the wind.

Ellie passed the church and graveyard; unwilling to face them yet. She needed to see the Long Man first. She had waited a long time for this moment, what would happen when she saw him?

The village gave way to open countryside then there he was.

Immediately a sense of power and significance and rightness filled her and Ellie knew she had been meant to travel half way around the world to this place deep in the heart of the English countryside. Excited yet afraid, Ellie stopped and stood still. What did it all mean and what would happen now?

At that moment, dark clouds obscuring the sky moved aside and the sun shone down upon the figure outlined on the green hillside. Golden light intensified and embraced Ellie with its warmth. As it did so, a powerful love for the beautiful landscape arose in her heart and she felt a shift in consciousness. All the years and her present life faded away and, for a moment, she became Anne looking out over the landscape she loved. She had finally come home.

Ellie came back to the present. Yes, returning to Wilmington had been the right thing to do. She knew it in every part of her body. Here were the answers she needed to make sense of the obsession which had come to dominate her life but would the figure on the ancient, sacred hillside reveal his secrets?

The clouds closed over again, darkening the scene. As they did so, Ellie became aware of the rustling of the trees behind her as a strong gust of wind swept over the countryside. She felt uneasy. Knowing she could no longer put off seeing Thomas's grave, she walked towards an old wooden gate a short distance away. Moving along the path, Ellie held her breath but then she saw the old yew tree, its dark shape spreading over the graves, its huge old limbs supported by wooden poles and its roots going down deep into history. Close by, as she had known it would be, lay the grave.

Ellie walked over and read the inscription: Thomas Marshall 1868—1892. She placed her hand on the headstone and intense love for the man who lay beneath flooded through her. Their passion had been larger than both of them and, with her, had even endured through time. A profound sorrow welled up for he was lost to her, lying lifeless in the earth. As if in mockery, a dry, brown oak leaf fluttered onto the grave. It crumbled in her fingers when she picked it up, the fragments blowing away on the wind.

The cawing of a crow echoed through the graveyard and Ellie shivered. She walked away and entered through the open door of the church into silence and stillness.

It took a moment to adjust to the dim light as she moved down the central aisle between the wooden pews. She noticed the white linen draped altar with its cross and candlesticks but a flash of colour drew her into the small side chapel and she found herself standing in front of the Bee and Butterfly window with its distinctive figure of St Peter. The glowing red plumage of the phoenix burned into her eyes and Ellie half expected to wake up on the bright beach under the strong Australian sun but she continued to stand on the old worn floor of the church surrounded by shadow.

It was at that moment, she realised. Everything she had done in the last few minutes had been a re-enactment of that dream on the beach, from looking at the Long Man and hearing the trees, to standing by the grave then coming in here and seeing the window! That dream hadn't been a vision of the past, as she thought, but of her future, *this* future, which she was living now, a premonition, one that, ironically, had opened up the past.

Ellie walked back into the main part of the church and sank onto a pew, overwhelmed by the enormity of it all. She glanced around. Several things had changed because of the fire and yet it still had the same atmosphere she remembered. As she allowed herself to relax, her senses reawakened to the deep stillness and aliveness of the place.

After sitting quietly for a few minutes, a subtle fragrance wafted through the church and she had the strong feeling someone sat behind her. She swung around but saw she remained alone. Ellie remembered the monks and Old Father who often used to come and how good she felt in the church. The place held a sacred beauty for her in that time, almost as if it existed in another dimension. For a moment, Ellie caught an impression of that again but then it faded. She felt a sense of loss and a wave of tiredness hit her. She really needed to sleep.

Ellie made her way out of the church. Although intending to return to the hotel, she found herself drawn back to the grave. As she stood staring down at it, an icy chill spread throughout her body and her mind filled with darkness.

She floated in the dark water of the lake, her arms clasped around Thomas. Broken fragments of the moon's reflection flickered all around them. Anne heard Helen running away but then that faded and the wood became silent.

And so she held him in the water. The broken light from the moon slowly merged back into a whole and she stared at it, cradling the lifeless body of Thomas. A long time passed. She grew cold and the moon faded before her eyes. Her strength drained away as her temperature dropped but she welcomed it, not wanting to live without Thomas. It would be good if they died together here.

But then two men from the village came. They plunged in, breaking the reflection of the moon, and tried to take Thomas from her. "No!" she screamed. She wanted to die with him. But they pulled him out of her grasp and dragged him out of the lake. Then more people came and someone gently led her out of the water to her house in the village. Two women sat her by a blazing fire and helped her into dry clothes. They gave her tea to drink but the hot liquid did nothing to dispel the icy coldness that engulfed her body. She couldn't cry, only sit numb and silent, sipping the tea and staring at the flames. For her, the world had become empty and meaningless. The two women left. Anne sat unmoving until dawn lightened the sky.

In the morning a group of people came. They told her two men walking back from the pub had found Helen just outside the village. Although hysterical, she managed to tell them what had happened. She still held the knife in her hand. They wanted to know Anne's side of the story. She answered their questions as well as she could. They stared at her coldly. No one had any sympathy. They blamed her for it all.

When everyone left, Anne lay on her bed and stayed there for several days. She missed Thomas. Every part of her cried out for his presence. All the times they spent together ran through her mind and she yearned to be with him walking on the hills, laughing, talking, lying together in their secret place in the woods. Her body craved his touch. With him she had been open and alive. There had been no barriers and she knew he felt that way, too. They had known a closeness that transcended them both. Their love had been sacred but came with a tragic human cost.

An awful darkness fell over her mind. Anne felt responsible for his death. If she had not come between him and Helen he would still be alive. She had also ruined Helen's life. First, Anne had taken her husband and now Helen faced a future in prison or worse. Anne did not know how to bear the pain of it.

Ellie, standing by the grave, realised that when Thomas died, all her joy and love for the world, the openness of spirit and aliveness she experienced as Anne, had been buried with him. For it had been these things that had drawn Thomas to her, driven him mad with passion, so much so that he no longer cared for his wife or his farm, and all of this had ultimately brought about his death.

Wracked with guilt, she had no longer felt deserving of the deep spiritual connection that had been so much a part of her life as Anne. Ellie realised this guilt had persisted into her present as the depression she had suffered since early childhood but never understood. And it was why she had returned to Wilmington. She had suffered enough. It was now time to finally move on, let go of the past and forgive herself for causing Thomas's death. Perhaps, then, the depression would finally lift and her spiritual connection could reawaken.

The sun went back behind the clouds and a chill wind blew but Ellie stood oblivious for the past took over her mind once again.

She stayed in bed for three days. Anne could not cry but lay there numb and empty. On the fourth day she rose and walked through the village, wild and unkempt, barely recognisable to those who saw her, and went to the woods. She passed among the trees but the place felt lifeless and empty. The darkness of her inner world spread out like a dark cloud obscuring the brightness and living beauty. She stopped and held onto a tree she particularly loved, an ancient oak, but no longer felt its life force. She slid down the trunk and sat at the base where she and Thomas had lain together so many times. And it was there she finally let the tears fall.

Anne cried for two hours. All the pain of the last few days flooded through her: intense grief for Thomas and deep guilt for causing such a tragedy. Anne did not think she could hold such a huge amount of pain. She considered taking her own life in the lake where Thomas died, but, as she sat in silence, felt the first fluttery kicks of her unborn child and knew she would have to find a way to live on. She did not want another death on her hands. She laid a hand on her abdomen. It was his child, their child. She had to bring it into the world and raise it.

But not in Wilmington.

When she returned from London it had been her intention to stay in Wilmington for the rest of her life but now Anne knew she had no other choice but to leave. It would be too difficult here for her now. No one would help her. The thought of leaving the land she loved so much wrenched her heart but it had to be. Yes, she had to go and soon but, one day, Anne vowed, she would bring her child back to Wilmington, back to the land where it had been conceived. Deep inside, she knew that this was its destiny.

Anne stood up. She took one last look at the trees that rustled in the wind and stared for a while at the carpet of soft grass beneath her feet, the bed for a passion that would be known no more. She said a silent farewell to the birds and animals, her friends in times of loneliness, then walked away.

She climbed the path that led up and over Windover Hill and stood above the Man to survey her beloved hills and valleys where she and Thomas had run and played as children and would always do so in her memory. It had been such a time of magic. These hills would always echo with their laughter and the ground would forever hold its memory of the times they had lain together as lovers.

Anne walked down the hill beside the figure of the Long Man. She returned to her house and packed a few belongings. Before the day passed into night, her cottage stood empty.

Ellie became aware again of standing in the churchyard. A tear trickled down her cheek and fell to the ground, soaking into the cold earth. Ellie thought about Thomas lying beneath her feet and knew only bones remained. *He* wasn't there.

If she lived again surely Thomas must, too? She longed to find him. She missed him now more than ever, even after all this time. Was it possible that he, like her, might also remember and be drawn to Wilmington?

As she walked past the yew tree, her mood lifted. Even though only just arrived in Wilmington, she had discovered more about her life as Anne, already making the journey worthwhile. What else might she discover?

Her head heavy and her eyes aching with exhaustion, Ellie managed to walk back down the hill. Knowing a soft bed awaited her back in the hotel kept her going. She entered her room, lay down on the bed without even pulling off her coat and fell deeply asleep. Day faded into evening, then night, and still she slept. She did not dream. It wasn't until the grey light of dawn spread over the nearby hills the next morning that she stirred.

Chapter 10

A S ELLIE SLOWLY CAME AWAKE, she heard birds singing and lay still for a while with her eyes shut just listening to the lovely sound. She stretched and luxuriated in the comfortable bed, so in contrast to the awful cramped seat of the plane.

After a while Ellie stretched and opened her eyes. Seeing the window, she rose to look out. Mist pervaded the garden, lending it a mysterious quality. Apart from the birds, no other sounds disturbed the stillness and she savoured the peace and quiet. It soothed her spirit and all tension drained out of her body. Ravenous, though, she hoped it wouldn't be too long before the hotel restaurant opened. She made herself a cup of tea and organised her belongings then took a shower and dressed in jeans and a soft angora jumper. By this time it was eight o'clock. Ellie let herself out of the bedroom and went in search of breakfast.

Her stomach comfortably full of cornflakes and toast, Ellie made her way up the hill through Wilmington. The sun had evaporated the mist. She walked past the church to the end of the village to look out over the lush, green downs at the figure of the Long Man. He stood watchful on the hillside, just as he had when she walked this landscape before.

Ellie went through a gate and into a field. As soon as she laid her feet upon the thick grass, she felt a kinship, a deep familiarity, with the earth. It felt like home. The intensity of the impressions transported her back in time. For a moment, she no longer felt jeans against her legs but the rough material of a long skirt. Her short hair became long and wavy and blew across her face as she moved.

Coming back to the present, Ellie felt a surge of intense joy. She ran over the grass until she came to the base of the Long Man. He looked enormous, viewed from this angle. How many times had she walked this way? She climbed up beside one of the staves. Half way, she turned and took in the vast sweep of English countryside below. Exultation gave power to her steps and she continued up the hillside. At the top, breathless but invigorated, she turned and savoured the cool wind blowing on her face.

Ellie gazed in wonder at the small trees and hedges, fields and houses below. She noticed buildings and roads not present in her time as Anne but it still looked familiar. Despite the passing of so many years, and even death, she had made it back.

Without warning, a feeling of emptiness replaced her joy. She hadn't brought him. It was too late. He had never run down beside the Man and played in the streams or laughed at the squirrels. She hadn't been able to bring her son, *their* son, here.

John.

As the name broke through to the forefront of her mind, Ellie became aware of being in the present wondering about the child but then the viewpoint of Anne intruded again. Past and present fought for transcendence. Part of her was Ellie, standing in jeans and a jumper who had a life in Australia thousands of miles away but, at the same time, she was also Anne who lived and loved here so many years ago. But, of course, Ellie realised, they were one and the same and, in that moment, as she stood on the top of the hill, she felt it. Her name and physical form may have changed but, in essence, she had endured through time and death.

The sensation of being divided into two people disappeared. Both lives merged into one and Ellie accepted the interplay of past and present. She stepped back and viewed everything from a point of stillness and clarity. As this happened, more memories and feelings rose into her consciousness and she knew what she needed to do next.

Without hesitation, Ellie strode down the hill. She remembered the way. Once down in the valley, she followed the road and then took a narrow track to the wooded area where she and Thomas spent so much time together in childhood and then as man and woman. She walked in among the oak trees. The wind sighed through the branches. The wood seemed unchanged, so quiet and peaceful, a sanctuary away from the world and Ellie felt it welcomed her. She walked to their special place. The ancient oak tree still stood there. Beneath its branches she saw a soft depression where the grass grew thick and old autumn leaves gathered. It had been there they had laughed and played as children and reached out to each other as adults.

Heat flooded Ellie's body as she remembered how it was when she and Thomas lay together here. The pain of his loss cut like a knife and she longed for him with all of herself. A wild cry came from deep within as the grief rose up. The wind blew stronger and carried it away. Perhaps he would hear it, wherever he was? Surely, on some level, he would know?

But it was futile and Ellie knew it.

And so she stood there under the tree alone. She looked around her and saw how beautiful the old oak trees were, especially the one nearest her. She reached out a hand and touched the bark, feeling its roughness beneath her fingers. In the past she had sensed the life essence within trees but could not feel it now. The experience remained a memory, something that no longer held any reality. She longed for a feeling of unity with nature just as much as she longed for it with Thomas but it had all faded the night he died.

Despite the brightness of the sun, a gust of cold wind blew. Ellie shivered and put on the coat she had brought with her but still couldn't get warm. She felt apprehensive, as if someone was watching her, but the wood seemed deserted. Through the trees, though, she noticed the lake. Although reluctant to go there, Ellie moved towards it as if drawn by some force beyond her control.

The cold intensified closer to the lake and the path became damp and muddy but Ellie ignored it, her attention focussed on the dark expanse of water ahead. In a few more steps, she stood on the small wooden jetty by the exact spot where Thomas died.

Ellie didn't want to go through it all again but the memory wouldn't be denied.

"I knew it was true." Helen screamed at Thomas. "How could you? She's just a whore."

Helen turned to Anne. "A whore!" she repeated, "A dirty whore." At that moment, Anne saw Helen held a knife. It glittered in the moonlight. She rushed forward and Thomas shouted, "No, Helen, No!" but she kept coming. Anne gasped at the intensity of hatred in Helen's eyes. Thomas moved to stop her and took the blow in his chest. He cried out and staggered, Anne screamed and Helen pulled back, the knife still in her hand, horror on her face.

Thomas swayed but remained standing. He turned and gazed at Anne with a deep sorrow in his eyes then fell backwards into the lake.

Helen fled and Anne plunged into the water, somehow pulling Thomas to the surface. "No, no, no," she moaned, over and over, until despair stilled her cries. Anne stared at the reflection of the moon, the only bright thing in a world gone dark, until the villagers came and took Thomas from her.

Ellie came back to the present, the look in Thomas's eyes etched in her mind. Grief and guilt surged through her body. She should have resisted her feelings for Thomas and turned him away then none of it would have happened but she loved him too much.

As these feelings flowed out, Ellie became aware of something hidden underneath, rage. Why had her mother forced her to leave Wilmington so that Thomas could marry another? Why, if they could not be together, did they crave each other the way they had? And why had Helen been moved to pick up the knife that day? What kind of God could let such things happen?

She hadn't wanted much, only to love Thomas and bring up their child. Suddenly the rage transmuted into something she hadn't wanted to acknowledge, something buried deep inside that cast a shadow on her life: hatred.

For the world.

For God.

The whole wood darkened with it. Ellie sank down, heedless of the dampness of the ground. "No," she cried out and put her hands over her face.

Ellie had never felt more alone. Why had she come? It was insane. This wasn't what she'd hoped to find, despair, but then Ellie heard a man's voice say softly, "Go through him and reach beyond." She scrambled to her feet and looked around. Ellie saw no one but she distinctly heard a voice. Or had she? Overwrought; she could have imagined it.

"Go through him and reach beyond?" What did that mean? Go through Thomas? As the words repeated in her mind, Ellie suddenly found herself able to access a memory that lay beneath the hate.

Anne stood on the hill with the ring of trees staring out at the landscape. Sensing the living presence of the earth beneath her feet, a great love for the world moved in her chest. She turned and saw Thomas walking towards her, so vital and alive. She loved the way he looked: the strength and firmness of his body, his curly, dark hair ruffled by the wind, his deep brown eyes and the way he smiled. He smiled now as he came over and put his arms around her. "I missed you," he whispered, looking into her eyes. "How are you?"

"Tired," she said. "Fred Taylor's pig escaped last night and got into the garden. Made such a noise it scared me out of my wits."

"I don't like you living alone." Thomas kissed her gently and held her to him.

"I'm fine."

"Come," he said. "I've found a place." They walked down the hill and along a track to a small stone barn. Anne followed Thomas inside.

"What if someone comes?"

"They won't. I know the owner. He and his wife have gone to Eastbourne for a few days. Her father died." Thomas put down the bag he carried. "Look, I brought a blanket and some food. We have plenty of time. Helen is at her parents' house today."

Thomas made a place for them on a pile of straw and lay the blanket down. Anne stood by the door staring out at the shifting accumulation of grey clouds above. Thomas came and put his arms around her. She relaxed against him and they both looked out over the countryside into the distance.

Anne loved the feel of him next to her. Just for once, they had time and so they stood there, being with each other simply and it was enough. Past and future fell away in the perfection of the moment. A flight of birds passed across the sky and the sun crept out from behind the clouds. A warm breeze caressed their faces. Sheep grazed peacefully in the distance. Anne smiled and looked at Thomas. "Thank you for this."

"Let's eat," Thomas said. They moved back inside the barn and sat down on the blanket. Thomas brought out some cups and poured cider from a bottle then handed her some bread and cheese. The food tasted good. After a while, Thomas laid their cups aside and gently touched her cheek. He moved closer and softly kissed her lips. She returned his kiss and slid her arms up and around his neck. Slowly they removed each other's clothing then lay back. Cushioned by straw, the blanket welcomed them with softness. No hard earth here.

Thomas reached out and touched Anne's mouth with his thumb then moved his hand through her long hair, watching the strands as they ran between his fingers. She loved the way he touched her, with reverence, as if she were something sacred. He made her feel special, beautiful. That was his way.

Suddenly he smiled and reached for something in the straw, a feather. With great care he slowly ran it over the contours of her face and then her neck. She reached out to caress him in return. "No wait," he whispered. "Just lay still." He moved the feather slowly all over her. She trembled and sighed with pleasure, her whole body awakening. He lay the feather aside and carried on touching her, this time with his lips, slowly, so slowly. Her senses responded in a way she hadn't experienced before. He lifted himself up and stared into her eyes for a long time, his gaze revealing the depth of his love. His body stirred with the power of his passion yet he held back to continue looking at her and it was an intimacy beyond actual lovemaking.

When he finally came into her she surrendered completely to the totality of the experience: the energy of it, the feel of him, his scent, his touch, the soft blanket and the cool air wafting over their skin. She still felt open and alive from being on the hill and, when their bodies moved together, the feeling intensified and she experienced an ecstasy that could not be described in words except as a deep communion with life itself.

Ellie became aware again of standing by the lake, her body resonating with the powerful sexual and spiritual energy she had tapped into. Tears filled her eyes as the feelings faded away. This is what she had unknowingly craved, to feel like this, she realised. As Anne, she had known such a depth of surrender with Thomas she touched the heart of existence itself but when he died, her grief and anger had been so great she drew back and shut down, losing the ability to sense the sacredness of life. She could not love a world in which such tragedy existed and so the deadening pall of depression descended.

And yet, her longing to reconnect with the spiritual awareness she once knew had never been completely lost but lay dormant, awaiting the right conditions to arise and force her to come to terms with what happened in the past. And so, in time, she had remembered her life as Anne and followed her impulse to return to Wilmington to find healing. It all made sense to her now.

Looking around, Ellie noticed the wood around her shone with sunlight. The dark night when Thomas died had long since gone. No moon reflected in the water now, only blue sky. The leaves rustled and the birds sung in homage to nature. People passing by would never know what had happened here all those years ago. The place teemed with life: trees, plants, animals and insects.

The experience of Thomas's death had been frozen in place in her memory but, in reality, the wood and its living creatures had moved on. Many cycles of birth and death had since played out. The characters in her drama, Thomas and Helen, had also moved on. This was the way of things. Thomas's death had not been the end. Ellie knew now only the physical form passed away and that something greater and deeper existed within each human being which could not be destroyed. And so, she had been reborn into a new life with another chance to find love and spiritual connection and so, too, had Thomas and Helen.

Ellie wondered what had become of Helen. Did she go to prison? What was the penalty for murder in those days? But one thing was clear. She was not in prison now. She, too, had the chance to find love and happiness in a new life. Ellie fervently hoped she had.

Now Ellie knew she could let go of the guilt that had overshadowed her life. She hadn't wanted to destroy Helen's happiness with Thomas and thereby cause his death. In fact, she had tried to keep away from him but the power of their attraction had been too great. Perhaps there hadn't been any way to stop what happened. Ellie had the sense that maybe forces beyond her control had been at work, moving and shaping events beneath the appearance of things.

Something powerful and uplifting lay behind life, she had sensed it as Anne, and perhaps could now reconnect with it. Physical forms were inherently transient but the essence of life, spirit, could not die. She knew this for she had survived death.

Ellie realised she need not cling to life but simply rest within the awareness that everything happened as it needed to, that the forces behind things flowed on and she and the others were all part of something deeper and greater, in which they could find peace, love and freedom.

As she thought this, Ellie opened up within, like a flower to the sun, and knew she could now embrace the world again. Her body relaxed and she felt a shifting and lightening inside as she let go of the pain and resistance carried for so many years.

Ellie saw now she had so much to live for but not with a heart heavy with sorrow, guilt and bitterness, for they isolated her from life. There were others to love now and new things to see and experience. She could build on the knowledge of her time as Anne and take that on into the future.

A powerful love arose within her and she knew it would help her deal with all the sorrows and tragedy of human life. All her grief fell away and, as Ellie stared around her, she saw the wood fill with light, not with her physical vision, but with an inner sense she could not explain. It was the living energy of the place. The vision lasted just a few seconds but it left Ellie forever altered. For the first time in her present life, she felt truly alive. And it wasn't just a memory but real in her now.

She stood up, oblivious to the mud that clung to her clothes. She took one last look around. The wood appeared ordinary again, no longer filled with light but no longer holding the tragedy trapped within it, either. Smiling, Ellie turned and walked away down the path, past the ancient oak tree and back to Wilmington.

Chapter 11

BACK AT THE HOTEL ELLIE ate a light lunch then decided to rest. She still felt tired and light headed from jet lag. She lay down on her bed but could not sleep; the longing to reconnect with Wilmington too strong to ignore.

Ellie left the hotel and walked up the main street. The light dimmed. She looked up to see heavy clouds drawing over the sun. It got darker the further she went. She reached the church and paused. The haunting sound of voices chanting emanated from within. There must be a service going on, she thought. Curious, Ellie decided to have a look. She moved along the path by the yew tree but the chanting had stopped by the time she reached the porch.

Careful to make as little noise as possible, Ellie opened the door and looked inside. Confused, she pushed it right open and checked all around the building but found no one. The chanting must have come from some other source, perhaps a nearby house, but somehow that didn't feel right. She felt certain it had originated from the church. Ellie felt uncomfortable, something about the place had changed, but she could not pinpoint what.

As Ellie walked back down the centre aisle, she saw it! An old carved cupboard had been moved forward away from its position by a wall. Behind it gaped a dark opening. She glanced around but still saw no one. Edging forwards for a closer look, she discovered steps leading down to a lower level, probably to a crypt, she reasoned. The person responsible for moving the cupboard must have slipped down them. A slight breeze came through the gap so it must connect to the outside. A smell of perfume, perhaps incense, wafted through. She had smelt that before but couldn't remember where.

Ellie looked down. *Was* it a crypt? She thought of the mouldering bodies it might hold and shivered. The air smelt sweet, though, not of decay.

The steps descended into darkness. Where did they lead? Knowing she probably shouldn't, Ellie went down the steps. At the bottom, she saw it wasn't a crypt but a passageway with stone walls which led off into blackness. She walked a few steps along the tunnel, stopping when it became too dark to see. There didn't seem to be any lighting installed.

Ellie shivered in the cold air and sensed the heavy weight of the church above. She wondered who had built the tunnel and why. A soft breeze ruffled her hair. There had to be another exit. Ellie decided to find someone to ask. Despite her intense curiosity, she knew she couldn't just go off walking into the darkness. Reluctantly, she went back up the stairs.

Coming out through the wall into the church again, Ellie felt dizzy. She walked up the central aisle but the sensation intensified so she stopped. As she did so, she became aware that the church no longer felt empty yet no one had come in. She stood still and shut her eyes. To her astonishment, she sensed the presence of a number of people around her. When she opened her eyes, though, the effect disappeared. It returned when she closed them again.

She didn't feel afraid; it felt as if she were picking up some kind of residual trace of people who had once been in the church. Ellie tensed as she heard voices. Now she did feel frightened. What was happening? Was she going crazy? Could they perhaps be ghosts?

Forcing her eyes open, Ellie saw the church still stood empty but the voices sounded louder now. Her heart pounded but then the door of the church swung open and a man and a woman walked in, to Ellie's relief, very much alive.

"Oh, this is lovely," the woman exclaimed. "I do love these old country churches." Ellie recognised them. She had seen the pair earlier at the hotel. By the distinctive sound of their accents, she knew they were American. They walked down the centre aisle of the church. The woman looked to be in her late fifties but the man was probably no more than thirty or so. Mother and son, Ellie thought.

"Oh, hello. Is it OK to come in here?" the woman asked.

"Yes, I think so." Ellie said.

"Didn't I see you at the Green Man Hotel?"

"Yes, I'm staying there."

"I know that accent. You're from Australia, aren't you?"

"Yes," Ellie replied.

"My name's Christine and this is my son, Derek."

Ellie nodded at him.

Christine went on, "And you're?"

"Ellie."

"Cute name."

"Short for Eleanor."

"Lovely, lovely," the woman repeated but her attention had flicked onto something else and she walked away.

Ellie smiled politely at Derek. She couldn't help noticing his good looks. Tall and clean-shaven with short dark hair, he looked the sort of person who had no trouble getting women and knew it. "Nice to meet you," he said, his brown eyes lingering on her for longer than Ellie felt comfortable with. She looked away and suppressed a shiver. She didn't like this man.

"Are you on holiday here?" he asked, blatantly looking her up and down.

"Yes." Ellie cringed inside.

"Derek. Come and look at this," Christine called.

To Ellie's relief, Derek went over to his mother. Ellie watched them as they stared up at the stained glass windows at the front of the church. They laughed at something and the man took a photo of his mother standing in front of the altar.

Ellie felt irritated by their intrusion. They did not see the church as a place of worship and sanctity but merely as a place of historical curiosity. It was time to go. She glanced over at the opening in the wall and stared in shock. The heavy cupboard had been replaced across the opening. It looked as if it had never moved at all.

She went over and touched the dark wood of the cupboard. Large and heavy, it wouldn't have been easy to move. How come she hadn't heard anything? Someone, maybe even several people, must have come up the passageway and moved it back, Ellie surmised. But how had they done it silently? She'd been distracted by the couple and it probably had handles on the back, she decided in the end and turned away but still felt uneasy. Anxious to avoid getting caught up with the Americans again, Ellie hurried to the main door and let herself out.

Outside, rain poured down. With nothing to protect her, Ellie ran back to the hotel. The rain looked set in for the day so she lay on her bed and looked through tourist literature picked up from the foyer. After a while, drowsiness overcame her and she closed her eyes.

She woke up at five thirty from a deep and dreamless sleep. She made herself presentable and went downstairs to the restaurant. She sat at a table and noticed the Americans seated a short distance away. The woman caught her eye. Ellie smiled then turned her attention to the menu. Later, when the waiter took her order, she noticed Derek staring at her. He made no attempt to hide it. Ellie felt uncomfortable and looked around the room, anywhere but at him. She hurried through her meal. Why did he look at her like that? She got up as soon as she could but, to her dismay, saw him and his mother also rise. They headed her way so Ellie ducked into an appropriately placed women's toilet. When she came out a few minutes later, Derek and Christine had vanished.

Ellie went into the bar next to the dining room and, after making sure Derek wasn't there, ordered a coffee. She settled herself at a corner table and took in the surroundings. She couldn't get over the age of the place, several hundred years at least. It had rough, stone walls and low wooden beams supported the ceiling. Ellie loved the antiques decorating the room: shiny horse brasses and a number of highly polished kitchen pans and kettles shining with reflected light.

She felt self-conscious but didn't want to sit alone in her room. Ellie quietly looked around her and absorbed the atmosphere. A number of people sat at tables and along the dark wooden bar. She listened to the soft buzz of conversation, enjoying the English accents.

Ellie sipped her coffee when it came and thought about the trip so far. She'd only been in Wilmington for little more than a day and yet so much had happened. She still felt uplifted from her experience in the woods. She smiled to herself, wondering if Thomas had been in this building. Strangely, the thought of him no longer seemed so heavily laden with pain, more a wistful longing. The trip had already been worthwhile but what next?

She wanted to explore the area more and do some research to see if she could find out what happened to her after Thomas died, especially whether the child had survived. Ellie felt a sense of frustration, so much of her life as Anne still lay out of reach. She also wanted to discover where the tunnel in the church led and find the hill with the ring of trees. Her mind reeled with it all. She felt excited. Wilmington held so many secrets, she thought.

Ellie became aware of someone standing by her table and looked up into Derek's penetrating gaze. "Can I get you something to drink?" he asked.

"No, I'm fine, thank you."

"Do you mind if I join you?"

"Well, I . . ."

"Ignoring her hesitation, Derek sat down and put his glass of beer on the table in front of him.

"I'm glad you're here. I wanted to talk to you."

"Oh?"

"This is going to sound stupid but. . . . ." Derek hesitated. "Well, I wanted to ask you if we've met before. You just look so damn familiar. It's driving me nuts. Have you ever been in the States?"

The room went out of focus. With the way Adam had recognised her still fresh in her mind, Ellie couldn't help but wonder if Derek could be someone from her past life. "No, I haven't," she managed to say.

Derek ran his gaze over Ellie's body and back to her face, not realising he had thrown Ellie into confusion. "I've not been to Australia so it doesn't make sense," he continued, looking at her speculatively. His gaze flicked down to her breasts, lingering for a few seconds before returning to her face. "It's been bothering me ever since I saw you in the church."

Ellie shifted uncomfortably. She doubted Derek recognised her. It had to be a pick up line but she couldn't help wondering. Thomas came into her mind but she rejected the idea. The man in front of her now couldn't be Thomas. Derek repelled her. But could she really be sure? Thomas would be different now. She herself didn't look the way she had as Anne.

Derek picked up his beer and Ellie studied him as he drank. She remembered the gentle kindness of Thomas, his loving smile. Derek came across as hard and sophisticated. They couldn't be more different.

Anxious to leave, Ellie tried to drink her coffee as fast as she could but the hot liquid scalded her mouth.

Derek put down his beer. "How long are you here?"

"Six weeks."

"On holiday?"

"Yes."

"Alone?"

Ellie hesitated. She knew where this was going and didn't want to encourage him.

"I . . . well, yes, but I have a fiancé back in Australia," Ellie lied.

"That's a very long way away," Derek said. "You're very lovely, you know."

"Thank you." Ellie sipped her coffee so she wouldn't have to look at him, desperately trying to think of an excuse to leave.

"Do you like it here in Wilmington?" Derek asked.

"Yes, I do. It's a very interesting place."

"I think so, too. It's odd but I kind of recognised it when I first got here. Do you know that déjà vu feeling?"

Ellie looked up at him, her stomach churning with tension. "Yes."

"Well, ever since I got here I've had it really strongly, especially around the church. I got goose bumps when I went there. It feels like I've been in Wilmington before but this is my first visit to England. Isn't that weird?" Just for a moment, confusion and uncertainty showed in his expression. He looked worried and Ellie felt he might be telling the truth.

"Yes, it *is* odd," she replied, calm on the outside but in turmoil within, as she began to consider the possibility this man *was* Thomas reincarnated. *Could* he be? No, it was too unlikely. But was it? She'd been drawn back here, why not Thomas? He'd felt strongly about the place, as well. Just because she didn't feel attracted to Derek didn't mean he couldn't have *been* Thomas.

Derek saw he had Ellie's attention. "It's the same with you, as I said. I'm sure I know you. That tells me we'd be good together. There's something between us. Can't you feel it?" He looked at her with undisguised desire. Ellie looked down into her coffee, her cheeks reddening. She didn't know what to make of this. Derek unsettled her; she now half believed he *was* Thomas. A sick feeling arose in her stomach. She had to get away.

Ellie put down her coffee. "Look, I'm really sorry. You'll have to excuse me; I've an awful headache."

"That's a pity. I thought maybe you and I could go into Eastbourne, have a look around. I've got a hire car."

"No, thanks, but no." Ellie stood up and hurried out of the closest exit. She found herself in an unfamiliar corridor. Reluctant to return to the bar, she carried on down it hoping to find a way out.

She saw an open door at the end and pushed her way through into a brightly lit modern kitchen.

"Can I help you?"

Ellie swivelled round. A young man stood watching her. He held a knife in his hand! Her eyes locked on to it. Already upset, she started shaking. The knife glinted in the light. The man came closer and all Ellie could see was Helen coming towards her that night by the lake. She tensed and a feeling of dread ran down the length of her body.

"Are you all right?" the man asked, concerned. Then he realised she was staring at the knife and laughed. "Sorry," he said, and put it down. "I'm just clearing up."

Ellie came back to the present, aware she had made a complete fool of herself. She'd found her way into the kitchen and this man was only one of the chefs who worked for the hotel. "Er, I'm lost, I'm looking for a way back to the hotel bedrooms."

"Well, that's easy, just go back the way you came and through the bar . . ."

"Um, is there another way? There's someone I don't want to see there."

"Oh, I see," the chef said with a knowing smile, "it's like that, is it? You can go this way." He held open a door that led out into the back garden. "There's a path round the building. Just follow it to the right and you'll find yourself in the carpark out front."

"Thanks," Feeling ridiculous, Ellie walked past him and outside. The young man stood and watched her as she hurried away. Unaware of his gaze, Ellie followed his directions to the front of the building and passed in through the main entrance. Scanning the lobby for any sign of Derek, she darted up the stairs to her room.

Ellie's head spun. He couldn't be Thomas, she'd know if he was. Wouldn't she? But she couldn't forget the intense look of desire in Derek's eyes. Thomas had wanted her like that. She turned on the TV, not wanting to think about Derek anymore. She prepared for bed, flicked through the channels and fell asleep watching an old black and white movie.

Chapter 12

Ellie sat up straight in the darkness completely awake. She had been dreaming of the Long Man. The images evaporated except for a feeling growing on the edge of her consciousness. It flowered into a strange desire: to leave the hotel and walk out onto the hills even though it was the middle of the night. She turned on the bedside light and looked at her alarm clock. Four a.m. Sighing, Ellie lay down and tried to sleep again but could not settle. She really wanted to go for a walk. Finally, in frustration, she rose from the bed.

She made herself a cup of tea and looked out of the window at the dark and silent countryside. The idea of walking wouldn't go away but she felt too afraid to go out in the darkness onto the hills alone. It was too risky, especially for a woman in a strange country.

There weren't any good reasons to do it but, without stopping to think any further, Ellie dressed, grabbed her coat and opened the door. Lights illuminated the corridor but the hotel stood silent. Feeling conspicuous, she made her way to the staircase and down to the foyer. The office was lit but Ellie couldn't see anyone. She wondered if she'd be able to open the front door, which would be locked, but had no problem. In moments, she was out and in the car park.

Ellie walked up the hill. A few ineffective streetlights did little to dispel the darkness. She wondered about her sanity as she moved away from the hotel. Part of her felt terrified but another, deeper, aspect knew it would be all right. As Anne, she had often wandered out at night, especially as a child. The further Ellie went, the more relaxed she became. Her senses heightened, attuning her to the night world, as she strode unseen up the street.

As she walked further and further from the hotel, away from the safe cocoon of her normal world: her room and possessions and her neatly structured life back in Australia, she moved more and more out on a limb into the unknown. Strangely, she felt protected, under the care of forces she could not understand but sensed on the periphery of her awareness. The impulse that had drawn her out became stronger as she headed up the main street. She *had* to do this; there could be no turning back.

Wilmington at night was a very different place to the one that existed in the daytime. Shrouded in shadow, it looked wild and mysterious. Occasional streetlights helped Ellie see her way but also added to the eeriness. Only the sound of trees rustling and her footsteps on the road broke the silence.

A feeling of excitement grew as Ellie walked up the hill. She reached the church, stopped by the gate and listened. Awed by her courage, which had sprung out of nowhere, she stared into the darkness. The churchyard lay quiet and still. Ellie could just make out the dark spreading limbs of the old yew tree. No ghosts walked in the churchyard. As she stared harder into the shadows, her fear melted away further as she sensed that there was indeed nothing to be afraid of.

Ellie turned away and walked on, knowing intuitively where she needed to go. A gust of wind moved through the churchyard, blowing old leaves along the path and against the graves. The church continued to wait in silence.

Passing out of Wilmington, she could discern the outline of the hills against the sky but everything else remained lost in the darkness. Now she was really out and away from everyone. Ellie knew the direction she needed to take, her feet remembered. She passed into a field and over towards the Long Man feeling an intense loneliness yet remained unafraid. She kept on walking, taking care not to trip on the rough grass or the stones that picked out the shape of the Man on the hillside. She revelled in being alone. Whilst others slept, she had the world to herself.

Enthusiasm fuelled Ellie's steps and she soon reached the top of the hill where she paused and stood still, allowing her heightened awareness to take in the experience. She felt the ancientness of the ground beneath her feet and sensed the presence of those long dead who had also stood in this place way back in history. Untold numbers of people had come and gone here, living out their lives before being laid to rest in the earth.

But again, Ellie knew she must move on and continued walking down a trail she could not see but sensed beneath her feet. Unused to the rough walking and steep inclines, she soon tired but carried on regardless until she reached the bottom of a different hill. Yes, this was the place, she could see the vague outline of trees against the sky, so began to climb, a cool wind dissipating the heat generated by her exertion. After ten minutes or so, she reached the summit.

Darkness shrouded the hilltop but Ellie knew she had found the ring of trees for she heard them rustling above her. The original trees had been planted in a circle many centuries before for what purpose she did not know. She felt exhilarated, having faced her fear of being alone in the darkness. She stood still, just allowing her senses to expand and felt a wonderful feeling of freedom as her focus dissolved away from herself. She sensed the presence of something much larger and more potent and in the feeling of it felt a powerful connection with the wider world. A loving energy came then, emanating from her heart, similar to what she felt as Anne before grief and guilt obscured it. But these had lifted now so it seemed as if her sensitivity had reawakened.

The sky lightened and the trees came out of shadow. Ellie walked to the edge of the ring. A flash of gold glowed behind a distant hill. She watched as the sun slowly rose up above the horizon revealing the surrounding countryside. As it did, she felt a unity with everything around her: the earth and sky and the restless trees.

Ellie smiled. She felt wonderful, truly alive, for the first time in her present life. She felt a pang of longing for Thomas, wishing he stood there beside her, but it soon faded. Her joy came from a deeper place than the sadness of his loss. She stood for some time, feeling almost weightless, as she looked out over the landscape and watched it come awake.

As the sun rose higher, Ellie felt hungry and decided to return to the hotel for breakfast. She walked down the hillside but, half way down, turned and looked back. A group of people stood where she had been standing moments before on the summit. Ellie couldn't quite make them out but sensed they watched her. For a second, she felt an impulse to go back and talk to them but dismissed the idea. It wasn't a good idea to approach strangers when alone. Her mother would be appalled at what Ellie had done already—walking out at night. All the same, something about the figures drew her attention and she looked back several times on the way down. They stood unmoving. When Ellie reached the valley and turned for a last look, they had vanished.

Spurred on by the thought of hot coffee, Ellie kept up a fast pace. She returned to Wilmington by a different route along a narrow country lane. Still too early for traffic, she had the road to herself and enjoyed the fresh quietness of the morning. The more time she spent in Wilmington the more Ellie loved it.

She arrived back at the hotel just before eight and, after making herself more presentable, went into the restaurant. She saw no sign of Derek or his mother but did see the young man she encountered in the kitchen the night before. He stood talking to an older woman. Something about him fascinated her and she found herself staring. He was certainly attractive but that wasn't it. She couldn't work it out. He looked to be in his mid-twenties and was slightly built with sandy coloured hair parted on one side which kept falling over his eyes. Suddenly he looked up and their eyes met. Ellie coloured. Had he noticed her staring? He smiled. Ellie smiled in return then looked away. When she glanced back, he had gone. She relaxed and ordered a large breakfast, ravenous after all that walking.

After her meal, Ellie decided to go out again. On her way through the hotel lobby, she paused to look at some tourist leaflets and noticed Derek talking to a woman at the nearby reception desk. Ellie hadn't been able to forget the previous night. Did Derek really recognise her or was he making it up? But why mention feeling that way about Wilmington, too?

Ellie studied Derek surreptitiously. Dressed impeccably in expensive clothes, he exuded power and control, in total contrast to the Thomas she had known who had been wild, often unkempt, strong yet gentle, loving and open. It didn't seem possible that someone could be so radically different. And yet, underneath Derek's controlled exterior last night she had seen something more genuine when, for a moment, he seemed confused, vulnerable even. It had thrown her, making her wonder if he really could be Thomas.

She leafed through a tourist guide but continued to study Derek. She decided he couldn't be Thomas. Despite Derek's good looks, she wasn't attracted to him at all.

Derek turned away from the woman and noticed Ellie looking at him. He smiled at her. She blushed and strode out of the hotel entrance, hoping Derek wouldn't follow. Luckily, he didn't.

Ellie kept walking. It was a beautiful day. Now recovered from her earlier exertions, she wanted to explore more, see it all. She noticed much of the Wilmington she had known before had changed. This was inevitable. A long time had passed. Some buildings were gone and others had taken their place.

She walked along the small lane she recognised as leading to the old farmhouse, the home of Thomas and his father. Disappointed, she found no trace of the place. Nothing but a field of grass remained where once had been a flint cottage and outbuildings. How could something so solid vanish so completely? She felt sad.

Ellie next sought out the old timber frame cottage that had been her home. She had a strong feeling about its location but when she arrived there found only a group of recent looking houses. She felt disorientated and disappointed then noticed a low flint wall. This she knew. It had formed a border for one side of the garden that surrounded her house. She walked over and laid her hand on the rough stone. The moment she did so, the past gained ascendancy in her mind.

She sat on a lawn speckled with small white flowers, daisies. Anne picked one, made a slit in its stalk then picked another and threaded it through. She attached a third flower to the second in the same way and repeated the process until a long chain hung from her fingers. Closing it into a circle, she placed it around her neck. She was six years old and waiting for her father to come home.

A middle-aged woman with a lined face and long straggly brown hair came out of the cottage, her mother, Martha. "Come help me, Anne."

Anne often helped her mother in the garden. She revelled in the feel of soft earth in her hands and planting seeds. Each day she would check their progress, waiting for the little shoots to break through into the light. They grew vegetables but also flowers of many kinds. Martha dug through a patch of soil revealing several rounded shapes. "You pick them potatoes out and mind you don't miss any." Anne retrieved all she could find, rubbed off the excess dirt and placed them in an old fraying basket.

Hearing the garden gate open, Ellie turned and saw him. A tall man with light brown hair came into the garden and laid down his canvas bag, her father, Alfred. Anne ran to him. He grabbed her hands and swung her up and around for a long time. When he stopped, she fell to the ground, dizzy but happy. Alfred ruffled her hair. "You've grown so much, little one," he said then went over to his wife. He kissed her on the lips. She wrapped her arms around him and they stood holding each other for a while. Anne smiled at them.

He left again just a few short weeks later. He worked on a ship. Anne watched as he kissed her mother then he bent down and hugged her. She held onto his legs but he prised her away, walked through the old gate and down the lane. She looked out for him every day but he never returned.

A long time later, her mother told her he had drowned but she hadn't believed it. People didn't die, she was certain of it. Once she saw him from her bedroom window. She ran down the stairs and out into the garden but he vanished. She wondered why he hadn't come into the house. Anne told her mother but it made her cry.

The scene faded out for a moment then came back.

She was older now, thirteen. A different man stood in the garden. He looked rough and unkempt. Jack. She feared him. Martha had married again. He went into the house. Anne heard him shouting then he returned to the garden. She hid behind a bush so he wouldn't see her. Jack stumbled off up the street, drunk again.

Anne sighed and went into the house. It needed repairing. Times were hard; money scarce. They barely had enough to eat. Anne climbed the narrow wooden stairs to her room in the roof. Sometime later Martha called for her to come down. "There's someone here to see you."

Curious, Anne went into the kitchen. Who was it? A short, balding man with a red face stood next to her mother. She had seen him once a long time ago. "You remember your Uncle George, don't you?" Martha said. Anne said nothing, uneasy all of a sudden.

Uncle George looked stern. He wore a dark suit and seemed out of place in the untidy kitchen. He watched Anne as she came in but didn't acknowledge her. He turned to Martha. "We'll leave right away," he said. Anne looked at her mother for reassurance but she would not meet her eyes and fiddled with the strings of her apron.

"Anne," Martha said after a moment, "something wonderful has happened. Your uncle, well, he works for a big house in London. They were looking for a scullery maid and he put in a word for you." Martha looked at George. "He's come to take you up there. It's such a good opportunity. You'll be earning money."

Shocked, Anne could not speak but stood, open mouthed, staring at her mother and uncle. The room went dark. This wasn't happening. She couldn't leave the countryside she loved and Thomas. She would die.

"But I can't go," she said.

Martha's eyes softened as she looked at her daughter. "I'm sorry, sweetheart, but Jack can't get work at the moment and everything is so dear. You're growing up now, you know."

George shifted irritably. "We have a long way to go, Martha. Gather the girl's things."

Anne's stomach churned with fear. She didn't like Uncle George.

"No!" she shouted and moved towards the door. Martha tried to grab her but Anne was too quick. She ducked under her

mother's arm and ran to find Thomas. He would know what to do.

She went to his house first but no one answered the door. Anne ran through the farm and surrounding countryside to all their favourite places. She scrambled up to the top of the Man, scattering sheep in all directions, and looked out but saw no sign of him anywhere. Tears streaming down her face, Anne ran down to the only other place where she thought someone might help her, the church. She pushed the door open with such force it banged against the wall. The sound echoed around the empty building. In that moment, she lost all hope and fell into despair.

She walked into the small side chapel and stood in front of the bee and butterfly window. Tears blurred her vision but she could just make out St Peter in the centre looking down on her. He looked sad as if he knew and cared about her trouble but how could he? He was just a figure in a window. But, as she continued to stand there, the deep silence of the church wrapped itself around her like a comforting blanket. She so loved this place. For a moment, her troubles faded as she relaxed in the familiar atmosphere. She could almost believe that everything outside the door of the church was a dream.

Anne felt a hand on her shoulder and a feeling of warmth flooded through her body. She turned. Old Father stood beside her. He looked at her with great love and compassion.

"My mother wants me to go away, to leave Wilmington." Anne said, her voice quavering. "What shall I do? Can you help me?"

"Alas, no, my child, your life is your own. I cannot interfere."

"But. . . ."

The old man pointed at St Peter in the stained glass window. "Look, he has the key to heaven. You too have the key. Remember it always."

Anne looked up at the figure in the window. "I don't understand."

"But you do."

Anne felt even more confused. What did he mean?

"Think of the way it has been for you here, what we have taught you. You carry that inside you. Does that all disappear

because you no longer walk these particular hills and lanes? Does your inner light, the light of truth, shine only here? How can it? Wherever you go it is there and, if you remember, it will transform everything. This is your lesson. Know it even exists in the darkness when all seems pointless suffering. Remember now and in the future that the light is within you and you will discover freedom."

Anne stared into the old monk's deep blue eyes and felt as if she was staring past the man into a vast space, and sensing something greater and deeper that on some level she recognised. And then she knew what he meant. The monks had told her many times she was not just her body, thoughts and feelings but spirit, and that this could not be confined but always remained free. She had felt this often out on the hills. Those had been the best times. She had been completely happy, loving everything around her.

"Open yourself up, child, let all your worries and cares fall away for they are not real. Nothing will be lost, for in losing you gain: you come to know the Presence in which all creation rests."

As she continued to stare into Old Father's eyes, Anne let go of the feeling of her body and the swirling play of fear and worry. She became conscious of the light of awareness within her and a glowing living energy. Anne felt the sense of herself as a separate body dissolve and, as she stood there, her consciousness expanded to include the presence of the monk standing before her, the church around them and even the world beyond. Anne felt unlimited, no longer trapped in the pain of her circumstances, and smiled.

"Always remember this. Even when you forget, remember," Old Father said.

Anne looked at him, confused again.

"Yes, you will forget. There will be times when life will swallow you whole but always remember that you have the key. Think back to this time, this place, and the memory will become a doorway for you."

Anne nodded.

"It is time to go." The monk stood and walked away from the window.

Anne followed but her eyes filled with tears once more. "I will miss you."

Old Father turned and looked into her eyes. "We will not be apart, my child. Not in the way that really matters."

They reached the entrance and the monk stopped. Anne walked forward and opened the door. The bright light of the outside world flooded in and she heard birds singing. She turned to say a last good bye but the monk had vanished.

Ellie became aware of the stone wall beneath her hand and the modern houses nearby. A few random thoughts passed through her mind and she could feel her body still but, in that moment, knew her essential self to be consciousness, unconfined, wide and open. It felt wonderful, more powerful than her experience earlier in the morning. She realised all she had to do was be aware and let go. Nothing needed to be done except what she was doing, nothing to be except what she was now and that everything would work out as it needed to do.

The experience intensified. This was how it had been for her as Anne walking this land as a child. Ellie had glimpsed it in her previous memories but what she felt now was real and not just a memory. Joy rose up within her. She stood and followed a familiar lane out to Windover Hill and walked along the top, looking down at the scenery below. Despite lack of sleep from the night before, intense energy flowed through her body. She felt happy and excited. She now knew where she had been during the missing years from thirteen: she had been sent to work as a domestic servant.

The experience of standing in front of the stained glass window with the old man shone bright in her mind, especially the figure of St Peter. He held the key to the gates of heaven. Now she knew why she so loved the small silver key she had brought with her to England, why she had used it in games to open doors in her house to access imaginary worlds far away from the painful reality of her life. Even just holding it had made her feel better when things at school became hard to bear. "Always remember," Old Father said and, at some level, she had. As a child, she had tapped into an echo of the scene in the church and the wonderful feeling of freedom she experienced that day even though the details of it all had been obscured.

Ellie marvelled at how her life had changed so dramatically in the last few months since that day on the beach. With the opening up of her memory she had learned so much. And she knew there was more to discover.

After a while, even though Ellie still felt uplifted, tiredness overcame her so she returned to the hotel. She ate a light lunch then lay down on the bed in her room, soon falling into a deep sleep.

Chapter 13

T HE AFTERNOON WORE ON. ELLIE stirred but did not wake for her mind had taken her to another time.

When Anne came out of the church she saw her mother coming towards her. She cast a last look back at the building and allowed herself to be taken home. Her uncle sat in the kitchen waiting. He scowled at Anne then turned to Martha. "I hope this is not a sign I am making a mistake recommending her?"

"Oh no," Martha said. "Anne's a good girl. You won't regret it."

Anne's mother helped her pack a few belongings into an old cloth bag. "You won't need much," Martha said. "They'll give you some nice clothes to wear."

The afternoon passed in a blur. A horse and cart came and Anne climbed onto it. Her uncle sat beside her and they started off. She glanced back and saw her mother wiping her eyes with her apron. They passed through Wilmington and then out into the countryside. What would become of her? Anne wondered. If it had not been for the calming memory of Old Father and what happened in the church, she would not have been able to bear it.

After some time, the cart stopped outside a brick building and George took Anne inside. Her uncle talked to someone and then they went through another door to the outside again where they waited with a number of other people.

Out of the distance came a strange and haunting whistle. It sent a shiver of fear through Anne's body. It came again with another sound she had not heard before. She clutched her small cloth bag tighter. She saw a cloud of grey smoke coming closer and closer. Anne stepped back at the sight of the great metal railway engine as it slowed into the station and drew up alongside the platform. It hissed and spurted jets of steam.

Anne trembled with fear. She had never been away from Wilmington and the surrounding countryside before, let alone travelled in such a terrifying manner. A hand gripped her arm and George propelled her through the people clustered around the train and up to a carriage door. He pulled it open and pushed her inside. Other people got in behind them and much jostling and shoving went on as people stowed luggage and found seats. Anne found herself squeezed in tight against the side of the carriage by the window.

The intense smell of stale tobacco, sweat and some sort of sickly sweet perfume assaulted Anne's senses and she found it hard to breathe. People shouted outside and carriage doors slammed. A whistle blew, the carriage jolted and they moved off.

They travelled fast, unlike the slow, gentle journey on the horse and cart. Anne stared out of the window in fascination as the train sped through the countryside. All she had ever known now lay behind her. Torn away from the soft fields and woods of her home, and from her mother and Thomas, in a few short hours her whole life had been turned upside down.

Anne felt George's leg pressed close to hers. She tried to move away but, wedged in against the window, could not. She glanced at him. He stared impassively ahead. She felt the coldness in his manner and wondered what had happened to make him so closed off.

She focussed on the world that passed by the train. She saw hills and fields, cows and sheep, rivers and villages. But then the countryside gave way to houses, rows and rows of them with hardly any trees. Soon they pulled into another station. George urged Anne out and they made their way to a different platform where a larger engine waited at the head of a long line of carriages.

Anne again found herself squeezed into a seat, this time between George and a large fat woman wearing a dress which pulled in tight at the waist and had a skirt so full some of it spread over Anne's legs. She gazed in wonder at the soft, shiny fabric and felt embarrassed by her own clothes, a rough grey skirt with a worn hem and a jacket with arms too short. Stains and mud covered her old shoes which also needed repairing. This had never mattered before, not to someone whose life had been scrambling up trees and wading in streams, but Anne had travelled a long way from that now.

The window took Anne's attention for most of the long journey as she stared out at the countryside and buildings of the towns they passed through. After a while, her eyelids drooped and her head fell forward onto her chest as the repetitive rattle of the train on the tracks lulled her to sleep.

The train stopped and Anne snapped awake. They had pulled into a very large station. George urged her out and they jostled through the crowds along the platform. Overwhelmed, Anne struggled to keep up with her uncle. She had never seen so many people or heard so much noise: people calling and shouting, engines hooting, whistles blowing. They were pushed and shoved several times before they reached the outside.

It was busy there, too, even though the day had now turned into evening. George took a firm hold of Anne's arm so she wouldn't get lost. She felt grateful for this, despite her discomfort at being with him, for she feared this new world, so very different to the tiny country village of Wilmington. People hurried about everywhere but also horses, pulling not only carts but carriages, some very shiny and fancy.

They walked for a long time, Anne staring around her in amazement as she struggled to absorb this strange environment. She had not realised such a place existed. Many of the buildings towered above her. Anne had never seen anything like them before with their pillars and carved decorations. She felt small and unimportant.

Anne stared at the people they passed. Some wore rough garments like hers but others had beautiful clothes. She could not believe the fineness of them: wonderful long dresses made from materials of all kinds and colours. They had folds and gathers, bows and lace. And then there were the hats: funny arrangements of flowers, lace and feathers.

The streets quietened the further they walked and George relaxed his grip. After a while they reached a small rectangular park with grass and trees fenced off by iron railings. Anne felt grateful for the presence of these living things in an otherwise hard world of stone. They reminded her of home. Her eyes filled with tears. She wondered what Thomas was doing. Did he know she had been sent away yet? Suddenly George stopped in front of one of the houses by the park and pointed. "We're here. This is where you are to live and work."

Anne stared up in awe at the huge brick house where her new life would begin. Several steps led up to a large black painted door with a shiny brass doorknob. The dark windows gave no indication of what lay within.

"You will never use this entrance," George said. "We go in another way." The house stood at the end of a terrace. He led Anne along the side of the building to a door in a brick wall at the rear. They went through into a garden with a lawn and a few small trees. They walked across a paved area and down some steps to another black door. As they passed through it, George turned to Anne and said, "Mind you do what you're told, my girl, or you will be out this door faster than you can blink."

He took Anne through into a large kitchen lit by gas lights on the wall. A number of people sat around a wooden table. They stared at her. No one spoke. "This is Anne," George announced. "She is to work here now." He turned to a large middle-aged woman wearing a brown dress and stained white apron. "I'll leave her in your care, Mrs Hall." With this, George left the room.

Anne stared anxiously around.

"Sit yourself down, love," Mrs Hall said. "Are you hungry?"

Anne nodded, grateful for this gesture of humanity in a world that made no sense. The other people got up and left. A few smiled but the others did not even look at her.

Mrs Hall set a cup of hot tea and a plate of bread and strawberry jam in front of Anne. She ate it without speaking, her eyes gazing around the massive kitchen full of bright pots and pans. Mrs Hall bustled around the room. Anne liked her. She had a smiling face.

A little later, a tall thin girl dressed in a black dress with a bright white apron came with a lit candle. She took Anne down a long dark corridor into a small room with two narrow metal beds. "You can sleep there," she said, pointing to the one closest to the door. She lit a candle on a shelf and left. A sudden draught extinguished the flame leaving Anne in complete darkness.

Exhausted and overwhelmed, Anne lay down on the bed and covered herself with the single blanket. Tears ran down her cheeks. This was surely hell. She lay awake for a long time, her heart breaking for the loss of her familiar life. She missed her mother already and longed to be at home. How could she remain in this place so far from the hills and fields of Wilmington and Thomas? What would he think? She cried herself to sleep.

Ellie's eyes flew open to the sound of knocking. She looked at the clock on the wall. Six fifty. The day had turned into evening whilst she slept. Ellie swung herself off the bed and opened the door. Derek stood there.

"Hello Ellie. I just wondered if, well, if you might like to come out with me tonight, maybe visit one of the local pubs, some are really quaint."

Still fuddled with sleep, Ellie stared at him, wondering how to get out of this. "What about your mother?" she said.

"Oh, she likes to go to bed early. She won't mind."

At that moment, her mobile phone rang. "Look, I don't really feel like going out tonight." Ellie said.

Derek gestured towards the phone. "Shouldn't you get that?"

Ellie moved inside the room and picked up her phone, realising her mistake as Derek followed her in.

"Hello?" Ellie said. It was her mother. "Can you just give me a moment?" She put her hand over the phone and turned to Derek. "Thank you for asking me but, as I said, I'd like to stay in tonight." She waited for him to leave but he walked over to the window and looked out.

"I want to talk to you but you go right ahead. I'll wait." Ellie seethed inwardly, couldn't the guy take a hint, for God's sake.

"She turned her attention to the phone. "Sorry, Mum."

"Ellie, have you got someone with you?"

"No, yes, it's one of the other guests, they wanted to ask me something. Mum, do you think I could ring you later? I was about to go down to dinner."

"Are you all right? We miss you so much."

"I'm fine."

It took her another five minutes to get off the phone, all the time intensely aware of Derek in the room with her. She didn't like it. When she ended the call, he came away from the window. Ellie realised the door had shut. When had that happened? Before she had time to think further, Derek moved closer. He didn't waste any time.

He looked up at her hair, then down at her body, then back to her face.

"You're beautiful. Did you know that?" he said. "Ever since I saw you in the church, I haven't been able to get you out of my mind. It's driving me crazy. You like me, don't you, just a little?"

Ellie smelt beer on his breath and recoiled but he bent close and tried to put his lips on hers. She pulled back sharply. "Look, I'm sorry, but I told you I have a fiancé."

"I don't think you do. Why isn't he here with you, then? Even if you have, he's thousands of miles away. Don't tell me you don't feel anything. I've seen you looking at me."

Oh God, Ellie thought, Derek noticed her staring at him in the hotel lobby earlier.

"I can't explain it but, being here with you, just feels so right." Derek picked up her hand. It looked so small in his. "What is it about you? I don't know. I only know I want you and I think you feel the same, you just won't admit it."

For a second, something in Derek's eyes made her think of Thomas and the passion they shared. She stared at the man in front of her, wondering and he saw this as his chance. He put his mouth on hers and kissed her passionately. The moment he did so, Ellie knew without doubt he wasn't Thomas. The feel of

Derek's lips revolted her. Thomas kissed her with sensitivity and love, considerate of her response. Derek's kiss felt like an invasion, rough and demanding. He sought only his own pleasure. She tried to push him away but he grasped her tight and shoved her against the wall, holding her there with his body. He pulled up her top and laid a hand on one of her breasts.

With Thomas she had known a profound love and passion; this was the complete opposite. Thinking of Thomas and how it had been with him, gave Ellie enough strength to push Derek back. She hadn't come to Wilmington for this. She twisted away and ran to the door. She opened it and stood there. "I want you to leave," she said, her voice firm.

When Derek made no move, she said, "If you don't, I'll scream."

He looked at her and then at the door as if weighing up his chances of still getting what he wanted. Deciding it wasn't worth the risk, he walked to the door. "OK, I'm going but you asked for it, you know." Ellie gasped. She felt like an idiot. He had misinterpreted her interest. Her obsession with finding Thomas had given him the opening he needed.

"I'm sorry if I gave you the wrong impression," she said, coldly. "I didn't mean to but it still didn't give you the right to do what you did."

Derek said nothing but looked at her with contempt as he walked out into the corridor. Ellie shut the door behind him and locked it.

She sat down on the bed, sighing in relief. What if Derek hadn't gone? She didn't like to think about what could have happened. A feeling of sadness welled up. The encounter with Derek made Ellie realise how special her relationship with Thomas had been, especially the physical passion they shared, so in contrast to what just happened. Ellie found herself pitying Derek. He had no idea how to arouse a woman. He thought he could simply take what he wanted but the result would never be true intimacy, not passion but emptiness.

Ellie sipped her orange juice, enjoying the feel of the cold liquid as it slid down her throat. She had been reluctant to leave her room after Derek left but, annoyed that he should prevent her doing what she wanted, Ellie had returned her mother's call and then gone down to the dining room, watchful for Derek but determined not to let him spoil her trip. After dinner she had wandered into the bar, drawn by the warm glow of the soft lighting and a desire to be with other people rather than alone.

She watched as the chef she encountered last night came into the room to talk to the barman for a few moments. He smiled at Ellie before he left. She sat alone listening to the conversation going on at the next table and looking at the antiques displayed around the room. An old copper kettle drew her attention. Highly polished, it glowed with light from the bar. Ellie saw her own reflection staring out as if trapped inside. She felt light headed and a little unwell then noticed her fingers felt odd. Flexing them, she saw they had somehow become red and raw. And her head ached. All of a sudden, Ellie felt exhausted. Despite being in the hotel bar, she laid her head down on her folded arms, desperate to rest.

She had been polishing for hours and now felt worn out. Tears gathered in her eyes. It had still been dark when one of the other maids pulled her out of bed. After a breakfast of porridge, Anne had been given a broom and told to sweep out the lower rooms. Next she had been shown where to get water and ordered to scrub the kitchen floor. Except for a brief meal at mid-day, she had not stopped working. It was now the afternoon of her first day in the big house. When would it ever end?

This was a nightmare. A tear fell onto the kettle she held. She sat at a large wooden table covered with newspaper. Several pans still waited to be cleaned.

Although windows existed in this underworld, they looked out onto stone walls a short distance away. The servants' rooms were below the level of the street. Anne could not see the garden at the back of the house or the open sky. She had become trapped in a subterranean world. She longed for the light of the sun, a fresh breeze and open fields.

Anne's eyes closed. She thought longingly of her bed. Sleep offered the only possibility of escape from this awful place. But there were all these pots to clean and Mrs Brightman, the housekeeper, would scold her if she caught her slacking. Anne had already been on the receiving end of abuse when she stopped scrubbing the kitchen floor to wipe away tears with her sleeve.

Drying white polish covered the kettle's surface. Anne picked up her rag and rubbed at it. The metal showed through, dull at first, but as she polished, it gleamed, revealing the reflection of her face. She had tied her long hair up in a bun behind her head but a few wispy pieces escaped to hang down around a face showing the strain of the last two days. Her limbs heavy with weariness, Anne felt defeated by this new world into which she had been unwillingly thrust.

She had lost contact with all she held dear: her mother, the land, Thomas and the monks. She tried to remember what Old Father had said in the church. She knew it was important but the memory wouldn't come. It lay hidden under fear and confusion as she struggled to cope with her new environment of strange, unfriendly people and backbreaking physical work.

Anne knew she had to put aside her thoughts of Wilmington and all she had lost. It hurt too much. And so she just kept rubbing until the whole kettle shone but then her eyes grew heavy and it all became too much to bear. She had to rest. Just for a moment. Anne pushed the kettle aside and laid her head on her arms.

"Excuse me, are you all right?"

Ellie opened her eyes and became aware of where she sat. Oh, God, she had fallen asleep with her head on the table in the hotel bar! She lifted herself up and came into eye contact with the chef. He looked at her with concern. Embarrassed, she said, "Oh yes, I'm fine, thanks." Christ, he'd think her drunk, she thought. With what happened the other night in his kitchen, she must look completely pathetic. "I . . . I was just so tired."

"I'm not surprised."

Ellie looked at him in confusion.

"I saw you this morning."

"Doing what?"

"Walking on the Downs in the dark."

"Oh, yes, I was."

He thrust out his hand. "I'm Alan."

"Ellie." She took his hand in hers, noting its softness.

"Do you often walk at that time of the morning?"

"Actually, no," Ellie said. "I've never done it before."

"What made you do it this time?"

"I, er, couldn't sleep."

"Some people watch TV or read books but you went out alone on the hills?" He gave her a speculative look. Ellie got the feeling he knew there was more to it.

Ellie evaded the question. "You were out, too," she said. "What were *you* doing?"

"Now that would be telling," he said and laughed. "I went out to watch the sunrise. I walked up the Long Man. You know it's a sacred place?"

"I thought no one really knew for sure what his purpose was."

"He's the guardian of the gateway."

Ellie knew of this theory from her Internet research but wondered what Alan meant by it. "What gateway?"

For a moment, Alan stared through Ellie as if she wasn't there. As she looked into his light grey eyes, she couldn't help wondering. Was *this* man Thomas? She liked Alan. He was different to Derek. She tore her gaze away. She had to stop this, people would think her mad and she'd get into trouble again.

Alan's attention snapped back. "The Long Man is a gateway through time."

As he spoke, a shock ran through Ellie. The Long Man had been the first thing she saw in the dream that started the opening up of her past life. Her mouth went dry and she found it hard to speak. "What do you mean?" she asked.

Before Alan could answer, the woman behind the bar called his name. "I need you to go down to the cellar, get some wine," she said.

Alan looked over. "OK," he replied then turned back to Ellie. "Sorry, got to go. You should get to bed, you look really tired." He started to walk away.

"Wait. Tell me more about the Long Man."

Alan stopped and gave Ellie a penetrating look. "We'll talk again."

"But. . . ."

"Soon."

Ellie watched as Alan walked away, his statement about the Long Man burning in her brain. She waited a while, hoping he would return, but he didn't. Finally, she got up and made her way back to her room.

As she undressed, Alan's words whirled around in her mind, "a gateway through time." In one sense, it had been true for her. The Long Man had been the recognisable and traceable element in her memories of Anne that helped her locate Wilmington. And since returning, more and more memories of her past life as Anne were surfacing.

But why would *Alan* say it? Perhaps he hadn't meant anything in particular by it but somehow she didn't think so. She decided to find Alan tomorrow and ask him.

Ellie climbed into bed and closed her eyes. Sleep eluded her for a while but finally she relaxed. Her mind filled with images of the dark servants' quarters where she had been sent to work as Anne. Ellie had the sense of a dark, despairing time when all hope of returning to the country had been lost. For a wild young girl used to her freedom, the big house was a prison. Ellie felt herself being pulled back there as she drifted off to sleep.

Chapter 14

*S*HE SAT IN FRONT OF *a black iron fireplace in one of the basement rooms, her eyes threatening to close. The moment she fell into her bed late at night it seemed like only moments before she had to get up and begin work all over again. The dark first days in this house had rapidly turned into weeks and now she had been in the big house three months.*

Anne finished sweeping out the ashes and laid newspaper and kindling wood in the grate ready for the next fire. Picking up her bucket of ashes, she went down the passage to the back door and out into a small yard. Anne breathed in the fresh air and looked up at the sky above. She wondered what Thomas was doing. She wished she could write him a letter but didn't know how and, anyway, what would she say? He would be upset to hear of her life here. But perhaps he would come and rescue her, take her away back to Wilmington. She could live on the farm with him. She cast a look at the back door. She dare not stay outside long; she would be missed.

Anne glanced up at the house, wondering what it was like on the floors above. She envied the housemaids who got to work up where the old lady, their employer, lived. She would hear them talking in the kitchen about it. But she was just a humble scullery maid, never allowed anywhere but the lower floors. Her Uncle George, a footman, spent a lot of time upstairs. Anne shuddered. Once he had reassured himself she wouldn't run off, he ignored her. She thought of running away but the outside world frightened her. How would she get back to Wilmington alone?

Anne emptied her bucket and hurried back inside. "Anne." Emily, a young girl only a year or so older than Anne, came hurrying up the passageway. "Mrs Brightman wants you to scrub the passage by the back door." Anne wearily gathered a bucket of soapy water and a scrubbing brush. Why did God hate her so? What had she done that was so bad she deserved this torture?

An hour later, her hands wrinkled and sore, Anne reached the back door. From her position on the floor, she saw a small patch of sky through a window. Its brightness contrasted with the dark passage that held her captive. She had been buried alive here, how could she go on? She simply couldn't, not one moment longer.

A door opened down the passage behind her. Bertha the cook called out, "Hurry up, Anne. I want you to peel some potatoes for me." Anne thrust her brush into the water, anger giving vehemence to her actions and scrubbed the last section of floor. Tears blurred her vision. As she cleaned into a dark corner, she heard a metallic sound. Lifting her brush, Anne saw a key covered with dirt. She rinsed it off in the bucket.

As she stared at the dripping key in her hand, Anne remembered.

The corridor vanished and she stood in the church at Wilmington, staring at the stained glass image of St Peter holding his key to the gates of heaven. Beside her Old Father spoke. "Think of the way it has been for you here, what we have taught you. You carry that inside you. Does that all disappear because you no longer walk these particular hills and lanes? Does your inner light, the light of truth, shine only here? How can it? Wherever you go know it is there and, if you remember, it will transform everything. This is your lesson. Know it even exists in the darkness when it all seems pointless suffering. Remember now, and in the future, that the light is within you and you will discover freedom."

But she had forgotten.

Old Father continued, "Yes, you will forget. There will be times when life will swallow you whole but always remember you have the key. Think back to this time, this place, and the memory will become a doorway for you."

In the church that day she felt something powerful arise within her, the same ineffable sacred Presence she felt when out on the hills, yet greater. As Anne remembered this, a miracle happened and she felt it again. Her sense of a separate self in conflict with a hostile world fell away and she no longer remained confined within her body. She still felt the cold, stone floor and the wetness of her dirty clothes but they no longer mattered for she knew her true reality was spirit, a love which knew no limitation. A wonderful peace and joy spread throughout through Anne's body as her awareness expanded. And in that moment, though trapped below ground, she found a greater freedom than she had ever experienced before.

For the first time in that place, a smile formed on Anne's lips and she felt a sense of love and gratitude to Old Father and the other monks who taught her so much. She realised she would probably forget again, when times got hard, but now she knew what to do: remember she had the key.

Anne stood, with the intention of replacing the key into the backdoor from which it had presumably fallen, but found a key already there. She drew it out of the lock and saw both keys looked identical. The one she found probably wouldn't be missed. Before going to peel the potatoes, Anne hurried to her room and placed the key under her pillow.

When Anne went to the kitchen and started work, it took her a long while to peel all the potatoes, her hands were so raw and sore from the scrubbing, but she felt so uplifted and full of energy she barely noticed the time it took. She smiled as she worked, finding satisfaction in cleaning away the dark mud and revealing the creamy white flesh underneath. She loved the feel of her body and its aliveness, the strength in her hands as she worked and the results flowing from her efforts. Even the soreness of her hands ceased to matter as much.

Anne sang softly to herself for she felt the Presence strong inside her even there in the gloomy kitchen. She no longer felt alone or trapped in suffering.

Later that day, Anne sat polishing a pan. As she rubbed, she became entranced by the beauty of flickering flames in the nearby fire reflecting in the metal. A few minutes later she savoured the feel of clean starched linen as she put it away and stopped to admire a rare sunbeam by the back door. Why, there is such beauty here, even in this dark place, she thought. Once awakened to it, she noticed more things of loveliness: a patch of blue sky with a passing cloud, glowing coals dancing with life, the sound of rain on the glass windows, and, of course, the taste of bread with her favourite strawberry jam at her next meal. All her senses came alive

That evening, while she sat eating, her uncle came into the kitchen. Like many of the servants, he made it his business to be unpleasant and ignored her as usual. Anne stared at him in surprise, suddenly able to feel the sadness locked in his chest and the wall of bitterness he had created which kept him imprisoned, isolated from others. Anne sensed he loved a woman who did not return his affection and felt a flowering of compassion for him. "Are you well today, Uncle?" she asked. He turned and glared at her but his expression softened at the smile she gave him.

"Yes," he said with a gruff voice before walking away.

As the days passed, Anne found the same thing happened with the other servants. When she looked at them, she sensed their pain. Many of them had received harsh treatment from life. They carried their suffering around with them as a heaviness she could feel in her own body. Anne tried to cheer them up if possible. Everyone wondered at the transformation of the quiet child who had been so miserable and lost in the beginning. How could she be so happy doing the most lowly and menial tasks? But she was. Her joy spread out and touched all those around her. People liked to be with her and treated her with more kindness.

And this is how it was after that. Sometimes, particularly at the end of a long hard day, she would find herself slipping into despair, when feelings of longing for those she loved arose or her back felt sore, but it didn't last long. Whenever she felt the cool metal of the key under her pillow, it acted as a reminder of her inner light and she let go of the darkness, allowing her emotions to rise and fall away unhindered. In time, she no longer needed the key to remind her and joy became the hallmark of all her days. Even though imprisoned in the big house, she embraced her situation and everything in it. In the light of her acceptance, the great love for life she held within her grew.

Despite the gruelling workload, her awareness of spirit enabled her to access powerful energy that carried her through the long hours of labour. She no longer minded the scrubbing and polishing. She grew to enjoy making things clean and shining.

A few months later, Mrs Brightman, the housekeeper, told Anne she had been raised to the position of housemaid. "You will be working upstairs. Your duties will begin today. Go and find Nancy. She will explain what is expected of you."

Anne followed Nancy upstairs for the first time, staring around her in amazement. Beautiful oriental carpets covered the floors, ornate carved furnishings filled the rooms and pretty patterned wallpaper decorated the walls. Anne gently touched a curtain. The fabric felt so, so soft. She stared in awe at the many wonderful objects around; statues of people and animals, delicate china flowers and vases with elaborate designs and fascinating wooden clocks, their pendulums swaying back and forth as they marked time. She loved the colourful landscape paintings and portraits of interesting looking people on the walls. Anne felt overcome by all the richness. It contrasted so dramatically with the drabness of the lower levels of the house.

Over the next few days, as she learnt her duties, Anne occasionally saw her elderly employer, Ethel Deacon, moving slowly and painfully around the house, helped by her personal maid, every movement causing pain, the result of a crippling disease that confined her within the house. Anne felt her sorrow and loneliness. Ethel had never recovered from the death of her husband, William, who had died fifteen years before, and still dressed in black. With no children and only one relative who lived a long way away, she spent most of her time alone except for the servants.

Anne loved being a housemaid upstairs although she still worked hard and for long hours. There were several fires to light and keep stoked during the day, hot water to be brought up from the basement for washing and then taken back down, chamber pots to be emptied and washed and endless cleaning. Anne spent her days sweeping, dusting, scrubbing floors, polishing and beating rugs. Heavy loads of coal also had to be carted up the stairs. Anne's back ached under the strain but she took it all in good part and often sang at her work.

One day Anne knelt in front of the fireplace in the upstairs sitting room laying a fire. She sang softly to herself, a silly little song she had made up about squirrels in the trees. Someone coughed behind her. She turned, aghast to see old Mrs Deacon standing there leaning on her stick. Anne had been told to do the fires well before her employer rose in the mornings. Mrs Brightman would be angry.

"I'm so sorry," Anne said, scrambling to her feet. "I'll be finished in just a moment." She remembered it was against the rules to speak to her employer unless spoken to first and fell silent. She stared at Mrs Deacon, suddenly uncertain. The old lady looked so old and tired, so defeated, standing there. Anne felt a wave of sympathy for her. Mrs Deacon swayed as if she might fall and Anne rushed forwards. "Can I help you or shall I get Agnes?"

"If I could just take your arm I would be grateful," Mrs Deacon said. Anne helped the old lady walk to an armchair next to the fireplace. As she helped settle her into it, Anne stared into Mrs Deacon's face. She sensed this woman had no joy in her life despite all her wealth. No one cared about her and she knew it.

"Carry on with your work," Mrs Deacon said, gesturing to the fireplace. Anne quickly knelt down and finished lighting the fire. She sat there on the carpet waiting for it to catch, feeling awkward in the old lady's presence. Eventually, the fire took hold enough for Anne to leave it alone so she stood up.

"Is there anything else I can do for you, Madam?" she asked.

"Tell me," Mrs Deacon said, "what makes you sing?"

"Sing?" Anne stared in confusion at the old lady.

"I've heard you singing at your work several times now."

"Oh, I'm very sorry, Madam." Anne said, suddenly afraid. Would she get into trouble?

"You seem so happy but how can you be happy cleaning out

fireplaces?" Mrs Deacon looked at Anne with curiosity.

Anne wasn't sure what to say but Mrs Deacon waited for an answer. "I, well, I like cleaning out fireplaces," she stammered.

"I've watched you when you thought you were alone," Mrs Deacon said. "There's something very special about you, you're different to other people."

"I don't know what you mean, Madam."

Mrs Deacon leaned towards Anne, staring at her intently. "Tell me," she said, "what really makes you so happy?"

Anne sensed the old lady was reaching out to her, that she felt lost and alone and frightened, despite all her money and material comforts. "I am happy," Anne said, "because I am alive and the world is such a wonderful place. It feels good to walk upon the earth, feel the life in my body, see and do things."

"But you have to work so hard and at the dirtiest tasks, doesn't it make you miserable?"

"Oh yes, sometimes, but I have the key to freedom, you see. I might feel sad and tired but I know those things cannot hurt me. They are simply passing clouds in the sky of myself."

"That's a funny thing to say. Whatever do you mean?"

"I'm sorry, I don't think I can explain it very well."

"Try."

Anne thought for a while. How could she put what she experienced into words? "Well, I know I am not just my body with all its aches and pains but spirit. And as spirit I am free and in communion with the world, with everything. Knowing this brings such joy I cannot help but sing."

"That sounds so beautiful," Mrs Deacon murmured, a wistful look on her face."

"Old Father helped me know this."

"Who is Old Father?"

"He was my friend. I used to see him and several other monks in the church at home and sometimes out on the hillsides."

"Where is your home?"

"Wilmington."

"Tell me about it."

"Well, it's a small village. I spent most of my time out in the countryside with my other friend, Thomas. But then I had to come here, live underground and work all the time.

"I hated it. I was so afraid and alone and tired. I forgot everything Old Father told me but one day I remembered. I found a key."

"A key?"

Anne told Mrs Deacon about finding the old key and how it reminded her of the last time she saw Old Father in the church when they stood in front of the bee and butterfly window. "He told me then to always remember the light in me, the light of spirit, even in times of suffering."

Mrs Deacon looked into Anne's eyes for a few moments as if searching for something. "You say the strangest things and yet I sense perhaps you have something others do not," she said. "Do you know, child, that I envy you? I only know emptiness now. I have no family, no friends. I think I will die soon. There is nothing to live for."

"Oh, don't say that," Anne said. Then she did something that in any other situation, at any other time, would have meant instant dismissal. She bent down and with great gentleness touched the old lady's hand. It was thin and cold. The veins stood out against the bones under the skin.

"It is easy for you to say, you are young; your life is ahead of you. Mine is done." Mrs Deacon said with bitterness.

"All life is special, worthwhile, however hard it may be." Anne said.

At that moment, Mrs Deacon's personal maid, Agnes, walked in.

"There you are, Madam," she said, stopping in surprise when she saw Anne's hand upon the mistress of the house. "What are you doing here?" Anne straightened up and moved away from the old lady.

"It's all right, Agnes. I asked her to stay and talk to me." Mrs Deacon said.

Agnes glared at Anne. "I think you had better get back downstairs," she said, coldly. "I'll speak to you later."

"She is not to be reprimanded," Mrs Deacon said. "Is that

clear?"

Agnes nodded, "Yes, Madam."

"I asked her to help me. She simply did as she was told." Mrs Deacon turned to Anne. "I want you to tell me all about your life in the country. Where was it?"

"Wilmington."

"Yes, and I want you to help me find what you have. Will you come to me tomorrow?"

Anne nodded.

"I will send for you in the afternoon. All right, Agnes?"

"Yes, Madam."

Anne looked at Agnes nervously. Seeing the disapproval plain on her face, Anne could tell what the other maid was thinking: <u>she</u> was the lady's maid, what was this child doing talking to the mistress. It wasn't right.

Despite opposition from Agnes and the housekeeper, Anne went to visit Mrs Deacon the next day. Anne got to drink tea in a fine bone china cup with a delicate floral pattern and eat cake from a silver cake stand. She sat on a soft armchair before the fire. Mrs Deacon sat opposite. Her arthritis paining her, she looked tired.

Anne gazed at the old lady, seeing the sadness in her expression and sensed her quiet desperation. She longed to relieve Mrs Deacon's suffering but how could she, a young girl with no schooling, find the right words.

"Tell me about your life in Wilmington," Mrs Deacon said.

And so Anne told the old lady about her village and the Long Man and her childhood on the hills with Thomas. "We climbed trees and played in the streams and watched the animals. When Thomas was busy, I used to talk to Old Father. It always felt so wonderful to be with him," Anne said. "He taught me so much."

"Tell me, do you believe in God?" Mrs Deacon suddenly asked.

Anne thought back to one particular day a few years back. She had fallen asleep in the church and woken to find the Sunday service going on around her. The vicar was talking. "Search your hearts. Find where evil has taken hold and mend your ways. Do not think you can hide your wrongdoing from God for

He will find you out. Heed my words, He will find you out. Repent now lest you incur His wrath and the fires of hell become your fate."

Anne had felt miserable and afraid. Who was this God who would turn against her if she were bad? Only eight years old and never having gone to school or church services before, she knew nothing of religion.

As soon as the service ended, Anne slipped away and ran to the hill with the ring of trees, even though a cold wind blew.

Fortunately, Old Father came. "You are sad, my child."

"I am afraid I'm not good enough and God will be angry." Anne told Old Father about the vicar's sermon.

"Sometimes those who seek to bring the truth to others bring confusion. Tell me, Anne, when we sit together, you and I, and when you are out on the hills, do you not feel the Presence of Love and Light inside you?"

Anne nodded.

"Trust that for it is God alive in you. He is always there, child. He does not stand apart in judgement. God is what you feel inside, He is your very essence and yet He is not confined. All things are one in God. When you know this and feel it, it makes you free and you need not fear for you are guided."

Anne told Mrs Deacon what Old Father had said to her about God.

"You're saying that God is inside me, part of me? Well, I have never heard of that before. But how can that be true?"

"But it is," said Anne. "He's not separate from you at all but your very being. He is the Light inside that gives you the power to see and experience everything. You are not trapped in your body; you are spirit that is free."

"Oh, I how I wish that were true," Mrs Deacon said, patting her legs. "You don't know how imprisoned I feel."

"Your body is crippled but <u>you</u> are not."

Anne watched Mrs Deacon's face as she struggled to understand. Anne could feel the old lady's fear. "Because you are spirit you need not fear death. You <u>are</u> afraid, aren't you?"

The old lady nodded. Her eyes filled with tears.

"Please don't cry." Anne reached for Mrs Deacon's hand. "You are never alone. Not in your deepest heart. Try to feel that this is true. Just be quiet and allow yourself to know it."

They sat in silence for a few moments. After a while, the old lady smiled. "I almost feel I can, sitting here with you, my dear. Thank you so much. Will you come and talk to me again?"

"Of course," Anne replied.

Anne visited Mrs Deacon every afternoon after that and they would spend it talking and laughing, although sometimes they just sat in quiet companionship. The other servants grumbled at first but Anne continued to be so cheerful and helpful, kind and caring to them the ill feelings soon dissipated.

Mrs Deacon arranged to have someone teach Anne to read and so a whole new world soon opened up for her, that of literature. She often read to Mrs Deacon who had weak eyesight. She loved to hear about the outside world and asked Anne to read newspapers to her. This broadened Anne's knowledge and the two of them would often discuss issues of the day. And so the months turned into a year. Anne grew very fond of the old lady. They became more than just employer and servant. A deep friendship developed between them. Anne still missed her mother and Thomas and the countryside of Wilmington but she made the most of her life, knowing the old lady needed her.

Mrs Deacon gave Anne an afternoon off a week and she took the opportunity to go out as much as possible. London amazed her. What a place it was. She loved the imposing buildings with their columns and intricate carvings and marvelled at the wealthy people dressed in fine clothes. The colourful dresses of the wealthy women fascinated her, with their elaborate bustles and bows, gathers and petticoats. Then there were the amazing hats decorated with feathers, flowers or lace. She would sit in parks and watch the wealthy people passing by, wondering how it would feel to wear such finery. The men, dressed in their smart suits, impressed her too, so different to what people wore back in Wilmington. The streets were often busy, bustling with various types of transport. The rich travelled around in shiny carriages, isolated from the harsh realities of the other side of London life.

In her wanderings, Anne soon discovered this other face of the city. One day she walked further along by the river than she had gone before and found herself in dirty, dark streets scarred by poverty. So many of the inhabitants looked sad, their faces lined with work and worry. Ragged children ran around the streets. They had no green fields to play in. Anne wished she could set them free in Wilmington.

She had walked a long way and a fog descended before she could get back to the house. It thickened until she could hardly see. These fogs were common, caused, so Anne had been told, by smoke from the coal fires. Anne mistook her way and found herself in a narrow alley. She heard a soft whimpering and almost fell over a woman lying on the ground. Blood ran down her face. Someone had dealt her a heavy blow. Anne tried to stem the flow with her handkerchief but the blood soon soaked through. She called out, "Help. Is there anyone who can help me, please?" Her voice sounded muffled.

A man came. He saw what had happened and disappeared. Anne sat with the woman, holding her hand. "Someone will come soon," she said, praying she spoke the truth. Fortunately, the man returned with a policeman. The woman described how she had been set upon by two men.

"They took my bag. It had me wages in it." Her eyes filled with tears. "How shall I feed my children?"

Anne had a few farthings. She pressed them into the woman's hand who whispered, "Bless you, love." The policeman gave Anne directions home and helped the woman away.

Eventually Anne saw the house she worked at materialise out of the fog and she ran downstairs, grateful to have returned safely. She missed the soft damp mists of Wilmington. No threats lurked within their gentle whiteness. She let herself into the servants' quarters and realised just how lucky she was. She had a good position with plenty to eat and, although she worked hard for long hours, was safe and protected.

Anne despised the poverty and violence but grew to love London. It had so much to see and do. She often walked through the markets, marvelling at all the things for sale on the stalls. Sometimes street entertainers enlivened the scene with their antics. Once, though, she saw a large brown bear goaded into dancing by its trainer. Anne had to turn away, finding the sadness in the creature's eyes too painful to watch.

She liked to walk down by the River Thames and look at all the boats. She often thought of her father, wondering what exotic places he had sailed to. Then there were the parks: St James's Park, Hyde Park, and Kensington Gardens. Here she found real earth to walk on, trees and lakes. In good weather, she sat on the ground. Sometimes she shut her eyes, breathed in the smell of the grass and imagined being on Windover Hill. But then she would hear people laughing and talking and London would enfold her again.

Her very favourite place was Westminster Abbey. She discovered it on one of her very first walks out around London. She saw the Houses of Parliament first, that day. As she passed, Anne stared up, overwhelmed by the majesty of the buildings and the incredible detail of the architecture. People with great power and authority gathered here. What must they be like? she wondered.

Then she saw the Abbey, so huge and magnificent, and immediately felt drawn to it. She walked over and admired the beautiful stonework. This was a house of God. She missed the church at home. Although the Abbey was on a completely different scale to Wilmington Church, it still brought back echoes of that special place and she felt moved to go inside. Would they allow a lowly servant girl to enter into such a royal looking place? She approached the doors and walked through. Amazingly no one stopped her.

Entering, she stared in awe, staggered by the beauty surrounding her. Never could she have imagined such a place. Stone pillars and arches drew her gaze upward to the most exquisite stained glass windows depicting angels and saints, soldiers, kings and queens and all manner of scenes, all in vivid colour, lit by the daylight behind them. Anne marvelled at the amount of work it must have taken to create such a place.

This truly was a wonderful monument to the Divine, Anne thought. She felt God's presence but also sadness. Every stone resonated with history and she knew many had come to this place, some in love and reverence but all too many in deep fear and suffering. Tears gathered in her eyes to think of it. How many had found what they had been searching for?

Anne passed through the Abbey staring in fascination at everything. Here were the resting places of English Kings and Queens, of people who had shaped the course of history. She marvelled at the stone tombs with the effigies of their occupants laid out on top and the many other beautiful statues and carvings. How had the sculptors managed to capture the human form so well? Anne wondered.

She walked around, touching the stonework and absorbing the sacred atmosphere. Even though she encountered several other people in the Abbey, Anne found a welcome stillness there. Despite her concern that she would not be allowed in such an important place, no one took any notice of her and she relaxed. She passed down a corridor and into a small empty chapel. Inside, it felt strange and the hairs stood up on the back of her neck. What was it about this particular place?

Anne moved to the centre and stared at the light coming in through the stained glass windows. A profound peace pervaded the room. As she stood there, Anne felt herself merge into that peace and become one with it. Her very being expanded and she opened fully to the awareness of the Presence inside her. She felt an enormous outpouring of love, so profound it brought tears to her eyes.

After some minutes, the intensity of the experience faded. As it did so, Anne became aware someone had entered the room. She swung around and saw a monk standing there, one of those she assumed worked in the Abbey. Feeling guilty and worried she had trespassed, Anne made her way to the entrance. As she passed him, the monk spoke, "You do not have to leave."

Anne stopped and looked at him. He smiled.

"You are welcome here," he said.

"Thank you," Anne replied.

The monk went on. "Those in whom the knowledge of God is great are always welcome within these walls."

Anne said nothing, staring at the monk in surprise at his unexpected words. He calmly returned her gaze. He reminded her of the monks in Wilmington. This man had the same tranquillity about him. Despite the strangeness of their conversation, she felt at ease in his presence, comfortable, as if she had known him all her life.

"You have done well, my child," the monk said.

"What do you mean?"

"The path you walk is that of truth. Those who open to the Light are so few. More are needed. Do not falter and, whatever happens, always remember you have the key."

Anne caught her breath in shock.

"Who are you and how can you know this?"

"I, too, hold the key." With that, the monk turned and moved swiftly out through the door, leaving Anne standing there, bewildered. As she stood watching the monk walk away, she felt a surge of joy. She knew deep inside her the monk was connected to Old Father, although how she could not possibly imagine.

Anne felt uplifted and joyful as she walked back to the house. After that, she often went to the Abbey to find some quiet corner where she could sit and absorb the peaceful atmosphere. Although she never saw the monk again, the small chapel had been imbued with the memory of him and she found inner strength whenever she returned there.

And so years passed and Anne grew into a woman. When Agnes married, Anne became Mrs Deacon's personal maid and the bond between her and the old lady strengthened. Anne continued to bring the world into the house for Mrs Deacon by reading to her and telling her all about the trips around London on her days off. The two women spent long hours in conversation about all kind of things and Anne taught Mrs Deacon to sit in quiet contemplation and feel the light of spirit inside her. And so the old lady found peace and freedom. She managed to accept her frailties more and find joy through the appreciation of the many blessings she still had in her life.

Anne had been working at the big house for nine years when she found Mrs Deacon unable to move or speak in bed one morning. She simply stared around the room blankly, as if she had receded away from reality. The doctor declared that nothing could be done. Anne stayed with her constantly, ministering to all her personal needs and keeping her company.

As the days passed, Mrs Deacon spent more and more time asleep. Anne still cared for her with love and dedication. She sensed the old lady slipping away so it came as no surprise when one morning she found her barely breathing. She reached for Mrs Deacon's hand and held it gently, hoping she would awaken. Anne knew it was hopeless but then, incredibly, the old lady's eyes opened. She looked at Anne and, miraculously, smiled. Anne knew she had come back to say goodbye. She squeezed Mrs Deacon's hand, the old lady's eyes closed and her breathing stopped.

Tears streaming down her face, Anne sat quietly by the bedside for a long while. She had grown to love Ethel Deacon a great deal and would miss her. The old lady had been a special person. Through her, Anne learnt to read and become knowledgeable about the world. In return, Anne eased Mrs Deacon's loneliness and made her last years more bearable.

The old lady had only one surviving relative, a nephew who lived in India. Not wishing to return to London, he put the house up for sale. Most of the servants were retained to keep it in order until a buyer could be found. One day a man in a dark suit came. He called Anne and several of the other servants into the upstairs drawing room. He stared at them with a sombre expression. "My name is Edmund Masters. I am the solicitor handling the estate of the late Mrs Ethel Deacon. I have come here today to inform you that a small sum of money has been left to each of you in her will."

Anne gasped when the solicitor told her the amount she would be receiving. She knew that if she invested the money wisely it could generate a modest income, perhaps enough to live on. Mrs Deacon had repaid Anne for her years of dedicated companionship; she had given Anne her freedom.

She made arrangements to invest her money and prepared to leave London. On her last day in the house, a group of men came and cleared the furniture. Before she left, Anne went to Mrs Deacon's sitting room. The room stood silent and empty but Anne smiled. The old lady was free now. Anne walked down into the hall where her belongings waited. She searched through her bag and took out the old key she had found all those years ago. It had opened up her mind and heart, enabling her to live the message of Old Father when she had lost all hope. She took it downstairs and left it on a window ledge near the back door. It belonged to the house. She no longer needed it.

And so, at age twenty two, Anne left the house she had worked in for nine years and walked through the streets of London. There was only one place she wanted to go. She had carried its memory with her ever since she had arrived in London as a terrified thirteen-year-old girl. She was going home to Wilmington.

Chapter 15

ELLIE OPENED HER EYES IN the morning with the whole of her life as a servant girl in Victorian London still clear in her mind as if she had only just lived it. She felt elated.

She thought back over what she experienced. What a hard time it had been for her as Anne, an uneducated young country girl suddenly taken from her home and thrust into service. But then she found the old back door key and everything transformed. She reconnected with the wisdom of Old Father and remembered the presence of spirit within her. Ellie felt grateful to have had her own special key in her present life to bring joy into her childhood world.

Throwing off the bed covers, Ellie stood and stretched, feeling open and free. She smiled then laughed for joy. It was a new day and she was here in Wilmington, miles away from her old routines, living an adventure she could never have imagined a few months ago. Alan's words the night before surged into her brain. She longed to find out how the Long Man was a gateway through time. Ellie hurriedly dressed and went down to reception. "Do you happen to know if Alan's around?" she asked

"It's his day off," the girl replied.

Disappointed, Ellie wondered what to do. She looked out of the window. Grey clouds threatened rain but she needed to get out in the fresh air. She ate some breakfast then walked out of the hotel and wandered up the road through Wilmington.

A fine rain fell, coating Ellie with moisture, but she didn't mind. The damp chill felt familiar and soothing, even though she had been brought up in the hot, dry environment of Australia. She hadn't been homesick once. She loved it here.

The soft rain brought back the memory of when, as Anne, she walked back into Wilmington after nine years in London. She had passed up this street carrying her heavy bag not minding the rain then either, although it soaked into her clothing.

Ellie's head swam as memories surged into her mind, overlaying the present. She made her way into the churchyard and sat down on a seat. As she did so, the past took command of her consciousness.

She walked to the end of the village and looked out over the welcome green fields. The Long Man still watched over the countryside. It felt good to be back. Anne turned around and headed down the lane that led to her home. In just a few minutes she reached the familiar cottage.

The door stood ajar. Anne pushed it open. The darkness inside made it difficult to see but her eyes soon adjusted. What she saw shocked her. A bed had been placed along one wall. On it lay a tiny, gaunt figure. Anne hardly recognised her mother who had been quite a large woman.

"Oh Mother," Anne whispered and hurried to her side. Martha's eyes had shrunk into her face. She seemed asleep. Anne lifted one of Martha's hands and held it gently.

"Anne." Martha opened her eyes. She recognised her daughter and smiled. "It's so good to see you." But then the eyelids closed as the effort to speak became too much. Anne had not known how sick her mother was. No one had thought to let her know. She looked at Martha's heavily lined face and pale skin and knew she had arrived just in time. How could this be? This would be so hard to bear so soon after the passing of Mrs Deacon.

Anne heard someone come in and turned. A thin elderly woman came over to the bed, Janet who lived in the cottage next door.

"Oh, my goodness, is it Anne?" Janet exclaimed. "I'm so glad you're here, dear."

"You've been looking after my mother?"

"Yes. She's been quite poorly as you can see."

Thank you. Where is Jack?"

"Oh, he's long gone. Didn't you know?"

Anne shook her head.

"Got kicked in the head by old Arthur Port's horse."

Anne did what she could, cleaning up the cottage, getting in some good food to make some broth for her mother and arranging for the doctor to visit.

It wasn't until the next day that Anne left Martha in the care of Janet and walked to Thomas's farm. She saw his father standing in the garden. Anne stared unbelieving into his eyes as he told her Thomas had gone with his wife to visit her parents. Thomas married? Anne had never considered the possibility but, of course, why shouldn't he be? Most people married.

Anne walked down the hill with tears in her eyes. She longed to see Thomas again, share all her experiences and perhaps walk out in the countryside with him but everything had changed.

She went to the church, hoping that perhaps Old Father or some of the other monks would be there, but it stood empty. She sat awhile in front of the bee and butterfly window, loving the brightness of its colours. St Peter still held his key. Anne smiled. She sat in stillness, one with the Presence inside her, allowing her awareness to range through the building and out to embrace the countryside she sensed all around. Her sadness fell away. She had watched the passing seasons, the plants and animals coming and going, for too long not to know the inevitability of change. It was the way of things.

Martha improved at first under Anne's loving attention but two weeks later she deteriorated again. Like history repeating itself, Anne stayed by Martha's bedside only leaving for a short time one morning to fetch the doctor.

Anne took a short cut through the graveyard. A man stood

alone outside the church. Although no longer a boy, she knew him instantly: Thomas. She walked towards him, her heart thudding in her chest, but then a pretty young woman came out of the church and slipped her arm in his, his wife. They laughed. Anne hid behind a tree suddenly shy. She couldn't speak to them.

Why did it matter that he was married? Anne asked herself. What difference did it make? But, somehow, deep down, she knew it did matter. It had always been Anne and Thomas. But she had been away; obviously he would marry.

Anne waited until they passed and carried on walking, her mind full of him. He looked just the same only broader and taller. His image stayed with her until she arrived back home with the doctor who spent quite some time with Martha. When he turned to leave, Anne could tell by the seriousness of his expression she had to prepare for the worst. She accompanied him outside. "A matter of a few days, no more," the doctor said. Anne nodded.

Martha passed the next day. Janet and another neighbour helped Anne organise the funeral and the old lady was laid to rest a few days later in a corner of the churchyard on a beautiful sunny summer morning. Although Anne's eyes brimmed with tears for the loss of one she loved coming so close Ethel's death, she knew in her heart they had merely moved on, their souls lifting free to blend with the higher dimensions of life that existed behind the appearance of the world.

Anne stood at the graveside listening to the vicar talking about her mother when she noticed Thomas standing with his wife amongst a group of villagers. Their eyes met and she nodded her head in acknowledgement. He kept staring at her and Anne knew he was shocked by her appearance, how time had changed her.

Thomas continued gazing at Anne until his wife pulled at his arm and he looked down. Something about the sight of their closeness disturbed Anne and she focussed again on the vicar. A little later, the service over, she searched for Thomas but couldn't see him.

She sought out her neighbour, Janet. "Have you seen Thomas Marshall?" she asked.

"Oh, he was called away, some problem at the farm, I think."

Anne sighed, disappointed. There had been no time to talk to him since her return because of her mother's illness but she still longed to do so, aching to know about everything that had happened to him in the years they had been apart.

The day after the funeral Anne went out walking in the wilderness, delighting in the countryside: the trees and grass, the flowers and animals, the wide expanse of hills against the sky. The Long Man still stood sentinel. She felt like a sponge, soaking up the beauty of it all. She had been away too long.

Up on Windover Hill, despite still feeling a soft sadness from her mother's passing, Anne felt a sudden surge of joy. She was free. She did not have to worry about making a living for she had enough income from her inheritance to live on as long as she remained careful.

Her thoughts turned to her childhood and she remembered standing here so many times with Thomas. How happy they had been. She wanted to tell him all about her experiences in London and find out how he came to meet his wife. Anne set off down the hill in the direction of the farm, hoping Thomas would be there. She saw no sign of him around the fields or in the barns so let herself in through the garden gate and knocked at the heavy old wooden door but it remained steadfastly closed.

As she stood there, she imagined Thomas and Helen out together, holding hands, laughing and talking. A pang of sadness touched Anne's heart, as she realised her own closeness with Thomas now lay only in the past. His marriage had changed everything.

And so she stayed away. Over the next few days she went for long walks or sat under the oak tree in the woods, either reading or simply watching the movement of nature around her. The deep communion with the earth and the living things around her that she had always felt in Wilmington intensified. The squirrels still played in the oak wood. They kept her company. At least some things remained the same.

She kept a look out for the monks but saw no sign of them in the church. She went to the hill with the ring of trees but found it deserted. She asked people in the village where they were but, strangely, no one could remember them. Anne thought it odd but accepted they had left Wilmington. She missed Old Father. It made her sad but she pledged never to forget what she had learned from him.

Anne felt happy and at peace but then came the day of the storm.

Ellie came back to consciousness of the present. The memories of all that had happened after meeting Thomas in the barn that day were still vivid in her mind. They had been ever since they first surfaced back in Australia.

She remembered sheltering in the barn and seeing Thomas walk out of the shadows. They had talked and remembered. And, in that remembrance, their link had been forged anew. She looked into his eyes and realised she loved him. She stayed away from Thomas because he was married, but one day he followed her to the old oak wood and the madness began. A passion came into being so strong it could not be denied and, on the night of the full moon, tragedy had been the result.

The rain intensified, wetting her clothes. She stood and looked around her. The rain fell silently from the misty grey sky. A smell of damp vegetation pervaded the graveyard. Ellie walked over to the grave of Thomas underneath the old yew tree and stared up. The yew had reputedly stood for a thousand years, perhaps even for longer than the church itself. Ellie laid a hand on a branch and felt a tingling in her fingers. She stepped back in surprise then replaced her hand. She could feel the life in the old tree.

Ellie felt a deep kinship with the yew. It had been here when it all ended for her and Thomas. The tree bore witness all those years ago when Thomas was laid to rest in the earth and she, carrying his unborn child, had walked on into the future. Her grief for Thomas welled up once again as she stood there and remembered.

Anne stood next to the newly dug brown earth underneath the yew tree, her bag beside her. Two women came out of the church. She heard their voices and knew they were talking about her. Everyone blamed her for what happened.

They soon disappeared, leaving Anne standing alone staring at where Thomas now lay beneath the ground. Tears fell unheeded from her eyes. Her soul had been buried with him. Her body longed for his, for the warm touch of his skin, the sound of his laugh, the love in his eyes when he looked at her. But his flesh had turned lifeless and cold. He would never reach for her again. How could she bear to live without him? Would she ever be able to stop crying?

But most of all how could she continue to live with the burden of guilt that now lay so heavy on her shoulders? The villagers were right. If it had not been for her, Thomas would still be alive, walking on the land, tending his sheep, smiling and laughing. But that was not all, for two deaths now lay on her mind.

Anne thought back to the day after Thomas died. Her neighbour, Janet, had come to the house and stood at the bottom of the bed where Anne lay staring at the ceiling.

"There's something you should know," Janet said. "Helen is dead."

Anne looked at the old woman and saw she spoke the truth.

Janet went on. "When the police came to take her away to Eastbourne she acted like a mad woman. She struggled so much she fell and cracked her head open against a wall."

Anne moaned, a low keening cry of despair, then turned over and buried her face in her pillow. She gripped it tightly with her hands as spasms of grief shook her body. Poor, poor Helen, she had not deserved such a fate. A vision of a happy young woman holding onto Thomas's arm came into Anne's mind and she felt sick.

Coming back to awareness of the graveyard, she shut her eyes and soaked up the peace and silence of the churchyard. She had lost more than just Thomas; she had lost her whole life, all the joy she felt in being alive. She had no right to happiness when two others lay dead because of her. Anne's pain and guilt grew so intense they darkened her mind and closed over her awareness of the living Presence that so sustained her before. Why could she not feel it when she needed it the most? Pain filled her whole being. Anne sighed. She deserved to suffer.

She did not know how she was going to carry the weight of it all but somehow she must for she had a new life to think of. She needed to keep living even though she now felt alone in a dull and empty world. Anne longed for Old Father but knew this time he would not come.

Anne faced an uncertain future. How was she going to

manage bringing up a child with no husband or other support? What kind of life could she give her baby? She wanted it to have the freedom of her own childhood but she would have to find some other place with woods and fields and wild places. She would never ever forget Thomas or Wilmington, they were both too much a part of her, but she needed to get away now, find a place to heal and a way to live and care for her child.

She picked up her belongings. It was time. Soon it would be dark and she had a long way to go.

Ellie became aware again of the present. She looked down at the grassed over grave and worn headstone. The intense guilt she felt after Thomas died had been too much for her to bear so she closed off from life and lost her spiritual connection.

She forgot the key!

Chapter 16

As Ellie stood underneath the yew tree, her memories of the past intensified. She leaned against the trunk for support as she found her mind taking her back to walking along a country lane, a heavy bag weighing her down.

Anne reached a railway station and sank onto a bench, exhausted. She waited, alone and empty, staring at the ground, until a cloud of steam heralded the arrival of a train. Somehow she boarded and shut her eyes, falling into oblivion until a guard shook her awake. She stumbled out onto the platform of a large station. A sign read "Brighton." Anne walked past it and into the central area of the building.

She stopped, uncertain what to do next. People walked around her, a few staring curiously at the sad, young woman who stood with nowhere to go. Anne had no relatives except her uncle but she did not want to have anything to do with him. He, like most people would condemn her. Becoming pregnant without being married had set her outside society. One thing remained in her favour: she had money. She could find a place and, if she lived simply, afford to bring up her child without help or needing to find work. She blessed Ethel Deacon for her generosity.

Love flickered into life in Anne's chest as she thought of the old lady. They had shared such a close friendship. Her face floated before Anne's eyes now. What would Ethel think of all that had happened? Would she, like everyone else, judge her? Anne wasn't sure. Ethel broke the rules of society by befriending a servant but could she have accepted what Anne had done? She doubted it. The thought saddened her and made her feel even more alone.

The day had turned into early evening. Anne approached one of the clerks at the ticket office to ask where she might stay for the night. He directed her out of the station and down a long sloping road to a terrace of tall narrow houses.

Number Fourteen displayed a wooden sign: The Bedford Hotel. Anne walked up several steps to the front door. It stood open so she went inside. The interior looked shabby but Anne did not care. She hoped they had a room. She just wanted a soft bed to lie on so sleep could ease her suffering.

Anne noticed a small brass bell resting on a polished wooden table. She rang it and a tall, thin woman in her fifties, dressed in a black dress that rustled as she walked, came into the hall. "Have you a room?" Anne asked.

"How long would you like to stay?" The woman scrutinised Anne, a sour expression on her face.

Anne felt uncomfortable. "I'm not sure, just a few days."

"Then I think we will be able to accommodate you." The woman disappeared through a door. She came back with a key in her hand. "Come with me." With a flourish of her long dress, she turned and led Anne up a flight of red-carpeted stairs. Faded wallpaper covered the walls. Anne noticed its design, an intricate pattern of pink wild roses. They were one of her favourite flowers and grew in her garden in Wilmington. Seeing them flat and lifeless in this place intensified her sorrow. They reminded her she had lost not only Thomas but also the land she loved.

They went up two flights of stairs and into a small room. The woman pulled the curtains and lit the gas light before handing Anne the room key. "Breakfast is served from seven thirty," she said and went out, shutting the door quietly behind her.

Anne stared down at the key in her palm. She gripped it tight until the cold metal dug deep into her skin. The words, "You have the key. Remember it always," came into her mind but with them came an image of the church at Wilmington and the newly dug grave. No, this time she didn't want to remember. It hurt too much. She had to forget. Anne put the key down on a small chest of drawers. She pulled off her shoes, lay down fully clothed on the bed and pulled the blankets over her. She relaxed into the soft mattress. All she wanted to do was sleep.

In the morning she woke facing the wall. She stared at it, confused. For a moment she wondered where she was but then everything flooded back. Tempted just to lie there, Anne forced herself up and went downstairs to a small dining room. After a light breakfast, she left the hotel and walked out into a grey and stormy day. She made her way down the street. After a while, she heard a strange roaring accompanied by a rhythmic crashing sound.

Anne followed the noise. She didn't have to go far. Just round a corner she saw a wide road. She crossed and stopped, captivated. A heaving expanse of moving grey, green water confronted her, the sea. A strong wind pulled her clothes tight against her body but the incredible sight before her took all her attention. She had never seen the sea before, having spent all her life either in Wilmington or London. Anne had seen pictures in books and in art galleries but none of it prepared her for the reality. A thrill ran through her body.

The ocean stretched out to the horizon, a vast mass of constant motion. As Anne watched, the water drew back, rolled over and broke onto the seashore in white frothy foam. She walked down some steps and onto the beach. Rounded stones shifted under her feet, making it hard to remain upright against the wind. She struggled down to the water's edge and stared out. Here was something she understood, the power of nature. Salt spray dampened her face but she did not mind. Anne allowed the experience of the sea to wash through her and, for a short while, it eased her pain.

Anne made her way along the beach, staring at the restlessness of the churning water. A short distance away, a pier extended out into the ocean. She headed towards it, marvelling at how a construction of wood and metal could withstand the power of the stormy sea. It even had large ornate buildings on it. She left the beach and walked out along the pier, looking over the side at the water that seethed in echo of the chaos of her thoughts and emotions. She gripped the handrail, disorientated by the blend of movement and the solidity of the metal that supported the construction.

She looked along the coast. Its beauty lifted her out of herself and Anne decided she wanted to stay near the sea. It was so different to the green hills of Wilmington. Maybe she could forget more easily.

The wind increased the further out Anne walked. Soon she reached the end and caught the full force of it. Barely able to stand upright, she clung to the handrail. The water rose up in a massive swell almost to the wooden floor then fell away, churning and frothing. Anne realised she stood in the presence of enormous power. She wouldn't last long in that swirling water. It would be so easy to lean out over the rail and allow herself to fall. No more pain. Anne stared down at the ocean bulging upwards again. It wanted her.

But she couldn't do it for she had the child. She touched her abdomen and felt a surge of love for the tiny being nestled there. She had to keep going and give it the best life she could. The ocean fell back. The water surged around the pier's metal supports, seeking to work them loose, but they remained strong. Somehow she had to stay strong as well. Anne turned away and walked back to the town.

She spent several days in Brighton, wandering along the beach and exploring the shops. She loved watching the ocean most in all its changing moods and looked around for somewhere to live close by but soon decided Brighton was too busy and noisy. The owner of the hotel, Mrs Hoskins, told Anne about her brother who owned property for rent in a smaller town called Worthing. She gave Anne his address and she caught a train to take a look.

Anne liked Worthing right away. She left the station and walked down the main street, past various shops and businesses, until she reached the seafront. The beach had rounded stones near the road like Brighton but the tide had retreated a long way out exposing a huge expanse of flat sand. Anne walked out over it towards the sea. The sun shone warm on her face and a soft breeze ruffled her hair.

Reaching the water's edge, her heart lifted. She loved the openness here and the calmness of the sea, stretching out to the blue horizon, the absolute peace. It eased the torment in her heart. Nothing enclosed her here and she strolled along beside the sea, staring around her in fascination. Tiny wavelets lapped gently at the sand. Numerous shallow pools reflected the sky. Looking down, she marvelled at tiny sea creatures scrabbling around in the water. When she nearly trod on an unsuspecting crab, it scuttled rapidly away.

After the bustle of Brighton, Anne welcomed the quietness. All she could hear were waves lapping and the occasional cry of a seagull passing overhead. She came upon two children paddling in the shallow water watched by their mother. The woman smiled. Anne imagined her own child here, running in the water and laughing. Yes, Worthing would be a good place to have her baby.

The sparkling sea stretched off to merge with a perfect blue sky and Anne relaxed. Thomas would have loved this place, she thought, and felt a pang of pain but then smiled. At least his child would know it. As she walked back to town, Anne felt at peace with her decision. She could make a life here.

Anne located the office of Joe Green. He turned out to be a short balding man in his late fifties. He shook her hand warmly and, picking up some keys, accompanied her to look at the two properties he had to rent. The first proved to be too expensive but the second seemed ideal: a small terraced house in a quiet street leading down to the sea with a rent just within her means.

The house had three rooms upstairs and three on the ground floor, space enough to take in a lodger to help make ends meet. When Anne saw it had a small backyard the decision was made. Although over grown, it had a beautiful lilac tree and a rose bush. Mr Green agreed to take her as a tenant. Anne smiled. She had found a home.

Anne moved in. Used to hard work from her time in London, she soon had the house looking nice, despite the shabbiness of the furniture. Anne knew all about cleaning. She told the neighbours *her husband had recently drowned whilst working at sea. No one questioned it. She took in a lodger, a woman in her late fifties just retired from domestic service. Rose Pritchard turned out to be a pleasant woman and the two became friends.*

Anne created a small but lovely garden in the area behind the house. She planted vegetables but also several flowering plants. She determined to make the most of everything and, in time, found many small joys in her new life, especially in preparing things for her child. But always, deep within her, she felt a profound sense of loss and isolation. She missed Thomas every day with a grief that did not diminish.

One day Anne went to a church a few streets away from her home. The moment she entered the place with its gloomy interior, stone walls and bright stained glass windows she thought of Wilmington and Thomas. She sat at the back and listened to the service. She enjoyed the singing but then the vicar gave his sermon. His words boomed out with a fiery eloquence calculated to stir the congregation to greater goodness. For Anne, listening at the back, it could not have been more devastating. His words cut into her like knives. "Only if you are pure in heart will you gain access to heaven." The vicar went on to describe in great detail the fiery pits of hell where those who sinned were thrown for all eternity at the end of their lives. The deaths of Thomas and Helen weighed on her even more after that. Anne left before the end of the service and never returned.

What had been done could not be undone. Sometimes the pain of it all became overpowering. At those times, Anne walked on the beach, sometimes for miles. She especially loved it at low tide when she would walk right out away from everyone and everything. She loved the sea, observing it in all weathers and marvelling at its constantly changing nature.

She longed to open her heart and feel again the touch of Spirit, the Presence that was life itself, but all sense of it had gone. For her now, the gates of heaven had well and truly closed.

Ellie's mind came back to the present. The rain had stopped and a small patch of blue sky appeared behind the yew tree. The despair and isolation she experienced as Anne hung around her like a cloud. For a moment, it threatened to overwhelm her but then Ellie let it go. Things were different now; she had remembered the key and embraced the full meaning of it.

She knew now that death was not the end. Within each individual existed an eternal essence, one with the sacred Presence that gave all things being, even though most did not know it. She and Thomas had reached for it through each other and so, when Thomas died, she felt as if she had lost life itself. The intensity of her pain and guilt obscured all sense of her inner light and she nearly lost her sanity. Perhaps she would have if not for her growing child. In her despair, she had forgotten the key, the symbol of freedom that Old Father gave her, but, luckily, it had not been entirely lost. The impulse to reconnect with Spirit remained hidden deep inside her, lying dormant until her rebirth. It revealed itself, first in Ellie's childhood games with her small key, but then later in the breaking open of her memory and her desire to return to Wilmington.

Now Ellie realised that, in reality, she had never lost that inner light, *could* never lose it, for it was her own infinite awareness. Standing in the churchyard as Ellie, knowing herself to be more than her surface personality and physical body, she allowed the last of the suffering over Thomas to release. It rose up and out of her onto the hillsides that bore witness to her love for him. The churchyard and hills appeared so beautiful in that moment it brought tears to Ellie's eyes. The pain turned into joy as the last resistance to what happened dissolved.

Ellie felt a wonderful feeling of freedom and a sense of eternal life and peace, perfect peace, but also forgiveness.

Only the physical forms of Helen and Thomas had passed away, the inner essence that made them who they were could never be lost. They were out there somewhere, following their own paths. She, Thomas and Helen had all come together to act out their respective roles in the drama that took place in Wilmington but the actors had now moved away to live out their destinies in other places and with different people. Ellie felt the presence of forces all around her moving and shifting, flowing from the past and on and out into the rest of the world.

The clouds parted and sunshine spread over the graveyard. Damp from the earlier rain, Ellie appreciated its warmth.

A blackbird landed on the old yew, sprinkling Ellie with dislodged raindrops. It looked down at her for a moment then flew off towards the Long Man. She reached up and pulled a small branch from the tree and placed it on Thomas's grave. She laid her hand on the earth in silent acknowledgement of all they had been to each other and final acceptance of his passing. Then she stood and closed her eyes. Everything felt right, just as it should be.

Ellie heard footsteps and opened her eyes. Turning, she saw Alan walking along the path. He came and stood beside her and looked up at the yew.

"It's a wonderful old tree, isn't it?" he said. "Some people believe it to be well over a thousand years old."

Ellie stared up at the tree's spreading branches. "Yes, I know. It's incredible."

Alan reached out and reverently touched a branch. "In pre-Christian times people considered the yew to be sacred. They saw it as the tree of death, believing it sent out a root into the mouth of every corpse in the cemetery."

Ellie shuddered. "Ugh, I don't like the sound of that idea."

"No, but they also saw it as the tree of regeneration, as well, new life arising from death. Early Christians also used it as a symbol of immortality. "You'll find yew trees in cemeteries all over Britain."

"Immortality," the word echoed through Ellie's mind. It had a new significance for her now. "You seem to know a lot about it," she said, looking at Alan.

"I like reading about things like that. I find the world a fascinating place. There's so much more going on than we know. But there have always been those who *have* known and they're the ones who built the sacred sites and wove the myths and legends that speak about the deeper truths of life, some of which simply cannot be expressed in any other way."

Ellie studied Alan's face. "What do you mean?" she asked.

Alan turned and looked at her. "Words have limitations."

"Yes, I suppose they do sometimes."

Alan abruptly turned and walked away. "Come in the church," he called back and disappeared through the porch.

Ellie followed and walked from the bright outdoors into

dimness and shadow. She went over to where Alan stood in front of the altar looking up at the window behind it.

"I love stained glass windows," he said, "but they're nothing without the light behind them."

"I wanted to ask you," Ellie said. "What did you mean last night about the Long Man being the guardian of a gateway through time?" She watched Alan's face carefully.

Alan looked at her. "This is a very special area. But I think you know that, don't you?"

"What makes you say that?" Ellie asked, curious.

"I can see it in your face, the way you look at things. It's just something about the way you are. And you walk on the hills at dawn. That tells me a lot."

"What does it tell you?"

"That you feel it, too."

"Feel what?"

"The incredible energy of this area."

Ellie stared at him. She didn't know what to say but something about his expression held her attention and she couldn't look away.

"You do, don't you?" Alan said.

She *had* felt the energy and the evolution of all that had happened to her *had* all sprung from being in Wilmington in her past life, being connected to the countryside here. Alan was right. This *was* a special place.

Ellie wanted to tell Alan all this yet could not speak of the way she felt, it was beyond words. She felt on the brink of something, something new and yet a continuation of everything that had gone before. In the end, she could only give one reply, "Yes."

Alan smiled and she realised that no words had been necessary, here was someone who understood.

An elaborate flower arrangement stood on one side of the altar. Two petals fell from a rose long since past its prime. Alan picked them up and caressed them gently with his fingers. Ellie watched. He had fine hands, musician or artist's hands.

"Not everyone feels it. You're very lucky, perhaps more than you know," Alan said. "Tell me, how did you come to be in

Wilmington?"

"It's a long story. I don't even know where to begin."

"I'd like to hear it but, before you tell me, was there one thing in particular you could say made you come here?"

Ellie considered his question. She came because of her love for Thomas and this countryside.

Alan went on, "Did it have anything to do with the Long Man?"

"Yes, I suppose it did," she replied. The whole unfolding of her life as Anne had begun with seeing the Long Man in that dream on the beach. If it hadn't been for the Long Man she would probably never have been able to identify where it all happened and come to Wilmington.

"I thought so," Alan said. "It was that way for me, too. And do you know why?"

Ellie shook her head.

"Because the Long Man is a sign, it marks a very special place, a place where miracles happen, where the normal constraints of time can be transcended."

Ellie felt a sense of unreality, as if she had stepped out of time herself in that moment. "How do you know this?"

"Because of what I've experienced here."

"Tell me."

"I believe the Long Man was created a long time ago to draw certain people here. I know; it drew me."

"How?"

Alan moved away from the altar and sat down on a pew. Ellie sat beside him. "About a year ago," he said, "I came on holiday to the area with two friends. We'd come from the Midlands where we lived. We were driving along the A27 on our way to a campsite near Eastbourne when we saw the Long Man in the distance. The others just laughed at it but it fascinated me. I persuaded Mick and Steve to let me take a closer look. We drove up through Wilmington and stopped in the car park at the top of the village.

"I got out and couldn't stop staring at the Long Man. I swear his outline glowed against the hillside. I asked the others what they thought but they couldn't see it. I wanted to walk to the figure, climb to the top of the hill, but it was getting late in the day. The others wanted to find the campsite so we left but I couldn't get the Long Man out of my head. The next day, even though the others wanted to move on, I persuaded them to wait for a day. They went to look round Eastbourne, I returned here alone.

"I will never forget that day. As soon as I got out of the car and walked across the fields to the Long Man, I sensed the power of the place, a sort of energy but subtle. The hairs stood up on the back of my neck and I instantly knew I was meant to be there, that the place held a profound significance for me, although I couldn't imagine what. It felt as if the very earth itself welcomed my feet. I know that sounds bizarre but I can't describe it any other way.

"As I climbed up the hill, the outline of the Long Man again looked brighter than anything else. I don't think I saw it with my physical eyes; it was kind of in my mind. Does that make any sense?"

Ellie nodded.

"It was a lovely day. I lay down on the grass inside the outline of the Man and stared up. The sky was incredibly blue, not even a single cloud. I heard a kind of buzzing coming from the earth and then I heard someone laughing. I sat up and saw a young girl running down the hill, her long, dark hair streaming out behind her."

An odd feeling came over Ellie. She swallowed and realised her mouth had gone dry.

"The girl was laughing. I watched her until she disappeared. Then I noticed clouds in the sky and I knew I wasn't seeing the same scene I'd been looking at before I lay down. There were sheep dotted about on the previously empty hillside. What had been a tarmac road had become a rough track. This wasn't the same Wilmington I drove into only half an hour or so before.

"I was afraid. I got up and walked down the hill, back to the car park, but it had, of course, vanished and my car along with it. I thought I'd lost my mind and didn't know what to do. I walked towards the village and came to the churchyard. I had the strongest feeling I should go in. I stood for a while underneath the yew tree but then I noticed the door of the church was open so I went in. I found people inside, monks dressed in robes."

Ellie gasped and Alan looked at her. "Are you all right?"

"Yes, I'm fine," she said. Could Alan be describing the same monks who had been her friends? "Go on."

"You probably think I'm crazy," Alan said.

"No, I don't, actually, far from it. You said there were monks?"

"Yes, several of them, of all ages, but one in particular drew my attention because he was looking at me."

Ellie couldn't help interrupting, "Was he an old man with white hair?" She laughed at the look on Alan's face.

"Bloody hell, you're right!" Alan exclaimed. "Was that a lucky guess or do you know something I don't?"

"You finish telling me what happened to you and then I'll tell you how I met him."

"You *met* him! But that's impossible. Wait, maybe it's not. If there's one thing I know now, it's that nothing's impossible. OK, as I walked in the door, this monk was over there by the altar looking at me then he beckoned me over.

" 'You have come,' he says, then, 'You are welcome.'

"As he said this, I looked around and noticed the others watching us. The old man spoke again. He told me to sit next to him. I was pretty scared, I can tell you, by then but, as I sat there, I felt a kind of change come over the church. It went dead quiet and I found I couldn't move. The old man reached out and laid a hand on my head and all trace of fear disappeared. I shut my eyes and an indescribable peace flooded through me. I'd never felt anything like it before.

"I'd always been pretty mixed up, been in a bit of trouble, drinking, you know, and moody a lot of the time. As the old man touched me, I relaxed deeply and felt at ease. It was wonderful, but then I opened my eyes and found myself lying inside the outline of the Long Man on the hill. OK, I know you're going to tell me it was just a dream but, I tell you, it was just too real for that."

"I wasn't at all," said Ellie.

"I still felt peaceful and it lasted for several hours. I felt like I'd come home. This was where I needed to be, I knew it, and that here maybe I could get over all the confusion I'd felt ever since I could remember. The thing is," Alan paused, "that was only the start. I had other similar experiences and came to realise they weren't simply dreams but I was actually seeing into the past as it existed well over a hundred years ago and perhaps even earlier. They all occurred when inside the Long Man and it became obvious to me that the Long Man was some sort of gateway, a place where the ordinary laws of past, present and future didn't apply.

"The whole area around the Long Man, including this church, I believe, is a sacred site, a place where the energy is such that people can see through the illusion of time."

"Anyway, I walked back down the hill that first day and went into the church. It was just as I had "seen" it on the hill. I half expected the monks to be there but they weren't. I decided then that I had to try to stay in the area somehow.

"I walked around the rest of the village, saw the hotel, and asked if they had any jobs going. I had quite a bit of experience working as an assistant chef in a restaurant up North. They didn't, but I got on really well with Janice, the owner. We chatted for quite a long time about Wilmington and I left my mobile number. I returned to Eastbourne. Being a seaside resort, it had quite a few hotels and places to eat. I started asking round until I found a café that would give me a job. My friends weren't too happy but went on without me when they realised I was serious, deranged, but serious. I got a room in a bed and breakfast place and started work.

"I came to Wilmington on my days off but, luckily, eight weeks later, Janice rang me. They needed someone and so I began working at the Green Man Hotel. After a while I rented a small flat in Wilmington and I've been here ever since. It's been about a year now." Alan paused for a moment, looking down at the rose petals he still held in his hand. "I've never regretted my decision. I always felt I was searching for something. I found it here." He left the statement hanging. It acted like a beacon to Ellie, drawing her to him. She longed to know more but Alan looked at his wristwatch and said, "I'm sorry, I have a shift at the hotel. Look, I'd like to talk to you some more, find out how you know about the old monk. Can we meet later, perhaps in the bar? I should be free after the evening meals, about nine?"

"I'd like that," Ellie said." Alan stood and walked out of the church. The noise of the closing door died away leaving her enfolded in silence.

Chapter 17

T HE TALK WITH ALAN TURNED Ellie inside out. He had somehow seen Wilmington in the past. He "met" Old Father and the monks. He also saw a young girl with long dark hair. Could it have been her as Anne? But, if so, what did it mean? Why had Alan been drawn to Wilmington? Was he, too, experiencing memories of a past life?

Who would have been watching her running down the hillside in the past? A shiver ran down her spine. Thomas. It had to be, surely? She certainly felt drawn to Alan, at ease with him, comfortable. He was very different from Thomas physically but, of course, he wouldn't look the same, he, like her, had been born into a new body.

Ellie felt dizzy. She stared at the altar. It looked strange. Her vision lost some of its clarity and everything shimmered. She blinked but the effect remained. A familiar grating sound echoed through the church then subsided. Ellie felt a soft breeze on the back of her neck and smelt the subtle fragrance she'd experienced before. She turned and, sure enough, the cupboard had been moved aside, revealing the dark hole. But that was not all. A figure sat on a pew near the back of the church.

Old Father! Ellie's heart beat faster, there was no doubt. She recognised him from her flashbacks! But he existed in her past as Anne. He would be long dead now. Did that mean she was back in the past? She looked down at her body but saw she was still dressed in the jeans she put on earlier. Ellie looked back at Old Father. He sat motionless in deep contemplation but then he raised his head and looked at her. He smiled and Ellie felt as if she had been touched by a sunbeam.

But then the church door opened and a man came in. Ellie glanced at him. He looked at her and said, "Hello, there. Sorry to disturb you but we have to get the church ready for a concert tonight." Two older women with flowers and cleaning materials also entered the church.

Ellie looked back at Old Father but he'd vanished. The cupboard again stood in front of the passageway. There hadn't been enough time for him to leave through the opening and replace the cupboard behind him! Ellie wondered if she had seen Old Father's spirit.

One of the women took down the old flower arrangement next to the altar. Faded petals and leaves fell to the floor. Ellie stood and walked away down the centre of the church, staring at the cupboard hiding the passageway. Had she imagined Old Father? Memory and present had become so mixed up in her mind, how could she know? Ellie moved past but then had an idea. She walked over to the man. "Excuse me, but are you the vicar?

"Yes, I am, Bob Greenway. How are you?" He reached out to shake her hand with a firm grip. Ellie welcomed the touch of living flesh in contrast to insubstantial images from the past.

"Did you see the man who was just in here? He was over there." Ellie pointed to the corner where Old Father had sat.

Bob Greenway shook his head, "No, sorry. I didn't see anyone."

"Oh, well, never mind. Can you tell me something, though? Where does the passageway behind the cupboard lead?"

The vicar looked confused. "Passageway? There's no passageway there."

"Behind the cupboard, you can't see it at the moment."

"No, I'm absolutely sure there's no passageway there."

"But it was definitely there just a few minutes ago," Ellie insisted.

The vicar looked at her with a furrowed brow and she knew he must be wondering if she had taken leave of her senses.

"There is a legend about one connecting the church with the priory but we don't know where it was. Here look." The vicar went over and, with a bit of effort, pulled the cupboard away from the wall.

Ellie stared at the unbroken stonework behind it. Why was there no sign of any passageway? It didn't make sense. "I'm so sorry to have bothered you," she mumbled, embarrassed, and hurried out of the church.

She felt confused by what had just happened. She could have sworn she hadn't been dreaming or simply remembering the old monk. He had seemed so real. But obviously he hadn't been, and neither had the passageway. She didn't understand. She looked forward to seeing Alan that evening and finding out more about what happened to him. Maybe he could help her understand what was going on.

The weather had improved so Ellie set off walking along the track that led to the Long Man. She felt a deep sense of fulfilment and joy as she walked. She loved this countryside so. Uplifted, she climbed up the hillside. Alan was right; this *was* a very special area. She reached the top and looked out.

She sensed the presence of the past all around her. She and Thomas were still running down the Man together, held in the memory of this land. Had Alan been able to tap into that memory or had he been Thomas there with her? Why didn't she *know* for sure? She felt disappointed. She had made a dreadful mistake thinking Derek had been Thomas. She didn't want to do the same thing again but she couldn't help wondering.

Ellie returned to the hotel and ate a light lunch in the dining room. As she sat sipping a cup of tea, pain clamped across her abdomen and she felt sick. She wondered if the food had been off. Fortunately, the pain faded and she forgot about it. However, a short while later, it returned, this time much worse. It didn't go and she made her way up to her room. There the pain increased and took on the recognisable nature of her period. Ellie took two painkillers and lay on the bed where she soon dozed off.

Anne stood on the beach looking out to sea. Grey clouds stretched across the horizon. A biting wind stung her face and she felt cold, despite the heavy woollen shawl she held around her. Back at the house it was warm and cosy with a good fire burning in the grate. She had been sitting in front of it when the need to step out and feel the elements around her arose. Walking loosened the bonds of loss that still encircled her heart. When she came to the shore, her suffering fell away and, just for a short while, she caught a breath of the freedom she knew in Wilmington. Her thoughts stopped whirling as she focussed on the solidity of the beach beneath her feet and the energy of the moving ocean. She loved watching the curving of the waves, how they foamed in whiteness as they broke on the stones over and over again. The seagulls gliding in the air above became her companions.

Huge greys waves threw themselves at her feet and the spray tasted salty on her lips. Without warning, a strong pain clenched across Anne's abdomen and the baby kicked. The discomfort faded away and she continued looking out over the ocean but the winter wind pulled at her without mercy and the chill ate into her body. The pain came again, this time stronger, and she knew she needed to return to the house. It was time. She wondered how long it would take.

Anne turned, hurried up the beach and along the promenade to the small street that led home. She passed through the front door and went over to stand by the fire. The warmth felt good. She watched the flames licking over the coals as she tried to get feeling back into her frozen fingers.

She began to think nothing more would happen when a strong contraction took hold. Anne clenched her teeth and sank down onto a chair as pain took possession of her body.

Rose, coming down the hallway, glanced through the door. She saw the grimace of pain on Anne's face and rushed in. "Anne, my dear. Are you all right?" Rose soon realised what was happening. "Shall I get Sarah Barnes?"

Anne took a deep breath and, as the pain subsided, relaxed. "Yes."

Rose ran her hand over Anne's hair. "You'll get through this and then you shall have your son."

Anne managed a smile. "I'll laugh when it's a girl."

"It's a boy, I tell you. I have my ways of knowing."

Anne smiled. Rose always talked as if the baby would be a boy. It was a joke between them. But in the next moment Anne no longer cared what it was for another surge of pain came and she could do nothing but allow it to run its course.

"I'll get Sarah." Rose went out, returning after a short while. "She's coming soon. Are you all right there while I get the bedroom ready?" Anne nodded.

A little later, Anne lay in bed. Flames flickered in the grate but she still felt cold. Rose built up the fire more. The wind blew a flurry of raindrops against the window and Anne shivered. The pain came again and Rose, seeing it, held out her hand. Anne gripped it, grateful for the support. "Where's the midwife?" she asked. The pains were coming close together now. It couldn't be much longer.

"Don't worry. She'll be here soon."

The afternoon passed into evening and Rose turned on the lamps. She saw Anne was tiring. A loud knocking came on the front door, heralding the arrival of the midwife. "I've done everything you told me to do," Rose said as she opened the front door.

"Good."

Sarah examined Anne. "The baby is well on its way. You'll be able to push soon."

Anne lay on the bed, overwhelmed by the strong contractions surging through her body.

"Go with them, they're carrying him to you." Rose's voice sounded distant but Anne held onto it through the pain which became almost beyond her ability to withstand. So this was her punishment for love: agony.

The urge to push came upon her and she strove to expel the child from her body. The urge came again and again but two hours passed and still the child did not come. Rose and Sarah looked at each other anxiously. They could see Anne weakening.

"Push, sweetheart, push," Sarah encouraged. "He's almost here."

Rose winced as Anne reached for her hand again and tightened her grip as the next contraction took control.

Anne's hair became damp and matted, her face tense with strain. The contractions came like waves in the ocean and she felt helpless, caught in their ebb and flow. She heard a voice but it came from far away. She couldn't stand this pain any longer. But she had to. She wanted to see her child: Thomas's child. It needed to be born. She was exhausted. Then, just as Anne thought she could go on no longer, she had a vision of Windover Hill in Wilmington. She walked up the Long Man. A figure stood on the summit surrounded by a bright light. She felt weightless, as if she were floating.

"One more push, one more push," came a voice and so she did. With everything she had, just before dawn, Anne thrust the child from her body into Sarah's waiting hands.

"It's a boy," shouted Rose, triumphant. Sarah cut the cord, wrapped the child in soft cloths then placed him into Anne's arms.

Anne had thought she would never love again but, as she stared into the dark eyes of her child and saw the damp, dark hair, she was lost. She gently touched his face. Rose stood beside her crying. Sarah quietly attended to cleaning up. In that moment, Anne once again knew joy.

After a while, Sarah came and showed Anne how to feed her son but she was so weak she could not hold him to her breast. Rose helped her. Anne cried out in pain as his jaws clamped onto her flesh. The child was strong and eager. She smiled at Rose. "He's so beautiful," she whispered.

"He is," Rose replied, watching the baby suckle.

Anne's eyes shut, she was so tired, but then she opened them again. "His name is John," she said.

"John," Rose repeated, "a fine name."

The baby finished feeding. "I'll take him," Rose said. "You need to rest."

"No," Anne said, vehemently. "I want to hold him."

Sarah came over. "Are you all right?" she asked.

Anne nodded and smiled. "Thank you."

"I'll be back later today. You get some sleep."

Anne opened her eyes and looked down at John. She touched

the soft hair on his head. She felt dizzy. The room went out of focus and she found herself back by the Long Man looking out over her beloved countryside, the place where it all began and she knew such joy and happiness. The scene faded and she looked down at her child. "I will take you there," she whispered, "one day." Then she shut her eyes.

This time she walked away from the Long Man towards the top of the hill. The figure stood waiting. It was Old Father. The light around him grew stronger, reaching out to encircle her. Anne felt as if she were vapour diffusing into the brightness.

Ellie came awake, her mind still full of the intense glow. The pain had gone but she felt insubstantial. She couldn't move. As she became aware of her body, it felt heavy, unfamiliar. She gazed at the ceiling, shaken by her vivid dream of the past. She had given birth to a son, John. He had been born strong and healthy but she herself had not survived. Ellie had just experienced her own death.

She forced her limbs into action and managed to sit up. She felt weak and her abdomen ached as in remembrance. Ellie felt awed. The vision of Old Father and the sensation of diffusing into the light remained clear in her mind. She found it hard to adjust to being in her body once again. She slid off the bed and stood but her legs felt weak so it took a while before she could walk. Now late afternoon, she realised she had slept for several hours.

After about ten minutes, Ellie became able to move about freely. She made herself a cup of tea and sipped the hot liquid. These last memories had been the most powerful so far. They felt more real than her present reality. Her whole body still cried out for the child she had so recently given birth to. She remembered the feel of his small body in her arms and longed to hold him. She felt empty inside. John. His name had been John.

Ellie longed to know what became of him. She felt afraid. Had he ended up as an orphan in a workhouse? She knew conditions in those institutions had been harsh. How could she find out? Perhaps John could be traced through historical records, although she didn't have much to go on. A lot of details about of her life as Anne were hazy and indistinct but she did know she had lived near the end of the nineteenth century. Queen Victoria had been on the throne, she remembered that from reading the newspapers to Ethel in London. She also knew that John had been born in a town called Worthing. If she could find the house, she would have an address. She would probably need his full name, though, to trace him, and that she did not know. Ellie could not remember the surname she had as Anne. It was very frustrating.

As Ellie finished her tea, she wondered if she would be able to find John himself but then realised her son had been born well over a hundred years ago, too long a time to still be alive. She felt desolate. How could that be when she so clearly remembered his birth? Her two lifetimes became muddled as past and present, no longer linear, merged. It made her head spin.

Perhaps, though, there had been other births. If John had children then *they* would most certainly be alive. She might even get to meet them. How odd that would be.

Chapter 18

ELLIE ORDERED AN ORANGE JUICE and sat down at a corner table in the hotel bar. She felt light-headed after her experience in the afternoon. She saw Alan across the room talking to other staff members. It was nearly nine, the time they had agreed to meet. Alan laughed. She liked him a lot, instinctively feeling comfortable and at ease with him, unlike Derek, who she noticed earlier in the dining room. He looked at her with such disdain it made her feel sick. She hoped he'd leave her alone.

Her thoughts returned to Alan. She couldn't wait to hear more about what had happened to him in Wilmington. He had experienced something similar to her. It felt as if their destinies were linked. As she looked at him, her heart lifted and she felt a flood of warmth towards him. She really liked him. A lot. Here was someone with whom she could share what had been happening to her. Alan caught her eye and waved. After a couple of minutes, he finished talking and made his way over.

"Hi. What are you drinking?"

"I'm fine, thanks," Ellie said. Alan went over to the bar and returned with a beer. He sat down opposite her.

"I've been looking forward to this all day. I couldn't stop thinking about you. You're the first person I've told about my experiences here. It's good to be able to talk about it. Most people would think I was crazy but you're different."

"I certainly don't think you're crazy." Ellie took a sip of her drink. "If I thought *you* were crazy," she said, keeping her tone even, "then I would have to accept that I was too."

"Tell me what you mean. You seemed to recognise the old monk I told you about earlier. What was that all about?" Alan gazed at her intently.

Ellie suddenly wanted to tell him it all, the whole story, just as it had happened right from that first day at the beach. She *needed* to tell him, share it with someone who would understand and, just maybe, help her make sense of it all.

"Like you, I was drawn to come to Wilmington. It all started with a dream." Ellie described seeing the Long Man on Windover Hill, then walking into the graveyard. "I looked down at the grave of a man. His headstone read Thomas Marshall and that he died in 1892. I knew that I had loved this man with all of my being. The grief I felt was like nothing I have ever experienced."

Ellie felt as if she were living it all again as she told her story: how she woke after the dream still mourning the man in the grave, a man she did not know, and all about the break-up with James. She explained how she experienced more and more intense memories of another life as Anne lived on the hills of Wilmington, a life in which she experienced a heightened spiritual awareness and a deep connection to the earth. She told of her memories of a childhood friendship with Thomas and the monks who worshipped on the hills and in the church. Then she described her passionate affair with Thomas when they became adults and how he died.

She held nothing back, only stopping occasionally to sip her juice when her mouth became dry. Alan listened without interrupting. He kept his gaze on her face the whole time. They both lost awareness of the bar and people talking around them.

Ellie described everything that occurred since she came to Wilmington, finishing with the latest memories of her death giving birth in Worthing. "The last thing I remember was seeing Old Father," she said, "then it all became white light." Ellie fell silent.

Alan said nothing at first, just looked at her.

"Say something," Ellie said.

"It's unbelievable," he said, finally. "I don't really know *what* to say. Do you realise what's happened here? Why it's. . . . ." He couldn't go on. His eyes filled with tears. Ellie reached into her bag to get a tissue. She too felt like crying. She wasn't sure why. Alan reached out and grasped her hand. She stared into his grey eyes and felt a powerful connection to this man and knew he felt it, too.

Ellie's lips formed the word, "Thomas," but dared not say it out loud. She looked deep into Alan's eyes searching, searching for the truth. This had to be Thomas, the love he engendered in her, even after only knowing him so little time, was surely proof. But it wasn't the intense connection she had with him before. This was different, a quiet, gentle love. Something was missing. She felt no physical passion for this man and yet she longed so much to be close. What did it mean? Ellie felt confused but also content to experience everything in its fullness, however it manifested, for here was something miraculous. Within her heart, she felt the arising of joy and a sense of completion.

Alan still held her hand. His touch felt soft and warm, perfect. A current of energy flowed between them and the moment expanded and enfolded them within it. Alan drew his hand away first. He picked up his glass and took a few sips of his drink. "This whole thing is incredible," he said. "All that you described, it makes sense of everything that happened to me. I think you and I have been seeing back in time, back into lives we lived before we were born. I can hardly believe it. And now we've been drawn together."

"Yes," Ellie agreed. "Tell me, what do *you* remember?" She felt an intense curiosity but also embarrassment, considering the nature of her relationship with Thomas. Did Alan also remember the intensity and depth of their physical passion in the past? Her face coloured at the thought.

"I've never seen things so spontaneously as you. My visions only happened when I was on the Long Man, at least in the beginning. I told you, I first got a job in Eastbourne?"

Ellie nodded.

"Well, I didn't get back to Wilmington for about a week. Anyway, when I did, I went and sat in the centre of the Man. At first nothing happened. I began to think I'd imagined it all but then I noticed some people walking towards me: a man and a boy. They were dressed in Victorian style clothing and I knew that a shift in my perception of time had occurred again. I called to them but they couldn't hear me. Again I went for a walk around the village. Everything modern had vanished. It was so weird.

"I went to the church and the girl I'd seen before was sitting there with some of the monks. She didn't see me but the monks did. I saw it in their expressions. When the girl left, they turned to me and smiled then continued to sit in contemplation. I went and sat with them. It seemed like the right thing to do. They didn't talk to me but I sensed their peacefulness. I stayed with the monks for what seemed like ages. The longer I sat there, the more peaceful I myself became. I'd always suffered badly with anxiety but that day it faded away completely and I felt an openness of mind, a new aliveness. After a while, the monks all stood up and disappeared through an opening in the wall, the same passage you saw. They never said a word in all that time but it somehow didn't seem important.

"I felt happy. I knew something miraculous had happened. When I went out of the church I saw the modern Wilmington again but I still felt good, light and free. I wasn't sure if the monks had helped me look at the world a different way or whether Wilmington itself, the Long Man and the church, in particular, had the power to affect my brain somehow and alter my perception. Anyway, it didn't matter; the effects were wonderful. I don't believe I went back through time physically, I just think I became able to *see* that time with my mind.

"As you can imagine, I couldn't wait until I could come back to Wilmington again. I hated leaving it. I visited Wilmington several times whilst I worked in Eastbourne and each time something similar would happen. I would go to the Long Man and, after a while, I began to see that other time. I would go and find the monks. They were usually around somewhere, in the church or out in the countryside. I felt such an affinity with them and also a growing sense of heightened awareness. And it was all by just being with them here in this place. I began to feel a part of the landscape and started to sense the energy of things. I felt it very strong in the past but I began to feel it more and more when I came back into the present."

"Anyway, after a couple of months, I was able to move here. After that happened, I became even more sensitive and started seeing the past in other areas of Wilmington. I no longer needed to go onto the Long Man itself."

A voice echoed through the bar. "Last orders, please."

"They're shutting," Alan said. "Look, would you like to come back to my flat for a coffee? I don't live far. I think we need to carry on talking about this."

"Yes, we do," agreed Ellie. "OK, let's go."

Alan and Ellie walked out of the hotel into the night. Ellie welcomed the caress of cool air on her skin. As they walked, she became increasingly sensitive to Alan's physical presence beside her. She wanted to reach out and put her arms around him, hold him close, but she did nothing.

"Did you go to the hill with the ring of trees when you remembered the past?" asked Ellie.

"Yes, I saw the young girl with the monks there."

"You saw her a lot?"

"Yes. I always seemed to see her. I felt drawn to her. She fascinated me. I felt she was important to me somehow. Later, I discovered just how important she had been." Alan smiled at Ellie. "And now I know who it was. You! That's why this is so amazing: that you and I are together, here, now.

"Yes, you're right, it is."

"I tried to talk to her," Alan continued, "but she never responded. She obviously couldn't see me."

Ellie felt a twinge of unease and disappointment. This didn't fit with her memories of being with Thomas. She and Thomas had been so close, why did Alan not remember?

"I would see her around the countryside, running or walking. She had such vitality. I felt I wanted to be with her but could never get close. The other people who lived in the village couldn't see me either. Only the monks responded to my presence.

After a few minutes of walking, Alan stopped in front of a red brick house. He opened the door and led Ellie inside and up a flight of stairs. "I have the whole top floor," Alan said. He put on the lights and showed Ellie into a small sitting room. "How do you like your coffee?"

"Milk and no sugar," Ellie replied. Alan went out to the kitchen and she surveyed the room, taking in the shabby old furniture and the bookshelves lined with books. As she walked further into the room, she noticed a number of paintings propped up along one wall. Ellie recognised various places around Wilmington. One in particular drew her attention, a view from the top of Windover Hill looking down the figure of the Long Man to the fields below. The colours glowed and the exquisite detail of everything took Ellie's breath away. The other paintings had been done in a similar way.

"You paint," she said when Alan returned with the coffees.

"Yes. I've always been interested in art but it wasn't until I came here that I started to get serious about it. I suppose it was the effect of the place on me. I fell in love with the landscape here and, this will sound stupid, but when I paint, I feel a deep connection to what I'm painting. I think, it's something to do with the enhanced perception I've developed since being in Wilmington. I notice things now in a way I never did before." He smiled. "I was blind until I came here but now I can't get enough of the world. There's so much beauty everywhere, even in the simplest things."

"It comes across in these," said Ellie, in admiration, as she looked at the paintings. "It really does. I love this one." She pointed to one of a cornfield. "You get a wonderful sense of perspective." In the foreground Alan had painted stalks of corn and vibrant red poppy flowers in incredible detail. The field swept back in changing shades of yellow into the green of the surrounding countryside. "I feel like the paintings are alive in a way. You're very talented."

"Oh, I don't know. It's only these I've done of Wilmington that are any good. The work I did before coming here wasn't like this at all."

Ellie suddenly noticed another painting half hidden behind a chair. She went over and pulled it out. It showed the church and the old yew tree. Shadowy figures stood in the graveyard: the monks. "Do you ever see the monks in the present?" Ellie asked.

"No, I don't. I've only ever seen them in the past. There are no monks here in Wilmington now."

"But I saw Old Father earlier," Ellie said.

"Yes, but you said he vanished quickly. You must have been seeing the past at that moment. I did some research. There haven't been any monks at the Priory for a very long time and you saw for yourself there's no passageway in the church now."

"Yes, you're right." Ellie conceded.

"I find it interesting that you describe similar altered states of consciousness as those I experience. Do you know what I think, Ellie?"

"What?"

"I believe that Wilmington is some kind of power centre."

"*Power centre?* What do you mean?"

"The earth has an energy system. In fact, we are ourselves energy and are very sensitive receivers. We sense and react to the energy of the earth. Well, in certain places, often where there're ancient monuments: holy sites, stone circles, churches, that kind of thing, the energy is such that it can, I believe, directly affect people, perhaps even alter their consciousness.

"These sacred sites are often connected by lines of energy running over the earth: ley lines. One runs right through Wilmington here. It comes across the Downs in a line directly through the Long Man, the Priory and the Church. I think that when you lived here in the past as Anne you were profoundly affected by the energy of this area. It opened you up spiritually, that and the friendship you had with the monks. They helped you to deepen your experience."

"I lost it, though, when I moved away to London," Ellie said.

"Yes, you were no longer under the influence of the energy here and all the suffering you went through obscured it. However, you never lost it, just your awareness of it."

"You're right. Old Father gave me the means to remember it when he told me that I too held the key to the gates of heaven like St Peter in the Bee and Butterfly Window. He told me to always remember the key even when I forgot. I didn't know what he meant at the time but I do now.

"When I found that old key in London as Anne, it reconnected me to the memory of what Old Father said to me that day and to the spiritual experience I had with him. It opened me up to Spirit again and transformed my life, at least, until the death of Thomas when I forgot it again."

"You loved him so much your grief cut you off from awareness of it then."

"And my guilt," added Ellie.

"Yes. All that pain blocked your spiritual connection. You also moved away to Worthing, out of the influence of this area. Then, of course, you died but deep inside, you still held the memory of the key. The impulse to awaken then started coming up through your memory into your present life."

"Yes, you're right, it did. When I was a child I actually had a small key. It was my very special possession." Ellie told Alan of the pain and anguish of her childhood and how the key she found unlocked a fantasy world that eased her suffering. In fact," she delved into her handbag, "I have it here. I found it in my bag on the plane. I'm still not sure how it got there. It belonged to my grandmother. When she died, my mother kept it for some reason, although she never found anything it opened. Anyway, it didn't matter to me. I just loved it for itself." She passed the key over to Alan.

Alan looked at it in the palm of his hand: a small silver key with a delicate design of entwined leaves on the handle. "It obviously triggered a memory of the key you had as Anne and the state of happiness that was linked with it then. It came out in your childhood fantasies.

"That was obviously the start of your awakening process. The actual memories came later, after your premonition at the beach and the break-up with your fiancé. And with the memories came the heightened spiritual awareness you used to feel as Anne."

"It was why I came back here. I felt that, in Wilmington, maybe I could explore that more." Ellie looked at Alan. The bond she felt existed between them had grown stronger. She longed to reach out and hold him, just in a gentle way, caressing way, let him know how much she cared for him. She could no longer ignore it. She had to know if he was Thomas. "To be honest, it wasn't the only reason I wanted to come to Wilmington," Nervous all of a sudden, Ellie sipped her coffee. "I was also hoping I might find Thomas here." She watched Alan carefully, waiting for his reaction.

"I guess that would be on your mind."

Ellie waited for him to say something more but he didn't. Ellie felt uneasy. "Alan? Do you . . ." Ellie tried to swallow but her throat felt constricted. She drank down the last of her coffee and tried again. "Alan, what else do you remember of your life in Wilmington, your *past* life, I mean?"

Nothing could have prepared Ellie for his reply.

"Oh, I didn't have a past life in Wilmington myself," Alan said.

Shock ran the length of Ellie's body. How could this be? "But you said you saw back into the past. You saw me and the monks, you must have been there at the same time."

"No, I wasn't. I only *saw* back in time. I wasn't reliving memories of an actual life in Wilmington." Alan saw the stunned expression on Ellie's face. "What?'

Ellie sat there, looking at Alan, unable to speak. The world tumbled around her. She couldn't tell Alan why she had become upset.

Alan stared at Ellie in confusion but then it hit him. "Did you think . . . God, did you think *I* was *Thomas?*"

Ellie remained silent.

"You did, didn't you?" Alan reached out and took Ellie's hand. "No, I didn't have a past life in Wilmington. I'm sorry, I'm not Thomas." He looked into her eyes. "I think you knew that deep down, though, didn't you?"

Ellie still couldn't speak, a profound confusion clouding her mind. Alan was right, she *had* been unsure, but there could be no denying the strength of love she felt for him, even now as she looked at him across the table. It made no sense.

Alan continued. "I'm not Thomas, Ellie. I'm John."

The room went dark and Ellie thought she would pass out. "What?"

"Yes, I'm John, your son, the child you bore as Anne."

Chapter 19

E LLIE SAT ON THE FADED settee next to Alan and the memory of holding a tiny baby came flooding back: his soft hair, the deep, dark eyes, so perfect. "Oh, my God," she whispered. "How is this possible?" She looked at Alan, her eyes wide. "How do you know?"

"I didn't experience a past life in Wilmington but that doesn't mean I didn't experience a past life at all. I did."

"I don't understand," said Ellie.

"After I'd been living in Wilmington a short while, I started to change, as I told you. I opened up to the world, became more sensitive. I was able see into the past of Wilmington but I also began to see other things. I remembered living a different life.

"I experienced being a young boy roaming along a beach and playing in the sand, building castles and digging channels for sea water to run through. We lived in a small house close to the sea."

"We?"

"My parents died so an aunt brought me up. Well, she wasn't really an aunt, I just called her that."

"Rose, was it Rose?" Ellie asked.

"Yes."

Ellie smiled. Rose had cared for John.

"She did her best but I was a wild one, always off out somewhere, getting into mischief. I hated to be confined."

"That sounds familiar." Ellie laughed.

"Aunt Rose made sure I went to school, at least most of the time, but I longed to be out in the open.

"I used to go for long walks along the beach. I always wondered about my mother, and, for some reason, I felt close to her, you, down by the sea. I used to imagine you as the wind, all around, touching me, but invisible. I visited your grave in the cemetery but never felt the same way there. It was odd."

Ellie shivered at the thought of her grave.

"When I became older," Alan continued, "Rose told me about you, how you loved the sea. I asked her about my father but she said you rarely talked of him. All she knew was that he died some months before my birth and that you suffered greatly over his loss.

"The memories of this life didn't come all at once," explained Alan. "Like you, they came in sections over a period of time. I would get glimpses that made no sense but I managed to piece them together.

"As John, I was restless, as if there was somewhere I needed to go or something I had to do but I never knew what it was. I didn't like school and so left as soon as I could. I tried various jobs but none of them satisfied me. I left home and got work on a farm outside Worthing and that was a good time. I enjoyed being out in the countryside and handling animals, especially the horses. I loved them, their beauty and power. I would often ride, enjoying the feel of the horse beneath me and the excitement of galloping fast over the hills and fields.

"There were relationships with women but none that lasted. Again, I'd feel unsettled after a while. I hated being tied down. I was only ever really happy when I went out riding. At those times I felt as if nothing could confine me.

"At twenty-one, I received money left to me by my mother and started my own business breeding horses, only a few at first, but over the years I made a success of it. I was happy to some extent although the vague sense of incompletion I had felt all my life never entirely left me."

Ellie listened, moved by Alan's story. He had been John, the tiny baby she had known just for moments in her life as Anne. He was here with her now and they were actually in Wilmington together. "This is just incredible," she broke in. "I can't believe this."

"But it's true. You brought us together here."

"I did?" Ellie looked at Alan in confusion. "What do you mean?'

"I know I said the Long Man drew me to Wilmington, that's still true, but it did so because of you."

"I don't understand,"

Alan stood up and went into another room. He came back with a brown cardboard box stained with age. "I came to Wilmington in this life because of this."

Ellie stared in fascination. "What is it?"

Alan carefully laid it on the coffee table between them. He gently lifted the lid. Inside lay an old, worn notebook. The edges of the pages had been decorated with swirling coloured patterns and it had a cover of frayed blue cloth glued onto board. Alan handed it to Ellie. As she touched it, Ellie remembered. She knew what it was and also what it contained. "Of course," Ellie whispered, "of course. But how did you get this?" Ellie turned a wondering gaze onto Alan.

"Well, I found it as John first. After I had been breeding horses for a number of years, Rose died. She had no surviving relatives, only me. I organised the funeral and then later sorted out the house. It was then that I found this in a cupboard. Rose hoarded things. The house was packed full of stuff, mostly rubbish. This cardboard box looked so unimportant I nearly threw it away but something made me look inside. I had no idea that it would change my life."

Alan stopped talking, his attention back in the past. He remained silent for a few moments then came back to the present and continued. "Anyway, I opened it and saw that book inside."

Ellie lifted the notebook to her nose. It smelled faintly of some kind of perfume. She opened it and leafed through some of the pages. It was full of neat handwriting. There were household hints, recipes, even little sketches of things: a vase of flowers, the scene through a window, a cat curled by a fireplace.

"This is what drew my attention." Alan reached out and took the book back. He extracted a piece of paper and gave it to Ellie. It was an etching of the Long Man of Wilmington. Ellie remembered getting it from a bookshop one day.

"I found the picture at the back of the notebook but I also found this." Alan handed Ellie another piece of paper, this one folded in half and yellowed with age. Ellie opened it.

"Read it out," Alan said.

Ellie's hands shook and her voice quavered. She didn't think she could do it but it got easier as she continued.

"To my child," she read. "I was walking by the ocean today and had the strangest feeling I should write to you. You are not yet born but I long to see and hold you.

I want you to know you are special. You came out of love, the deepest love that I believe is possible. This love grew out of the hills and valleys of a place I also loved. Part of me still runs free in the countryside there, especially at night in my dreams when I dance like the wind as I used to do as a young girl.

"This place is like no other and I want you to know it, too. We will go there one day, you and I. We will walk together up and over the great Long Man. There you will know the joy I felt in that place.

"A heaviness lies upon me today and I fear the future, that maybe the tides will turn against my dreams. If I am gone when you read this, know always that I love you and go there one day, go to where the Long Man of Wilmington watches and waits for you."

Ellie's eyes filled with tears. One dripped down onto the letter. She hastily wiped it away with her sleeve. "Where did you get this?" Ellie asked. "You said you found it when you were John, how come you have it now?"

"I'll get to that. I wasn't sure what to make of the letter when I found it as John but I treasured it because it came from my mother. I took the notebook back home with me. The Long Man of Wilmington had been special to my mother, so much so she had written to me about it. I wondered why.

"The wondering stayed with me and opened up a feeling inside me, a sense of mystery. It made me feel a strange excitement. Also, I always wanted to know more about my mother. She loved this Long Man so it was a connection to her, to you." Alan looked at Ellie and smiled. "I determined to go there the first opportunity I got.

"However. . . ." A look of pain came over Alan's face.

"What?" Ellie asked. "Tell me."

The very next day after returning to my stables I was called up."

"What do you mean "called up?"

"Conscripted into the army. It was 1917, the First World War had been going on for three years." Ellie sensed a rawness in Alan's voice as he spoke and it shook her. Ellie, sensing she wouldn't like the next part of Alan's story, felt a feeling of dread. She was right.

"After the memories of being John surfaced, I started having vivid dreams. First, I found myself on a boat travelling across what must have been the English Channel. A lot of other men accompanied me. I remember the smell of urine and vomit. It was a rough crossing and we all huddled inside. We sailed on a tide of fear but some laughed and joked. They kept the rest of us sane.

"The next night I dreamt we marched, walking on and on through a beautiful countryside. I heard birds singing and looked up at a clear blue sky. The world seemed perfect but soon the sound of loud explosions echoed across the fields and the knowledge of our destination weighed heavy on our minds.

"After several days we came to an area of devastation. All too soon, the most dreadful chaos you could imagine engulfed us: explosions, smoke, men screaming.

"I killed a man. I never thought I would ever do such a thing. All I wanted to do was to return to my own land and my horses but this German came at me and I shot him. Just like that. I saw his face. I *still* see his face." Alan's features tightened with tension. "I had several nights of dreams like this. I experienced bombs exploding close by, cries of pain, confusion, being covered in mud but at other times we waited in silence, sometimes for days, until it all started up again." Alan's voice faltered for a second. "I'm sorry, but I feel I have to tell you this."

"It's all right," Ellie said. "Go on."

"I lived in filth for days, cowering in dark holes, never knowing with each sunrise whether it would be my last.

Alan took a deep breath. "And then one day it was. I lay in a trench. A huge explosion turned the world upside down. It threw me some distance away and I passed out. When I regained consciousness, I had a tremendous pain in my back. I couldn't see anything except smoke: dark, black smoke. I heard people calling out but no one came. I couldn't move. I knew this was it and, oddly, felt calm. I can't describe it. I sensed the battle still raging on around me, heard people shouting and more explosions going off but, where I lay, it became completely still." Alan's expression took on a faraway look and, strangely, he smiled. "The smoke started to clear and I saw the blue of the sky, such a deep, deep blue. I felt it went on forever. I stared up at it, watching the smoke fading away. Soon I saw nothing but blue and that's the last thing I can remember of my life as John.

"I think these memories were buried deep in my unconscious when I was reborn. I always felt a heavy feeling I could never define as I grew up. Now I know about John, so much in my life makes sense.

"Anyway," Alan's smile widened, "everything is different now. I've found peace here and so much more. Also, I've found you."

"So, as John you never made it to Wilmington," Ellie said.

"No. No, I didn't but the seed of it had been sown in me by your letter. And I never forgot it. I held it inside me whilst I endured those dark days of war. Each night, I dreamed that one day I would walk on the hills of Wilmington and see the Long Man as my mother wanted me to. It became a bright beacon of hope for me when things were awful. I'd imagine how it would be: the sweep of pure, green grass, the silent figure of the Long Man watching and waiting, the joy I would feel knowing my mother had walked on that place and loved it, that I, myself, came out of it. This bright vision took me away from the broken and burnt fields I endured. And you would be there with me on the bright hill in my imagination.

"I believe this powerful image, mixed in with such strong emotion, drew me here to Wilmington in my present life. When I passed by with my friends on our way to Eastbourne that day and

I saw the Long Man, I recognised it at some deep level, remembered it from my connection to you in my past life as John.

"When I sat on the Long Man that first day and saw a young girl in the past I had no idea who she was. It wasn't until I heard your story that I realised who she had been: my mother in my past life, you. So, because of you I am here."

"I fulfilled my promise after all, then," Ellie said.

"What promise?" Alan asked.

"Just before I left Wilmington after Thomas died, I swore I would bring you back here one day so you could know the beauty of this place. I'm glad. Tell me, how did you get the notebook in *this* life?"

"As John, I lived in a small cottage near the stables where I bred my horses. When I had to go and fight, I worried someone would break in while I was away. I gathered important things together in a metal box and hid them under the floor before I left.

"When the memories of being John surfaced, I remembered doing it and so I went to where I thought the house was. I hardly dared hope it would still be there. Even if it was, I doubted I'd be able to gain access to my hiding place. How would I explain what I wanted to the occupants? Even then, I had no guarantee the stuff would still be there.

"I had trouble finding the house at first; the area had changed so much. A small wood had grown up round it. Anyway, I managed to locate the house and found it abandoned. The roof had fallen in and a pile of rubble covered where I left the things. It took me the best part of a day to shift it."

"But the box was obviously there," Ellie said.

"Yes. I couldn't believe it when I prised up the boards and saw the box. I took the book out and read your letter and it all became real. I mean, I knew inside me it was true, but another part of me doubted, even thought I was delusional. To have visions of a past life, that's hardly normal, is it?"

"No," agreed Ellie. "I felt like that, as well."

Alan stopped talking and neither spoke, both in awe at the forces at work in their lives. Ellie broke the silence first. "And so here we are."

"Yes, because of you, and I can't thank you enough, for here in

Wilmington I have discovered something of inestimable value. As soon as I came here, I realised how special this area is and the power and significance of the Long Man. I, like you and Thomas, have now experienced the power of this place where time is fluid and dreams can be fulfilled, albeit in the most bizarre ways. I am grateful you drew me here so I could know powerful joy and be opened to receive a deep truth: the knowledge of my own true reality, for that is what I gained here."

Alan came and sat down next to Ellie on the settee. He put his arms around her and pulled her against him. She felt his heart beating beneath the soft wool of his jumper. They sat holding each other for a while, mother and child finally reunited, albeit a long time later and in different flesh.

After a few minutes, Alan pulled away. "You know, I can't help feeling there's something more to all of this. Most people don't remember their past lives. Why did we? And the monks, haven't you ever wondered who they are, especially Old Father? There's something very unusual about them, don't you think?

"Well, yes, you're right. I never thought about it as Anne but now, looking back, I can see what you mean."

"Mmm." Alan stood. "Would you like another coffee?" He looked at his watch. "God, it's two thirty in the morning. Do you want to go back to the hotel?"

"Not really," Ellie replied. "I don't think I could sleep. I'll have that coffee, unless *you* want to sleep?"

"No, I feel the same." Alan disappeared into the kitchen.

While she waited, Ellie reread her letter. She remembered writing it now. She had been filled with a deep sadness and yearning for Wilmington, for Thomas, that day. She woke in the morning filled with a nameless dread and, to escape it, walked down to the beach. She did not succeed. On her return home, she wrote the letter.

Ellie realised that, at some level, she had known what was going to happen and what she had to do. Somehow she had accessed an inner knowing, the deeper intelligence Ellie now knew lay within each and every person, always present and supporting even though most people were unconscious of it. We are all held gently in the web of life, she thought, playing out our parts, fulfilling our destinies. The letter had enabled her to reach out into her child's life, despite her death, and guide him to Wilmington. Her love for him had reached through time. She smiled at Alan as he entered the room.

They sat together, sipping their coffee. Neither felt the need to speak. To be together was enough. Ellie finished off her drink and set the cup down on the coffee table. As she did so, she became aware of an overwhelming urge to go out, walk into the darkness and breathe the cool night air. She sensed something just beyond the reach of her consciousness calling her. "Let's walk," she said to Alan.

Alan looked out of the window then back at Ellie. "OK." They went downstairs and out into the night. As they walked through Wilmington, they saw a soft glow coming through the windows of the church. They looked at each other. "That's odd," said Alan. "What's going on there in the middle of the night?"

"Let's take a look," Ellie replied.

They turned off the road and into the churchyard. Ellie sensed the spreading weight of the old yew tree above her as they passed. Alan reached out and found Ellie's hand and they walked over to the church.

The door stood ajar. They pushed it open and stopped on the threshold in amazement. The glow came from dozens of candles placed all around the interior of the building. Their flames flickered. Ellie and Alan looked at each other. They both knew something extraordinary was happening. As they moved further in, they saw the church stood empty. Ellie became aware of the strange perfume she smelt each time the passageway had appeared. She swung around. Sure enough, the entrance gaped open, a dark hole in the wall of the church.

Chapter 20

ELLIE NUDGED ALAN'S ARM. "LOOK. Can you see it?"

Alan turned and nodded. "Come on." He let go of Ellie's hand and picked up two candles. He handed one to Ellie."

They walked over to the opening. Ellie stared at the stone steps leading down and her body tingled as if in the presence of static electricity. Alan looked at her and they started down, taking it slow and carefully.

"The vicar told me this afternoon a passageway is supposed to exist leading to the priory although he didn't know where," Ellie said. "But Alan, he pulled out the cupboard and this passage wasn't here. It was just a wall. What does it mean?"

"I think we're no longer in the present." Ellie looked at Alan in amazement and realised he was serious. His features stood out in stark relief in the flickering light of his candle. He seemed different: intense, excited.

Could what Alan said be true? Ellie looked down at her body. But she was still wearing her modern clothes. This couldn't be a memory but happening to her now. Now but somehow linked to the past? She couldn't cope with the implications of it so Ellie turned her attention to their surroundings. They reached the bottom of the steps and saw stone walls disappearing off into the darkness. The strange scent smelt stronger now. Ellie shivered in the chill air as they moved forward. The tunnel curved around and downwards for a while before straightening again. Then they came to a place where the tunnel branched in two directions.

"Can you get a feel of the direction we're taking?" Alan asked.

"Well, I should think this one leads to the Priory." Ellie walked down one of the tunnels a short way. She couldn't see anything. It felt cold and damp; a smell of mustiness pervading the air. Ellie sensed the presence of death and decay. She walked into the other tunnel. There she felt a soft movement of air and smelt the strange odour. "This way," she said, "we need to go this way."

Ellie walked forwards, Alan followed. The tunnel stretched ahead.

"This is amazing," Alan said, after a few minutes. "I wonder . . ."

"What?"

"Well, I've a feeling we're heading towards Windover Hill?"

"You mean this could lead under the Long Man?"

"If I'm right, it will, but it's hard to gauge it."

The walk went on and on. Ellie sensed the tunnel growing warmer and the smell intensified. The static electricity in the air also increased and so did the tingling in her body.

Finally, when they thought the tunnel would go on forever, they reached the end. It opened out into a large rectangular chamber lined with stone. "This is definitely under the hill," Alan whispered. Pillars and arches supported the ceiling. "This has obviously been here for centuries and no one has ever guessed."

As Ellie and Alan walked out into the chamber, an aura of sacredness enveloped them and they fell silent, staring around them in awe. Chills ran up and down Ellie's body. At the far end they saw an altar on which stood a cross and two burning candles. The further she went into the room, the more Ellie's consciousness expanded from the confines of her body as if she were somehow dissolving into the walls of the chamber. It felt right to be there.

They came to a standstill halfway into the room and noticed an opening on the right side of the room. As they stared at it, they saw the faint glimmer of approaching light. Ellie held her breath.

Figures came into view, monks dressed in distinctive brown robes and carrying candles. As they emerged from the tunnel, they looked at Ellie and Alan and bent their heads in acknowledgement. Ellie recognised several of the monks as those she knew when she had lived as Anne.

The room filled with light from the candles. Ellie counted twenty monks gathered around them. They all simply stood and waited. She hardly dared breathe. Then, after a few minutes had passed, a single figure, dressed in white, came out of the tunnel. "Old Father," Ellie whispered. She could not believe this was happening.

The old man walked towards them. He had a gentle smile upon his face. "Welcome," he said. "Now it can begin."

The moment he said this, the monks around the room began chanting, a series of haunting notes that not only filled the room but resonated throughout Ellie's mind and body. The old man smiled and motioned for Ellie and Alan to follow him. He turned and led them towards the altar on which they now noticed stood a glass vase of pink wild roses next to the simple wooden cross at the centre. On the other side, white smoke curled and coiled its way up to the roof from a metal incense burner. Ellie realised this had been the subtle fragrance wafting from the passageway into the church.

She stared at the delicate colour and soft fullness of the roses. Their image burned into her brain. Behind and around her came a powerful crescendo of sound. It vibrated through her whole being and her awareness, already heightened, expanded even more. It moved through the dense rock and earth above to encompass the figure of the Long Man stretched out on the hillside. Alan had been right, incredible power existed in the chamber.

The knowing came to Ellie that this place held the power to help those within it to break through the chains of identification with physical matter and transcend the limitations of space and time. The roses in front of her, so simple and beautiful, were also infinitely complex, an expression of the majestic cosmic forces she sensed at work in the whole of creation in that moment. All her thoughts and feelings, worries and concerns about life fell away and she stood in the purity and perfection of the present moment. Nothing more was needed other than to be here with these people.

And still the sound echoed around the room. Ellie's awareness rose higher into the night sky and the image flowed into her brain of the darkness of space speckled with stars stretching beyond the clouds. And still she expanded, onwards and outwards, as if she were speeding to the centre of the universe itself, yet paradoxically remained very much herself standing next to Alan in the cavern with the monks chanting and the candlelight dancing on the walls. Outside became inside as all barriers in her perception dissolved in a monumental upwelling of love from the centre of her chest. After a while, the old man turned and smiled and the voices fell away into a silence that was itself as full and profound as the sound had been.

Ellie knew they all stood as one united being in that glorious moment, living expressions of the infinite intelligence that she now knew to be her very essence. The sense of Living Presence became so strong tears of joy flowed unrestrained from her eyes. Ellie knew she would never forget this as long as she lived. She felt light and free and energised. She found herself smiling as a bubble of joy rose from within. She saw Alan smile too. He looked around and squeezed her hand.

They stood like this for several more minutes but then Ellie realised the monks were leaving. As they came past, those she had known in her life as Anne smiled before walking back into the tunnel from where they came. Eventually, only Old Father remained.

"You have many questions, I know," he said. He turned to Ellie. "Do you remember the young girl who ran over the hills and reached out with her heart to the earth and sky?"

"Yes, I do," said Ellie. "And you were with me then. You taught me to be still inside, to be open and free, yet part of the world. And such a world it was, so beautiful and alive."

"Yes, we were teaching you, helping you know the truth of your real self. You learned well. And then there was your young friend."

"Thomas," Ellie whispered.

"Yes. He too was open and alive, in tune with the earth. He was never able to see us but, through you, he came to understand much. You embraced him with your joyful spirit. It drew him to you and made his love so strong, especially later. For him, you were a link to something larger, greater, that he sensed but did not understand."

"Why could Thomas not see you?"

"Because he did not have the inner eyes to see us. We did not live in his time, Ellie, just as we do not live in yours now. We lived a long time ago."

"But . . ."

"You've come out of the past." Alan said.

Old Father looked at Alan. " No *you* have come *back* to the past," he said. "You have the ability to reach back into the history of Wilmington. This is possible because of the intensity of energy here. You sensed our presence and we are able to respond to you because of your receptivity. All those that come to Wilmington who are ready will see us."

"We belong to a secret spiritual order of people drawn here by the energies present in this place. We attained understanding of many secrets of the universe but what we discovered was not ready to be known by the majority and so we stayed here underground.

The Long Man is a sign to those who are searching for understanding. This has always been a place of pilgrimage for here people can remember who they are. Here are the gates of heaven for those who are ready to pass through.

"There have been many over the years who have come here to learn, those who had the sensitivity to perceive us. This place only draws those who are ready. They stay for a while and are taught our ways. They then return to their lives, taking the knowledge with them."

"I still don't understand how we're able to see and hear you if you don't exist in our present?" Ellie said.

"You can do it because this place is a portal through time. Certain very powerful energies exist in and around this hill. They make it easier to open to the truth of the spiritual dimension in which many more things are possible than you can conceive of at this time. You are able to attune to us because of your awareness of the spiritual dimension within you."

Old Father looked back at Ellie. "You were especially receptive when you were Anne. We taught you throughout your childhood until you left Wilmington. We helped you become aware of the truth of your inner being, that you were much more than the physical body, that in your spirit you were never alone but connected to the whole of creation. And you lived that truth in your life, in your response to the world, and it was a joy for us to behold. You also drew Thomas into your vision and understanding. But then you were tested."

"My mother sent me away to London," said Ellie. "That was so hard. I felt as though my life had ended."

"That happened because you missed the powerful energy of Wilmington but also because you were in a large city cut off from the healing presence of nature and surrounded by large numbers of people, many struggling with difficult lives. You could not help but feel overwhelmed by the heavy atmosphere of London at first."

"I forgot everything you taught me. I became lost in my own suffering," said Ellie.

"But then you found the key in the basement of the house and connected with Spirit once again. You were able to bring light into a dark situation where hope had been lost."

"Ethel?"

"Yes, but you also helped others in the house. You lifted their lives by your example. You did well."

"But, Old Father, how can you say that? Look what happened when I returned to Wilmington. What of Helen and Thomas?"

"You and Thomas had a destiny to fulfil. He saw in you something he craved, a greater life and communion with Spirit. He did not know but sensed, with his emotions and his body, that through loving you he could connect with this.

"You taught him so much: with your openness and love for life, with your surrender and powerful love for him. And so you were both able to open out and embrace, not only each other, but the world. However, you both needed to learn something more: that what you really sought lay inside you, not in the other. And so the greatest test began."

"Yes," Ellie said sadly. "When Thomas died, I blamed myself for it. I even blamed God. I lost the light again. Old Father, why could I not hold onto it when I needed it the most?"

"But you never lost it. You only lost your awareness of it when you became locked in your pain. You felt you no longer deserved to live and know happiness, not when others had died because of your actions, and so you fell into darkness. But you still had the key that I gave you and so, in time, and through a new birth, you started to remember. The truth can never be completely denied, only temporarily forgotten when the search for it is in the wrong direction. And so your mind, bit by bit, broke open. The memories of Wilmington came back and you returned here to reconnect with the truth of who you are.

"Old Father, why could I not see you when I returned from looking after Ethel? I thought you had all left Wilmington."

"You had been out of the area of the Long Man for so long you were no longer attuned to our presence. After that, your focus was on your relationship with Thomas and, later, your grief when he died."

"You only started to perceive me again when you returned here in your present life and your grief and guilt lessened."

"The voice I heard by the lake telling me to reach through Thomas, that was you?"

"Yes. As you opened up, you became more receptive to me again."

"What you said helped me resolve my guilt over the deaths of Thomas and Helen."

"Yes. Death is not the end. People are not trapped in their lives but can use them to experience what they need to learn to come into awareness of their own deeper nature. Helen and Thomas were following paths they had *chosen.*

"Now you have fully awakened to your inner truth. You will not forget again."

Old Father turned to Alan. "And you are here because the woman who gave you birth as John loved this place and the truth contained here so much that she wanted it for you. She passed her vision of it on despite her death and it lay dormant in you until the time and conditions were right for its physical expression. Nothing happens by accident and now is the time you both need to be here to finally realise your true potential."

"Old Father? How can you know all about us like you do?" Ellie asked.

"When I look at you I do not see only the physical person but your whole being and life through time."

"But how?" Ellie persisted.

"We are all one, everything exists in consciousness. It is given to me to know these things so I may guide you to the fulfilment of your potential."

"Who *are* you?" Alan asked.

"I am simply one of the guardians of the gateway here. I help those who are ready to become aware of their true nature." Old Father paused, then continued, "So few realise the gift that lies within them, the treasure that holds the power to transform their whole experience of life. People seek happiness only in outer circumstances."

A brief look of sadness passed over Old Father's face then he smiled again. "But you are here and it is a miracle. The world needs those such as you.

"There are some who *are* beginning to understand, who realise the material world alone does not fulfil their deepest longings. And so they look around them for answers. Those who know must point the way."

"But how can we do that?" asked Ellie.

Old Father looked at her, "You can tell the story."

Ellie stared blankly at him. "What story?"

The old man went on, "The story of a young girl whose heart was wide open, wide enough to contain the whole world. Write of her love for the land of her birth and also her love for the person who shared it with her. Describe Thomas and your longing to bring his son into the world and to this place where the Long Man stands watching. Tell of your pain for it echoes the suffering of so many. Write about how you felt, how you became aware of the living Presence that gives you, and everyone, your very life. Tell how this inner light can see through the deadening mind and illuminate the miracle and intrinsic purity of every moment. Write about those things. Bring Wilmington alive for them so they can live it too, so they might then look within themselves and realise that the truth, the living Presence, does not just exist in you but in them also."

Old Father turned to Alan, "And you can paint the truth. Paint your new vision. Show others the world as you see it. Let your paintings speak to people of what they know but have turned away from."

"Yes, you can do it, "Ellie said to Alan. "The work I saw at your flat is amazing."

"I do love painting," Alan mused.

"You both have other work to do but that will become known to you in time."

Alan turned to Ellie. "Do you think you could write your story?"

The idea whirled around in Ellie's consciousness. She'd been good at writing at school. *Could* she write her story? It was certainly worth trying, she decided.

"Use words to paint the landscape of your experience for them." Old Father said. "Bring others into your truth."

"Old Father," Ellie said. "What of Thomas?"

"He has never returned to Wilmington."

Ellie took a deep breath. "Do you think he remembers?"

"Sometimes it is necessary to remember to go forwards. For you both," Old Father looked over at Alan then back to Ellie, "this was so but most people do not remember their past lives, not consciously. It would be too much for them. They need to focus on their path in the present until the time is right for them to know." Old Father looked at Ellie compassionately.

"I see." Ellie felt a profound disappointment. The meaning behind Old Father's words was clear. Thomas had no recollection of their time together. She had to let go of the idea they would ever meet again.

"So now I need to let go of the past, don't I?" Ellie said.

"No, you build on it. You have the gift of all you have learned and experienced here to illuminate your life in this moment."

"Yes," Ellie smiled. It was true. She knew now that the ultimate source of all the love she could ever crave was already inside her in her own living conscious being. She felt that love now as she stood with Alan and Old Father deep under the Long Man.

The roses bloomed, the candles flickered and the incense curled its smoke to the ceiling above. Old Father fell silent and shut his eyes. Ellie and Alan joined him in his stillness. It deepened the longer they stood without moving. And they took that stillness with them when Old Father opened his eyes and gently laid his hand on, first, Ellie's head, then Alan's, in blessing. They both felt the Divine energy flowing through his hand. Then Old Father gestured towards the ceiling. "The dawn breaks. Go in peace and live in Truth."

Old Father smiled one last time and walked away into the tunnel where the other monks had gone.

Ellie and Alan stood alone in the chamber for a while, soaking in the beauty of the atmosphere. The air remained warm and perfumed but then Ellie felt a cool breeze waft over her cheek. It came from the tunnel where Old Father had disappeared. "It's time to go," she whispered. Alan nodded.

"Let's go where the monks went," Ellie said. "I think it may be another way out."

"OK."

They took one last look at the chamber then turned and made their way over to the tunnel. The passage looked similar to the one they had come down before except that water trickled down the walls in places. They encountered several openings. These led into small rooms containing simple pieces of wooden furniture. They saw no sign of the monks.

Ellie and Alan walked for a long time. Finally the freshness of the air intensified and the tunnel ended in a roughly hewn cave in the natural rock. They discovered a narrow fissure large enough to permit them to pass through. They blew out their candles and, leaving them in the cave, squeezed out of the opening into the grey light of dawn.

They found themselves struggling through dense undergrowth. It took them quite a while to reach a clearer area, then it became obvious where they were, the small wood where she and Thomas spent so much time together. She had never known that an underground passage existed there. Ellie stared around. The place seemed different somehow. Just as this thought came, a wave of dizziness engulfed her. She put out a hand to steady herself on a nearby tree but it became insubstantial and Ellie fell into darkness.

Ellie opened her eyes first. A soft natural light filled the church. She felt stiff and cold. Alan stirred beside her. They both sat together on a pew near the back of the church. She shook Alan's shoulder. "Wake up." He opened his eyes and stared at her without comprehension then he turned and looked at where the passageway had gaped open the night before. The cupboard was back in place. They stared around the church. The candles had all gone. Nothing remained to indicate that any of the previous night's events had ever happened.

"What do you remember?" Alan asked.

Ellie described what she had experienced: going down the passage, meeting the monks and Old Father, the extraordinary chanting. She still heard the sound in her mind and felt again its uplifting effect.

"That's exactly what I experienced too. My God!" Alan ran a hand through his tousled hair. He looked at Ellie. He had tears in his eyes. "The chanting it . . ." he said and stopped.

"I know," Ellie said.

They went over to the cupboard and shifted it to one side. Alan inspected the wall. "I reckon this has been very carefully sealed over. Whoever did it went to a lot of trouble to find stone the same as the surrounding wall. I wonder why? Look, though," he pointed. "You can just make out the slightly different shade of mortar here. A passage definitely existed here at one time."

"I still can't get my head around all this," Ellie said. "Everything that happened last night seemed so real."

"It *was* real. We went back into the past when the passageway actually existed and was used by the monks. The unique energy of this area made it possible."

"Yes, but it still seems incredible." Ellie looked around at the church that had borne witness to it all. It stood silent, unwilling to yield its secrets.

"I'm starving," Alan said. "Come back to the flat. I'll make us breakfast."

"That sounds good."

They replaced the cupboard and let themselves out of the church. Neither spoke as they walked down the road. Ellie drank in the sights and sounds of the early morning. She felt energised, as light as air, yet completely in tune with her body. Miracles met her eyes wherever she looked: a blackbird that eyed her speculatively from a branch, the subtle blue of the sky, the sound of birdsong, a garden of colourful flowers.

They reached Alan's flat. Ellie sat down in the lounge while Alan went off to the kitchen. He made some tea and toast. When he returned, he found Ellie lying on the settee fast asleep. He gently covered her with a blanket and left the room.

Chapter 21

ELLIE OPENED HER EYES TO a room dark except for a small crack of bright sunlight where the drawn curtains didn't quite meet. Her neck felt stiff from sleeping awkwardly. She raised herself to a sitting position and got up. Walking through the flat, she discovered Alan had gone out. A clock in the kitchen showed twenty past three. She had slept for most of the day.

In Alan's bedroom, Ellie found more paintings of Wilmington. She looked at them for a long time. One in particular caught her attention. She bent down to take a better look. It reminded her of the very first dream she had of Wilmington. It was of a group of tall trees through which Windover Hill and the Long Man, bathed in golden sunlight, could be seen. She loved the beautiful shades of green and Alan's characteristic depiction of fine detail in the foreground. Ellie wondered if he would sell it to her.

Old Father was right about the value of Alan's paintings, Ellie thought. They had something about them. They looked as if illuminated from within. As she turned to leave, Ellie noticed a painting of a young girl holding a bunch of wildflowers. She had a light in her eyes and a joyful smile on her lips. Her skin had the golden sheen of one who spent her days out in the open.

Ellie heard a key turn in the front door and went out into the hall just as Alan let himself in. "Hello. Did you have a good sleep?" he asked.

"Yes, I did, thanks. What about you, did you sleep at all?"

"For a few hours but I had to do a shift at the hotel. Would you like something to eat?"

"Yes, please."

Ellie followed him into the kitchen. Painted a dull green, it felt oppressive. Alan saw her looking around and said. "Yes, it's disgusting, isn't it?"

One bright spot, however, drew Ellie's attention. A small painting sat on a shelf. It featured a group of wildflowers nestling amid stalks of grass. Their bright colours lifted the gloom of that part of the room. "I love your use of colour. It's remarkable, you know," Ellie said. "You must keep on painting."

Alan followed her gaze towards the picture. "Well, yes, I would like to. I enjoy painting and drawing, especially out on the hills here. There's so much to see. I guess painting's my way of connecting to the environment."

"But it's more than that," Ellie said. "The paintings I've seen here reach out and draw me into them. You can see the love you hold for what you paint. It makes me feel that way too."

"Thanks," Alan said. "I never thought about them much, just had fun with them."

"Who was the girl? I'm sorry, I went into your bedroom looking for you."

"Don't you know?"

Ellie stared at him.

"It's you," Alan laughed at her expression, "as Anne."

"I never knew I looked like that," Ellie murmured.

"It's how I saw you."

While Alan made some sandwiches he explained that he'd got into trouble for missing the breakfast shift. "I've got the rest of the day free now, though. Would you like to go for a walk?"

"Yes. Let's go up Windover Hill. When I was pregnant, I imagined going up there with you. It seems appropriate to go there together now, don't you think?"

"Definitely."

A little later, Ellie and Alan walked out along the main road. Ellie stopped by the churchyard. "Do you mind if we go in here first."

"Not at all."

Ellie walked over to a far corner of the churchyard and stood by a grave. She read the headstone: Martha Darby born 1817 died 1892, her mother. Bright yellow flowers grew over the grave. The beauty of it touched Ellie's heart: the physical body welcomed back into the earth from where it came, the spirit liberated to be reborn elsewhere and nature continuing on in the wildflowers and grass.

Seeing Alan waiting underneath the yew tree, Ellie went over. He was looking down at the grave of Thomas. "'I wish I'd known him," he said. "From what you've told me he sounds like a remarkable person. I think I did see him with you a few times when I went back into the past. Did he have dark, curly hair?"

"Yes. I had no other friends so if you saw someone with me that was Thomas."

"I never saw you as adults, only as children."

"I suppose you saw what you needed to see."

"Mmm."

They left the churchyard and passed over the fields to the base of the Long Man. They walked in silence, simply content to be in the moment with each other just experiencing the warm sun, blue sky and grass stretching away from them. They walked up the centre of the figure. Ellie thought of the dark space underneath and the monks filling it with their sacred sound.

Finally, she and Alan reached the summit. They stopped and looked out over the Sussex countryside. Ellie stared at the so very familiar green fields and hedgerows beneath her. She loved this land and would always do so but, Ellie realised, it no longer mattered where she was because she knew Spirit, the Presence she felt so strongly again, was inside her and in all things everywhere. And it was then Ellie knew that she, like Thomas, now had to move on and into the future to find her place in the landscape of her present life. For her, as Ellie, this was Australia.

But not yet, she still had several weeks before she had to return home and there remained so much she wanted to explore: more of the area around Wilmington and, of course, Worthing where she had borne John and died as Anne. Did the house where she lived still exist? Then there was London. She couldn't wait to search out places known to her in her past life, especially Westminster Abbey.

The future, both immediate and more distant, beckoned. For her the world had come alive. Ellie realised just how mediocre her existence had been before, how overshadowed by suffering. But now, no longer imprisoned in her mind and physical body but in touch with the reality of spirit, she felt a new vitality.

"Let's walk down to the wood," Alan said. "I want to see if we can find the tunnel."

"OK." They set off down the hillside and on towards the wood. Arriving at where Alan thought the tunnel entrance must be, they stopped, uncertain. It seemed so different now.

Alan scanned around. "The fissure we dreamt we came out of was on the side of a small hillock. Could that be it?" He made his way over to an area of raised ground and pushed through the dense undergrowth. Ellie followed more slowly. She felt a sudden chill despite the warmth of the sun. The coldness around her increased and she felt a sense of foreboding despite the light infused beauty of the wood.

A flash of red caught her attention. A robin sat watching her on a branch. Ellie stopped and admired his simple beauty until he flew off. She looked around for Alan but he had disappeared.

Ellie stood still, uncertain which way to go, but then heard Alan's voice. "Over here." He appeared from behind a tree. Ellie went over and he showed her the crevice hidden under the bushes. It led down under a small hillock. Ellie followed him through it into cool darkness. The smell of damp earth filled her nostrils and she heard a scampering sound as a small animal scurried away.

"The entrance to the tunnel should be over here," Alan said. Suddenly the cave filled with light.

"I didn't know you brought a torch," Ellie said.

"Yes, in my backpack."

Something brushed Ellie's shoulder and she jumped. Looking up she saw roots hanging down from the roof.

"This is definitely where the entrance was but it appears blocked "Here, you hold the torch." Alan went outside and came back with a piece of wood. He gouged at the earth and dust filled the air. "Someone definitely didn't want anyone to find the tunnel."

"Perhaps we should leave it alone." Ellie still felt uneasy.

"No way." Alan continued pounding at the soil. "Look, I'm going to get a spade. There's one in the garden shed back at my place?"

He clambered out of the opening. Ellie followed. "I'll wait here," she said.

"Okay, I won't be long." Alan pushed his way through the bushes and disappeared.

The wood fell silent. Ellie saw the old oak tree where she and Thomas used to meet. She walked over and sat down with her back against it. She sensed the tree reaching up towards the sun and stared at the light flickering through the shifting leaves above. Ellie relaxed against the trunk and felt the plunging of its roots deep into the ground. She sensed the movement of the earth spinning around the sun and it made her dizzy. Still tired from the night before, Ellie drifted off to sleep.

Anne opened her eyes. A figure stood against the light. She could not see his face but knew him. He sat down beside her and pulled her close. She loved the feel of his arms around her. "I love you so much, Anne," he whispered. Then he kissed her.

She reached up and ran her fingers through his curly hair then moved her arms down to pull his body closer. She wanted to hold onto him forever but he moved away.

"I'm sorry, I cannot stay. I am expected back." Thomas cupped her face in his hands and kissed her gently. Anne's eyes filled with tears. One ran down her face. Thomas wiped it away with his finger then put it to his lips. "We will be together one day, I promise." Then he rose to his feet, turned and vanished.

Ellie woke. She still remembered the feeling of Thomas's arms around her and longed to dwell in the memory of him but heard Alan calling her. She rose and went over to where he stood by the crevice. "Did you have a good sleep?" he asked.

"Yes."

They squeezed through the opening. Alan had wedged the torch behind a tree root. Its beam shone against the side of the cave. A dark hole gaped open. "Fortunately it was only soil. It didn't take me long to clear it." He took hold of the torch and shone it through. Ellie saw familiar stone walls stretching back into darkness.

"I'm not sure we should go down there," she said. The sense of foreboding she felt earlier returned. "I want to remember it as we saw it last night back in time."

Alan came forward and held her by the shoulders. "There's nothing to fear. Nothing. You know that, don't you? Don't you?" Ellie stared into his eyes and knew he spoke the truth.

"OK," she said. "Let's go."

Alan took the lead and they walked down the long passage. Their footsteps echoed on the floor. After a while, Ellie sensed the weight of the hillside above and then soon after the corridor ended in darkness.

They came to the entrance of the underground chamber and stood side by side. Alan shone his torch up to the ceiling then over the numerous stone pillars that supported the roof. Finally, he shone the light down to the ground and into the sightless eyes of a human body.

Ellie screamed and Alan dropped the torch, plunging them into darkness. While Alan searched for it, Ellie stood in the pitch black, the face of the corpse etched into her mind.

Alan found the torch and once again they stared at the body. Only the head and one hand could be seen, decaying brown material covered the rest. Alan went closer but Ellie stayed back.

"It's one of the monks," he said. "He's been dead for hundreds of years, I would guess." Alan shone the torch over the rest of the chamber and they saw several other bodies sprawled around the floor, all lying with their limbs at different angles. Ellie and Alan picked their way through the room.

"They were taken by surprise," Alan said. They counted twenty bodies, mostly decayed into skeletal remains. Barely any flesh clung to the bones.

Ellie shuddered, "Who would have done this?"

"I don't know. My guess would be that someone objected to

their teachings, saw them as a threat in some way."

"Threat? How could they be a threat?"

"Think about it, they taught that the light of God is within each and every one. Old Father told us they lived long before Anne's time, several hundred years before, I would think. In those days, the idea of ordinary people being able to achieve personal experience of God would have been heresy. If people had that knowledge, the power of the church as an intermediary would have been diminished.

"Yes, I see what you mean."

"I did some research into the priory next to the church when I first came here. I couldn't find much out about the monks that used to live there. It was what was known as an alien priory, an offshoot of an abbey in Normandy. As far as I can tell, Wilmington Priory was mainly a base for managing their English land. Land was power in those days. However, a lot more went on than was ever recorded. In fact, someone went to a lot of trouble to ensure all this under the Long Man remained secret.

"I reckon, looking at it, that this chamber, at least in some form, has been here for thousands of years. I think that maybe monks sent to Wilmington discovered it and after spending time here became profoundly affected. The energy of this area raised their level of consciousness until they became able to experience the Divine in themselves. This area has probably always drawn certain sensitive people and Old Father and the monks would have taught those they encountered. They probably lived down under the Long Man in those rooms we saw."

"Only someone, perhaps church officials, found out about them and . . ."

"Murdered them," Ellie finished for him in a voice heavy with grief as she scanned the room. "And all done in the name of religion?"

"Those that did this probably wouldn't have seen it like that. To them, they would have been protecting what they saw as the truth. Countless thousands have been killed over the years in the name of religion, or, at least, to protect the outer trappings of religion, the real kernel of truth at the heart of all faiths is something quite different.

"But something exists here that could not be erased: the power of their presence. Their realisation of the Divine within them had become so strong and so powerfully linked in with the energy of this area, we were able to sense it and connect back to the time here when they were physically alive."

Ellie's eyes streamed tears now. Here were the bodies of her friends from the past. Alan noticed her tears and came over. He took her in his arms. "Please don't cry. Don't you see they are not dead?"

"Yes, yes, you're right, of course, they're not."

"They weren't even physically alive when you knew them in your time as Anne," Alan said. They had been dead then for a long time already."

They both fell silent and simply stood, looking around at the scene. Ellie kept remembering how it had been the night before, so alive and joyous, the monks chanting and the light flickering, the incense burning and the delicate beauty of the roses.

As she remembered the flowers, Ellie looked at the altar. A body lay just in front of it. She walked over. Alan followed. He shone the torch down and they saw that the cloth shrouding the remains had once been white.

"Old Father," Ellie whispered.

This corpse was different to the others. The flesh still remained although the skin on his face had shrunk back against the skull. He looked to be sleeping. A deep peace lay upon his features. There had been no struggle but complete surrender. Ellie and Alan stood looking in awe. How had Old Father's body remained free of corruption? It was a miracle.

Ellie stared for a long time at the remains of her friends lying around the floor and, as she did so, the macabre nature of the scene subtly altered and she understood, really understood, that those who had thought to destroy them had not succeeded. They could not. What was real about those that lay here could not be destroyed. These bodies were mere shells, no longer needed, falling back into the earth from where they arose. What was vital and living about the monks had not gone but still existed, held in the heart of life itself and would be born again. Also, the monks' legacy of truth had been taken into the hearts and minds of those taught by them and so had passed out into the world.

She smiled as she remembered the vitality of the living roses that bloomed in the vase that now lay dusty and empty, all water long since evaporated. Those flowers still lived in her memory and echoed in countless other blossoms that bloomed now on the surface of the earth. Similar roses even flowered in her mother's garden back in Australia. The thought linked Ellie back to her native land in her present life and knew the truth existed there too, in every stone and leaf and person living and breathing.

"Why are you smiling?" Alan asked.

"Because there is no death, simply change of form and that out of physical decay springs new life and because we are here, very much alive and can remember the monks and what they showed us."

Ellie stopped talking and they both stood listening to the silence. It was a sacred silence, not empty but full, and it held them both gently inside it. Ellie felt the sense of living Presence strong inside her and her whole body tingled with the energy present in the chamber. How strange it was that in this place of death she had found life. They stood for a few minutes but then Ellie touched Alan's shoulder. "Let's go now," she said.

Alan and Ellie turned away from the altar. As they walked back through the room, shadows cast by the pillars moved over the corpses creating an eerie impression. Ellie suddenly longed to be in the light and fresh air once again. They looked behind them one last time then turned and made their way back through the tunnel. As she walked, Ellie felt strangely elated and excited at the thought of being back out in the open as if she were about to be reborn once again. In one sense it was true for, as a result of her experiences here in Wilmington and in the womb of Windover Hill, she had been irrevocably changed.

The air freshened and they arrived back at the earthy cavern. They squeezed out through the crevice into the undergrowth. Pushing through the branches, they came out into sunlight. Ellie felt complete openness and freedom. No trace of the guilt and sorrow that had haunted her life for so long remained and she knew she was ready to walk away from Wilmington and into a new experience of life in this present birth.

Chapter 22

DEREK STOOD BY THE HOTEL entrance waiting for his mother. Their suitcases were already loaded in the hire car. He looked around the foyer. He'd be glad to see the back of the place and looked forward to moving on to London. Wilmington had not lived up to expectations. He hadn't once had a good night's sleep and wasn't feeling that well. He decided to get a check-up as soon as they returned home.

The dreams hadn't helped. They started the first night here and continued every night, always the same scene. He walked down a long dark tunnel deep underground. Others walked beside him. They held burning torches and long swords that glinted in the light. As they progressed along the passageway, Derek heard a strange sound he couldn't identify.

Eventually, they reached a stone lined chamber with an altar on which two candles burned. Several monks chanted, on and on, a strange chant, an unearthly chant. It filled his mind and slowed his steps but then the monks saw him and there could be no turning back. It had to be done quickly. He and his companions knew what to do and they did not hesitate. One by one, the monks fell to the remorseless thrusts of their swords and the sound died away until just one man chanted, a lone voice singing in the darkness. The sound wound its way right into Derek's heart and he knew deep inside that what he was doing in this place was wrong. But that could not be. What kind of people worshipped in darkness underground?

The last monk, an old man dressed in a white robe, carried on chanting, his eyes shut, seemingly unaware of what was happening but then one of Derek's companions thrust a sword through his heart. Derek always woke at that point, hot and sweaty, with a feeling of unease.

But last night the dream changed. The same events had run their course until Derek's companion plunged the sword into the last monk's chest. A red stain spread across his white robe but he did not fall. He carried on standing for a while then opened his eyes and looked at Derek. He could not move, held captive in the old man's gaze. They stood like that for some moments as if time had stopped. Derek felt exposed, knowing the old monk saw deep inside him.

Derek had woken with the monk's face still vivid in his mind. He knew he would never forget those eyes and what he saw in them: forgiveness and compassion. Derek felt a soft sadness in his chest. He wasn't sure about anything anymore. This trip had unsettled him, made him realise he didn't really like himself very much or the life he led. He noticed Ellie coming towards him through the hotel foyer and felt a pang of remorse. He felt sorry about the way he'd come on to her now. Derek sighed; he was such a bloody asshole. No wonder Janine left him.

He thought of his daughter, Rebecca. He hadn't seen her for several months. He'd visit her when he got back, he really should see her more. Maybe that was what was missing from his life.

As Ellie walked by him, their eyes met. Derek wanted to say something but could not, then she moved past and walked away.

"OK, let's go." His mother swept past him to the car. Derek followed more slowly. He cast one last look around Wilmington then climbed in and they drove off.

As Ellie walked away from Derek, the expression in his eyes made a deep impression. He looked different. No trace remained of the arrogance that had so repelled her. It had been replaced by uncertainty. He looked vulnerable, lost even. She found herself feeling sorry for him. She wondered what had happened to make him so changed. Ellie didn't have time to think any more about it for she saw Alan standing next to a small red car. She and Alan had arranged to drive to Worthing, the small seaside town where Ellie spent the last months of her life as Anne.

They decided to say nothing for the time being about their discovery under the Long Man yesterday. The time was not yet right. They wanted to hold the knowledge to themselves for the moment and rest in the peace and beauty of Wilmington as it was. If they told the authorities an army of experts would descend and tear open the entrances, probing and violating the sacred silence beneath the Man.

Ellie enjoyed the drive through the Sussex countryside and then along the coast to Worthing. She recognised it instantly. Although some of it had changed over the years, much of it remained the same. Ellie felt a pang of sadness. It had been such an emotional and difficult time for her here while she mourned the loss of Thomas and carried their child. She looked round at Alan as he drove through the town. In their previous lives, they had been mother and son but for so brief a time. And yet here they were again, although in different bodies, drawn together by destiny.

They found the cemetery where Anne had been buried and Ellie found herself looking down at the grave of her previous mortal body. She stared at the plain rectangular headstone and read the simple inscription: Anne Darby 1869–1893. Had she really lived in different flesh, in a body that now lay as dry bones beneath her feet? Ellie still found it hard to comprehend at times. When she thought about it with her mind, it seemed impossible but in her heart, her inner self, she knew it to be the truth.

They had only stood a few minutes before Alan started to walk back to the car. "I'm going to get some flowers for the grave."

"No." Ellie didn't want to think of bright fresh flowers being left to fade and die until the wind swept them away. Living grass blanketed her body. It was a fitting memorial. "Don't. There is nothing to mourn here," she said.

They left the cemetery and drove to find the house where Ellie had lived as Anne. Ellie recognised the street right away. The small house had been painted a different colour but otherwise looked very much the same. Here she had brought her son, John, now Alan, into the world. She laughed.

"What's so funny?" Alan asked.

"Isn't it just bizarre how it's all worked out, how we've been drawn back together?"

"Not when you know about reincarnation. It's quite logical that it should occur when souls have things they need to work out together."

They stood looking at the simple terraced house, still with its original dark slate roof, both remembering their time there. Ellie looked down the road towards the seafront. "Let's go down to the beach."

It took them only a few minutes to reach the promenade. Ellie stared around her as they walked down over the stones and out over the sand. The tide had retreated far out in the distance. She had walked here as Anne in all weathers. She had loved the sea almost as much as the hills of Wilmington.

Low lying grey clouds stretched in all directions overhead but a warm breeze ruffled their clothing. Ellie felt as if no time had passed and she was Anne again waiting for her child to be born.

Long water breaks stretched out from the beach, their wood worn soft and smooth by the tides. Water gathered in the ripple marks in the sand and in pools that reflected the sky. Ellie slipped off her shoes. The touch of the sand felt soft and cool. She shut her eyes. She could be on her local beach in Australia. The feel of the sand felt the same. When she returned to Adelaide, she would walk on the beach and think of Worthing half a world away.

Ellie opened her eyes. Two seagulls fought over a dead crab. As Ellie and Alan approached, the birds flew off screeching. Similar to those in Australia, they too reminded her of home. Finally, they reached the sea. Calm, it stretched out to a distant horizon. Only a slight lifting of the water's edge suggested the presence of the tide. Ellie felt completely happy within the quiet gentleness of the moment. Tomorrow heavy waves might pound the shore and fling seaweed high up on the stones but today it was serene and still. Everything went in cycles, Ellie thought: calm and storm, light and dark, birth and death, and she and her companions in life moved along with them.

Over the next few weeks Ellie spent as much time as possible with Alan. When he wasn't working, they walked over the Downs, glorifying in the open countryside and exploring other nearby villages. On days Alan did work, Ellie would walk alone. She welcomed the chance to be on her own. She experienced everything more intensely then. Sometimes she would find a place to sit and contemplate the world around her or the sacred space within.

She started writing down her impressions of Wilmington in a notebook. She also spent a long time taking photographs of everything that meant so much to her: the Long Man and the wonderful view from the top, the old oak wood, the church and the hill with the ring of trees.

On several occasions, Ellie took the train to London. She was disappointed to discover the house she worked in as a maid and companion to Ethel Deacon had been bombed during the Second World War. However, many of the places she used to visit on her afternoons off remained.

Ellie spent a fascinating time walking through Westminster Abbey in awe of the majestic architecture and beautiful sculptures, just as she had when Anne. Marvelling at the tombs of kings and queens and other memorable people who had shaped so much of human history, she sensed the weight of that history as she explored, all the accumulated suffering but also hopes and dreams of those who had gathered there over the years.

She shared the abbey with hundreds of milling tourists. She walked down several corridors until she found the room where, as Anne, she had encountered the monk. No one was inside. Ellie slipped in, grateful for the chance to be alone. She half expected the monk to slide out of the shadows but the room remained silent and empty. Ellie wondered who that monk had been and how had he known so much about her. "Always remember you have the key," he said. His words had echoed those of Old Father.

Ellie wondered if the monk had come from Wilmington but did not remember him as one of those she had known there. Then an idea occurred to her: perhaps he had been someone who belonged in Anne's own time who visited Wilmington and also experienced Old Father. Could Old Father have known somehow she would be drawn to Westminster Abbey and told the monk to look out for her? She would never know but Ellie had no doubt that Old Father had the power. Ever since she and Alan had talked to him in the chamber under the Long Man and seen his uncorrupted body, they had known he was no ordinary man.

Later that evening, Ellie met Alan in the bar of the Green Man Hotel. She told him about her visit to Westminster Abbey. "I'm sure the monk I saw there in my life as Anne was somehow connected with Wilmington." Ellie told Alan her theory.

"You could be right," he said.

"Do you think we'll see Old Father and the other monks again?" Ellie asked. Three weeks had passed since their last encounter with the monks in the chamber under Windover Hill and neither had seen any sign of them.

"I rather suspect not," Alan replied, "I don't think we need them anymore."

Ellie thought about what he said. She sat quietly for a moment and felt the truth of his words. Through all that had happened, she had reconnected with the reality of her own spiritual nature. It was now far stronger than it had ever been, even when she had been Anne living in Wilmington. This time Ellie knew she would not forget. "No, I don't think we do."

The monks' work was done. To them she would always be grateful for they had given her so much. Now, perhaps, it was her turn to give to others.

"There's something I wanted to show you," Ellie said. She delved into her bag and brought out a pad of lined paper. "I've been writing down some of my feelings and impressions of Wilmington. I'd like to know what you think."

Ellie sipped her drink while Alan read what she had written.

He finally looked up. "This is good. You have a way with words."

"Oh, I don't know about that," Ellie said but she had enjoyed searching out just the right words to convey the sense of what she had seen and felt. It brought it all the more alive for her.

"You have to write it all down, Ellie. This shows you have the ability. Old Father wanted you to. Bring others into our experience here, show them it's possible for them to find what we have found."

"I'll try."

Ellie filled her days with exploring the area around Wilmington. She and Alan visited other tourist sites in Sussex as well. One day, she felt it was time to visit Laura Cox, her relative in England, the sister of Ellie's grandmother, Nancy. Ellie rang and talked to the old lady's daughter in law, Irene, who told her that Laura was keen to see her. The next morning, she caught a train to Haywards Heath, the closest station to Laura's house and Ellie found herself in the centre of a rather uninspiring town, an impression not helped by a heavy, grey sky.

As Ellie walked out of the station, a soft rain dampened her clothes. She noticed an area of brightness: a profusion of flowers displayed around the entrance to a florist shop. She went in and smiled when she saw a container of Australian banksias. Every so often she would get a reminder of home like this, as if the two places were merging in some indefinable way, at least, in her mind. Ellie bought some for Laura and also some beautiful orange lilies.

Back outside, Ellie looked around. She stood near a noisy and busy main road. It seemed a long way from the quietness of Wilmington. She needed to get to the small village of Lindfield where Laura lived. Noticing a line of taxis, she made her way over.

After only a few minutes of driving through the town, the taxi rounded a bend and Ellie saw a wide expanse of a park and then a large pond surrounded by lovely old houses. The taxi drove up through the centre of Lindfield. Ellie stared out of the window, fascinated by all the different building styles, many very old. She loved the quaint thatched cottages. Right at the top of the village, a church steeple rose up from behind the houses.

The taxi turned right and along a narrow lane close to the church. It drew up outside a small house built of red brick and tile. It appeared to be several hundred years old. The roof sagged slightly but it looked well maintained. It had leadlight windows and a beautiful creeper of some kind climbing around the front porch. It looked enchanting. Ellie loved the old buildings of England; they had so much character.

She paid the taxi driver and walked through a white wooden

gate into a small front garden full of flowers of all kinds and colours. Ellie didn't know what to expect. Laura was ninety-one but still able to live alone with the help of her son, Andrew, and his wife, Irene, who lived a short distance away.

Ellie smelt a beautiful fragrance as she walked up the front path. She pressed the bell and waited. Nothing happened. She wondered if Laura had gone out. Ellie lifted her hand to ring again but then the face of an elderly woman appeared at one of the windows. She stared at Ellie for a short while before disappearing then the front door opened a crack.

"Hello, Laura? I'm Ellie."

"Who?"

"Ellie." She said it louder this time "From Australia." The door swung open and Ellie found herself looking into smiling brown eyes in a face heavily wrinkled by time.

"Oh, my dear, come in, come in."

Ellie walked through into a narrow hallway. She felt huge next to the tiny, frail looking Laura. The old lady looked expensively dressed in a soft cream blouse and a lilac woollen skirt. She had soft, wavy white hair. Laura shut the door and led Ellie through into a pretty room with pale blue walls on which several paintings hung. On one side, she saw a highly polished piano and a dark oak sideboard. In the middle of the room, two armchairs and a settee had been arranged around a coffee table. Glass doors led to a garden with a small sweep of lawn surrounded by flowerbeds filled with flowers. "What a lovely garden you have," exclaimed Ellie. "You hardly need them but I brought you these." Ellie held out the banksias and orange lilies.

"You can never have too many flowers. Thank you." Laura clasped the cellophane with fingers distorted by arthritis. She pointed to the sideboard, "If you could just look in there for a vase, we can put these in water."

Ellie found a large cut glass container. "Do you want me to put the flowers in for you?"

"Please."

Ellie found the kitchen and quickly arranged the flowers. She came back into the lounge and placed them on the sideboard.

"Sit down, dear. Irene will be here soon. She'll make us some tea.”

Laura sat in a large armchair with a floral design and crocheted covers. So English, Ellie thought, as she sat on the matching settee. She stared around the room, taking in the profusion of china ornaments. Then she saw it! In a dark corner , a small painting had been hung. Ellie couldn’t believe it. Inside an ornate, gold frame, the unmistakable shape of Windover Hill and the Long Man in his familiar pose had been painted in exquisite detail.

“Wilmington. You have a picture of Wilmington,” Ellie exclaimed.

Laura leaned round in order to see the painting. “Ah, yes, I was born there, a long time ago now.” She laughed.

Ellie stared at her in amazement. How could this be? But then came the thought, she should be used to the bizarre by now after all that had happened.

“That’s where I’m staying at the moment. Where did you live in Wilmington?” Was it possible Laura knew any of the people Ellie had known as Anne? A quick mental calculation told her, no, not directly, but maybe another member of her family had, a mother or father.

“We lived in Rose Lane. Do you know it, Ellie?”

“No.”

“I lived there until I married, then I came here. I was twenty-three. My Robert, he was so handsome.” Laura chuckled.

Ellie wanted to know more about the time before Laura married so she gently steered Laura back. “Your parents,” she asked, “do you remember much about them?”

“Oh, my goodness, I can see my mother as clear as I see you now. I didn’t like her, really. She was always cross, didn’t have much time for my sister and me. Neither did my father, he was a doctor and always at work.” A look of sadness passed across Laura’s face. “My mother died while I was still quite young. It was hard. But my grandmother moved in with us and things were better. I loved her. She used to sing to Nancy and me and take us walking over the Downs to gather wild flowers. She read us stories and taught us to read.

“We had a cook, Betty, and a maid, Norma, who took care of

the house. They were happy times, then. I had a lovely red velvet dress with a white lace collar. Nancy had a blue one. We wore them to church on Sundays."

Laura was off and running. Ellie sat quietly and listened. Laura had been born in 1912, about twenty years after the time Anne had moved away to Worthing, so it was unlikely that Laura had known anyone connected directly with Thomas or Anne.

The elderly lady was obviously enjoying her reminiscing. "One day we went to Eastbourne and stayed in a hotel. Very posh it was. The place had a ballroom and one night Nancy and I were allowed to stay up late so we could see the dancing."

Ellie continued to listen but then remembered the silver key. She took it out of her bag. Although it had belonged to her sister, Nancy, there was a small possibility Laura would know what it had opened.

As soon as she could, Ellie gently interrupted. "Laura, I wonder, you don't happen to remember this, do you?" She held out the small silver key. The old lady reached out and took it. Ellie explained how it had been found in her grandmother's things and how nothing had been found that it opened.

Laura sat looking at the key without speaking, a mixture of emotions passing across her face, but then she spoke, "Well, I never. I thought this was lost. Oh, my goodness. You say Nancy had it? She always denied taking it but I knew she had. I knew."

"What did it open?"

The old lady didn't answer. She slowly rose to her feet and walked to the door. "Come with me."

Laura went out into the hall and struggled up a narrow staircase. Ellie followed, afraid the old lady might fall at any moment. Ellie breathed a sigh of relief when they arrived upstairs. Laura went into a bedroom with built in cupboards all along one side and pointed up. "Look in that top one on the left by the wall. I'm sure it's still in there."

Ellie located a chair to stand on and opened the cupboard. All she could see were piles of paper, yellowing books and old blankets.

"I'm afraid, you'll have to take that lot out. It's probably at the back."

"What is?"

"A wooden box, it's got a silver pattern on it. Can you see it?"

"Not yet."

Laura sat down on a bed while Ellie took out some of the stuff from inside the cupboard. It took a few minutes, but then she saw it: a dark, wooden rectangular box. Ellie reached for it. As she touched its surface, her fingers tingled. She pulled it out and saw it had been inlaid with a delicate design of leaves in silver metal matching that of the key. She climbed down and put the box on the bed.

"If you wouldn't mind just putting the stuff back, dear," Laura said.

"Of course."

Laura went back downstairs. Ellie stowed everything back in the cupboard then picked up the box again. It wasn't that big but felt quite heavy. It obviously had something inside. She shook it gently but couldn't hear anything. The lid was locked. Would her key actually fit? Ellie couldn't wait to find out. She hurried downstairs and laid the box on the coffee table. Laura sat back down in her armchair. She held the key out. "You open it, dear."

Laura watched intently as Ellie reached out and took the key then carefully placed it in the lock. It resisted for an instant then slid right in. She looked at Laura, smiled, then turned the key. It moved half way around then stopped. She applied more pressure and the lock turned with an audible click. Ellie carefully lifted the lid. A single musical note sounded, followed by a grating sound that lasted for a few seconds. She pulled the lid fully back and gazed inside. Another note sounded followed by silence.

"A musical box," Ellie said. Inside, she saw a shallow compartment lined with purple velvet. The music mechanism obviously lay underneath. The box contained a delicate but yellowed folded lace handkerchief. Ellie lifted it out and felt something hard inside it. She carefully unfolded the material and saw a band of dark metal. "A bracelet," Ellie said and removed it so she could take a closer look. It was badly tarnished but she could see its outer surface had been etched with a delicate pattern of interweaving flowers and leaves. It had a hinge and clasp so the bracelet could be opened and then fastened around the wrist.

Ellie examined the inner surface. It had a clear hallmark which made it silver but something else caught her attention. Two letters had been engraved in the metal. They were interwoven and elaborately curled but quite clearly an "A" and a "T."

"That bracelet was always in the box. Grandmother said we had to keep it in there. I used to wear it sometimes. Luckily, Nancy didn't like it much or we'd have argued about it."

Laura leaned forward and pulled on a short length of purple ribbon Ellie hadn't noticed. The bottom of the compartment lifted up, revealing the music mechanism. It still looked in surprisingly good condition, although somewhat dusty. "Turn that." Laura pointed to a small key on one side. Ellie put down the bracelet and did as requested. She turned the key as much as she dared, afraid of breaking the clockwork mechanism then released it. A cylinder covered with tiny pins turned and music echoed around the room, a pretty little tune Ellie didn't recognise. It ran for a full five minutes before it wound down.

Ellie and Laura sat entranced. Ellie spoke first, "How lovely."

"Yes," said Laura, a wistful look on her face. She reached out, lifted the box onto her lap and ran her fingers over it. "I really loved this box when I was a child. I used to play it all the time." Her expression darkened. "But Nancy said it was hers. We used to argue over it. I would hide it but she always found it. The box didn't belong to either of us, of course. It was my grandmother's. We were supposed to share it. One day the key disappeared and so no one could use it. I always suspected Nancy had hidden it but she always denied it. When I married, just after Grandmother died, I took the box but I never found the key. Nancy obviously had it all the time. I meant to get a new key made but never got round to it." Laura's eyes filled with tears. "Nancy married a year after me and she and her husband went to Australia. Somehow the key went with her and you found it years later. And now here you are. It's amazing."

"Yes," Ellie agreed. She looked down at the silver bracelet in her hand. "This is beautiful." It would be even better cleaned up, she thought, and wondered who the initials "A" and "T" engraved inside stood for. How odd the initials were these particular letters after all that had happened. They could stand for Anne and Thomas. Of course, they didn't, but it felt a little strange, even so.

"What was your grandmother's name?" Ellie asked.

"Florence."

"Who do you think these initials stand for, then?" Ellie handed the bracelet to Laura. "Obviously not her."

At that moment, the front door opened and a short, plump woman dressed in a tracksuit and breathing heavily came in. "Been running, a bit puffed," she explained. "Hello, I'm Irene, you must be Ellie."

"Yes, hello."

"What've you got there, Laura?"

"It's my old musical box. You won't believe it, but Ellie here had the key. It had been lost for years."

"But how did she come to have it?"

"My sister, Nancy, took it to Australia with her." Laura explained how they argued over the box.

"My mother found it in Nancy's things." Ellie said.

"You're joking, how odd." Irene reached over to the box. "Can I?" she asked Laura.

"Go ahead."

Irene wound up the mechanism and once again the tinkling notes chimed out.

"This bracelet was in the box. We were trying to decide who owned it." Ellie said. "It's got initials inside: "A" and "T.""

"Why don't you look on the family tree?" Irene turned to Ellie. "My husband's interested in genealogy. He's researched the family right back to 1612. Laura's got a copy." Irene disappeared for a moment, returning with a large folded up sheet of paper. She opened it out on the coffee table. "Right. Well, there's Laura and her sister, Nancy. Their mother's name was Mavis. She was the only child of William and Florence."

"Florence was my grandmother. She had the bracelet," Laura said.

"So we are looking for a woman before or around her time. There's no one with the initials "AT.""

""AT" might stand for the names of a couple. My Robert gave me a ring with our initials on, "L" and "R," Laura suggested

"You could be right." Irene scanned the sheet. "I can't see any names beginning with an "A" or "T," though. Oh, wait a minute. Florence's brother, Mathew, he had a son, look, Thomas."

"Thomas?" Ellie leant forward to look where Irene's finger pointed on the family tree. As she did so, everything else except the writing went out of focus. It couldn't be, she thought, but the words burned clear: Thomas Marshall, 1868—1892.

Chapter 23

"ARE YOU ALL RIGHT, DEAR?" Laura asked.

Numb with shock, Ellie stared at the sheet, unable to speak. How could this be? She became aware of Laura and Irene looking at her. "Yes, yes, I'm fine. What were you saying, Irene?"

"Thomas's wife's name was Helen so the bracelet didn't belong to her." Irene continued scanning the names. "There aren't any others" She straightened up. "Perhaps the bracelet never belonged to anyone in the family, Laura. Your grandmother just bought it or got given it."

"Maybe it didn't belong to Thomas's wife but someone else he knew," Laura said, an odd tone in her voice. The others looked at her. "Thomas was killed, murdered. I remember my grandmother telling me. It happened before our birth but the story fascinated my sister and I. It caused a huge scandal in Wilmington. Thomas was killed by Helen, his wife. She caught him with another woman. Helen herself died a few days later, I'm not sure how. Anyway, maybe Thomas planned to give the bracelet to his mistress. Laura paused for dramatic effect then continued. "Her name was Anne, "A" and "T," Anne and Thomas."

"But how would your grandmother have got the bracelet,

Laura?" Irene asked.

"My grandmother told me she looked after her brother when his son Thomas died. Mathew was distraught. He never recovered from the loss and died just over a year later. My grandmother would have sorted through Thomas's things when Mathew died. She inherited the farm.

Ellie had been standing silently all this time, her mind reeling with the implications of everything the other two women were saying. "Can I look at it again?" she asked. Laura passed her the bracelet and Ellie stared at it in her hand. Could it be true? Had Thomas intended to give this bracelet to her but died before he could do so? She ran her fingers over the pattern and stared at the letters etched inside. My God, she thought. What if it were true?

"Have it, dear." Laura said.

"Pardon?"

"The bracelet." Laura said. "Would you like it? It's no good to me and you seem so interested in it."

"Oh, Laura, I would love it but are you sure?" Ellie put the bracelet on her wrist. Was it possible that Thomas's gift had finally been given?

"Look, it fits perfectly," the old lady said with a smile. "It looks right on you, dear. I just have a feeling you should have it."

"Thank you so much. And, of course, you must have the key. It belongs with the box."

A broad smile lit up the old lady's features. "Yes. I still can't get over how you came to have the key. It's unbelievable."

Ellie wondered whether it really was. She suspected finding the key, and now this box with the bracelet inside, hadn't been an accident. She now knew many hidden forces were at play in the world.

"Let's have some tea," Laura said.

"Sounds good to me," Irene replied. "I'll get it. You sit and talk." While she clattered about in the kitchen, Ellie sat with Laura. They played the musical box again. Ellie smiled at the pleasure in the old lady's face. It would be strange to not have the key after all this time but she no longer needed it. All she had learned in Wilmington had become a living experience, a deep knowing inside her. The key had done its work. Not only had it helped to unlock her past, it had brought her a gift from Thomas down through the years.

Irene brought in tea and cake. Ellie described her life in Australia and Laura talked about the family. However, Laura could not remember anything more about Thomas. Whilst they sat talking, a grey squirrel bounded across the lawn. Ellie laughed as it stopped and nibbled a nut it held in its paws. "We get them here all the time," Laura said.

When the old lady said she needed a rest, Irene took Ellie on a brief tour of Lindfield. She loved the beauty of the old village with its attractive historic buildings and picturesque church. Irene took Ellie to her house to meet her husband and showed her photos of their two sons, now moved away. Irene suggested they polish the bracelet and found some silver cleaner.

Ellie smeared the white creamy liquid onto an old cotton rag and rubbed it over the bracelet. Slowly the black faded away, revealing the silver underneath. It took a while but in time the bracelet shone. The two initials became clear to see: "A" and "T," Anne and Thomas.

"It's gorgeous," commented Irene.

Ellie clipped it back on. "Yes, it is." She loved the look of it on her wrist.

They returned to Laura's house. Ellie stayed for a short while longer but then it became time to say goodbye. Laura gave her a bunch of sweet peas from her garden to take away with her. To Ellie, their soft, fragile petals and fragrant perfume expressed perfectly the essence of an English country garden.

Ellie hugged both Laura and Irene. All of them had tears in their eyes as she boarded the taxi that came to take her back to the station.

It had been a truly amazing day and Ellie couldn't wait to tell Alan about her visit. He was working when she got back but they met later in the hotel bar. Ellie showed him the bracelet on her wrist and described how it had come to be with Laura.

"It's certainly incredible that you have this family connection to Thomas but you can't be sure this belonged to him or that he meant to give it to you, " Alan said cynically. "Sorry, but it could have been given to Laura's grandmother by anybody.

"It belonged to Thomas, I know it did," Ellie replied, irritated by his cynicism.

"Mmm." Alan still looked sceptical.

Ellie twirled the bracelet around on her wrist, disappointed, but knew Alan could be right. She wanted it to be from Thomas but that didn't mean it was. All her feelings for him rose up in that moment and she felt a profound sadness, knowing she would never see him again. She realised she still felt a deep connection to Thomas. "There is one thing I *can* do," she said, looking at Alan. "Do you remember me telling you about my meeting with Adam, Thomas's father in his past life? He might know about the bracelet. I have his phone number. I told him I'd let him know how I got on if I went to England." She looked at her watch and did a rough calculation. "It's early in the morning in Australia at the moment. I'll do it later."

She reached over and touched Alan's hand. "I'm going to miss you when I go back."

"We still have a week." Alan smiled. "Anyway, we'll see each other again, I'm sure of it." He squeezed Ellie's hand. "I've treasured these past few weeks more than I can possibly say."

"Me too."

Neither said anything for a few moments then Ellie spoke. "What are you going to do in the future? Are you going to stay in Wilmington?"

"I've thought about it a lot. Yes, I'm going to stay here," Alan said. "I walked up on Windover Hill early this morning before work. It was so beautiful up there and I felt the energy of the whole area pulsing through my body. I don't think I could ever leave here."

"I love Wilmington and I always will," Ellie said, "but I know that it's only part of a much larger world. I was awakened here but I know the Light is within me and in all things everywhere. I've been feeling that more and more the last few weeks. It's odd but I keep seeing things that remind me of home in Australia. I think I've done what I needed to do here."

"It's different for me, Ellie. I really feel this is where I need to be. You notice we haven't seen Old Father or any of the other monks since we found the passageway under Windover Hill?"

"Yes."

"I don't think we'll ever see them again, not in the same form, anyway. It all changed once we found the passage under the Long Man."

"Yes, I feel that as well."

"I think that some sort of a shift has occurred. I felt it today walking across the Man. I think that others will be drawn to Wilmington now, especially when the passageway under the hill becomes known. New guardians are needed and I plan to be one. I don't know how or what that means but I believe I'll find out."

"When will you tell the authorities about the chamber and the monks?"

"Do you want it to be now?" Alan asked. "Do you want to be involved?"

"Actually, I'd rather not. I'd like to keep it to ourselves for just one more week, until I leave. Do you mind?"

"No. That's what I feel, too."

"And, when I get back, I'll write my story." Ellie said.

"Good. The story of this place needs to be told." They smiled at each other then Ellie became aware of a woman standing next to them.

"Sorry to interrupt, but, Alan, could you just take a look at the roster with me?"

Alan stood. "OK." He turned to Ellie. "Sorry, I have to go. Come round in the morning. I'm not working."

"All right. Goodnight, then."

Ellie watched Alan disappear behind the bar then hurried up to her room. She watched TV for an hour then reached for the phone. It would now be about eight in the morning in Australia. She hoped Adam would be there.

"Hello? Adam? It's Ellie."

"Hi. How are you?"

"I'm fine. Look, I'm ringing from England."

"My God, you went."

"Yes. I'm in Wilmington."

"How is it?"

"Just as you described and I remembered. I found Thomas's grave," Ellie paused, "and my own."

Ellie briefly described everything that had happened since she saw Adam, ending with meeting Laura. "It's incredible, her grandmother was your sister, when you were Mathew, I mean. She inherited everything you left when you died."

"Florence, yes, I remember her. Christ, it's weird, isn't it? I haven't thought much about it all since I saw you. It seems to be finally fading out, a bloody relief, actually."

"Sorry to bring it all back up again." Ellie said.

"No, it's OK. It's good to have my story validated. No one ever believed me, except you. I think that meeting you helped to release it all. That's why it's fading now. I'm beginning to focus more on the present."

"Oh, Adam, I'm so pleased for you. Anyway, there's just something I wanted to ask you then I'll leave you alone. Laura had something that Florence found in the things you left behind when you died in your past life. We think it belonged to Thomas, though." Ellie told Adam about the key and the musical box. "We found a silver bracelet inside marked with the initials "A" and "T." Ellie looked down at her wrist. "It's a solid band with a hinge, there's an engraved floral design on it. Did you ever see anything like that?" She waited for his answer. It didn't come. "Adam? Are you still there?'

"I remember it."

"You do?"

Ellie waited but Adam remained silent. "Are you all right?" she asked.

Adam spoke, "It was in his pocket."

"His pocket?"

"The night Thomas died."

"Oh my God!" The room went out of focus. So, the bracelet *had* come from Thomas. He had been going to give it to her that night. Ellie stared at the bracelet. It had been in his pocket, on his actual body.

"They brought him back to the house. Put him on his bed. Two women came the next morning to lay him out. They found the bracelet. I heard them laughing. They stopped when I came in. I took it from them and saw what it was. I knew it had been for you and I hated you more than anything then. You had taken everything from me. Helen killed him but it never would have happened if you hadn't come back. They were happy together. She really loved him." Adam took a deep breath. "Sorry, I know, it wasn't that simple. I don't hate you now. Thomas is probably reborn somewhere like you and I.

"Florence was there that day. She took the bracelet from me. I didn't know what she did with it and I never asked. I thought she'd thrown it away but she obviously kept it. I wonder why."

Ellie's hand shook as she held the phone. The bracelet had been with Thomas as he died. She remembered again holding him in the dark water that night.

"Ellie?"

"Sorry, Adam, what did you say?"

"I said, I wonder why Florence kept the bracelet."

"I don't know but there's one thing I *do* know: nothing happens by chance. We're all playing our parts in some elaborate drama. It's a remarkable chain of events. Because Florence kept the bracelet and put it in the musical box, Laura and her sister found it. Laura kept the box but my grandmother, Nancy, kept the key, out of spite, I think. They argued over the box when they were children. Nancy took the key with her to Australia, probably accidentally mixed in with her jewellery. I was born into the family and found the key, treasuring it because, obviously, I associated keys with being uplifted in my life as Anne. Eventually, the key helped me unlock my memory and led me to Laura and the bracelet.

"Adam, Laura gave it to me. I'm wearing it now."

"So Thomas was able to give the bracelet to you, after all."

"Yes. In receiving the bracelet, I feel as if he's reached out to me."

Ellie and Adam talked for a few moments more about Wilmington then Adam said, "I've got to go. When are you getting back?"

"Next week."

"Give me a ring, perhaps we can have lunch or something."

"I'd like that."

"You can meet Mia. We got back together.

"Oh, Adam, that's great."

Ellie put down the phone. She twirled the bracelet on her wrist. Thomas had wanted her to have it. Now, years later, his wish had been fulfilled. God, she'd loved him. Why was he not here in Wilmington like she and Alan? Ellie sighed. It was late. Still wearing the bracelet, Ellie went to bed and fell asleep. She dreamed of walking with Thomas over the sunlit Downs.

The next morning Ellie walked to Alan's flat. "The bracelet *did* belong to Thomas," she said, as soon as he opened the door. She repeated what Adam told her.

"So he was going to give it to you the night he died?"

"Yes."

"That's incredible!"

Ellie followed Alan into the kitchen. "Coffee?" he asked.

"Yes, thanks. I still love him, you know. Finding this bracelet has kind of brought it more into focus for me. Ellie reached for something in her bag. "I wrote this." She drew out a slip of paper and handed it to Alan. He took it and read what she had written.

THOMAS

On the sacred green hillside,
where the Long Man stands watching,
I found you.
In the old oak wood
where the ancient trees bore witness,
I loved you.
In the still waters of a dark lake,
under a full moon,
I lost you.

But, where the sun burns down
from a clear blue sky,
I remembered you.
Surely a love like ours cannot die?
And so, on the sacred green hillside,
where the Long Man still stands watching,
I await you.
Will you come again?

"Oh, that's beautiful," Alan said softly.

"I really thought he would come, you know, but he's not going to, is he? He's most likely living a life somewhere oblivious to what happened here." Ellie sighed. A look of sadness passed over her features but then she smiled. "When Thomas and I lived our lives in Wilmington, we were reaching out for more than each other. I'm lucky. I found what I was looking for, a greater love, that of Spirit, the essence of life itself. I know Thomas and I are united within that and always will be. If we are destined to physically meet again we will, if not, well, I have a whole new life to lead."

"Yes, that's right," Alan said.

"I don't think I will ever forget him, though. I hope Thomas is happy wherever he is."

"He's doing what he needs to do just like the rest of us," Alan said. "He'll find his way." Alan reached out for Ellie's hand. "Because of you and Thomas I was drawn here and found my life path and for that I can never repay you."

"You don't need to. I believe it was meant to be, all of it."

"Yes."

They hugged each other then Alan pulled away. He finished making the coffee and handed one to Ellie. "I've got something to show you. Come into the lounge."

Ellie saw the painting as soon as they walked into the room. "Oh, Alan," she exclaimed. It was Old Father. The painting was only half finished but there was no mistaking his distinctive face. "It's so life like." Alan had painted the eyes in such detail Ellie felt as if the old man could actually see her. A gentle smile played about his lips. She felt embraced by a feeling of love emanating from the painted figure and she sensed an echo of the familiar presence.

"You're very talented, Alan," Ellie said.

"Thanks. I don't have to work today. I thought I'd go sketching around the hill with the ring of trees. Would you like to come?"

"Oh, yes."

Ellie had been lucky with most of the weather on her holiday and today was no exception. The sun shone and only a few light clouds floated in the sky. Alan packed some sandwiches and, a short while later, they passed through the village. All her trips around Wilmington had a special poignancy now for she only had a short time before her flight home.

They walked past the church and along the road by Windover Hill where the Long Man stood. Ellie soaked in the sights and sounds of the countryside, drawing them inside to carry away with her when she left. Soon they came to the track that led up to the hill with the ring of trees and they started the climb. Alan stopped half way and took out his sketchpad. "I'd like to draw the view from here."

Ellie walked on up and stood in the centre of the trees. As she listened to the sound of the breeze rustling through the branches above her head, a memory flashed into her mind.

She danced around and around, whirling through the trees, the wind in her hair, the earth beneath her feet and the exuberance of a child flooding her body. Old Father stood watching. Finally, exhausted, she flung herself down at his feet. "Never forget the stillness in your dancing," he said and smiled.

As Anne she hadn't understood but now she knew. She started to dance again, moving through the trees, in time to the rhythm of life around her. She felt the world spinning through space and everything moving on its surface but, within her, existed stillness, an absolute peace and unity with it all. The wind blew and the long grass moved gently in the fields. White clouds drifted across the sky and a lone bird flew up from the ground and into the distance. Alan saw her from below and waved. Ellie waved back and continued dancing.

Ellie stood on top of Windover Hill looking out over the Sussex countryside. In two hours Alan would be driving her to the airport. It had been a lovely last few days, walking the countryside with Alan and talking, sometimes until long into the night, about their lives, their hopes and dreams and all that had happened. As she surveyed the scene before her, Ellie realised she had taken in as much of Wilmington as she needed. It was time to go home.

She walked down over the Long Man to the church. She let herself in and moved through it, absorbing the sacredness of the atmosphere. She went over to the Bee and Butterfly Window and stared at the vivid red phoenix at its base, a mythological bird that represented regeneration and rebirth, and thought how appropriate it was she had dreamed of it that day on the beach, for she had, indeed, been reborn, not only physically but spiritually.

Ellie turned away and walked outside to where Thomas lay buried. Where was he now? His face came into her mind and she remembered the feel of his arms holding her. As she stared down at the grave, all the love she had for Thomas flowed out of her, embracing the earth, the yew tree above, the beautiful old church and the nearby hillside where the Long Man surveyed the surrounding countryside. "Thomas," she whispered. "Why did you not come?" It seemed impossible that they should not be together in the place they both loved so deeply. "Will I *ever* see you again?" Eternity was a very long time. If they had been drawn together so powerfully once, surely it would happen again? Not now, in this place, but maybe one day, somewhere? Ellie stood in silence for several minutes then took one last look around and walked away.

Chapter 24

Ellie stared at the figure of the Long Man etched in the grass of Windover Hill, blue sky behind, oak trees in the foreground. Ellie loved looking at Alan's painting. It hung on the wall of her apartment. He gave it to her on her last day in Wilmington. It was a wonderful reminder and connection to Alan and the place she still held sacred.

The doorbell rang. Ellie gathered her luggage together and opened the door. She followed the waiting taxi driver to his car.

The drive to the airport took only a short while and soon Ellie flew high over the brown landscape of Australia, so in contrast to the soft greenness of the Wilmington landscape in her painting. Nevertheless she loved it. Since her trip to England three years ago, she had become more aware of the beauty of the world and now experienced a deep connection to the land of her birth as deep and powerful as the one she felt for Wilmington.

As Ellie sat on the plane watching the clouds and landscape speed past, she reflected on how much her life had changed since her return.

She had arrived back to a cloudy and wet winter's morning. All her family were at the airport, her mother grateful her wandering daughter had survived the perils of a trip overseas. They came back to Ellie's apartment, keen to hear about her adventures but she told them an edited version, not ready to tell the whole story yet. She was grateful when everyone left and, despite being tired, welcomed the chance to visit the beach.

Warmly dressed against a chill wind, she walked down onto the flat sea washed sand. So much had happened since she last walked this beach. The day of her visit to Worthing came to mind. She looked down. The sand *was* the same here. The memory served to unite the two experiences into one and she felt a deep affinity for the whole earth.

No flashbacks had occurred since leaving Wilmington but her memories remained vivid and so, often at night, she allowed her mind to drift through them. Sadness remained for the man she loved and lost but it rested gently within the deep peace that had become her new reality.

A few days after her return, Ellie met up with Adam and his girlfriend, Mia. Ellie showed them her photos of Wilmington.

Adam looked at them one by one. "It's just as I remember," he said. "Yes, I know that place, and that. You say the farm wasn't there?"

"No, it's been pulled down."

"That's a shame."

"The whole thing's incredible," Mia commented. "I didn't believe Adam at first but now, talking to you, well . . . It makes you think, doesn't it?" She nudged Adam gently. "Do you think I was there, too?"

"It's entirely possible," Adam said and laughed.

He finished looking through the photos, tidied them into a neat pile and handed them back to Ellie. "I no longer feel the weight of that life. It's falling away more and more. I'm at peace. I've got things to look forward to in this life now." He smiled at Mia.

It pleased Ellie to see his new happiness.

A week after her return, she started back at work but hated the dull routine and couldn't settle. She still had a fair amount of the money from her share of the house she bought with James so decided to leave her job. She needed time to adjust and work out what to do next.

Ellie went for long walks along the coast and into the hills and finally, one stormy night, unable to sleep, started writing about her journey to Wilmington and everything that happened. She began by describing her first dream on the beach in which she saw The Long Man of Wilmington and found Thomas's grave. The story flowed freely, as if merely waiting in her mind for the opportunity to find expression.

One day, about six months after her return, Ellie entered a café in the centre of Adelaide. She saw two familiar figures and stopped, "Hello, James, Catherine."

They looked up from their plates of food, surprised and uncomfortable to see Ellie standing there. They made a good couple, she thought, James in his dark suit and Catherine in her beautifully tailored jacket and skirt, her make up immaculate. Ellie immediately felt untidy but shrugged the feeling off. What did it matter? She was glad to be free of the constraints of being an up and coming professional.

"How are things?" James asked.

"I'm well, and you?"

James glanced at Catherine. "We're married now." Ellie looked at the woman who stole James from her and the two of them stared at each other. And in that moment, Ellie knew who she was. The unmistakeable triumph she saw in Catherine's eyes sent a chill down Ellie's spine and her mind travelled back through time to a night by a dark lake when, as Helen, this woman had tried to kill her! In the past, Ellie stole someone Catherine loved, now, in the present, the roles had been reversed; Catherine had taken James from Ellie.

Catherine's eyes flicked away to look at James. Ellie doubted she consciously remembered her past life as Helen but, nevertheless, impulses and emotions had persisted into the present.

Instinctively, Ellie reached out and touched Catherine's hand. "I'm sorry, really sorry," she said. Catherine looked at her questioningly for a moment but then nodded. Ellie straightened. The drama had played out, the debt paid.

"Good luck," she said to both of them and left.

It took her the best part of a year, but Ellie finally finished writing the story of her experiences. She called it *Reflection of the*

Moon. It took a while to find a publisher but, eventually, one company showed interest and published the work. It met with success both in Australia and England. Ellie didn't know what she wanted to do next, perhaps continue writing, but the money from the book meant she had more time to make a decision.

And so here she was on her way back to visit Alan in Wilmington. A lot of interest had been generated when he told authorities about the monks under the Long Man. Research still went on to determine who they were and the age of the chamber under the hill. The tunnel had been found to be unsafe so few people had so far been allowed inside.

Alan still painted his wonderful paintings, now quite sought after by collectors, but spent most of his time running a residential meditation retreat he set up in an old house close to the Long Man in Wilmington. He often took people onto the Long Man or to the hill with the ring of trees to meditate and tap into the unique energy of the area.

"I feel it's what Old Father wanted," Alan told Ellie on one of their frequent long phone calls.

"I think you're right."

Alan's centre had gained quite a reputation as a place where profound transformation could occur. Guided by Alan, people let go of their suffering and opened up to life, responding to the peace and vitality present in Wilmington. Ellie hadn't seen the centre yet and looked forward to visiting it.

Thinking about the Long Man reminded Ellie of Thomas. He still often came into her thoughts, even now, three years later. Whenever she met someone new, Ellie would look in their eyes and wonder if they were him. After all, it was entirely possible, she had already met Mathew, John and Helen who had been with her in her past life, so why not Thomas? And yet it hadn't happened and so she had now accepted it may not be meant to be. She'd been out on a few dates with men but each time there had been no spark, no depth of connection, beyond friendship and the unconditional love she felt as an integral part of her.

The plane descended and Ellie looked out of the window at the impressive view of Sydney stretched out beneath her. She had been booked to give a talk about *Reflection of the Moon* at an arts festival so was spending a few days in the city before flying on to

England.

Ellie noticed the tiny but distinctive form of the Opera House in the distance. In just a few minutes, the plane landed and Ellie sat in the back of a taxi driving through the streets of Sydney. Soon after arriving at the hotel, Ellie went out walking through the Botanic Gardens to the Opera House. She walked alongside the now huge building to a nearby café, ordered a coffee and sat on the waterfront, drinking in the sights and sounds of the harbour and breathing in the ocean smell on the breeze.

Planes flew by in the sky, cars rushed along the nearby road and boats sped over the shining, blue water. People milled about everywhere. Busy, modern life surrounded Ellie and yet, inside, as always, she felt stillness, the infinite Presence she first became aware of on the hills of Wilmington. She smiled at the kaleidoscope of events going on all around.

Acting on a sudden instinct, she turned. A man stood watching her. Their eyes met and she knew they shared the same experience. For a timeless moment, they both rested in the quiet acknowledgement of Truth. She never thought she would see him again. He smiled and raised his hand. Ellie lifted hers in response then he turned and walked away to disappear into the crowd. He had been only a young man, perhaps twenty or so, but, to Ellie, he still seemed old. She would always remember him the way he appeared to her as she roamed the green hillsides of Wilmington in another life.

She sipped her coffee, her mind reeling with the enormity of what just happened. To see Old Father again, here now, reborn into a new physical body, as she was about to return to Wilmington seemed more than coincidence. What could it mean? Her thoughts turned to the Long Man and the secret chamber where she last saw Old Father, such a sacred place. Would Old Father return there now? She wondered what he was doing in Australia.

Ellie gave her talk that evening, describing the awakening of her past life memories and her journey to Wilmington. Several people she spoke to afterwards told her how much they had been uplifted by the story. She came away feeling that writing the book had been worthwhile.

Two days later Ellie boarded another plane, this time bound

for England.

The taxi drew up in front of a wide sweep of newly mown lawn. A short distance away, stood a large old house with flint walls and white window frames. Before it, a wooden sign read "Gateway House Meditation Centre." Ellie got out and stood for a moment looking at the building. She remembered passing it when she visited Wilmington before. It had been dilapidated then. Alan had done a good job renovating the place. Ellie took a deep breath of fresh air and looked around her, absorbing the familiar surroundings. It was a lovely summer's day. She saw the Long Man in the distance standing sentinel, as always, on the hill. It felt good to be back.

Ellie paid the taxi driver and walked along a stone path to the house. Several large trees rustled in the breeze and a floral fragrance wafted from a cascading spread of honeysuckle on a nearby wall.

The front door stood open. Ellie went in and found herself in a spacious hallway with honey coloured, polished floorboards and white painted walls. She sensed the peacefulness of the building right away. A hint of incense hung in the air. The place looked deserted. Ellie put down her luggage and stood still, blissfully absorbing the quietness. She had spent too many hours listening to the drone of aircraft engines.

Several of Alan's paintings hung around the walls. Ellie went over to look at one. Delicate wild roses hung in profusion over an old brick wall. An open gate showed a view of the Sussex countryside stretching into the distance. Everything had been painted in intricate detail. Ellie smiled as she noticed a small red and black ladybird clinging to a leaf. Drops of water on the foliage shone with reflected light. The quality of the work had improved enormously since she saw it last.

"Ellie!" She turned and saw Alan behind her. He looked just the same. They hugged each other for a long time; they had three years to make up for.

"It's wonderful to see you," Ellie said, releasing Alan. She looked around. "This place is just lovely."

"Yes, a lot of it thanks to you." Ellie had contributed a large amount of the money she received from her book to help Alan set up the centre. "It took a lot of work but it was worth it. We're quite successful now," he said.

Alan's expression caught Ellie's attention. He had a wide grin on his face. "What is it?"

"I'm just really happy to see you," he said. Ellie looked at him suspiciously. That wasn't it, she felt sure. He was hiding something.

Alan picked up her case. "I'll show you where you'll be staying." Ellie followed him up some stairs and along a short corridor. "The place is empty at the moment but another course starts the day after tomorrow." They went into a small but pleasantly decorated room.

"This is nice." Ellie walked over and looked out at the view of the Downs that met her gaze. "It's so good to be here. Oh, Alan," she turned back to look at him, "I saw Old Father." She described her recent encounter in Sydney. "It all took just few moments but it was definitely him."

"I've always believed he'd be reborn somewhere." Alan said.

"What I don't understand is, why he hasn't returned to Wilmington in a new physical life to continue his work of teaching and acting as a guardian of the gateway?"

"Because he doesn't have to."

"What do you mean?" Ellie asked.

"He doesn't need to because, many years ago, a sensitive young girl spent time on the hills here and listened to the silence inside her." Alan smiled. "Helped by the powerful energy here she psychically tapped into the presence of the monks in the past and received their teachings.

"Then she fell in love and, through that love, I was drawn into the picture, also connecting with Old Father and receiving knowledge. You and I were physically reunited and discovered the chamber under the Man. This discovery brought publicity to the area and I started my meditation centre to teach the ideas I received. And you wrote your book. What better way to communicate spiritual ideas than through a simple story about the lives of real people who lived and loved and discovered truth on a hillside? People like a good story. How powerful is all that?

"In the days of Old Father's physical existence here, the world simply wasn't ready for his ideas. The monks were killed and their place of worship blocked up but their spiritual truth could not be destroyed. It lives on through us and the other people whose lives they touched. You know the night we spoke to Old Father in the chamber?"

Ellie nodded.

"Do you remember him telling us we would have other work to do?

"Yes."

"Well, I believe he meant us to be the new guardians. I'm trying to stay involved with the investigation of the site under the Long Man. I've got to know the director of the research team very well, Stephen Mills. He comes here to meditate with us. He's felt the energy under the Man and understands its special significance. We are working to make sure the chamber is protected. I believe that one day, when the tunnel has been properly assessed and strengthened, it may be opened up to the public.

"Why don't you stay and work with me here, Ellie? The centre is becoming very popular and I could do with all the help I can get."

Ellie stared out of the window at the countryside and considered Alan's words. Stay here? She imagined herself working in the centre. She listened to the silence inside her and remembered being with Old Father and the other monks, how good it had been to be with people who loved life and felt the same way about things. Yes, she *would* like to be involved in something that helped people become more spiritually aware.

"OK, I will," she said, "at least, for a while."

"Great."

"I expect Old Father will teach people where he is now," Ellie said.

"Yes, I'm sure he will. And that's what the world needs. People need to know there's a spiritual dimension to life and that it's accessible everywhere, that it's actually inside them, even as they are now. People can't tap into the truth because they don't know it's there."

"Yes," Ellie said. "When I went back to Australia, although I missed Wilmington, I still felt the same spiritual connectedness there. I wrote about it at the end of my story."

"I know. I liked the way you did that. It was important. Wilmington is a special place and, perhaps makes it easier, but it's not necessary to come here to realise the truth because it is present *everywhere* and in *everyone*."

"Do you think there's any likelihood the monk's bodies will ever be properly buried?" Ellie asked. She knew they had been taken away to be studied.

"Stephen says it'll happen one day but not for a while yet. We're hoping they can be placed in the churchyard here in Wilmington."

"Do they know who built the chamber yet?"

"No. They know it's several thousand years old but not who originally built it." Alan moved towards the door. "Anyway, let me show you around the rest of the place."

As they walked through the top floor of the centre, Ellie caught Alan looking at her in the same odd way he'd done earlier—with an air of suppressed amusement.

"The upstairs is all guest accommodation," Alan said. "There's more in a new addition out the back. Let's go downstairs now."

Ellie admired the beautifully decorated meditation rooms on the lower level and then the dining room in the new wing. "This place is so beautiful. I love the natural materials you've used," she commented. They went out into the garden. "Oh, Alan, this is breathtaking." Ellie went over to a circular stone pond and stood looking down at the goldfish swimming around. A central fountain jetted water a short way up into the air. Ellie shut her eyes for a moment and listened to its soft sound. As she did so, her whole body relaxed.

After a few moments, she moved away and walked around the rest of the garden. The trees and bushes had been specially planted to create secluded areas.

"We encourage people to meditate in the open air." Alan explained. "When the weather permits," he added. Ellie laughed.

They went back inside the building and Alan led the way along a central hallway. "The only place you haven't seen now is the office." He opened the door a crack then stopped. "Look, there's something I have to do. You go in and I'll be right back." He walked away, smiling broadly. Ellie stared after his retreating figure. Something was *definitely* odd about Alan's manner, she thought.

Pushing open the wooden door, Ellie moved into a spacious office. The first thing she noticed was a painting on the wall in front of her, another of Alan's. An exquisite white water lily, glowing with an interior light, floated on the surface of a dark pool. Her attention taken with the powerful image, she failed to notice the person standing by the window gazing at her.

When she finally turned to look around the rest of the room, all colour drained from her cheeks. Physically he couldn't be any more different. This man was older, in his mid to late thirties, his hair light and straight, his features finer, softer, his body tall and thin, and yet it was him. She saw the truth of it in his eyes and felt it in her heart.

"Thomas," she whispered.

Chapter 25

"YOU'RE SO DIFFERENT." THOMAS SAID.

"You too."

They both fell silent and stood there, looking at each other, too overwhelmed to speak. Memories swirled up out of the past of when they had been together before: running in the wind, rolling down the Long Man, climbing trees, then later as adults meeting in hidden places, touching each other, kissing, expressing the deep passion that existed between them. It was all there, present in that moment.

Finally, Ellie said. "You remember?"

"Yes."

"All of it?"

"All of it."

"I know who you are but perhaps I should introduce myself," the man said with an ironic smile. "My name is Simon, Simon Grange."

Ellie stood motionless, her mind numb. She had thought about this moment so many times over the years but none of it had prepared her for the reality.

"I read your book," Simon continued. He spoke rapidly, as if he needed to fill the space between them with words, "Three weeks ago, now. I saw it on display in a shop. The picture on the cover drew my attention."

The publishers had been reluctant to use an image of the moon reflected in a lake at first but Ellie convinced them it was the best design and she had been pleased with the final result.

"I bought it, although I don't normally read much. I'll never forget that afternoon. I came home and sat in the lounge. It was raining. I made myself a coffee but forgot to drink it. I read the book in one sitting. The moment I began it, memories poured back: of living near the Long Man, of being a man named Thomas in another time," he paused, "of being with you."

Ellie flushed.

Simon continued, "I remembered things you did not write of, could not know from your perspective. I knew all about Thomas, what had happened for him, the power of his passion for the woman who showed him her soul.

"A lot of things finally made sense. I'd always felt something missing in my life. Nothing I ever did, or any relationship I had, seemed to satisfy. As a young boy, I had dreams about the Long Man, strange dreams that made no sense but left me with a feeling of sadness. I also never liked being near ponds or lakes with dark water. When I read your story, I realised why.

"The next day I got in the car and drove down here. It was a long drive, I live in the Lake District, but I had to come. I booked into the hotel, found Alan at the meditation centre and told him who I was. We talked for a long time about everything that happened to you and him. We got on well. He offered to let me stay here and we spent several days talking and walking around the place. I felt as if I had come home. It all seemed so familiar and I remembered more and more the longer I remained here.

"Alan showed me the chamber under the Long Man. I had no idea of its existence when I lived here as Thomas but I certainly sensed there was something special about the area. I'm sorry I used to tease you about your monks but I never saw them and no one else I knew seemed to know who they were."

"It's OK," Ellie said. "I had no idea they weren't living, they seemed so real, but they'd been dead a long time, even then."

Simon continued. "Anyway, Alan offered me a job working here. I said, "Yes." Then, a few days ago, he said you were coming." He trailed off and stared at her for a moment, as if really seeing her for the first time. A look of confusion passed across his face and he looked uncertain. Ellie knew his mind struggled to match her physical reality with what his heart told him. She understood for she felt the same.

Simon pointed to Ellie's wrist. "You're wearing it."

She looked down and ran her fingers over the etched surface of the silver bracelet given to her by Laura. "Yes."

"I had that made for you in Eastbourne. I was going to give it to you the night that . . ." Darkness clouded his features. "I knew I should stop seeing you but I couldn't. I just couldn't." Tears filled his eyes. "I did care for Helen. She didn't deserve any of it. She was a sweet person but couldn't bear it when she found out about you and me. She became so angry and bitter, someone I didn't know. She made me swear not to see you again. She was so upset I agreed but I couldn't keep away from you.

"I nearly didn't come that night because Helen and I argued. She wanted to know whether I was still seeing you. She shouted and screamed and I hated her then, just for being there." Pain distorted his features. "God help me, I hated her. She finally went to bed but I said I had to check on a sick sheep. You and I had arranged to meet in the wood. I had to see you, tell you and try to find some way out. I wanted to give you the bracelet so I put it in my pocket and came to find you. Helen didn't believe my story and followed.

"When I saw you at the wood, all I could think about was holding you, touching you. I couldn't help myself. But then we saw the light and went to the lake. It all gets hazy at that point. I just remember the reflection of the moon in the water and then Helen came and I was falling . . ." Simon faltered and his face took on a distant expression. "I fell down into darkness, a deep darkness, but then I saw a bright light and that's the last memory I have of being Thomas."

Simon focussed back on Ellie. "Why didn't you tell me about the child?"

"I was going to that night but never got the chance."

"This whole thing is incredible, isn't it?" Simon said.

"Yes, it is." They both fell silent.

Ellie had yearned for this man through time but now, as she stood there looking at him, she didn't know how she felt. A mixture of emotions surged up: love, sadness, guilt, anger, grief. Her legs felt weak. She couldn't believe it was happening.

"Are you all right?" Simon looked concerned.

"Yes, I'm sorry. I'm overwhelmed. I'm not sure how I feel."

"It's OK, neither do I, but it doesn't matter. We don't have to feel anything. We'll just see what happens."

"Yes, that's a good idea. One thing, though, are you. . . ." she hesitated, reluctant to ask.

Simon guessed. "Married?"

Ellie nodded.

"I was," Simon smiled, "but I'm not now."

A knock came at the door and Alan peered in. "You two have met, then."

"You could say that," Ellie said and they all laughed. "Now I know why you were looking at me in an odd way. You could have warned me."

"I considered it, but thought it better if you didn't know. Anyway, I've organised some lunch for us all. We've got a lot to talk about."

Ellie and Simon followed Alan into the dining area and over to a table on which a meal had been laid out. They sat down. Alan looked at Ellie and Simon and smiled. "I can hardly believe this is really happening, that we should all be here together like this, but we are and I feel it's the fruition of something that started a long time ago." He turned to Simon. "Ellie has agreed to stay and help us here in the centre." Then Alan looked at Ellie. "I believe it's what Old Father wanted. I don't think you'll regret it."

Alan poured each of them a drink from a green bottle. "I know this is only apple juice but I'd like to propose a toast anyway." He raised his glass in the direction of Windover Hill, "To the Long Man."

"The Long Man," they all repeated and laughed.

"Help yourselves," Alan said, gesturing at the food.

Ellie didn't feel like eating. For her, the whole world had turned inside out. She truly believed she and Thomas would never meet again yet here he was.

She glanced at Simon. Ellie knew he was Thomas, the man she had known and loved, but he looked so different and it unsettled her. She longed to be alone with him so they could talk and get to know each other again, yet felt hesitant and afraid. Such a long time had passed and so much had happened. She had loved him with all of herself. He had filled her thoughts and possessed her heart with such intensity she had even remembered him through death, but they had both lived new lives with other people, what if they discovered they no longer felt the same? How could she bear it? It would be like losing him all over again.

But the moment she thought this, Ellie felt the sacred Presence of Spirit within her and knew this held them both in its loving embrace. The realisation came that, if she simply and honestly opened her heart to this man with no expectations, this freedom would allow them to discover naturally whether their destinies were still entwined.

After the meal, Alan brought them coffees and put a plate of biscuits in the centre of the table. Ellie and Simon both reached for the last one at the same time and their fingers touched. She pulled her hand back as if burned.

"Sorry," Simon said. "You have it." He smiled with such a familiar look, tears came into her eyes. It was real. He really *was* Thomas, the one she had loved and lost. He had revealed himself to her in the gesture and, as she watched him talking to Alan for the next hour, she saw Simon as Thomas more and more: the way he held his head, the way he cleared his throat, laughed and sighed, nuances of expression unique to him. But it was more than that. As she let go and relaxed, she realised she *felt* him, not physically but his essence. It was definitely him, her energy field recognised his and remembered. His unique signature vibration felt home to her, as familiar as her own. Her lips lifted in a soft smile.

Simon stole glances at the woman across from him. She looked happy. He heard Alan talking about the centre but all he cared about in that moment was Ellie. He had been agitated all morning waiting for her to arrive. Part of him wanted to run away. What would he think? How would she be? What would he say?

His life had changed utterly the day he entered the book shop looking for a gift for his nephew. His eyes had scanned the shelves but only one book drew him, the one with a reflection of the moon shimmering in the dark waters of a lake.

The moment he saw it, pain gripped his chest and his breath caught. Darkness filled his vision and, afraid of a heart attack, he leant against a bookshelf. Thankfully, the sensations lessened and he managed to breathe again. The pain faded and he could almost believe it never happened.

As he picked up the book, he shivered, icy cold despite the warmth of the day. Thinking he might be coming down with something, he hurried out of the shop but not before he paid for the book entitled *Reflection of the Moon.*

He arrived home and lay down on the sofa and started to read. His present life dropped away as his mind opened up and, in his memory, he roamed the South Downs, meeting and loving a woman with long, dark hair with whom he became obsessed to the point of losing all reason.

Simon studied her now. She was different, with hair shorter and a lighter brown and she was taller and thinner, but he saw a distinct echo of Anne in her face. Her eyes had transfixed him the first moment they met, the way she looked at him. He had fallen through those eyes, down and down, and a deep part of him had resonated with recognition at what he sensed beneath her gaze. He felt something fall into place within him as if, now she had come, everything in his life made sense and, yet, his mind still found the whole situation crazy.

Ellie, Alan and Simon spent several hours talking: about their past and present lives, the monks, the future of the meditation centre. As the afternoon wore on, Ellie continued to watch and listen to Simon as he talked. She recognised the way he held his head, the expressions on his face, even his laugh sounded the same. Amazed so many mannerisms had survived through death, she found herself becoming more and more drawn to him, but one thing began to disturb her. Would he feel the same? So much had happened to him since the night he died by her side. He had loved another woman.

The doubt swelled and became a heaviness causing her eyelids to close and her head to slump. Simon looked at her with concern. "You look exhausted."

Ellie smiled at him and their gazes locked but dizziness clouded her brain and it became too much: the long flight and finding Thomas here after all this time. She needed a break, time alone to adjust to the powerful emotions running through her. "I'm really tired," she mumbled. "I think I'll go and lie down, if you don't mind."

"Of course not," Simon said.

Ellie stood and walked out of the room as fast as she could. The two men watched her go.

Ellie woke the next morning to the sound of the dawn chorus, having slept over fourteen hours. Despite it being only six in the morning, she rose, put on some warm clothing and went downstairs. The house was deserted. Restless, Ellie let herself out of the centre and walked through Wilmington. She had the world to herself. Although cool now, it looked as if the day would shape up to be dry and sunny.

She reached Windover Hill. The moment she set foot on it, her spirit soared, high up into the sky and all around the surrounding countryside in exultation at the glory of being alive. The sensation intensified as she walked up beside the Long Man. The wind blew through her hair, the blue sky stretched on forever and the earth felt like home beneath her feet.

Ellie reached the top and turned to look down at Wilmington and the landscape beyond, love for this special place swelling in her chest. At that moment, she sensed someone coming from the opposite direction and knew it was him. She felt his nearness, remembered how, in the past, she had yearned for his approach.

"I thought you'd be here," Simon said. "I hope you don't mind me disturbing you?"

Ellie turned and looked at him. He looked unsure, worried, as if she might tell him to go.

"No, no, it's OK," she said.

"How are you feeling?"

"Better. I had a good, long sleep."

Simon stood beside Ellie and looked out. "We had some wonderful times here, didn't we?"

"Yes, we did."

"Let's walk," Simon said. As they made their way down the hillside, they talked of the things they had done as the young Thomas and Anne, laughing as they remembered and pointing out familiar landmarks. They did not mention the later years; neither ready to go there yet.

After a while, they came to the area of open ground where Thomas's farmhouse had been. "I can't believe it's gone," Simon murmured. "Tell me about my father, Adam, I mean. How is he? I can't tell you how strange it was to read about you meeting him in your book."

"He was pretty messed up by it all at one time but he's put it behind him now. He got married recently. He and his wife seem really happy."

"That's good." Simon ran his hand through his hair, another mannerism he'd had as Thomas. Ellie noticed tears in his eyes. Her heart moved with compassion for him. She knew his mind had drifted back to the past, to his life in his home, the place he shared with his wife. Ellie longed to put her arms around him but could not.

"I'm sorry about Helen," he said.

"Don't be. She's fine."

Simon looked at her in surprise. "How do you know?"

Ellie hadn't written about the incident in the café with James and Catherine. Catherine wasn't fully conscious of her past life and Ellie hadn't wanted her to read about it in a book. She told Simon about her relationship with James and her realisation that Catherine was Helen.

"Are you sure it was her?"

"Yes."

"And she was all right?"

"Yes. I think she's a very successful woman, a lawyer and, of course, she has James. They're very well suited."

The tension in Simon's face eased. "I'm sorry, it must have been difficult for you."

"Don't be. I'm glad. James and I weren't meant to be." Ellie reached out and laid a hand gently on Simon's arm. "It means you can let go of it now."

"Yes, you're right."

Simon looked down at her hand. Ellie withdrew it. "Let's move on now," she said, feeling awkward.

They walked to the hill with the ring of trees. As they neared the top, Ellie felt light and energised. She hurried on ahead and walked in and out of all the ancient oaks. Simon sat down and watched. "You were always happy here," he said when she came and sat down on the grass beside him.

"Yes." Ellie turned towards Simon and stared into his eyes, Thomas's eyes. Simon smiled and he *was* Thomas, fully and completely and, for the first time since meeting him, the physical yearning she used to feel in the past stirred. There had been no barrier between them then, not even his marriage to another woman. Only death had parted them. But only for a while for here he was.

Ellie felt uncomfortable and embarrassed, though, unsure of what to say or do. Simon had given her no indication of the way he felt. This wasn't how she had imagined their reunion. She glanced at him. He was still looking at her but his gaze gave nothing away. Their passion in the past had been intense. The memory of it hung in the air between them now, unexpressed, but no less real for that. What was he feeling? Ellie wondered. She felt everything flowing out of her control. To break her growing tension, she jumped to her feet. "Let's go and get something to eat." Ellie couldn't look at Simon again and hurried down the hill.

They decided to call in for a meal at the Green Man Hotel. They sat out to eat in the garden. A few white, painted metal chairs and tables had been placed on a patio overlooking a lawn. They had the place to themselves. They kept their conversation focussed on lighter matters and Ellie told Simon about her recent life in Australia, finishing with seeing Old Father before flying to England.

"I wish I had known him, too," Simon commented. "I can hardly take in all that has happened. I thought I understood life, believing it followed predictable, physical laws: that we lived, and, if we were lucky, loved, had children then died. Do you remember anything about . . . your death?"

"No, I don't, only some kind of light at some point and a figure waiting on a hillside then being here again as a young child in Australia. Life was normal for me until I dreamt of the Long Man much later, and, of course, you. I started to dream about you all the time." She watched his face for some kind of reaction but he simply drained his coffee so she said, "Let's keep walking."

They left the hotel and went back up on the Downs. "Tell me more about your life, Simon," Ellie asked.

"Well, until two months ago, I lived in Keswick, working in a landscaping firm. I always loved gardening so it had been a natural career choice for me. I hated it when I became the manager. I no longer did the hands on work so much. The only thing I miss in coming here is my garden at home but the grounds are going to be my responsibility at the meditation centre so I'm looking forward to getting into that. I've got some ideas for the landscaping I want to put into effect."

They crossed a field and came to a barn Ellie remembered from her time as Anne. As they passed it, a forgotten memory came into her mind.

She and Thomas had been together and were walking back towards Wilmington when they heard a cry of pain. Huddled over by the wall of a stone barn, they saw a sheep in obvious agony. Thomas went over and laid his hand upon it. The animal calmed. Without hesitation, he reached inside the creature's body and grasped the lamb trapped inside. It slithered out onto the grass, wet and bloody, the cord wrapped around its neck. Thomas released it and laid the tiny animal close to the mother who cleaned it but the lamb remained limp and unresponsive. Anne felt a wrench of pity for the sheep, its labouring had been in vain, but Thomas kept massaging the lamb's tiny body and, in time, it took a breath and moved its legs.

Anne went over to Thomas where he knelt by the lamb and put her arms around him, uncaring that blood covered his hands. Together, they watched the mother care for her offspring and smiled when they saw the lamb respond. Anne loved Thomas so much in that moment: his strength and gentleness, the obvious joy he felt tending his animals and working the land.

"Any interest in animals?" Ellie asked Simon.

"Yes, I've always had a dog. Do you remember Ben?"

"Ben, yes." She had watched Thomas as a boy learning to herd the sheep with the old sheep dog, his father looking on.

"You know, I can see him in my memory as clear as if it was yesterday. It's astonishing. Once I'd read your book, it was like a door opened in my mind and more and more memories came up out of the past. Coming here has helped bring it all into focus." He fell silent. Ellie wondered if he was thinking of how it had been between them.

"You said you were divorced, any children?" she asked.

Simon's features clouded over. "Yes. We had a son, Andrew. He was killed by a car when he was five."

"Oh, my God, I'm so sorry."

"It happened four years ago. It should have drawn me and Joanne closer together but it drove us apart. We hadn't been getting on well for some time before that. She didn't like my moods, my need to spend time alone in the garden. It's easier now with Andrew, knowing that death is obviously not the end, but it's still damn hard. I miss him so much."

"Yes, I can imagine," Ellie said.

"I envy you your spiritual connection. I always had a great affinity with nature, with animals and working the land as Thomas, and I certainly longed for something deeper, in my present life, too, but I didn't feel what you talk about in your book. The only time I ever felt really connected and uplifted was with you in the past when we were . . ." he paused, searching for the right words, "together out in the countryside."

He looked at her. "You took me beyond myself. You had something about you. I loved your spirit, your vitality, how you felt the energy of the earth and the plants. I saw the light in your eyes and couldn't leave you alone. I couldn't leave you alone," he repeated. "Sorry." Suddenly aware he was staring, he turned away. "Anyway, I feel good being here now. I'm working with Alan, meditating, walking on the hills, reading and I'm beginning to understand so much more."

They were passing the church. "I suppose you've seen where

you're . . . Thomas, is buried?" Ellie asked.

"Yes, when I first came here. It was a bizarre experience."

"I know. I visited my grave in Worthing. It still hardly seems possible sometimes but the memories are so real they're a part of who I am today."

"I feel the same. I'm still Thomas, although my name has changed. And my body," he added and laughed.

"Can we go inside?" Ellie asked.

"Of course," Simon replied. As they passed the yew tree and his grave, he could not help but shudder. How had it happened that he now lived and could remember that life? Because of its intensity, he realised, then glanced at the woman beside him, because of her. His love for her had been all consuming. As Anne, she used to move him in a way that broke him open, brought his senses alive and touched his soul. She had something special: her beauty, her love for the world and gentleness, but more than that, her very presence. It had a depth, something indefinable: a stillness, a sacredness. And as Thomas he had longed for that himself. Yes, he who had worked the land with calluses on his hands, a rough man, used to the ways of men and hard work, nevertheless, had always yearned for softness, silence, peace.

Simon glanced at Ellie. He sensed those qualities in her now, if anything they had become fuller and richer. He still longed for them in his present life. The death of his son remained a heavy grief locked inside him.

He followed Ellie into the cool, dimness of the church and they wandered into the small chapel to the Bee and Butterfly window. They sat down next to each other and stared at St Peter with the red phoenix rising from the ashes below.

Ellie studied the figure holding the key to heaven in his hand. She no longer had her small key but no longer needed it. How like her life the window was. The original window was destroyed but a few fragments had survived and been incorporated into the new design. So too her life with Thomas had been destroyed but fragments of memory remained and they had become part of her present life, drawing her back to Wilmington.

She felt a sense of rightness. All the pieces of her life were now back in place. Those separated by tragedy: she, Thomas and their child, were reunited. Despite the fact she knew Old Father was thousands of miles away, Ellie sensed that he too was with her at that moment and was smiling.

Ellie turned and noticed Simon staring intently at the window, an expression of profound sorrow on his face. "Are you alright?" she asked.

"Yes, I . . . it's just . . ." Simon's head swam and he felt dizzy. He stared at the phoenix. Its glowing shapes and colours blurred together then the wings of the bird began flickering as if ablaze. A memory arose of sitting in this place. When Anne got taken to London he had felt so lost and alone. Knowing she loved the church, he used to go there and sit by the window, as if, somehow, it would connect him to her. When she did not return, he stopped coming but never forgot the girl who had been so much a part of his childhood. They had shared so much together. Now that past feeling of loss merged with the grief he felt for his son. Darkness filled his vision and, for a moment, he thought he might pass out.

Simon looked round and stared at Ellie, as if searching for something in her eyes. "I feel sort of lost, as if I'm looking for something that I can never find. Do know what I mean?"

Ellie saw the yearning in his eyes, not for her, but for something deeper and nodded.

"Everything's OK," she said. "It's always OK. You have come through death, we both have, and yet we are here, now." She gestured up at the phoenix, "Death is not the end, nor is life, there's something else, Simon, and it is with us always. It's what you seek and it's here, now, in you, in me. It is our essence, our true life."

The quiet voice of the woman beside him, the beat of his heart and the sound of his breathing all merged into one, then Simon noticed a sense of clarity behind his pain, a spaciousness, an absolute peace without condition, and knew she spoke the truth. The awareness of it grew and the knowing came that it had always existed in him and always would. He felt the subtle presence of his son then and knew that, in this peace, they had never been parted.

Beside him, Ellie fell silent, sensing that spaciousness also within herself and they sat together for some time by the Bee and Butterfly window, both bathed in coloured light and resting in the knowledge of the Great Stillness that had come upon them.

Chapter 26

THEY ARRIVED BACK AT THE centre in time for the evening meal. Neither had spoken much on the way back, both still held in thrall by what occurred in the church. A mixture of emotions ebbed and flowed within Ellie's chest as they walked towards the table in the dining room where Alan awaited them. Simon glanced at her and smiled. "I enjoyed today." His eyes lingered on her face in a way reminiscent of Thomas and she blushed.

"So did I."

While they ate, Alan and Simon talked about the research going on into the chamber under the Long Man of Wilmington and the general state of the world. None of it interested Ellie in the slightest. Her brain listened to the conversation and she made occasional replies and comments but her awareness remained on Simon, sitting so close she could reach out and touch him.

This man was Thomas, in his essence, the man she had loved and trusted and opened up to in a way so complete she lost her sense of separate self in his embrace. During the afternoon, she had found herself responding as she used to as Anne, feeling more and more physically attracted to him. Then, when they sat in the church and shared something far, far deeper than passion, she knew that, for her, the differences in appearance no longer mattered. Now, having him so close physically, memories of their times in the oak wood kept intruding into her mind.

Did Simon keep remembering too? she wondered. He had been reticent at first but then she too had felt that way. Today, though, as they spent time together, his gaze had lingered on her more and more. They had both shied away from discussing their time as lovers. What it meant she did not know.

Alan said something to her but Ellie made no sense of his words. She felt light-headed. "I'm sorry, I have a bad headache," she said. "I think I'll get some fresh air." Ellie stood up and hurried out of the room. She found an exit leading into the garden and walked over to the fountain. The sound of trickling water soothed her chaotic emotions and she relaxed in the soft, early evening light. Ellie loved the long English summer days.

Ellie saw Simon come out of the building but wasn't ready to face him, not the way she felt. She slipped behind some trees and saw a tall hedge running the length of the garden. In it, she saw a wooden gate. Ellie went through and found herself in a quiet lane. She started walking, needing peace and quiet, a chance to think, time to breathe and allow her feelings to settle.

She hurried along the road and down a narrow, country lane leading out of Wilmington. She walked for a while then realised where she was headed. It had been unconscious but now it seemed appropriate. She looked behind her, breathing a sigh of relief. Simon hadn't followed.

Ellie entered the old oak wood where she and Thomas spent so much time together. The familiar presence of the old trees that still stood, despite having passed through so many seasons, calmed her. She found the tree where she and Thomas had lain together in the distant past and sat down with her back to it as she had done so many, many times before. Ellie sensed the oak's living energy. It flooded through her body and she felt a powerful connection to both earth and sky. A deep sense of peace permeated the wood and all need for anything other than the soft rustling of the oak leaves above fell away.

It was nearly dark when Simon found Ellie lying fast asleep. He stood and looked at her, his gaze travelling over her body. He noted how the soft fabric of her long dress flowed over her limbs, sculpting itself to her form. His mind conjured the image of Anne in the past lying naked, staring up at him with passion in her eyes. He had come to her then and the world disappeared as they became lost in each other. But what of now? So far Ellie had kept her feelings veiled.

She looked so beautiful in the dim light, like an ethereal being. Yes, she was different but she *felt* the same to him, not physically, they had barely touched, but what her presence evoked melted him. He felt a depth of love he had never stopped feeling swell into fullness again, a love that encompassed more than the simple human being before him. It reawakened the powerful kinship he felt in the past for the land, the trees, the sky and, even more, for life itself. Tears filled his eyes at the beauty and miracle of the feeling.

A deep silence fell over the wood and he sat down beside Ellie. He could not leave her, not again.

Ellie opened her eyes. Simon sat watching her. She had known at some level he would come. Had she wanted him to? Of course, it was inevitable. They had both known this moment had to come but neither had been ready. It took all the courage she possessed to meet his gaze and not look away but she had to know how he felt.

As they sat motionless, staring into each other's eyes, time slowed then rewound back over the years and they were once again Anne and Thomas, their bodies yearning for the touch of the other. Thomas bent forward and, with exquisite gentleness, their lips met, like two feathers brushing together. As their kiss deepened, they brought their arms around each other and, in that embrace, their souls flowed into a depth of union they had never reached before. The love that had bound them together for so long radiated out, expressing itself in a profound passion that urged their physical bodies closer. They pulled off their clothes until no barrier remained and, in naked innocence, reborn for each other, they came together.

Hours later, Ellie opened her eyes. Darkness had fallen. She lay cradled in Simon's arms. She shifted and felt him move in response. The wood was silent. "Ellie," he said slowly and lovingly, as if saying it for the first time. "I like it. The name suits you."

"I think you'll always be Thomas to me," Ellie said.

"You can call me anything you like," Simon laughed, "as long as we're together." They kissed and held on to each other. Ellie didn't want to let him go but, finally, they drew apart. There would be other times. There was nothing to stop them anymore.

They stood and dressed but then Ellie froze and a feeling of dread came over her. "Look," she said. A light shone in the darkness. She had seen that light before.

Simon pulled her into his arms. "It's all right. Things are different now. Come." He led her down the path and to the bank of the lake where they had stood all those years ago as Thomas and Anne. A full moon floated serene in the sky above. Its reflection swam in the dark waters below.

They stood there, with their arms around each other, their faces illuminated with silver light. This time no one came, Thomas did not fall and the reflection of the moon in the water remained whole.

www.ingramcontent.com/pod-product-compliance
Lightning Source LLC
Chambersburg PA
CBHW020958120726
47905CB00009B/2751